I0679817

Poohsticks Bridge would not have been possible without the help of these wonderful people listed here. Happy Herbert for her editing skills, Sydney Blackburn for a cover design that appears exactly as Poohsticks bridge appears in my head, Jim Harnock just because, Glenda Cooper, Pip Cooper and Phil Beach for being the beta readers, and Valerie and Roy Birch for making me exist in the first place. So many others who have shown interest – I am always indebted to you all for your interest and encouragement.

And Helen, who would have been the most beloved twin sister in all the world, this is written by you, and for you.

My love always,

Andrew R Birch, August 9th, 2018

Edited by Happy Herbert

Published by OCTOSQUID

Poohsticks Bridge.

Winter 2041. The End.

The old man, feeling every second of his seventy five years, sat down slowly on the small familiar bench. The November air had a cold bite to it, but after coming here for over seventy years, he was used to the chill. He settled his elderly frame and took in the scene, bowing his head slightly against the frosty air. The little clearing in the woodland that ran behind the house held the familiar sights and smells that had been his home for seventy five years. Their home. He turned to the empty place at the side of him on the bench for a moment, and remembered another time. Another sound. Another smell. Listening contently to the thaw of the frost on the barren trees, he began to idly trace his finger over the curled design of the bench's ironwork. It reminded him of something. Something from a long time ago.

The little boy's fingers idly traced the curled design of the station wagon's leather bench seat. It was worn and old, but curved and twisted almost like a railroad track over the leather and fabric.

In the driving seat, his father honked the car horn angrily as the truck turned sharply in front.

"What the hell is that guy on," he growled to his wife, "did you see that?"

"Just calm down Ed, its fine," soothed his wife, holding the infant close to her chest, "there's no harm done."

"Guy should lose his licence!"

Madeline closed her eyes softly. Ed was a good driver, but he had such a short fuse as soon as he got in the car. He always seemed to take out all of his stresses when he was behind the wheel. That truck that had turned in front of them easily had the time to make the turn, but Ed, like usual, had seen red. Madeline guessed it was the stresses of work. The two of them lived in the family ranch house, the Belle Starr, and Ed was trying without much success to keep the business going. They'd already sold off a few acres of land to developers wanting to build industrial units, but even so things weren't that much better. At one time, Decatur Road had been pretty famous, with the old ranch houses stretching quite a ways. Now there were only four left, with another one abandoned and a couple more demolished and the land sold off. Old Jonesy at the end of the road had tried to open his as a tourist attraction for city folks, but they were just too far out in the sticks to attract that kind of trade. Plus, it wasn't like they were mid-west and enjoyed heat

4

and warm summers. It was September now and the middle of Fall. The kids already had sweaters and mittens on. They lived in a little bubble all of their own out here it seemed, and the harsh realities of Vietnam and Attica seemed to take place in another world. Madeline looked to the back seat. Her eldest son John was sat looking through the window of the Dodge station wagon, oblivious to the family's financial troubles. John was four years old, and today was his first day at preschool. Madeline had loved being at home with John, and spending time with her little son, but with his little brother Ed junior demanding her attention, they decided it was time for John to go mix with other kids. The problem was that Belle Starr was relatively isolated from the neighbourhood, and apart from his mom and dad, the little boy had largely been happy in his own company. When Ed junior had been born, John had been happy enough with the baby, even if he had been a little jealous of the attention the baby had received.

John loved to go in the car. The long ride down Decatur road to the intersection was boring, with just old ranch gates and fields and nothing to look at. He usually played with the window turners. At the intersection, there was usually plenty to look at though. There was a yard off to the left, with some old school buses parked in it. John had looked at them every time he'd come past in the car, and they never moved. He wanted to ask his dad to drive closer by so he could take a look, but he knew what his father would say and so he kept quiet. From the intersection it got more interesting, depending on where they were going. If they were headed into town, it was only a short ride to the next turnpike and there wouldn't be much time to watch stuff. There were usually trucks on the highway though, and sometimes a wrecker or snowplow parked on the turnpike.

He knew where they were going today. Something called school. To talk to other kids.

"Do what your teachers tell you, and be a good boy," Mom had said.

Another big heavy truck passed them on the highway, and John clambered to the other window to watch it go past, looking at all the moving parts as it roared by. Dad drove so slowly, at least to him. Always in the inside lane, never above fifty, and as the trucks always passed, it got him a good look.

"Quit clambering around" came a stern voice. John sat down in his seat, and began to play with the window turners again. They were embossed with the Dodge logo, and reminded John of a steering wheel. He imagined he was the driver of a big Dodge truck, and sat quietly playing with the turner until the car pulled sharply into a car park,

"This is the place," confirmed Ed, mainly to himself.

The large yellow and red sign was emblazoned with the words "Little Adventurer's Day Club" and Ed maneuvered the large Dodge into a parking space at the end of the parking lot.

"Looks nice," said Madeline.

"Yeah nice and stylish," replied Ed, "Are you ok with this. I know it's hard the first day?"

"It'll be fine. He needs to mix with other kids. That way kindergarten won't seem such a shock next year"

Kindergarten. John didn't know what that meant as he trotted alongside his mom, but it sounded horrible. He looked around him as they waked to the elegant, old fashioned looking brick building.

It was single story, made of red brick with a red painted roof, and a colored sign out in front. In between the street and the pre-school was a small paved walled area for outside play, with a small set of swings, a slide, some climbing equipment and a few ride-on pedal cars.

It all seemed strange and exciting to John, as he looked around. There were plenty of other kids too. There was one kid near to him, a boy with blonde hair, wearing a huge orange coat with a hood, carrying a teddy bear in one hand and a plastic bag with some food in the other. Across the other side was another kid, a dark haired boy in a blue shirt. He looked older somehow, like he knew what to do here. John had some snacks in the pockets of his red and black check shirt, but his father had advised him to leave his toys at home. Walking across the other side of the car park was a little girl, who looked small, like she was younger. She had a pretty green dress on with little red sandals, her blonde hair done up in pigtails. She carried a brightly painted tin box that said "Hair Bear Bunch" on the side. Her mom didn't look too good though, like maybe she didn't have any money or something. They hadn't come out of the car park; they had walked up the street, maybe they lived close by.

The Little Adventurer's Day Club was lots of fun.

The lady who looked after them, Miss Shelia, made the children laugh right away as she sat them all down. Then they did some games with numbers and had to shout things out, which was fun. There were colored things on the walls, paintings and drawings and posters of ducks and animals. Pictures and paintings of some guys with beards and wearing suits. John didn't know who they were. Sometimes when Miss Shelia was talking that morning, John's attention would drift to the walls and the colored paintings. At other times, he would watch the street. Over the tops of the houses, he could see the turnpike, and the tops of the trucks as they sped by on the highway. He'd already decided that one day he would be a truck driver. How exciting that would be, just like in that movie he'd seen at the weekend with his mom. The truck had exploded at the end though the driver got away. That was a shame, John had thought. Would have been nice to keep the truck.

Then, Miss Shelia said that it was time for a break, and to go play outside. The blonde kid, still wearing his orange coat, had stood near John, asked him if liked cars. John nodded.

"I like big trucks better" he said, "I'm gonna be a truck driver one day"

The kid had shook his head,

"They're too slow", he answered, "I'm gonna be a race car driver. You wanna play race cars?"

John nodded. He loved cars and trucks and things with wheels. The blonde kid was quiet, but seemed to have no friends apart from John and the dark-haired kid who John had seen going in before. The three of them played Indy 500, running by making race car noises. It seemed like hours of play to John, but in reality it was only about five minutes. He was soon bored with being a race car, and began to look around. The little blonde girl was sitting alone on a swing with her tin box. John thought it was weird that she was sat there not swinging. Swings were fun to go on. He wondered if she wanted a push and went to ask.

"You wanna push on the swing" he said, stuffing his hand in his pockets.

She shook her head.

"Momma gave me some snacks for my box", she replied, "you hungry?"

He'd already eaten his own biscuit, but he was hungry and nodded. So that was what was in the "Hare Bear Bunch" box. He stood near her and saw how neatly packed it was. There was an apple, some grapes in paper wrapping, two biscuits and a cardboard carton of juice. In the corner was a small red teddy bear.

"You want a biscuit, or some grapes," she asked?

"Biscuit please" he said and took it as she offered it. He unwrapped it, and remembering something his father had done with his mom a while back, he broke it in half, and offered the girl the other half. She laughed and took it from him, popping it in her mouth with one of the grapes.

"They like race cars" he said, watching his two friends running around.

The girl nodded slightly,

"I like coloring," she said, "and painting pictures and stuff"

They finished the biscuit together, and Shelia came to take them back inside.

"Mom told me I had to shake hands and be polite," the little girl said as they walked in together. She stopped, and in a practiced motion held out her hand.

"Pleased to meet you," she said, "My name is Melissa George, and I'm nearly five"

John didn't know what to do with the hand, so he grabbed it and they held hands back into the classroom.

"I'm John," he said.

After playtime, they took their jackets and coats off and went to sit in their seats again. His new friend Melissa sat at the back near the little cupboard on her own, whereas he sat with the two boys he knew by now. He wondered whether to move seats to be sat with Melissa, but he didn't know if that was allowed. And so he stayed where he was put. Miss Shelia began putting trays of crayons on the desks. John fingered them with interest. They smelled good, almost good enough to eat, though he knew from experience that they tasted sour. Suddenly remembering his playtime half biscuit, he looked across to Melissa who had a tray of crayons on her own. Miss Sheila gave them pictures from a small coloring book, one between two children. With each child needing a partner, she was pairing them up as she came back through the class, until she came back to the table of three boys. Both John's friends had paired up for the task, and Miss Sheila seemed to be looking around.

Always a bright boy, John seized his chance and asked,

"Could I go sit with my friend Melissa?"

Miss Sheila smiled, and touched his head.

"Of course honey," she said, "there's a seat there right at the side."

He stepped down from his chair, and moved to where the little blond girl sat with the crayons, looking at her paper.

"We got a forest," she said, "I like coloring"

"We got a real forest," John replied looking at the picture, "behind the house. And a creek too, with a bridge. Dad takes me there sometimes. I want to fish, but he says there's nothing in it."

The little girl nodded.

"You got a bridge and a creek and a bridge? Can you play poohsticks?"

John didn't know what that was.

"You sit one side of the bridge with a stick," she explained. "Then you drop it in the water and run to the other side to watch it come out. Momma read it to me from a book."

"I never tried", he replied. "That sounds like fun"

"Yeah," nodded Melissa, "Momma said ya gotta pay attention to whose stick is whose, otherwise they all look the same."

"You could color them in?" John suggested.

"I tried," she said, "I got lots of crayons at home. But it doesn't work. It still looks brown in the water. Maybe you could use other stuff, like from home. Like a carton. I dunno. Some stuff doesn't float though."

John made up his mind to try it out, and opened his mouth to tell his friend so, but at that moment Shelia came over to them, and touched both their heads,

"OK chatterboxes," she said with a twinkle in her eye, "can either of you tell me what I just said to the class?"

Neither of them had even known Miss Sheila had been talking. They shook their heads, downcast.

"It's ok this once," she said sternly, "but if I'm talking, then I want you to listen to me. Now each of you pick a color and take it in turns to color a section in. Decide what color you want it to be."

They looked at their picture. Of the pictures from the book, theirs was perhaps the least interesting. The pair of girls in front of them had a clown's face. The boys to the right had a peacock, those to the right of that had a couple of race cars. Their picture was of a field, a small forest, and some animals standing around eating grass.

"I'll get the green one," Melissa said, "Forests have to be all green."

"Good," said Miss Sheila, keeping the two on the task in hand, "what about you, John, why don't you do the animals?"

"Brown, right?"

"Good boy," said Miss Sheila, "let's see a good picture from you two."

Miss Sheila returned to the front, and John watched as Melissa picked up her green crayon and started coloring the field. He watched her hand as she gently colored. She had neat little hands, as most of the other little girls seemed to have, but hers, he noticed, seemed a pinker color, somehow closer to his own. He watched her fingers. She was good at coloring. Then she slid the paper across to him,

"You wanna take a turn," she asked?

"Yeah," he replied, "I'll do these cows."

"I don't think they're cows," she replied, "I dunno what they are, but they don't look like cows. I'll ask."

Melissa raised her hand like they'd been taught that morning,

"We got cows at home," he admitted, "used to have loads of them."

"In the house?" Melissa asked, her hand still raised.

John put down his crayon,

"No", he replied laughing, "in the fields and stuff. On the ranch. It was my granddads, but dad sold most of em off. Said they weren't making him money"

"How do cows make money?"

"I dunno. I think maybe dad grows em from babies and sells em."

"Yes Melissa", asked Miss Sheila, "what is it?"

The little girl had forgotten her hand was still up, and as Miss Sheila came over to her, she wondered what she had wanted her teacher for.

"Forgotten, honey?" asked Miss Sheila, amused.

"Maybe if you both spent less time chattering together and more time coloring," she said, "then you'd remember things, huh?"

Coloring. That made her remember, and she looked down at her discarded green crayon,

"Oh yeah", said Melissa suddenly, "we didn't know if these were cows or not. Cows grow on ranches and he says this doesn't look like a ranch. So maybe we were doing it wrong to color them in brown".

Miss Sheila stifled a smile and looked over them,

"They're deer I think," she said looking at Melissa's neat work with the green, "it doesn't matter what they are, just do a good job with the coloring."

She left them to it. Privately, she was glad little Melissa had found a friend. Her momma had told her that the little girl was very quiet, and needed bringing out of herself. And here she was chatting and talking away to her new friend. That should cheer her momma up. Melissa's mom had looked terribly ill. Miss Sheila and the director of the little preschool had both noticed it. She watched as the pair had downed their crayons once again and were busy discussing something, their little hands gesturing as if to make a point to each other.

"Chatterboxes in the back" she said loudly, "I want more coloring and less talking, otherwise I'll find a seat here in the front."

She watched as crayons were picked up hurriedly and coloring began.

Lunchtime came and, for the little ones, that was the end of the day. Melissa held her new friend's hand as they walked out the school to where their folks were waiting,

"Is that your mom?" he asked, looking at the tall woman in the thick coat and furry hat.

"Yeah, we only live a couple blocks away so she can walk to get me. Is that your dad in the truck there?"

John looked over at the red pickup that had the name "Mason Ranches Belle Starr" on the side,

He shook his head,

"That's Peter," he said, "one of the ranch guys. I guess Dad's busy and Mom has a new baby now."

"Oh. Sorry. Well will I see ya tomorrow?"

"Yeah. Can I sit with you again?"

She nodded, then as her mom gestured to her, she went running.

"Bye John," she shouted, "see ya tomorrow."

He watched her run to her momma. Peter the ranch hand was still reading "Sports Form" and hadn't noticed him. Melissa's mom picked up the little girl and hugged her close, listening intently as the little one told her something. Her mom nodded with a smile and looked over at where John stood. She waved to him and he waved back.

1999

John was alone in the cemetery. It was winter, and patches of melted snow still lay on the ground. It had been a year or so since he had been here, he hadn't come back to his hometown since...he just couldn't. He'd walked out on the family business. Walked out on the family ranch, the Belle Starr house, everything. That had been handed that over to his sister. His life seemed like such a blur now, a maelstrom of events that seemed to be played at too high a speed. His mind seemed to play tricks on him. Things seemed wrong since...he fingered the headstone, daring himself to look down at the name, the name that he never could bear to look at, though he'd been here more than once, he never had looked upon the name on the stone.

He knelt in the dirt, feeling the wet earth soak the knees of his suit pants. His hands shaking, his eyes blurred as he ran his hands across the engraved letters on the granite,

Suddenly he remembered the box. The "Hair Bear Bunch" lunch tin. Where the hell had that memory come from. John's hands shook as he knelt there on the soil remembering her and that little tin. He couldn't move now, he was just a shaking monument of grief and anger. It had been over a year, and still he felt unable to deal with it. He'd been back here twice, to this cemetery in his home town, unbeknown to his family, and the pain was still as great as before. He still remembered every inch of her, every expression on her face, every tiny movement of that hand coloring that picture that first day he met her with that fucking lunchbox she carried. They said that in time he would forget. They lied. They said in time the pain would ease. They lied. They said that in time he would love again. They fucking lied. Every single word out of every well-meaning mouth was a fucking dirty bastard lie. He hadn't forgotten her, he hadn't moved on, the pain wasn't better, it hadn't gone away, if anything it had gotten worse. He wouldn't love again and never could because the one that was the other half of his soul was underneath this wet frozen ground beneath this piece of granite. He still wanted to dig down under the earth, climb in the coffin at the side of her, hold her and go to sleep at her side.

He felt that pain in his head again, the stabbing pain that had been there since before...well for a long time anyway. He figured it was just all of this, and he shook it off, closing his eyes. The pain faded and he opened his eyes. Steeling himself, he wiped his eyes and forced himself to look upon the name on the headstone. It was the hardest thing he'd ever done.

1971, September

"I think he likes it," he heard his mom saying from the kitchen, "he made friends with a little girl. They shared a biscuit"

He heard his dad snort.

"No guys at that school?"

"It isn't the fifties," mom said airily, "and you're not your father."

John stopped listening. He was playing with Legos on the floor. The baby was asleep in the corner of the big living room. He was trying to build a truck using the wheels and the yellow and red bricks, but it just wouldn't come right.

The morning after, it was a different ranch hand who took John to the pre-school. With a lot of the land, and some of the cattle being sold off, there were less ranch hands now, and those who were kept on the books didn't have that much to do. This was Jake, a gangly, wiry man with a permanent hand-rolled cigarette dangling from the corner of his mouth. He was a much more casual driver than his father, with one arm resting on the rolled down window as they sped along.

He glanced over to the small boy.

"Hear you got a little girlfriend?" he said smiling. Jake winked conspiratorially.

"She gave me a biscuit", John said looking around him as they drove down the turnpike.

Jake laughed.

"Yeah," he said, "way to a man's heart is through his stomach. Just wait till ya grow up and she has her hand on your wallet as well as your heart."

John didn't know what Jake meant, and didn't answer. Jake patted his head with a smile,

"Ah, he breathed, "don't worry about it. Just enjoy being a kid, and be good to your friend."

They pulled up on the sidewalk outside the school, the pickup being a little too big for the pre-school's playground. John looked out the window at the moms waving their kids goodbye. There was the blond kid, Ian he was called, running into the playground. Melissa was there, holding her mom's hand and gripping the Hair Bear Bunch lunch tin with the other, looking around. Her mom caught sight of the pickup and pointed to it. Melissa looked up and nodded, saying something to her mom.

Jake opened the door, and lifted John down from the seat,

"You ok, little guy?" he said.

John nodded, and went to where his friend was standing.

"Pick you up later," shouted Jake. John waved and went to his friend.

"Hi," he said.

Melissa smiled.

"I got you another biscuit" she said.

Mom looked down at her laughing.

"One each this time," she said with a twinkle in her eye, "I can spare an extra biscuit for you both."

"Thanks," said John, looking at his friend. She was wearing the same little dress she'd worn the day before, only the pigtails had been brushed out and mom had given her a bright red Alice hairband.

"We got extra grapes too," said Melissa, "mom says we gotta have fruit."

"You have to stay healthy," her mom said, "both of you."

She knelt in front of her little girl.

"I have to go now," she said, "You be good. Look after each other and I'll see you soon."

"Bye Mommie" said Melissa.

"Goodbye maam", said John, "thanks for the biscuit and the grapes."

You're welcome honey," she said and walked away.

That morning, they spent a really boring hour learning about numbers. They had to learn about counting, and because Miss Sheila watched them intently, there wasn't much time to talk. John had wanted to ask his friend about Legos, whether she had any and if she knew how to make stuff, but he didn't have the opportunity. Shelia came around and placed a wooden object on their desk; an abacus, to add numbers with. There were three metal rails on the abacus, and on each metal rail were a series of counters, on one rail there were blue counters, on another red and the other one yellow.

The counters slid along and interlocked with each other. John was listening as Shelia explained what it was for.

"That one goes to Yonkers," whispered Melissa.

"Huh" said John quietly.

"See," see said smiling slightly, "they're subway trains. The yellow one goes to Yonkers."

She slid the counters along with her finger. She was right. It did look like a subway train. John loved trains. Not as much as trucks, but he loved trains too.

"The red one goes to Harlem" John replied, moving the trains along with his finger.

"Hurry. The Yonkers train is waiting."

John chuckled as the red abacus train moved along its rail to its connection with the Yonkers trains. Then the Yonkers train with its imaginary passengers moved back along the rail.

"Where can the blue trains be going?" asked Melissa?

John thought for a moment,

"San Francisco airport" he said. He'd heard his dad talking about it. Uncle Allan lived near there in California, so he remembered.

"The airport express," said Melissa, forgetting to whisper, "it has to go real fast."

She whooshed the blue train to the other end quickly.

And it hit the end of the abacus with a clack.

"Oh no there's been a crash" said John.

"Yeah it's come off the lines and everything."

Melissa laughed.

"Maybe it was a bomb like that one in Alaska?" she asked.

John didn't know anything about a bomb. He heard about his parents discussing something about a plane, but hadn't cared. He didn't like planes so much. In any case, the airport express was soon fixed and they whooshed it back along the rail to the station...

...where it was met by Shelia.

"Are you guys having fun?" she said, a stern look on her face.

"We're playing with the train", said Melissa sweetly, "the red one goes to Yonkers, the yellow one goes to Harlem and the blue one is the Airport train."

"No," corrected John, "you jumbled it up. Miss Shelia, the yellow one goes to Yonkers."

"Oh yeah," broke in Melissa, "it's the yellow one that goes to Yonkers, and the red one that goes to Harlem."

"And," continued John, "the airport express crashed, but it's ok again."

Shelia sighed.

"Anyway", she began, "when you two are finished playing trains, I'm explaining about numbers."

She turned to the rest of her small class.

"Class," she said, addressing the infants, "who can put their hands up and explain about how to count to twenty for the purpose of John and Melissa here who haven't been listening."

The little ones giggled and turned around to look at those who had been playing instead of paying attention. Melissa blushed slightly, and gently returned the abacus trains to their starting position.

The rest of the half hour they spent quietly doing basic counting and a little adding quiz in their workbook. The two of them learned, when Shelia wasn't watching, to work together and get the work finished faster. If he didn't know the answer, he poked her arm with the end of his pencil, and she in turn poked him with hers. After four simple sums, this began to develop into a finger poking war, until a gentle cough from Shelia in their direction stopped them in their tracks. Nevertheless, their quiz was finished quickly and, more importantly, correctly, and they went out to play happy and laughing.

After break, where they again shared their biscuits sat on the swings, to John's delight it was time for Legos. John loved Legos. For the Legos, the kids were in the other room. The playroom they called it. There were no tables or chairs in the playroom, and the kids sat cross legged on the floor, or knelt. Melissa selected a spot next to John, and knelt down. The rest of the kids were already busy making houses, or miniature forts, or dens, or race cars.

"Do you know how to do Legos," he asked her?

She nodded,

"I have some at home," she said, "I made a house. I have no wheels though."

"Houses don't have wheels," John said, "unless it's a trailer. I think those have wheels."

"Yeah," she said, "they do. And those other things too, I dunno what they're called? Like little trucks with curtains and windows."

"Winnie something?" John suggested.

"Yeah," she nodded, "they have wheels too."

"I got loads of wheels at home," he said, "I could bring you some"

Melissa nodded again,

"Then I could make a winnie out of my house."

"I'll tell mom to get some" he answered, "let's build one of those now. With a big truck front and loads of wheels."

And so they did. Whereas it hadn't worked for him before playing on the lounge floor, with her fingers to help him, together they did it. Their creation, as that was all it could be called, had a huge truck bonnet, side walls, a roof, a veranda and about eighteen wheels.

Miss Shelia came looking, marvelling at the 'wonderful' creations.

"Oh my," she said, "what on earth is that beast? It looks like a huge juggernaut."

"It's a Winnie trailer," said Melissa proudly, "like a truck, but with beds and stuff."

"You mean a motorhome?" laughed Miss Sheila, "a Winnebago."

"Yeah," replied John, "one of those. She has a proper house at home, so I'm gonna get my mom to bring her some wheels to make it into one of those."

"You can't make a real house into a motorhome, honey," she said patting John's head.

"No," Melissa corrected, "I made a Legos house, but I don't have any wheels."

"I got loads of wheels," broke in John, "so I'm giving her some."

"Then I can make a winnie…," she struggled to get her tongue around the word,

"Winnebago" corrected Miss Sheila with amusement,

"Yeah," answered Melissa, "one of those. I'm gonna turn my Lego house into one of those".

Shelia laughed to herself at the little pair on the floor. All the kids loved the Legos, but these two seemed to be getting more out of it. What imaginations they had. True, John and Melissa could be considered chatterboxes, and sometimes a little naughty, but privately she loved their little earnest faces when they were telling her one of their long rambling tales.

Over the course of the weeks, friendships came and went, as the little ones formed new friendships, and learned how to interact with their little groups. Apart from one pair who stayed solidly locked together in friendship. In a way, Shelia was glad to see this. John and Melissa spoke to other kids, but they were firm friends, and over the course of the weeks, it never occurred to either of them to move seats. In fact, apart from once, they had never argued.

That argument had come one morning playtime, when Melissa had been sat on the little swing at the bottom of the play yard. She was sat talking to another little girl, a quiet Asian girl who always sat at the front. John didn't know what to do. Why was his friend talking to some other kid? He stood around wondering what to do, and watched as Melissa turned to him, and seemed to scrutinise him, before saying something to the Asian girl and laughing. That made John mad. He watched as the Asian girl got up, and wandered over to Shelia to ask her something. John felt suddenly as if the whole class were laughing at him for something. What had Melissa said? He had thought they were friends, and here she was laughing at him, and saying stuff to other kids? He suddenly felt horrible inside. He stomped over to her, his face a mask of pain and stared at her, sitting there on the swing. He heard the words of his father in his head as he had smacked a ranch hand once.

"This is how Mason men deal with things."

She looked up at him, almost surprised that he was there. He reached out hard with both hands and pushed her violently backwards off the swing. She fell off the swing and sat down in the dirt, hard, the Hare Bear Bunch lunch box spilling everywhere. He didn't know if Miss Sheila had seen, but at that moment, he didn't care. He was too furious and too angry to care. He stalked away as she sat there in the dirt. Then, after a moment he turned and looked at his little friend. Her eyes were looking straight at him, and as she surveyed the wreckage of her snack box. He saw her eyes fill with tears. Little as he was, he saw the look of betrayal and the look of hurt in his friend's eyes, and felt the sudden blackness of pain engulf his little shell.

"I made my friend cry," he thought, and stopped there watching as she sat there, tears streaming down her cheeks.

And then suddenly, the little boy was crying too, as he saw the pain and hurt and betrayal in her face. If anything, he was crying harder than her. He walked back over to her, knelt beside her, and, in a technique copied from his mom to cure him from tears when he'd fell down, he put his arms around her neck and kissed her on the cheek. For a moment, they hugged each other, relief in both their little hearts that their friendship was intact. Somehow not wanting to let go, they both became aware of the spilt contents of the little tin box, and letting her go, he helped her to pick up the contents and pack the little box until it was good as new.

"Why'd ya push me?" she said puzzled, "was it a joke?"

John shook his head sadly, his little face still full of tears. She held his hand.

"No," he said, "you made me mad. I thought you were laughing at me. My dad always pushes people around who tick him off."

"I was saying to Kim that you were the one I shared my biscuits with, cos you were my best friend."

John was silent, and as he remembered her sitting down in the dirt, the tears came to his face again.

"I'm sorry I hurt you," he said, his sad little face earnest.

"It's ok," she said, "You're my best friend. I forgive you. Ya want a biscuit? They're a bit dirty, but I don't think they're too bad."

They sat down in the dirt together and unpacked the sand coated biscuits, eating them and laughing now.

The little boy thought hard. Doing things the way he'd seen his dad do them had made his friend cry. That had been the worst thing he'd ever seen or felt in his whole short life. He'd never ever felt so bad. It made him feel weird. John had always tried to copy his father, to be like him, tall and strong and tough. But this made him feel horrible. Being tough had made his friend cry. He knew, even if it meant he was never like his father, he would never do that to her again. He wondered if his Dad had been wrong.

It was too complicated for him to think about, and so he did what he'd started doing a while back to comfort himself: he put his arm round his Melissa and hugged her. She returned the hug, and in this position they stayed until Shelia called them in. She'd watched the whole thing, concerned, but hoping the two of them would sort it out between themselves. They were very young, yet very close to each other and she had hoped that the little boy would learn a lesson. By the look on his face, and the care he took of his little friend, he had learned the lesson and fast. The remainder of the day Shelia turned a blind eye to the constant chattering of Melissa and John during lessons, leaving them, for once, unattended to talk and dream and play at the back of the little classroom. By the end of the day, they were laughing and chattering in pleasure, all memory of the incident gone.

Jakes little pickup rattled more than the newer one did as they sped home that night, with the old ranch hand at the wheel.

"Something on your mind, kid?" he said with a look of concern to John.

"It's just," began the boy, "I pushed my friend in the dirt. I made her cry."

The very thought of the memory made his eyes fill with tears again, and he cast his head down. Even though the two of them had forgotten the incident completely, he remembered it now.

"Huh," said Jake, "By the look on your face, ya already realised that was the wrong thing to do?"

"Yeah," said John sadly.

"And have you said sorry to her?"

"Yeah, straight away. I kissed her on the cheek like mom does and then we were friends again. I'm never doing that again."

Jake looked at the little boy with affection.

"Good boy," he said, "I'm proud of you. There's guys way older than you have never figured that one out."

"Dad does it with you guys sometimes, don't he," said John, "I always thought he was cool. Tough."

Jake could see the boy was confused, and John missed the look on his face when Ed Mason was mentioned. Maybe when he was older. He thought of something wise to say,

"Listen kid," he said, "your Mom and Dad love you a lot. Don't forget that. But they can only teach you so much. Some things ya gotta learn on your own. Like today. You learned that pushing people around is bad. It makes them feel bad, and it makes you feel bad. If the whole world knew that, we'd be in a lot better place right now, let me tell ya."

"Is my Dad wrong?" said John suddenly.

Jake blanched. How the hell to even approach questions about Ed Mason.

"Did you enjoy hurting your little buddy?" he asked.

John shook his head firmly.

29

"It was horrible," he said, "I cried harder than her. Then we laughed cos we had cried so much."

"So do you think its right to push people around? Would you push her again if your Dad asked you to?"

John couldn't imagine his dad asking him to do that. But the answer would be the same if he did

"No sir" he said, "I'd refuse. I'll never hurt her again. Never."

"Good boy", Jake replied, "we'll make a man outta you yet."

2001

The diner was run down. He could see that. Past its best. Crumbling. Nobody wanted to go there anymore. Bit like him, he thought. John sat and drank the foul tasting coffee that had been served to him in the Styrofoam cup and watched the trucks go by on the interstate. He began to wonder how his life had led him here, alone and widowed in a dreary run down truck stop in the wrong state in the wrong part of the country. As he considered this, he noticed a little girl sat beside him,

"What you want kid," he said brusquely, "where's your mom?"

"At home," she replied in a matter of fact tone, Dad's in the hospital. In a coma. Had a bad car wreck."

"You here alone," he asked looking around for her parents. She seemed only about seven or eight. For a fleeting moment, noting her scruffy beatnik pants and battered sneakers, she reminded him of…no….that was years ago. He'd locked those memories away a long time ago.

"Yeah I'm alone," she said, "sucks, doesn't it? I was an orphan till my folks chose me. Who knows why they chose me? I wouldn't have chosen me."

He smiled, sipping his coffee.

"They musta had their reasons," he muttered, "You want a coke, kid?"

She shook her head.

"And then he goes and rolls his car on the freeway," she said sadly, "he's in a coma now. She doesn't know what to do with herself. He won't wake up. How's that for luck. Just as I get folks to love me, he goes and does that. Now she can't keep the big house going without him on what she makes and we might have to move into an apartment."

"Sorry, kid," he said staring at his cup, "sometimes I forget there's other folks in the world whose lives aren't so great. For what it's worth, I lost my special one too, a long time ago. She was the thing I loved most in the world. But you know what, at least we had a short time with them...knew them for a little while. Better that than nothing, huh kid?"

He looked up. But the little girl had gone. The diner was near empty and how much time had passed he didn't know. He called for a refill.

1972, February

"President Nixon today met with Mao Zedong in what is a historic visit to the peoples..."

John's mom flicked off the radio.

"Hey I was listening to that," Ed replied. "Just 'cos you have no interest in the news."

"China?" replied his Mom. "Why would I be interested in that? I do have some news for you though."

"Oh," replied Ed. looking up from his paper. "What's that?"

She looked around the kitchen to make sure John's little boy's ears weren't listening, and then she leaned in closer to her husband.

"You remember that woman from John's pre-school?" she said. "The one you said looked like death warned up?"

"Yeah I remember," replied Ed,

"She's the mom of that little g rl John shares those biscuits with."

"That's her," replied his wife.

"What about her?" asked Ed, looking back at his paper.

"Found her dead this morning. Husband walked in the bathroom and there she was. I heard it from Danny, who was delivering the papers around the corner. Dan and Barbara's kid goes to the same pre-school."

"Geez," said Ed shaking his head. "You never know when your time is up, do ya?"

"No," said John's mom sadly. "That poor little girl."

"Yeah," nodded Ed, looking back at the paper. "Hey have you seen this? The initial designs of the Space shuttle are in the paper here, some artist drawing. Can you believe it? We'll be living on goddamned Mars in ten years."

1973, September

John turned into a solitary, sometimes moody little boy. He was six years old now, and had been at elementary school for a year. His friend Melissa never returned to the pre-school after her mother's sudden death. At first, he missed her terribly, but then her memory began to fade. Elementary school was bigger, and more exciting, with more stuff to do, but sometimes he was lonely. He still played with the blond kid whose name was Ian, John had discovered. But he usually preferred to be alone, and when playtime came, the little boy could usually be found sitting on his own on one of the benches, dreaming to himself. And when he wasn't at school, he was usually with Jake. With John's mom pregnant again with a third child, his parents had little time for their eldest son. Jake the ranch hand, kept on at Belle Starr even though a lot of the land was now sold off and all the cattle gone, was mainly an odd job man and maintenance guy. But John's parents entrusted the care of their son to him when he wasn't at school, and he taught the little boy to fish and how to survive in the open, camping like cowboys. Compared to school, which was quite a miserable experience, John loved spending time with Jake. The ranch hand apparently had no family of his own, although he had heard his father talk about him finding women in something called a "whorehouse," though the little boy hadn't known what that was and hadn't liked to ask.

The long summer vacation of 1972 had been lots of fun. Jake had taken him camping, and his mother and father had taken him to Chicago to see the newly completed Sears tower. It was loads of fun. And he'd even had some new Legos as a gift from his uncle. Legos didn't seem to make him happy any more, as they reminded him of his friend Melissa, who he hadn't seen for over a year. Not that he hadn't asked about her: he had, but his mother had either said she lived with her grandmother or that they had moved. Apparently, Melissa's father had taken his wife's death rather hard.

And then came the new school term. Jake didn't take him anymore. Ed had managed to convince the school bus to make a detour down the bumpy pothole-ridden Decatur Road to pick up his son, along with the rest of the kids. And so there John stood with his satchel, packed neatly with his lunch wrapped up in a paper bag, and his Star Trek pencil case. Most of the kids would already be on the bus when it detoured down Decatur Road, the old road that had once held some of the finest ranch houses in the district. Now there were only three left. Jonesy at the end had died during the winter, and the bank intended to demolish his property and sell the land to build a new turnpike for the highway.

As John watched, he saw the bus come bumping along the dirt road. The driver waved to him, then swung the huge yellow bus into the driveway, pushed a lever that John, knowing about such things, was reverse, and eased the bus backwards.

"Wonder who I'll sit with," thought the little boy with sudden anxiety as he saw the full bus. "I guess I could just stand there at the front."

Decatur Road was narrow, and the maneuver was a hard, tight one. But there was no other turnaround until Jonesy's place right up the road. The bus reversed and turned, the driver opened the door and John climbed aboard.

"Morning, young man," said the driver in a friendly way. "Go take a seat. Fourth row back, little lady on the left wanted to know if it was you we were picking up. Think you got an admirer, huh?"

John thanked the driver, and trotted to the fourth row back, wondering who it was that knew him. Might be Janelle, or Katie. They both fussed over him, as little girls sometimes did.

But it wasn't. She now had her blonde hair loose, and cut with a little short line of bangs across her forehead that meant he didn't recognise her at first. But he recognised the lunch box.

Hare Bear bunch!

Both of their faces broke into smile when they saw each other. He sat down; staring at the best friend he hadn't seen for a long time. Suddenly he hugged her tight, and she returned the hug eagerly.

She looked quite modern, though her clothes weren't as clean or as flashy as Katie or Janelle's. She had on a green military color jacket, denim jeans with flowers on them, white socks with cute little bows that dangled, and shiny red sandals. John, who had worn his old comfortable red and black check shirt and the pants his mom had left out for him, felt scruffy by comparison.

"I asked the driver if it was you when we turned this way," she said softly.

"It is me," he said, looking at his friend.

"Yeah I know," she laughed. "I can see ya."

Suddenly the world of elementary school seemed like fun again. And they had years of it. Years and years of playing and having fun and laughing. She could come to his house and play on the land with Jake, and he could go see her mom....

He turned to her quietly, and touched her hand as it rested on the seat.

37

"I'm sorry about your mom," he said looked down at the bus floor.

"She slipped her little hand into his and squeezed it tight.

"Thanks," she said quietly. "Mommy was ill. She'd told me that. Grandma looks after me now. She lived with my dad. He can't cope with me on his own."

"I missed you," he said. "I got some new Legos."

Her face lit up.

"What ya get?" she replied.

"Fire trucks, with cabs, and wheels. My uncle sent it."

"Wow," she said. "I missed last year, spent it at my Grans in Detroit. Do we play with Lego in school here?"

"No," he said sadly. "Just learning and stuff. I don't have anybody to sit with, so you can sit with me if you want."

She gripped his hand tighter.

"Yeah," she replied. "Shame about the Legos though. Don't we play at all?"

"Naw," he shook his head sadly. "Just loads of lessons. You can come to my house on Saturday though if you want. We can play there, or at the bridge. You know, the Poohsticks Bridge?"

"Yeah," she said excitedly. "I'll ask Grandma. She can bring me. I have loads of paints and colors now, so I can paint some sticks and see if they float and we can see them when we play Poohsticks."

Elementary school with his best friend was a new experience for John. He and Melissa were inseparable. She sat next to him in every class, and played with him at playtime. They played with other kids too, of course, but if they hadn't seen each other for a few minutes, they would look around and go find each other. He was a changed boy, confident and smiling for the first time. Melissa was a quiet little girl. Her teachers had been told that her mother had recently died, and they had been watching out for her. But they saw her with a friend, and though she was still prone to be quiet at times, with the little boy from Decatur Road she seemed happy. Not as bright as John in lessons, Melissa was interested more in the art lessons. Painting and coloring she would work laboriously at, skimping on other work to make more time for the art that she loved.

The first week was fun, and the weekend was something they had both been looking forward to excitedly. Her Grandma hadn't had time to come deliver her, and his father and mother had not the time to go get her, so John had asked Jake. And so, in return for helping him sweep out the barn and wash down the pickups, Jake had set off at ten am to the estate in the suburb to pick up John's friend and bring her here. John was excited! His friend from school and preschool was coming here, to his house! He'd worn his favourite shirt, even though his mom nagged that it was getting too small. Though it was nearly fall, it was warm enough for shorts, and he wore his smartest blue shorts and sneakers. Jake seemed to be away for ages, and John watched constantly out of his bedroom window for any sign of the returning pickup. He'd tidied his room, even without any nagging from his mom, picked up his toys and tied them, rebuilt his Lego fire trucks, and arranged his bear smartly on his bed. Where was Jake?

Then Jake was here, the little truck bouncing up the drive. John looked out of his window eagerly. At first he couldn't see her, but there she was, looking out of the window with interest at the ranch as they came up the drive. He bounded down the stairs, almost into his mother.

His mom, glad that her eldest son had found a friend, had made some snacks and a lunch for them to have before they left for the bridge by the creek, at the rear of their land. John's mom felt sorry for the little girl without a mom, and wondered whether she would have eaten properly. And so she made more of a fuss than she perhaps otherwise would have.

"Careful honey," she said smiling. "Best behaviour now."

"I know, mom!" he said, going to the door. He watched as Melissa climbed out of the truck and jumped down before Jake had time to go around to help her. The little girl thanked Jake, then looked up at the big old white house. John ran down the porch steps to meet her. Like him, she was wearing shorts, a sleeveless orange t-shirt, and brown leather sandals. Her hair was held back by pins and stuff. She carried a little brown duffel bag over one shoulder.

"Hi," he said greeting her.

Her face was filled with wonderment at the big old house. It had seen better days, having been built before the turn of the century when the big boom in ranching and cattle had hit. A two story wood construction house, it had four huge windows upstairs, the center two of which led to a small balcony terrace. Downstairs the entrance of the property was pretty grand, with fake pillars surrounding a porch area. Four huge chimneys made from brick extended from the roof. Everything was painted white, as had been the fashion with the big old houses. At the front, the driveway circled around and to the side of the house where the garages were, and the front garden extended down the long driveway to Decatur Road way at the bottom. The front garden had once had an orchard and ornamental gardens, but now it was just tufts of grass and dead old trees. Surrounded on one side by trees and a wood, the other side was littered with farm implements and a couple of barns. The little girl loved it straight away. It looked like a big old happy house, not one of the flat concrete things she and her dad and Grandma lived in, all squished down flat.

"What ya got in the bag?" John said to her as they walked to the doorway.

"I made us some poohsticks with Grandma last night," she said excitedly. "I painted them and everything. And a bottle of juice."

"Come on in, you two," his mom said. "Before you do any of that, you're eating lunch."

"Pleased to meet you, Mrs. Mason," said Melissa politely, holding out her hand.

John's mom took the offered hand.

"It's lovely to see you, sweetheart," she replied to the little girl. "How are you and your daddy now that Grandma's come home?"

Melissa sighed as she climbed the steps to the porch.

"Dad doesn't like Grandma being at home. He doesn't like work either. Grandma is nice though. It's nice to have her living with us. Detroit made her grumpy."

"Well you're always welcome here, dear," Mom said, touching the girl's shoulder.

41

She was glad John had a friend. Ed was amused that it was a little girl and not a little guy, but his wife had said the same, as she always did, to stop being so fifties. Times were changing, anyone could see that. A little guy could be friends with a little girl now. How things changed. John's father heard someone coming in the house, and turned up the radio.

"...this Thursday a landmark game between Champion Bobby Riggs and Billie Jean King ended when ...."

He flicked the radio, and the report of the tennis match off, and listened to the commotion.

"I hope you like our house," his wife was saying.

In the hallway, the little girl said she did. It was amazing. Much bigger than her own, homely and old, with bits of the wood needing to be replaced. She wiped her feet on the mat as they entered.

"Should I take my shoes off?" she asked nervously.

John's mom laughed.

"No honey, you're fine. It's far from being a show home. The floors are torn up in the other hall, so you might get splinters."

Melissa nodded, and John, seeing that Melissa was nervous, took her hand.

"Come on," he said. "Mom says we gotta eat. We'll have our lunch and then go and explore."

They had a good lunch of hot bread rolls, cheese, a bag of corn chips each, and a large drink of juice. John's mom packed Melissa's back pack with chocolate and snack treats for the afternoon, and after thanking his mom, they set off outside.

"I'll show ya 'round the house later," he explained. "It goes dark at four, so we have to be in by then. What time ya have to be home?"

Melissa shrugged.

"Grandma didn't say," the little girl replied. "She works till late and Dad only gets home at eight from work, so I guess eight."

John was happy inside. That meant ages and ages with his friend. She reached her hand out and grabbed his, and hand in hand, they walked 'round the side of the house, past the garages and around the back. At the back, under the French doors that led to the kitchen, there was a swimming pool. That was empty now: it hadn't been used this year at all. Behind the pool was a huge long garden surrounded by the forest trees. They walked to the bottom of the long garden, their little feet getting buried in the long grass. It had been raining the day before, and the grass was wet. Melissa felt the raindrops wet her feet through her sandals, but as it was a warm day, it felt good, and she began to kick her feet through the long tufts.

"Where we going?" she said.

"The path to the creek starts at Decatur road," he explained, "but to get there, you have to go down the drive, turn right and walk down a way, only to come back up the forest path. So I just go out the bottom of the garden and through the bit of broken fence. Leads right to the path."

"And your dad owns all this?" she asked in amazement.

"Yeah," he nodded. "It was my grandpas. The land used to extend for ages and ages, but now on the other side, Dad sold a load of it. We still have the woods though, cos nobody wanted that."

"I wonder why," mused Melissa. "Woods are better than just boring old fields."

"Yeah," he said. "You can make dens and stuff, and the woods have the creek. But cows can't live in woods, they have to have fields."

"Ah," said Melissa nodding.

They reached the very bottom of the garden, where the fence had fallen down and, climbing between the broken pieces of fence post, they squeezed through and into a heavily wooded thicket. Melissa's bag caught on a branch and for a minute she was held up. John saw her, freeing her.

"It got me," she laughed. "Must have been goblins."

"You're not scared, are ya?" he asked.

She shook her head.

"I'm not scared of the goblins, and the dark or stuff like that," she said as they struggled through the thick underbrush to the woodland path.

"What are ya scared of?" he asked, looking into the little girl's eyes.

"I dunno," she said. "When momma said she was ill, I was scared of her going away and not seeing her any more, but now that's happened, I don't know what else I got to be scared of."

He saw her eyes grow sudden tears, and he remembered this was a day of happiness. He turned to his friend and hugged her suddenly.

"You got me," he said. "I won't go away."

"Ya better not," she answered. "You still owe me for that biscuit."

They followed the woodland path for a while, Melissa looking up at the trees for woodpeckers, thrushes and wrens who went about their daily business, unconcerned by the two human interlopers. Melissa absent mindedly picked leaves from bushes as they walked along. One had a caterpillar on it, and she poked John to show it to him.

"Wow," he said. "He's having his lunch."

They watched the caterpillar as she held it aloft. Afraid of them, it curled up into a ball. She gently poked it to make it move, but it did not.

"I better put him back," she said, "so he can carry on eating his lunch."

"Yeah," replied John. "Put him under a leaf somewhere so the birds won't eat him."

He watched as she clambered down under a branch and carefully set down the little left. They watched for a few minutes as the caterpillar eventually unfurled itself and scurried away into the undergrowth.

"He'll be safe now," said John. "Go and hide someplace."

"Yeah," she replied. "Maybe when we come back in spring, he'll be a butterfly."

"Why would he be one of those?" asked John, puzzled.

Melissa laughed.

"Mommie told me about them. They turn into something called a 'Chris list.' Then after that they come out of the Chris list and they're a butterfly. Like magic."

"Wow," he said. "I didn't know that. You're smart sometimes, ya know?"

"Yeah," she said. "It's just what my mom told me."

As they walked, one thing occurred to John. She had said 'when we come back in spring.' He had been worried that his friend wouldn't enjoy her visit to Belle Starr, but he had forgotten his anxiety as they explored the woodlands and the path. She seemed at home here. Somehow, it was as if, before, Belle Starr hadn't been right in some way. Now she was here, this was the thing that was missing.

He made up his mind to ask Jake about it. They were near the creek now. The red bushes were the giveaway. He didn't know what they were, but that they had red berries on that you couldn't eat. They only grew near the creek. The path widened a little, and there was the little bridge.

It was a small wooden footbridge over the small creek that ran the breadth of the Mason's land. Painted white, with stout footboards and a handrail, it stood proudly over the small creek. On one side there was a banking that led down to one or two rocks and the creek itself, and a small clearing, where you could sit and fish. On the other side, the red berry bushes grew a little more.

"Oh it's beautiful!" she exclaimed and ran onto the bridge, poking her head through the wooden handrails to the trickle of water a few feet lower."

"Yeah," said John. "I come here sometimes. Jake says you can fish here, but dad says there's no fish in the creek. I just like to sit here."

She looked all around her, her eyes taking in the whole quiet, tranquil scene, then sat down on the deck cross legged, setting the bag down before her.

"Poohsticks Bridge," she said.

"Huh?" he asked.

"Poohsticks Bridge," she repeated, "that's what we'll call it. When we're all old and married, we'll come back here every year to meet at Poohsticks Bridge, like they do in the movies."

John was suddenly sad, and she looked at him puzzled.

"We can think of a different name if you want," she said.

"I don't want to just come here once a year," he said, "I want to be here every day. I missed you last time you left."

She laughed.

"Then we'll come here every day. Maybe we could pitch a tent and live here like hobos."

John smiled a little.

"What about your husband?" he asked. "He'll want to come."

"He can stay home and look after my kids," she said dreaming. "Or else I'll just marry you and we can have our kids with us here."

He laughed loud now, and sat down in front of her, mimicking her cross-legged pose.

"How many we gonna have?" he asked.

"I dunno," she said. "Dad says I'm a pain in the ass, and one's too many. But your mom and dad are gonna have three, so I dunno."

"I don't think you're a pain in the ass," he said. "Dads are wrong sometimes. Mine was wrong once."

"I think he's just sad," said Melissa. "Grandma says I remind him of mommy. I think two kids would be fun."

"Four would be better," John said decisively. "'Cos then the two girls can play together and the two guys can too. That would leave us free to play here."

"That's a good idea," she returned, "but the guys can play with the girls too."

"Yeah," he said, having forgotten that his best friend was a girl. "Shall we tell my mom when we get home? Tell her we're marrying each other."

"Sure," said Melissa. "We'll tell her later. Maybe they'll say its ok for us to come live here."

"Poohsticks Bridge," he confirmed.

She nodded, suddenly remembering the sticks she had made. Rummaging around in the little rucksack, she found two sticks. She had filed the ends into points, and one was painted neatly yellow with a green stripe, and the other red with a white stripe.

"You have the red one," she said handing it to him.

"You made these?" he said examining the little stick.

"Yeah," she said. "I got my paints out and Grandma helped me."

"They're real good," he said. "Where'd you get the sticks?"

"I went looking for some," she answered. "The old man at the corner has a big oak tree in his front yard, so I went and broke some branches off of it. He used to trim it, but his wife just died so now he doesn't."

John didn't want to remind her of her mom again, and death, so he changed the subject.

"Let's see how they float," he said uncrossing his legs and standing. She followed him to the edge of the footbridge, stick in hand.

"Let's drop them and see who wins when they come out the other side."

They got onto their tiptoes so they could reach over the rail and held their sticks.

"One...," she counted, "two....three!"

They dropped their sticks in unison, and watched as they fell into the stream. Both sticks bobbed around for a little bit, then the yellow one seemed float away and under the bridge. The pair ran to the other side of the footbridge and watched as the yellow stick emerged first.

"Ha-ha," she laughed with joy. "I won! I won!"

He laughed too, and they watched as their little sticks caught on some rocks.

"C'mon," she said. Let's get em back and go again."

"How do we get em back?" he asked.

"Go in the water, dummy," she said, smiling.

"But it's cold and you'll get wet," he replied.

"Usually happens in water," she said.

He watched as she lifted her foot and unbuckled her sandals, leaving them on the deck of the bridge. The girl walked to the banking next to the wooden railings, and onto the grass.

"You coming?" she asked, watching him with amusement.

"Yeah," he said, though he wasn't sure if he was supposed to go near the water or not.

"You gonna get those sneakers wet," she said, sounding like his mom.

Reluctantly, he kicked them off and followed her barefoot through the grass. It felt cold and squidgy and damp. When he got to the banking, she was already halfway down and nearly at the small stream. He followed her to the banking. Melissa waded out to the water, holding out her hand for him to hold so that he could steady her. He planted his cold feet onto the banking and held her hand as she bent down to pick up their sticks. Having retrieved them, she placed them in her shorts pocket and started to splash.

"Come on in," she said. "It's lovely and cold."

He did so, and joined her in the water, paddling about amongst the stones and sand. They started to splash each other and pretty soon, tired, laughing, and soaked through, they clambered back onto the banking and up the grass verge back to the bridge. The early afternoon sun had broken through the trees now overhead and was baking the timbers of the bridge. She sat down on the bridge, taking the sticks out of her pocket. The paint was intact, apart from one or two places where it had chipped off.

"Shall we go again?" she asked.

"Yeah," he said, sitting facing her, "in a minute. Let's dry off first."

"Yeah," she replied. "We can have a snack."

She reached in the bag and fished out two biscuits, and gave him one. They ate them hungrily.

She leaned back against the white painted post of the bridge, and stretched out her feet. The little boy folded the paper of his biscuit, and touched the bottom of her pink foot with the edge of the paper.

"Hey," she laughed. "That tickles."

"Are you ticklish," he asked, touching the paper to her other foot until she jumped up and sat cross legged, hiding her vulnerable feet underneath her.

"Yeah," she said, leaping at him, "are you?"

He didn't know. Turned out he was. She grabbed for the sensitive bits of flesh underneath his arms and he squealed with laughter as they tickled each other. He grabbed for her bare foot again, and in defending herself, she kicked out and accidentally smacked him in the side of the head with her bare heel.

"Ouch, geez!" he shouted, rubbing his head and falling back.

She suddenly looked worried.

"I'm sorry," she said. "It was only an accident."

He saw her little face suddenly grow concerned, and have the beginnings of upset on it."

"It's ok," he said smiling, "Ain't nothing up there anyway, only dust and gravel. Dad said so."

"That explains why it felt like I kicked a rock," she said rubbing her heel.

He laughed.

"Besides," she said, looking at him with those green eyes. "Call it payback for smacking me in the dirt that day on the swing."

They both laughed. He'd never had a friend before, and not one like this, who he could laugh with. Accidents could happen, and they had the ability to laugh it off and have fun.

1973, October

The little boy couldn't imagine what life had been like before her now. Most weekends they came to what they called Poohsticks Bridge. John had begged his mom for the tent, so Melissa and he could camp out and have a night time sleepover, but his mom said they were too young. If they were having a sleepover, Melissa had to sleep in the guest room. In the house, she'd added firmly. They were inseparable at school too. Most of the kids had a special friend now. Janelle had Katie, Ian had David, and John had Melissa. The little girl, though she spent time with her Nan, spent most of her time in John's company, or in the company of his family. His mom, feeling sorry for how thin the little girl looked, had started to feed her alongside her own children and over the weeks she grew healthy and stronger. The late summer air browned their skin as they spent all their time in the woods or at the bridge.

The little girl was excited. Halloween was here. Though her Mommie had taken her to trick or treat, she'd never been since...since her Mommie had gone away. This year would be no different, it seemed. Gran didn't agree with knocking on folks' doors and disturbing them, and Dad was either too busy or didn't seem to care. But Melissa was wrong. This would be very different. Janelle's mom, deciding that trick or treating was so old fashioned, had decided to let her daughter have a party for all her elementary school friends. Naturally, Melissa had received an invite, and so had John. Somewhat afraid to ask her grandma permission, John asked Jake to mention it on one of the occasions he picked his friend up from her house.

Grandma had been dubious,

"She seems a little young for parties," she's mused.

"It'll be fine," Jake had reassured her. "My little guy is responsible. He's been my right-hand man up at Belle Star since he could walk. His mom and dad are right proud of him. He'll take care of her. I'll pick her up in the truck from school, she can have dinner with the folks, go to the party and everyone's happy... and you get a kid free night on Halloween."

That did sound tempting. A kid free night.

"Even better, she can sleep over at Belle Starr. We got plenty of room. Excited post-party kid taken off your hand too. Give you and your son a little peace, huh?"

"Well," grandma mused, "it's not been easy since..."

"I know," replied Jake, taking a long drag on his rolled-up cigarette. "Can't be easy. Have a couple nights off. We'll take care of the little one for ya."

And so Grandma had agreed. Thanks to Jake's nicotine stained silver tongue, Grandma had even agreed to make Melissa a costume. The little girl was already developing a somewhat skewed sense of humour, and specified, in a most earnest voice, a zombie outfit, something from *The Night of the Living Dead*.

The little girl was ages in the bathroom at Belle Starr getting ready. John's mom helped her, and though the older woman was shocked at the costume, she helped apply the makeup and the blood.

"I'm not sure it's ok for you to be watching movies like that, honey," she chided.

"I haven't watched it," Melissa replied. "I just saw the movie poster at the theatre in Detroit with my grandma last year. Do I look really freaky?"

"I think you'll win the costume competition hands down, dear," said John's mom. "Even I don't know if you're living or dead."

The little girl did indeed look freaky. Dressed in her old jeans, brown leather sandals and white stained t-shirt, her entire outfit was covered in grime, blood and fake scars. John's mom had done her face make-up for her. Her eyes were surrounded by death-like dark eye makeup and grey foundation, making the blonde girl look more like a freshly dug corpse than a healthy little girl. By comparison, John had visited the costume store and selected a red suit of sorts, with a mask covering his eyes, and a red tail. He was a red devil and loved his costume. He had wanted fangs too, but mom had said no. She didn't want the kids to mess with their teeth.

He watched as Melissa came out of the bathroom, imitating the stumbling zombie walk. She held her blood stained mouth open and gasped,

"Brains...I need to eat your brains."

As she walked towards him. The little boy looks terrified at first, and then he laughed nervously when he saw how realistic her outfit looked.

"You know," chided his mom, "for a little girl who has only seen a movie poster, you know an awful lot about that zombie business."

She looked warningly at the little girl, who did not meet her gaze.

"You look good too," Melissa said to her friend. "I love your tail."

"Thanks," he said. "It's a pain to walk with. Keeps tripping me, but I like the costume. Don't you have a tail?"

"I think she had quite enough, with all that blood," reminded his mom. "Go step into the living room you two. Dad wants a picture of you in your costumes."

John was surprised. His dad always hated Halloween. Something had happened though, after a row between Dad and Jake, though John didn't know what about.

"Come on kids," Dad said, ushering them into the room "Careful Melissa, don't bleed all over the walls."

The little girl chuckled.

"Brains..." she gasped again. "I need brains."

"Ha," laughed Mr Mason, "then I don't know why you're hanging around with my son. Not many of those in there, huh kid?"

"Ed, don't be mean," chided his mother. "Just take their picture."

"Yep," he said. "Step right over here and I'll take a snap. And in years to come, when you two are married with kids of your own, I can bring this photo out and embarrass you with it."

The two kids giggled and stood together holding hands as John's dad focussed the Nikon and snapped their picture.

"All done, you guys," he said. "Mom's gonna drop you off, and I'll pick you up at ten."

"Not Jake?" John asked.

"No," said Ed Mason, blanching slightly. "Jake's night off. Mom's doing the kid taxicab tonight."

"Be good," dad chided, "and look after your girlfriend."

They trotted outside.

"Yeah," snickered Melissa. "Be good to your girlfriend. Kiss kiss kiss."

"Shaddap you," he replied, laughter in his voice. "You can always turn into a real zombie you know."

"Just try it," she said, sticking out her tongue. "I'll just kick ya in the head again."

They couldn't wait to get in the car. They both knew what was coming, though mom did not. As she drove carefully down the driveway in the Dodge, she heard a series of loud squeals and giggles from the back seat as a full blown poking war had broken out.

"Kids," she chided, "I know it's exciting, but just be good. "I'm not as experienced in the car as your dad!"

The poking war did not subside, but turned into a pinching war, and John's mom felt wriggling and kids' movements from the back seats.

"Owww," came Melissa's voice, followed by a "Hey" from her son. She stopped the car at the bottom of the drive.

"If you two have to behave like preschool babies," she said turning around exasperated, "then you'll be treated as such. I can just turn this car right around and put you both to bed early."

They didn't' want that and, suitably chastised, sat quietly in the car, the poking and pinching war suspended for now. She resumed the journey. A stifled giggle from each of them from time to time was all she heard on the rest of the journey.

Melissa's costume was a massive hit. All the kids (and their moms and dads) gazed at the zombie girl. One little kid, someone's baby sister was really scared and started to cry, but when he saw that the zombie wasn't real, and it was just make up, he was fine. The party was fun too, with dancing and presents and laughing and fun. John especially liked the apple bobbing. There was a big tin bath set out on the table, with apples in it. The kid had to dip his or her face inside to grab an apple stalk with their teeth and pull it out to get a prize. Each kid had a go, and each kid got his or her face a little wet. Some got prizes, some didn't. John got his nose and chin wet, but didn't get a prize.

"I'll get us one," said Melissa confidently when it came to her turn.

With the rest of their school friends cheering her on, she dipped her face in, but it was impossible. John watched her as she tried and tried to no avail. Then he saw something that, years later, he would see again and again, and was one of the reasons that he always kept her close. He suddenly saw the determination in her eyes, the refusal to back down and be beaten no matter what. He saw that in her right there, and he held her hand to encourage her. She dipped her face in further, until her whole head and her long blonde hair was dipped fully into the water, in order to get an apple out. Their friends laughed, and some of the parents did too, as they watched the little zombie girl dip her head into the water fully.

But she was victorious, and emerged with an apple in her mouth held by her teeth with its stalk. Her makeup was ruined, and was streaked with red and black across her face, and her face and hair dripping. John was ecstatic, and the rest of the partygoers cheered.

John hugged her.

"You won one," he said.

"Yeah," she replied. "I guess I had a wash too."

One of the adults went for a towel for the dripping girl while another handed her a candy bar as a prize, which she stowed in her pants pocket. He'd imagined she would either share it with the other kids, or take it home, but she did neither. Later on, as the kids were getting ready to go home, she grabbed John's hand and they trotted outside, making sure that Janelle's mom didn't see them sneaking away. Janelle had a little swing attached to an oak tree in the garden, and Melissa and John sat on it together. They had a half hour yet before they were being picked up, but both were tired out by now with all the fun. They leaned on each other sat on the swing. He watched as she pulled out the chocolate bar, unwrapped it, and broke a bit off, handing it to him.

"Thanks," he said, "but it's yours. You won it fair and square."

"You're welcome," she replied, "but it's half yours."

"Why is it?" he asked, "I didn't win mine?"

"But," she answered, her little face earnest, "If you had, you'd have given me half."

"Yeah," he said. "I think that's what we gotta do, look after each other. Jake says that's what being a friend is about. Sharing stuff."

"You promise?" she asked. "Always look after me, and treat me right?"

"Yeah," he said, his little face solemn and remembering suddenly pushing her in the dirt. "I'll always be your friend. Life's fun 'cos of you."

"We'll be friends when we're old and married," she said, dreaming of far off times.

"NO," he reminded her. "We're getting married, remember? And living on the bridge."

She nodded in earnest.

"Yeah," she said. "I remember. Yeah we are. I think I wanna live in a house sometimes though. I guess we'll have to get jobs."

"Yeah," he replied. "And I'll have grandpa's trust fund then."

"What's that," she asked looking down at the water.

"I dunno really," he said. "Grandpa left some money for the kid that got married first, to start him off in life, so dad says."

"Wow," said Melissa. "That's cool. I guess you can buy a ton of Legos then."

"Hmm," dreamed John. "I'll buy you some too."

"Cool," she said smiling. "We'll have to get married then, won't we?"

They sat dreaming together for a minute, quiet and thoughtful, then she looked at him silently, broke off some more chocolate and gave him another piece, popping some more into her own mouth.

"That was worth getting wet for," she said.

"Yeah it was," he replied. "But r ext time, I'll get wet and give you the chocolate."

They laughed.

He flicked the radio off. Music hadn't seem the same since he'd hit middle age. Maybe he was just stressed. The girl had only been in his life for a few weeks. Taylor had only been released from prison a short while ago. For fraud as it happened. It seemed that she hadn't learned her lesson, for as soon as she'd dug her way into his affections, she'd screwed his life up and played holy hell with his finances, his friends, and his business partners. But that was all in the past now.

The taxi ride didn't seem familiar to him. The town had changed so much since he'd escaped to DC. Bits of it he recognised. Bits he didn't. It all seemed so very strange. And he still got the terrible headaches. Shaking it off, he watched the road as they turned onto the turnpike that would lead to Decatur Road. Eight years. He'd been away for eight years. He'd signed the deed for the Belle Starr over to his sister Cassie, and her husband Dougal, and they were trying to make a go of the land as a farm and a riding center for disadvantaged kids. Cassie had been married for six years now, and had two young kids of her own. With his brother Ed, Junior having a daughter, eldest brother John was the only one childless.

The car turned off Decatur Road and through the big gates. New gates, he thought, looking up at the Black and Gold automatic gates that opened as the cab approached. The initials BS, standing for Belle Starr were embossed onto the black wrought iron in huge golden metal letters. The long front garden was gone, replaced with children's activity areas and a car park for parents. And the house itself. The barns were all gone, demolished, and stables and a petting area were added. The huge ranch house itself looked just as nice as he remembered it, only its white paint had been refreshed.

His sister met him at the door of the house, running down the stair way and embracing him warmly.

"I didn't' think you'd come," she said smiling.

He looked at her warmly. She was still as beautiful as the day she was born, when he'd looked into her muslin wrap and seen his baby sister. She had black hair and dark eyes, like him, only her features were not as angular as his were, and there was no shadow hanging over her, as there was with her elder brother. She seemed smartly dressed in a short pale yellow dress and white sneakers.

"I promised, didn't I? And here I am."

He caressed her cheek, stroking the lock of short hair on her forehead,

"What happened to the ponytail?" he said smiling,

"Kids happened," she laughed, "and I only have time for a pixie cut in the morning now. Don't you like it?"

"You're still beautiful," he said, looking at her.

As Cassie watched his face, she saw his features darken as his eyes turned to the woods to the left of the house. His sister reached out and touched his hand.

"I'll come with you if you want to go," she said.

"No," he replied. "I'll go alone. It's fine. I have to face it sooner or later. Let's be honest now, it was a long time ago. Hell, I've even dated."

"I heard," said his sister, ushering him inside. "Is she back in jail now?"

"Best place," he said, not thinking of his previous girlfriend and how he'd been swindled. "It's in the past."

"And Melissa?" asked Cassie, almost afraid to say her name.

His features darkened again.

"It's almost as if my mind has blocked her out," he replied, going into the refurbished lounge with Cass. "It's like, sometimes there's parts of her I don't remember, bits of things I've blocked out."

"I think about her a lot," Cassie admitted, "Mom and dad were...well...You know. What they did was wrong."

"I know," he sighed, embracing her. "They did what they did, and I guess they have to live with that. But you...I'll never forget the way you sided with me over them. Never."

"I'd do it again," she smiled. "Brother and sister huh? Weren't we supposed to fight?"

"I'd be scared," he laughed. "You were a pretty tough little brat."

"I've had to be even tougher. Two kids and Dougal...hell, I should perhaps say three kids."

"I hear my name mentioned?" said a voice from the doorway. It was Dougal.

"Hey there guy," he said coming in. John held out his hand, but Dougal embraced him warmly.

"Good to see ya," he said. "It's been too long."

"Yeah," murmured John non-committally. He liked Dougal, and he sure made Cass happy, but this house...despite their revamp of it and the fact that they'd made it their own, it was too strange for him. It was like Cass and Dougal had got his life. His life with Melissa, here, happy with their children. And now he was watching from a distance while someone else lived his life.

"I like what you did with the house," said John. "Looks real nice."

"I just finished the roof," replied Dougal, stroking his beard. "Was a hell of a job."

"Looks good," John admitted, smiling. "You did a good job. Taking care of my sister, now that's the type of thing that a guy needs a medal for."

"Hey," objected Cass playfully punching her brother. "I'm low maintenance!"

"Really?" laughed Dougal. "When does that begin, honey?"

They shared a husband and wife moment, and suddenly, though he smiled with them, his sister saw the dark shadow descend over her elder brother. He'd never gotten over her death, not completely. He seemed to change overnight, darker, and meaner. He laughed or smiled so rarely that his smile and weak joke just then made her feel a relief that maybe he was beginning to come to terms with things. But then the shadow would descend over him like it had just then.

They enjoyed a dinner together. Cass and her brother and husband sat in the newly rebuilt kitchen. Her children were excited, they rarely saw their Uncle John, and had never seen him at Belle Starr. Alistair and Jessica were twins, dark hair and eyes like their mom, and with an inquisitive excited nature.

"Can I show you the creek, Uncle John?" said Jessica. "There's woodpeckers and everything. We think they're nesting."

"In the creek?" laughed John. "Won't they get wet?"

The family laughed, but Cass knew he'd made the silly joke to hide the fact his face had blanched at the mention of the creek.

"No," continued Jessica. "They nest in the trees. They take the berries that grow on the banks to feed their babies with. The creek feeds the berry bushes and helps them grow."

"We learned that at school," broke in Alistair. "We even had a nature walk through our woods to the little bridge."

"Poohsticks Bridge," he muttered to himself, and no joke in the world could disguise his face from turning white. He dropped the fork he was using to eat with, and stared at his plate for a second,

"Are you ok, buddy," asked Dougal concerned. "I know my wife isn't the best cook in the word, but…"

This time he smiled at the joke.

Cass sighed a mock sigh.

"If I had shoes on, I'd kick you under the table, you bastard," she laughed.

"Why d'ya think I don't let her wear shoes in the house?" Dougal said to John.

"I know," John replied. "She has a kick like a goddamned mule. I was black and blue as a kid."

Alistair and Jessica laughed, Uncle John's temporary upset forgotten. They continued to eat, making light-hearted conversation, each of them trying as hard as possible to lighten the mood.

But it was there at the back of his mind. He knew what was coming, and couldn't get away from it, couldn't turn around and face the other way to pretend it wasn't there. The damn place was still there, and although these kids and their friends and classmates had made it their own, something he was glad about, it was still their place. He hadn't been there since...since that day. Couldn't face it. But that was why he was here, at least one of the reasons. The business he had in town could have easily been done by fax or email, but it was time. Time to face things. He was forty after all. Officially middle aged now.

He decided to take a walk early the next morning, Sunday, before the house had officially woken. The rear garden was mainly stables and things for the children's riding stuff, and John had a hard time finding where the old gap in the fence was. Alistair and Jessica's father had rebuilt the wall, and put them a little gate on, with which to get into the woods, instead of the old broken board that John and Melissa had used. Opening the little gate and steeling himself, he went through. The woods were just waking up and the birds were singing their early morning chorus, a cacophony of calls from the roosting thrushes, woodpeckers and crows filled the wood with the air of life. For him, living a long time in the city, this was noise he was no longer used to. As he walked down the path, their calls and sounds came louder and clearer.

They were calling for her. They were singing a mournful lament, a massed chorus of birds and insects, all shrieking and crying their lament as the chief mourner in their funeral procession made his way along the well-trodden path to his destination. Feeling a hundred pairs of eyes on him, he brushed aside the growing vegetation as he caught a glimpse of it through the branches. Then there it was, the white painted handrails showing through the forest growth.

Poohsticks Bridge.

It made him shudder. Not from the early morning cold, but a shudder from deep inside him, as if the hurt that had been welling up inside him for as long as he could remember was making him shake as he fought to control it and remain standing. Taking a breath, he stepped along the path and into the clearing where the little bridge stood proudly over the creek.

The forest now stood in silence. Birds and creatures held their breath as he walked into the clearing in silence and ran his hands over the well-worn handrails.

"Should we paddle," she'd said at the side of him.

"It's six am," he remembered. "The water will be freezing."

She laughed a wicked laugh, her eyes sparkling and kicked of her sneakers, making her way down the bank, splashing into the creek."

"Come on," she laughed. "Don't be soft."

He turned away from his memories, and made his way down to the water's edge. The water was higher now, it was mid spring and the creek was at its highest. He watched the flat section of earth intently.

She laughed.

"What's the worst that can happen?" she laughed weakly. "I'll fall in the water?"

He looked at her with concern, making sure her hat and coat were still fastened to keep her warm.

She shivered in the autumn air.

"That was a joke, honey," she said lightly.

"I know," he said to himself, imagining she was still there, sat in the small folding chair he'd brought for her. The wood was still silent. He looked at the empty patch of earth.

"I don't think I can joke," he said to himself.

"Come on" she chided. "You being miserable isn't gonna make me better. Truth is, we have to face up to things. I don't know how long I can...I just want to be happy. This was our happy place."

"I know," he said. "I'm sorry. I'm just not as strong as you. I can't do this. I can't do it."

He remembered her hand reaching out weakly to his, and he'd grasped it tightly.

"Just don't be sad forever," she said softly. "This was our happy place. When you come here, remember our laughing, and our camping out, and being bitten by bugs and dropping our sandwiches in the water. Remember to smile again someday."

He turned around, as if there was someone with him. There wasn't. He was alone in the morning air.

"We ate them all the same," he said to nobody, smiling at the memory.

She smiled, weakly.

"Hey...Captain Miserable smiled again," she said mocking.

He smiled fully now.

"How can I not smile and be happy when I'm around you?" he said.

He turned around, expecting her to suddenly appear at the back of him. He looked around the little clearing, the creatures silent in their vigil of this little place, and he sank down and sat in the dirt, hugging his knees. He closed his eyes, and not for the first time, willed himself to be somewhere else, anywhere else. Anywhere but here. This had been a mistake. He couldn't be here. She was everywhere, the smell and the thought of her, and the ghost of her. He couldn't escape it, could never run far enough away. The pounding in his head threatened to make him black out, and for a second he became aware of a face leaning over him.

"Uncle John?" came a voice.

It was Jessica.

"Are you ok?" the little girl asked, concern on her face. "Mom said I could come look for you. She figured where you'd be at."

He nodded weakly, the pain subsiding. He took the child's hand and pulled himself up off the ground. Looking around at the place for one last time, he turned to Jessica.

"Let's go get breakfast," he said, sealing himself off from the pain of the place. "I'm done here."

1977, September

Summer was drawing to a close. It had been a big year of changes. Jimmy Carter was in the white house now, and Elvis, John's mom's favourite had died, way too young. The kids knew none of this, as they sat together at what had, for the past five years, been known as "Poohsticks Bridge." For the whole of elementary school, they'd stuck to each other, their friendship solid and unbreakable. Christmases had spent together, as were weekends and holidays. But now, as they sat there one early September afternoon, both their young eleven-year-old hearts were filled with dread and despair.

"Big school."

Their little elementary school had bidden them goodbye at the start of the summer. The pair hadn't cared as they played on the bridge, or on the land, or walked about town, as they were now allowed to go alone. Middle school and September had seemed so very far away, with the long hot summer of Belle Starr to look forward to. And they'd enjoyed it. The ranch was quieter now. During 1975, John's dad had sold off some more of the land, and gotten out of ranching for good, setting up a trucking business, to John's delight. His good friend Jake was one of his foremen still, though the business, known as "Mason Corp" was based in town. The house still had surrounding grounds, the woods and the bridge over the creek, but most of the rolling pastures and fields to the right were now sold and rumoured to being developed for agriculture and commercial industry. Belle Starr was now one of only two ranch houses left since the others had all been demolished. Jonesy's place at the end was now the new turnpike for the highway, forcing a lot of traffic down the newly widened, resurfaced and now busy Decatur Road. John's brother, Ed, Junior was in elementary school now, although he and John didn't really get on. This had started when most of John's old toys had been given to his brother, including his precious Legos.

"You don't need them dear," his mother had said. "You spend all your time with Melissa."

She was right. He didn't need them. They had more than enough to occupy their time, sitting by the bridge, or exploring the woods, or hanging round the new shopping mall. But he still didn't like the way his brother had taken them without even saying thank you. Melissa still said thank you when he gave her stuff, even though she didn't need to.

No, John didn't like his brother. But his baby sister Cassie he adored. She had dark eyes and dark hair, just like him. She was beautiful, and looked at her elder brother as if he was her hero. She was too little to play with though, so apart from giving her cuddles and buying her cuddly toys whenever he and Melissa went to the mall, there wasn't much they could do with her.

And so they sat at their little bridge, their feet dangling through the rails to the water below. The red berry bushes were in full bloom, and they sat quiet as the birds had their fill of the free harvest before the autumn and the cold came in. Today, on this day in September, they were both quiet. He wondered whether he should tell her about a conversation he'd overheard his mom and dad having before, but decided against it. Not being one to eavesdrop normally, he had heard his name mentioned from in the living room.

"All I'm saying is," his mom had said, "that he should be with other boys, other friends. Not just her all the time."

"Leave the kid alone," Ed Mason had replied. "They've been friends for a long time."

"I know," she answered, "but it's not healthy for him. Plus, she's becoming a woman, and who knows what might happen."

"He's barely eleven, for Christ's sake. Anyway, they're about to go to middle school. I'll bet you five bucks that after a month or so being there, he's hanging around with the guys, she's at the mall with her girlfriends, and he'll be all 'Melissa who?'"

John had backed away from the conversation after that, his heart suddenly full of terror. He was silent with her on the walk from the house to the bridge, but she was silent also. He suddenly wondered if this was the end of their happy little friendship, as his dad had said it would be, as it had been the end of their happy schooldays. Suddenly, as he sat on the bridge with her, he felt the dizzying blackness take a hold of him again.

As if echoing his thoughts, after a long while quiet, she spoke.

"I guess this is it," she said softly.

"Yeah," he replied sadly, "I guess so. Thanks for all the biscuits."

"It's ok," she answered. "I enjoyed sharing them with ya."

"Middle school's gonna suck," he said. "I just know it. High school will suck even harder. Big kids, work, growing up."

"Growing up's gonna suck," she said. "I hate it already. Dad says I'm gonna be hanging out with girls, and making new friends."

"They said the same to me," he replied, watching his feet as the dangled over the water.

"You want to go in the water?" he asked

She nodded, and silently and slowly, they took off their shoes and made their way solemnly down to the water's edge. At one time the pair had laughed and joked, but today there was no laughter in either of them, only the sense of changing times, friendship's end, and impending doom. They stood in the water quietly, letting the cold trickle of water lap about their ankles. For some reason, he remembered the time, years ago, when he'd pushed her in the dirt, and felt the tears well up at the back of his eyes.

"I won't share my biscuits with anyone else, ever," she said looking down.

"Fuck this," he said, swearing for effect. "I think they're wrong."

She looked at him sadly.

"Me too," she replied. "I don't want new friends. I like what I've got. I mean, I'd like new friends, but I'm not gonna give the one I got up to get them."

"I don't want any new friends," he said firmly. "I just don't. I like this...this here. Swinging our legs out here, standing in the water."

That moment in time, that September Saturday in 1977, was a moment he would always remember. Not because he stood there hugging her for what seemed like an eternity, as if to let her go would be to lose her forever, not because of that. It wasn't the first time first time they'd hugged. It was for another reason. That was the first moment he realised his mom and dad were wrong, and in his eleven-year-old brain, he knew that, from that moment on, he would put her first every time, his friend ever since he could remember, his companion since that little tiny preschool. His eleven-year-old mind knew that his parents did not really know him, or how much he valued her friendship, how much he cherished it and would always hold it dear, no matter where their lives led them. No matter how far away they would roam, he could always hold her close to him; she would always be a part of his heart and his soul and his being. And from that moment on, although young John still loved his parents and would obey them in most things, in that one thing he would not. In that one thing, his parents had lost him forever. Melissa would be his very best friend, he would hang out with her at the mall and not some dumb guys, he would do things with her.

"I'm still gonna be your friend," he said. "I don't give a shit what they think. If you still want to be friends with me?"

"I don't want to do growing up if I can't do it with you," she answered. "I think sometimes I'd just like us to run away and leave."

"Where the hell would we go?" he asked, his face earnest.

"Right here?" she suggested, "like we used to say, we'll come live here."

He laughed.

"They'd find us," he replied. "We're always down here playing. It's just...I only want you as my friend. You're fun to be with; you make me laugh and stuff. I don't want to be around some stupid other guys. But if you want to be friends with girls and do girl things, then that's ok."

To answer, she hugged him tight, right there in the water.

"I don't make friends easy," she said with a watery laugh. "You might have noticed. Besides, this has been the best time out here hanging out with you. I don't want that to change. If it does, I'm just gonna run away somewhere."

"Let's make things not change then," he said firmly. "Then we don't have to run away and be hobos."

She looked down at her torn jeans and old shirt.

"Kind of look like one anyway," she laughed.

It was true. These days, with her grandma now too old to look after the girl much, Melissa's jeans were torn, her sneakers old and her hair long, blonde, and sometimes ratty. She had the look of a beatnik, especially with the beads she had gotten woven into her hair at the mall that summer. She had developed her style along a different path to the other girls. Whereas Janelle, Katie, Mai, and the others they had grown up with were experimenting with high heels, and party dresses, Melissa now had her first pair of Doc Martens boots, of which she was extremely proud. Although John's mom had taught her how to wear makeup, the girl rarely wore much, if any. Most of the money she got from her dad went on pencils and art supplies for her drawing, which was rapidly becoming a passion. She wrote and drew a little comic, titled "The adventures of Tweedle-Dum and Tweedle-Dee," which was basically her version of a diary. In this little comic strip, she catalogued the adventures of John and her. Some she'd shown him, some she kept to herself in her small bedroom.

They waded out of the water in a slightly happier frame of mind.

"What about boyfriends," she said suddenly as she slipped and slid her way back up the banking.

"I don't want a boyfriend," he said, with a sly sideways smile of amusement on his face.

She chuckled.

"I don't mean you, dummy," she giggled, "I meant me."

"Have you got one?" he asked, scrutinising her.

"No," she answered, "of course I haven't!"

"Do you want one?" he asked, still studying her face.

"No!" she replied again. "I'm way too young for that."

"I don't get what you mean then?" he said.

"I mean," she explained, "we're going to big school. That means boyfriends and making out and stuff...you know? What if, I have this boyfriend and he wants me to come out with him, and I'm playing with you down here?"

"What would you rather do?" he asked, his face a mask of concern. Was this the first true test of their friendship? He didn't know.

"I'd rather be here," she said in a quiet voice. "But my dad says that I'll change when I start to get older."

"We'll both change," John said looking at her. "But I can't change without you."

She looked at him and, no matter how old she grew, and how many other things happened in their lives, she would always remember the next phrase from his eleven-year-old lips, as if it were engraved in her very brain.

"It's like," he began, thinking of his words. "You've become part of me. I can't remember what life was like out here before you were around. It's almost like they carved a bit of me out and dumped it, so you could fit into my body right at the side of me. You know what I mean? I sound so dumb sometimes? The words are there in my head, but when they come out my mouth, they come out in a different order?"

"I fit into your body right at the side of you" she said with a little smile on her face, "that's not so dumb."

"So I guess," he said as they sat down on the deck, "even if we have boyfriends and girlfriends and stuff, its ok."

"Yeah," she said, stretching out her wet feet and resting them across his legs. "'Cos I fit right in there at the side of you."

He smiled and dried her feet with the edge of his t-shirt. School still seemed scary; there was much to be concerned about. But today, there was one less thing. She fit right in there at the side of him. At least that was going to be ok.

That night, after Jake had taken her home, Melissa sat in her room with a piece of paper, and her pencils, sketching furiously. She hadn't known what it was gonna be, most of her stuff so far had been neatly done, but after another silent dinner with her father and grandma, she'd escaped to her room, and for some reason, started scribbling. It had begun as a sketch of a man, but had now grown huge, with two heads and an enormous belly. She continued to scrutinise the drawing, sketching without even seeing now as her eyes blurred and the lines of the drawing blurred into one. She could see it in her head. The image. Inside the body of the man, she began to form two figures, thin, smaller humans.

"You fit right in there at the side of me."

That was going to be the title. Inside the huge body of the man she had drawn, the little figures were huddled together, cowering in what looked to be fear. The huge man they were hiding inside
78

carried a schoolbag in one hand, and a briefcase in the other. She labelled this one "growing up."

After sketching, she coloured it, with more care this time, to get the shading and the feel of it correct, according to the image in her brain. The clock downstairs struck twelve, and her father came thudding up the stairs.

"You asleep?" he asked through her closed door.

"No," she shouted, "drawing."

He opened the door.

"Can I come in," he asked softly. She nodded.

"What you drawing?" he asked.

"Just something in my head," she said, showing him. He hadn't shown much interest in her drawing before.

He studied the drawing.

"You and John," he said, looking at her.

She nodded again, and at first she imagined that he was going to tear the drawing in two. But he didn't. He sat down on the bed.

"Can I ask you something," he said looking at her.

She nodded again.

"You're a good girl, aren't you?" he asked. "He's not touching you, is he? Cos if he is…"

She didn't answer. How could he even think that?

"I'm just worried about you," he said. "You two spend a lot of time together. I want you to be a good girl."

"I haven't done anything," she said, taking the drawing from him.

"That's all right then," he said, not looking reassured. "Your mother wanted the best for you."

"My mom wanted me to be happy," she said quietly, looking down at her socks.

"And that makes you happy?" he asked, his voice rose in exasperation. "Mooching about that old ranch all day in the dirt and rain? What about when he gets guy friends at high school and drops you like a stone?"

"We won't do that," Melissa said, still looking at the floor. Her dad was stubborn. She had realised a while ago that arguing with him solved nothing.

"Don't come crying to me," shouted Dad, "when you're stuck here with no friends and no career and he jets off round the world"

"I won't," she said. "You're the last person I'd go to."

He stared at her for a second, taking in the enormity of what she'd said. Anger rising, he tore the drawing violently from her hands and ripped it into pieces, wadding up the bits and scattering them on the floor. Looking at her small desk with her pencils and art things laid out, he swiped across it with his hand, and sent everything scattering onto the floor.

"There you go," he said decisively. "That's the end of it."

He stomped out of her room and slammed the door so hard it nearly came off its hinges.

She knelt on the floor, and picked up her crayons and pencils silently and neatly. Collecting the fragments of her drawing, she flattened them out. Her hands shaking with upset, the tears wouldn't come. At first Melissa wondered why. And then she realised.

It didn't matter. This angry man didn't matter anymore. In fact he hadn't mattered for a long time. He didn't understand or know her, and hadn't made an effort to connect with her since her mother had died when she was four. Melissa thought that he might resent her for holding him back from finding some replacement for mom, but the truth was, she didn't really care. Her drawing was important, her friend John was important, and in the space of ten minutes, this...this man had tried to smash beyond recognition both of those things that were precious to her. Things were different between them after that. Both were stubborn, and eleven-year-old Melissa had inherited her father's mean streak. Her father had little to do with her, apart from giving her an allowance and, when Grandma hadn't felt up to it, ordering dinner from take out. Neither of them cared enough, or were sorry enough to make amends.

School came, and the worry and fear that had eaten away at them during the final few days of the summer holidays melted away. The pair were resolute that this new middle school experience wouldn't separate their friendship, but in truth, all their school friends who they'd known since kindergarten knew them well enough, and knew that these two were best friends, and didn't try to come between them. All the same, there were new interests. Shoreline middle school had an art and printing club and Melissa was soon roped into helping with the printing of the magazine, and producing sketches for the banner. John's sports coach realised that the boy had an affinity for baseball, and he was asked to join the team. Over time, the two were accepted into their social group as a pair.

81

Sure, Melissa would join Janelle and Katy and her friends at the mall on a Saturday, but only if her friend was close by with the baseball guys. And after a while, the whole group would meet up in the café and milk bar. The guys would go off after this to check out the record store, or comic books, the girls would go do their thing, all the time never noticing that John and Melissa had slipped away together, mainly to sit on the little bench at the top of the stairwell and watch the people shopping until it was time for the bus to come.

1980

Melissa had just had her fourteenth birthday. This year, they had celebrated it alone. Her father had just given her ten dollars and left it at that, while John's parents hadn't seemed interested either.

"It's time we realised we don't have four kids" was all his mom had said. Dad was either busy with the "Mason Corp" trucking business, which was why mom was stressed, or in D.C. playing politics, his new passion.

And so they had spent her birthday alone. John, fourteen and a half, was a clever young man, and earned extra money for himself by looking over the business's books and receipts, and dealing with things for his father. And so he'd had plenty of money to spend in making the day special for his friend. They spent it down at the bridge, he took her a cake with candles, and they ate it sitting on the bridge deck, staying there until darkness came.

The high school was in the other part of town, close to the commercial district, with the stores, the new shopping mall and the picture theater advertising the new Star Wars movie. But things were changing in their home town, at least in this part of it. One afternoon, when getting changed after a workout with his baseball team, he noticed a couple of guys in a sedan hanging around the side gates. Several kids went to the car, handed some cash over and came away with something in their hand. John, a strong wiry young man, what with all the training, was confident now, and he went over to the eleven year old and asked what the kid had got from the guys,

"Uhh," said the little kid, scared. "Nuthin."

"Bullshit," John snapped back. "Open your hand."

The little kid didn't, and john grabbed his hand, forcing it open.

"Oww!" he shrieked. "You're hurting me. They told me to keep it quiet."

"Uh huh," nodded John. "How much you give them?"

"Twenty bucks," he said. "Got it out of my mom's purse. Half price, they said, special introductory offer."

John examined the small bag of powder. He wasn't quite sure what it was, but it sure as fuck didn't look good. He gave it back to the kid. Not his problem. But it was about to become his problem. His baseball workout finished, he was waiting for Melissa to finish up in the art room, before they would walk to the ice cream bar together to get something for the bus ride home. After a minute, waiting around a corner of the brick built school gym, he watched as more little freshmen came to the car window. Then he smiled as he saw his friend come bouncing happily from the art room, her old brown satchel under one arm, her art folder in the other. As he watched, he saw one of the guys call to her. She glanced to her right at the sedan, but continued walking. They shouted again. Again, Melissa ignored them. Then, one of the guys got out of the car and started to come closer to her, grabbing her shoulder. John left his hidden spot and marched over to them. The man from the car, wearing a cheap polyester petrol-blue suit was speaking harshly to the girl.

"You answer me when I'm talking to ya, ya hear me?" he said fiercely.

He was an ugly-looking man, with a pencil thin moustache and wiry, curly black hair. He had the appearance of a man who slept in his suit in a motel bedroom.

"Whatever you're selling," Melissa replied, "I don't want it."

84

"Oh is that a fact," he snarled, twisting her shoulder till she began to buckle under his grip. She dropped the satchel just as John got up to them. He felt himself shake with fury, and the dizzying blackness enveloped him, the towering fury of his rage making him seem older and taller than his fifteen years.

"Touch her again," he whispered under his breath to the man, "and I'll fucking kill you."

Despite John's youth, he snatched his hand away, before looking at the boy up and down and laughing.

"Jeez kid," said the man. "You had me there for a minute. Thought you were the fucking feds. I'm just chatting to your little girlfriend here."

He laughed, and sneered a little as his hand went to Melissa's crotch. She stepped back suddenly.

John kept his face stony straight.

"Like I said," he said quietly. "You touch her and I'll fucking kill you."

The man looked at John warily. Despite his youth, the man could see something about him. Something dangerous. The kid of a mobster maybe? He beckoned his friend from the car as back up.

John laughed as Melissa moved to the side of him.

"What's the matter," he said. "You such a pussy that you can't take a kid on without your fucking boyfriend."

"You got a big mouth, kid," said the man. John noticed the beads of sweat and the furtive looks on his face. Obviously a dealer, the kid thought, and using too, by the looks of his pupils and the beads of sweat. His friend was bigger, and had a receding hairline and an expanding waistline.

"What's the matter, Carl?" the big guy said. "This shithead giving you trouble?"

"I'm just explaining to him," said the guy in the blue suit, "how we're gonna get his girlfriend to suck our dicks and make him watch. And if she's good, maybe we won't carve our names in her tits."

John felt her move closer to him. He maintained his posture and looked Carl straight in the eye.

"I'm gonna give you a warning," the young man said, maintaining his composure. "You come near her again, or even look at her wrong, and I'll kill you both where you stand."

At that moment, as John had known he would, the principal came around the corner to where his car was parked close by. The fat drug dealer poked his friend in the arm.

"Come on," he hissed. "The goddamned teacher is coming. Fuck him."

"Yeah," snarled Carl. "We'll be seeing you later, big man."

He turned to Melissa.

"And you," he said running his fingers through the wiry, curly hair. "Your luscious lips have got an appointment with my dick."

"To bite it off," she hissed.

The man came towards her, but standing as she was at John's side, she didn't flinch. As the principal approached, the men went to the car and sped off.

"Trouble, John?" he said as he approached?

"No, Principal Harolson," he lied, "Just some friends of my dad's. Wanted to say hi before they left town."

"I see," replied Haroldson. "I've been seeing those guys around recently."

"They're gonna be leaving town real soon," replied John.

"Well, I hope things work out. See you both tomorrow."

He bid them good bye and went to his car. When he was out of sight, John put his arm around Melissa and hugged her.

"You ok?" he asked.

"I'm fine," she lied. "But what about when they come back? They're gonna come looking for us now. Especially since you called them out. Hadn't we better go to the cops?"

John shook his head.

"You gotta stand up to bullies," he replied. "Bullies are just cowards."

"Cowards with guns," Melissa mused as they walked to the ice cream store.

"They're not the only ones with guns," he muttered as they walked.

"Huh?" she said, not catching what he said.

"Nothing," he replied. "Just thinking aloud."

And he was thinking. This was the first time he'd kept something from her. He knew he would tell her after what had to be done was done. If he had the mettle to do it. His father had told him, not long before, that bullies had to be dealt with the old fashioned way. Hit them before they hit you. And hard. Jake had said the same thing.

"If somebody tries to hit you," Jake had said, "or your little friend, hit them back twice. Make sure they remember who they're fucking with."

He had heard through his father about a lot of nasty stuff starting to happen in the dirtier part of the city, and he hadn't liked it. Young as he was, he wasn't having her mixed up in any nasty stuff. They ordered their ice creams and watched as the buses came and went. John would get on the bus that took Melissa home, then walk from there down the side of the highway and onto Decatur road and home. If she had noticed he was quiet, then she didn't say. Having forgotten all about the incident, or at least pretending to, she chatted more than usual about the stuff she was doing for the school magazine, and her comic stuff. He wasn't really listening, though he always found the sound of her voice comforting.

Al the same, he was glad when he was alone and walking down the lonely Decatur road towards Belle Starr. He loved this place, really loved it, and he watched as the thrushes and Cuckoos began to start their evening roosting rituals. There was something missing, he realised as he walked alone in the fading late afternoon sun, and at first he didn't' know what it was. Then he suddenly realised with a smile, it was her at his side, the sound of her voice in the air that somehow complimented the calls of the cuckoo and the song thrush.

The day after,

BANG!

The shot rang out in the alley behind the school.

BANG!

Another shot fired. Then a whimper.

"Jesus no," the voice cried. "Please Jesus no. Take the money; just take the money, please. I'm sorry."

"You're sorry?" said another voice, the voice that held the silver Colt handgun. "You're sorry for saying that you were gonna make a fourteen-year-old girl suck you off and that's supposed to make it alright?"

Carl, panicked and bleeding heavily, knew full well who was under the knitted ski mask, but didn't say, for fear he would get shot again.

"Let's just call it quits, huh?" said the fat man, down on his knees a little further down the alley. The figure with the gun turned.

"Am I talking to you, fat buddy?" he asked before pumping four bullets into the man's gut and neck, killing him instantly.

Carl whimpered.

"He was my friend," he cried out.

"Maybe you'll get lucky," the gunman said. "They might even bury you together."

The shot came from the colt at that moment, piercing Carl's skull and brain and killing him. Stowing the gun in his jacket, the killer walked calmly away.

A few days later, Saturday had come around again, and she lay with her legs dangling over the bridge, her sandals kicked off and forgotten. He stood over her, leaning on the rail. The shooting incident of the two lowlifes had been the talk of the school, but the gunman had never been found. Principal Haroldson had been interviewed after they had suspected him, but they found nothing. Not even the gun.

"What did you do with the gun?" she said, almost in passing.

"In the bottom of my closet," he said with nonchalance. "It was dads. He thinks he left it at the shooting range."

She almost smiled. Almost.

"I keep wondering if there was another way," she mused softly.

"Me too," he replied. "There wasn't. You can't bargain with lowlifes. I didn't want to risk your life or mine. My dad said to always stand up to bullies."

"Ya sure as hell did that," she said smiling.

He knelt to face her.

"Are you ok with it?" he asked. "I just...I just couldn't see another way. If we'd have got the cops involved, it'd just mean more trouble, going to court, and bullshit like that. I didn't want to risk them hurting you."

"I know," she nodded. "And I was a little scared of going the cops too. I've heard what happens to people who go against guys like that, girls being raped and cut."

She sighed a deep sigh.

"I'm ok with it," she said seriously. "But in future, if you're going all Charles Bronson, kind of let me know first huh? Instead of letting me piece it together?"

"I didn't want you getting involved," he replied. "If it all went bad and I went to jail or got killed, then you weren't involved."

She smiled, looking at his serious face. She knew as he had said this that he had risked his life for her. He would have given his life for their friendship, as she would have done also. Melissa realised that she had been right to move apart from her father to spend more time here. This was the person who would be loyal to her, this was the one who would never hurt her, the one who would always care for her and keep her safe, who would amuse her and make her laugh. He was her family. He was almost sixteen now, and had grown into quite a handsome young man, so she thought. Even though he was her friend, she often wondered how he would react if she kissed him or slipped her hand into his as they had done when they were younger, though didn't any more. As she debated this, he came close to her and she thought for a moment he was going to kiss her. He didn't. He merely brushed a stray long lock from her face. She flushed slightly.

1981, July

Things were changing. Reagan was now in the White house, the eighties had begun in earnest, and the heady days of the sixties were over ten years gone. Melissa and John were still friends, nothing had ever happened with the two dead drug dealers found in the alley, the cops simply thought it was gang related. Round about a quarter of their way through their final year of high school, a guy from their school year named Tyler Brookes managed to convince Melissa to come to a comic convention with him, on a date. As John had been helping his father that weekend with some business stuff and couldn't go with her, Melissa reluctantly agreed. She was in two minds about the whole thing. She had dismissed the whole thing of suddenly finding her friend attractive as a girl crush and nothing more, and nothing had come of it. They had never kissed, though they still hung out together more often than not, although both of them now had their own friendship groups and were not in each other's pockets quite so constantly. But she had badly wanted to go to the comic convention and meet the artists, and perhaps get them to look at her work, and so Tyler offered to take her. He was about John's height, and with similar colored hair, though it was cut shorter, and he was thicker set, being, as he was, on the football team. She'd had a good time at the convention, several artists had given her contact numbers, they had all praised her work and agreed that she would be good enough to work in comic art if she kept up the practice. Overjoyed, when Tyler, sensing victory on his unofficial date, leaned in for a kiss. Normally, Melissa would have perhaps thought twice, worrying about what her friend would think. But they were growing up, perhaps this was the time. And so she responded and let him kiss her

After that they dated for a while. He was Melissa's first proper boyfriend, and, though she was often disappointed with some of the things he did, she put that down to her own over high expectations, with spending so much time with John over the years. They still hung out, though not as much, now that she had a boyfriend, and he was kind of hanging around with Connie. Connie was in a year below, and lived on the ranch next door. Small, dark haired and an only child, Connie was a smart quiet girl, much different to Melissa's own scruffy easy style. John's parents seemed happy with their eldest son's new interest, though Melissa realized that it was perhaps that the girl was the heir to a profitable family ranching business, rather than any happiness for their son.

It was a rainy Sunday afternoon when John and Melissa met up. She'd blown Tyler off, after being irked at him dragging her to wrestling the night before and getting drunk and bragging to his friends how he was 'banging' her. Nevertheless, somehow she'd been reluctant to come see John. Always at home at Belle Starr, she felt like a spare part now that Connie was only next door, her boyfriend being an excuse for her to be constantly in the kitchen of his family home. Was this it? Had they finally grown apart like their families had predicted they would? Or was this just another step in the friendship that would see them through their life. They were both quiet as they walked the path that they had walked for over ten years as friends. Though they no longer held hands, she still brushed his shoulder as they walked.

She sat down on the deck of the bridge and dangled her legs over the edge. He leaned on the white painted railing. It was so peaceful.

"Penny for em?" he said.

"Hmm" she murmured, "I was just thinking, next year is a big year for us, both of us"

She was right. They left school this year, she as doing a further year studying art and drawing, which was her passion, and he was doing as two year business course ready for taking the reins of his father's company when the time came. Their lives were altering, they were becoming adults.

Poohsticks Bridge was quiet, the birds didn't sing in the trees today, as if they sensed things were changing.

"Exciting times, huh", he muttered, watching the water"

"Yeah", she said quietly, her head down."

"Well", he said with amusement in his voice, "try not to show too much enthusiasm"

"It's not that", she said sighing, as he sat down beside her, "it's just...it's hard to explain?"

"How is it hard", he asked, "how long have we been friends now? Since we were four, five years old? Just say what the hells on your mind?"

She sighed again,

"It's just", she began, "I've been coming here since I was a little kid. This is kind of my happy place, not at home with my dad, or at the fucking mall with some stupid girlfriends trying on clothes, but here. I dunno why, but I've enjoyed it. Good times"

She looked at him, and she knew he felt it too. He put his arm around her, and turned away so she would not see the emotion in his face,

"I wouldn't want to have grown up anywhere else" he said. Damn, his voice cracked with emotion, and gave him away.

"Everything changes, I guess." She said sadly.

"Does it?" he said, in that way he had, "I'm not suddenly gonna want to not hang out with you. Some of my favorite times have been sat here with you."

94

"Yeah", she said, "but you know how it is, people go to new places, they meet new people, stuff happens and old friends go from hanging out every day to hanging out once a year. I just...I just feel that this is the end of things...how things were. I have Tyler...for now, and you have...well...you know?"

He drew her closer,

"Didn't we go through this when we left elementary school?" he smiled, "didn't we say our tearful goodbyes only to find out that, when we started high school, that you virtually lived here at Belle Star?"

She smiled but did not answer.

Here's what's gonna happen", he said firmly, "I dunno how it's gonna be with other people, but I know this. I'm gonna keep you close to me. Very close. In fact, I'm never gonna be more than a half mile away from you. If you need me, I'll be right there by your side."

She smiled, but remained quiet. Both friends knew and felt there were suddenly unspoken truths between them, and that it was linked to their pasts, and their futures. It would come out when the time was right, but for now, they were content to comfort each other and watch the water flow.

Heading back up to the house, they were still quiet. She looked down at her feet as she walked. Despite his assurances, she could still sense the smell of things ending. It had been fun though, she had thought. She couldn't have wished for a better childhood. Her hands shook a little at the thought of not coming here anymore, of him being here with his girlfriend, or his wife and his kids. As if almost reading her mind, he looked at her,

"Connie hates it down here", he said, "says there's bugs and crawling shit. I don't bring her down here. This was our place."

95

'This was our place'. There it was. Not 'this is our place'. Was. They reached the end of the path, where they cut through into the hedge and the back of the house, and she turned, her face oddly pale.

"I'm gonna go down here, get to the road", she said suddenly.

"What about dinner"?" he said, we always eat dinner Sundays? There's a place for you?"

"I'm fine", she answered, "I can get to the road down here. I'm fine honestly."

She turned to go down the path.

"Melissa" he shouted to her disappearing form.

Squaring her shoulders, she paused.

He couldn't do this any longer. No more fucking around. He'd wanted to date Connie for his parent's sake; they had been keen for him to date other people. And he'd tried. Tried real hard. But he didn't want her. He'd known who he wanted at the side of him since he was a tiny kid. He watched her shoulder, hunched in defeat as she paused on the path in the rain.

She turned, her eyes awash with unshed tears

"Remember", he began, "when we used to hold hands as we walked along here?"

She nodded,

"They've been good times", she said sadly, "but I can't do it anymore. I just can't. Its fucking with my brain too much. Let's just say we had a good time, some good memories to tell our kids, and when we meet in the street in years to come, we'll say hi.

He put his head down, and suddenly felt as though his world were ending,

"I couldn't bear that", he said, "just to say hi and walk away from you and leave you...leave you to go home to someone else. To laugh and have fun with someone else, to dress up as that zombie on Halloween with someone else. To give half your biscuit to someone else"

He grabbed both her hands as they stood under the forest canopy in the rain,

"Those fucking biscuits are mine" he said, "we don't belong to other people, we never have. Don't you see? That's why we're always miserable when shit like this happens. We start to shake and cry and we feel the roof is falling in on our lives, cos we're both so afraid it's gonna happen and some shit is gonna tear us apart. Well it isn't gonna happen anymore. I'm never letting you go; I'm never letting you walk off alone down some path in the rain. We walk together down that path or we stay home. In our home."

He embraced her wet and soaking form, and kissed her softly on the lips.

She held his face in both her hands and returned the kiss. Her body stopped shaking and she relaxed into his embrace.

"Are we serious about this", she said, "cos I can't fuck about with this anymore. My head won't cope with it. You've always been the only thing in my life that I wanted, the only thing in my life that I wanted to hold onto no matter what. I'd rather say goodbye to you now than have just a piece of you. I want all of you"

He smiled at her, stroking her head,

"I love you", he said softly, his voice barely a whisper.

She held onto him close, as if to break away would destroy the moment,

"I want to remember that", she said, "no matter how old I get, I want to remember you saying it to me tonight, when I was ready to give up"

"You won't have to", he replied, kissing her again, "I'll say it to you every day. When I wake up at the side of you in the morning, I'll kiss you on the forehead and tell you I love you."

"And then bring me breakfast in bed?" she suggested, smiling.

"Don't push your luck", he laughed, looking deep into her green eyes, "I don't love you that much."

She laughed, moving away from the embrace,

"I enjoyed all this," she said, moving along the path a little, "I just couldn't do it any more John, half having you and half not. I got to the stage where I figured it was a girl crush. Then, after Tyler, I realized it wasn't. I'd had you so close to me for so long in my life I can't live without you. I can't share you with anyone else I won't share you. I want you for me. I want you to wake up at the side of me, I want you to hold me all night, I want you, and you alone, to do things with me, and to me that no other man ever will. I want to be the one at your side."

"Remember what I said," he answered, looking at her, "right there at the side of me."

She nodded, "This is for real then? For keeps? I can only do this once, I know I'm only young and people will say I'm dumb as dogshit, but I mean it. I'm only gonna say this once in my life."

He held her hand.

"Just like when we were kids," she said, "We always held hands."

"Dunno why I stopped it," he replied, looking down at her neatly manicured short nails and slender, cold fingers.

She looked at the floor, at the rain that was beginning to subside.

"I love you", she said softly, "I always have. Sometimes I didn't know it, other times I did. You were the only one who I knew would never hurt me, the only one I knew would always love me, and stand by me. You're the only one that has ever made me laugh, has ever made me excited to be around, the only one who makes me tingle when you touch me"

"I make you tingle," he said smiling with that sideways smile he had.

"You're doing it now," she laughed, "Christ, you don't even know you're doing it. It was first when you stood up for me in the playground that time, with those...you know."

"Yeah," he said, his face darkening, "I remember."

"Well it was then," she continued, "not the first time though. But the guy said he wanted me to suck him off, and you touched my shoulder and I had this thought. That there was only one guy who I wanted to suck off that night."

Despite his lack of innocence, he blushed slightly.

"I wish you'd have said," he laughed softly.

"So do I," she admitted, "but we've got plenty of time for that."

"Yeah," he said, embracing her again and stroking her hair, "you're all wet."

She felt the tingle again that she hadn't felt with Tyler, and she stroked his hair with her hands. Then he kissed her. Not just a soft kiss this time, their lips and tongues met for their first time, embracing finally their true destiny and sealing the union that they both knew would last them a lifetime. He kissed her for a long time, not wanting to let her go. They had both known this moment had been coming, and there in the rain on the forest path they devoured each other hungrily as their passions took them.

At last she needed to take a break, and, holding her head close to his, looked at him.

"We can't exactly do it here," she said bluntly.

He was always taken aback and amused by her directness.

"It's a little wet," he admitted, "we'll probably get colds."

"Or I'll get one," she replied, "and when we...you know, I'll give it to you."

"I don't think my parents will be thrilled if we go back to the house," he said, thinking aloud.

"No," she answered, "I guess not. They don't exactly like me. I wonder how they would react, if they came home to find you and me fucking on the lounge sofa."

He laughed hard.

"I almost wanna do it just to see," he said kissing her again, "but no. They're home. And yeah, you're not the favorite person right now. Connie's probably with mom too, which is a mess. I'll have to handle that tomorrow."

"I'll tell Tyler tomorrow too," she said, realizing she technically had a boyfriend.

"Then I dunno", he answered, "I guess we could borrow Jake's truck, go to a motel or something. It isn't perfect, and not very romantic, but I can't stand the thought of lying in bed alone after what we've talked about tonight."

"You're not going to bed alone," she said firmly, "not ever again. You go to bed with me."

"I love it when you do that," he laughed, "all firm and strong."

They walked down the path to the clearing at the side of the house and crawled through,

"Not the only things that's firm and strong," she replied quietly.

He laughed, and grabbed her hand as they went to the side of the house where the workshop was. As John suspected, Jake was working on the pickup truck, as he often did when he could find a floozy to spend his night with. Jake had been distant for a long time now, and usually tried to distance himself from John for some reason. When he had been little, the two of them had been friends, but something had happened between Jake and his dad and things hadn't been the same since.

"I'll ask if we can borrow the truck," he said, knocking on the slightly open door.

"Yeah," came a slightly grizzled voice.

"It's John and Melissa," shouted John, "Can I take the truck?"

He appeared at the door, his face dirty with oil,

"You need to take her home," he said brusquely.

"No," he said looking at the floor, "It's just that I want to...that is...we wanted to..."

"I'm busy kid," he snapped, "spit it out."

"I'm gonna take her to a motel and...we're gonna spend the night there. You know?"

He eyed at Jake with a look, and Jake realized what was happening. The older man's face softened suddenly, and John saw a look of love and respect from the older man.

Jake sighed,

"Thank the good God for that," Jake said laughing, "I was wondering if you guys were ever gonna get together."

"SO you approve?" John asked."

Jake nodded.

"You two always went so well together," he replied, "It won't be easy. Relationships never are. Are you're both so damn young. Respect each other, listen to each other and remember why you were her friend in the first place."

"I'll never forget what's important," John said, his face watching Melissa.

"I'm proud of you, son," Jake said, his face pulling an expression that John didn't understand, "but you ain't taking your lady love to no motel."

"But we want to..." began Melissa.

"I know, I know," Jake said holding up his hands, "and you can. I know what it's like when you're in love. And I wouldn't recommend going in there."

He gestured to the house.

"I don't," replied John sadly.

"Look," continued Jake, "I can work in the barn round the other side just as easy. Got tools in there and some stuff for me to do. You can stay in the back of the workshop here, where the little restroom is. It's not that comfortable, but there's a little sofa that can be pulled out into a bed, and a TV. Some bourbon if you feel like a drink."

Melissa touched his arm.

"Thank you," she said.

Jake nodded.

"Just be careful with each other," he muttered, blushing, "Remember what they taught you in school."

"Yeah yeah…" John assured, also embarrassed.

Jake bid them goodbye, and watched as they went inside. He was happy for the kid. He'd only ever seen him smile when he was around her, and likewise, she was such a happy, smiling girl when he was around. They seemed born to be together. He walked across towards the barn, flicked the light on and going inside, began to fiddle with some engine parts. He'd hang around for a while, then go back to his rented apartment. Fiddling in his pocket, he reached for his cigarettes and lighter. Damn. Jacket pocket, along with the car keys. Realizing that the jacket was slung over the sofa bed at the back of the workshop, he sat down on the tractor step and looked around for something to do. No way was he going to disturb those kids.

Three hours passed. It was now ten o clock. Luckily, Jake had found an old trade magazine with some cars inside, and had read it cover to cover, even the adverts inside the back. Finding some cigarette papers, tobacco and some matches in the tractor, he'd rolled some unbelievably thin cigarettes and treated himself to one every half hour. Christ, how much stamina did these kids have anyway? He suddenly realized that they might have dropped off to sleep, but he couldn't let them sleep in there all night. Although John was pretty much left to his own devices by now, he was still expected to call or let them know if he was staying out.

At that moment, Jake heard a noise come from the main house nearby. He opened the barn door a crack and saw with horror, it was Ed Mason in his cardigan and slippers,

"Jake's still here, honey," he shouted through the door to his wife, "the cars here."

Madeline Mason appeared at the door, shivering in the cold night air.

"I hope he realizes he's not being paid for this," she said.

Fuck you, bitch, Jake thought. What a mistake you were. Then, thinking of the young man in the barn, he chided himself for that statement. Then he shook himself.

"Christ," he thought, "If Ed looks for me in the workshop, guess what he'll find..."

Panicking, and not wanting John to be found out, he left the barn, shouting to Ed loudly.

"Hey Ed", he bellowed, "over here. I guess I lost track of time. Sat reading an old magazine in there, kind of sucked my attention."

"Huh," grunted Ed," wondered who the hell was out here."

"Figured I'd be in there, huh?" shouted Jake, hoping his voice would warn the kids.

"Why you shouting," Ed grunted again, "you going deaf?"

Ah," laughed Jake, "It's this old workshop."

He banged loudly on the door.

"Made of tin, guess I lost my hearing a little."

Ed Mason wondered what was going on. He figured that maybe Jake had a tart in the workshop and didn't want him to know. Ed decided to play a trick on him, and find the tart in the workshop. Not that he gave a shit what Jake did in here. The two of them had finally reached an understanding, and each man stuck to his own business. Even so, Ed decided to have a bit of fun and find the floozy. He pushed Jake to one side and opened the workshop door.

"Left my cigarettes in here earlier," he said, going in.

104

Jake watched, aghast, and followed Ed inside.

"Somebody in here," Ed said, going to the back of the workshop where the camp bed was.

"Ed," Jake began, "don't…"

But Ed had. He went to the camp bed, and stopped in his tracks. Melissa shot upright from under the little grey cover that was thrown over them. For a moment, Ed Mason stared at the girls naked breasts, and wondered, almost in a trace, if it was Jake that was banging the girl. Christ, she wasn't even sixteen.

"What the hell are you…"he began, but then he saw Melissa's bed partner.

John sat up also, and covered Melisa with his hand.

At that moment, John's mother walked inside, and saw the scene.

"Oh Ed. Oh my god, what's he done."

"I knew it!" exploded his father, "I knew what you two were doing all this time, you dirty little bastards. How long has it been going on!"

"Oh John honey," said his mother, "I knew this would happen. I told you she was a bad influence and she would trap you. Now all she has to do is to go to the police and you're in big trouble."

"You're in jail," bellowed dad, "all because you couldn't say no when a dirty little whore showed you her tits?"

"Now wait a damn minute," Melissa said, throwing her top on and clambering out of the bed, looking for her socks and sneakers.

"No more from you," shouted Madeline, "I've heard your voice around here for too long, and seen you enchant my son with that spell of yours, you dirty little tramp."

"I've had enough of this," said John rising, and pulling on his shirt and boots, "would you two listen to yourselves? You don't know me, you don't know how I feel about her, and what we've been through."

"Been through," exploded dad again, "You're a kid. You've been through nothing, and you know nothing. You're wet behind the ears, and you've let yourself be seduced by this tramp."

John stood face to face with his father and reached for the wrench on top of a nearby filing cabinet.

"John, no," chided Melissa."

 "Call her that once more," the young man snarled, "and I will smash your skull in."

Jake interjected.

"Hey!" he said putting himself in between father and son, "you don't mean that. Come on, son. Take her home before anything else happens. Thing will be better in the morning. Don't do anything everyone will regret."

John and his father continued to face each other off for a second,

"Look what you've done to them," said his mother to Melissa and starting to cry, "you've caused this with your ways. Splitting them apart."

"Me?" shouted Melissa, "what's his favorite food? Favorite record? What's his batting average this year? Do you know any of these things? Did you bother to find out? What's his biggest fear? What, you don't know? How come you don't know? I know all of these things. "

"Come on," Jake said again, "John, take her home. It's gonna be fine. See her safely home and then come back here. I'll sort things here."

106

"You," shouted Ed, "you're to blame for this. Letting them use the workshop to do that? He's under age and going with a fucking tramp!"

John flew with the wrench, and only Jakes quick reactions stopped the young man from killing his father with it.

"Hey," Jake shouted to John, "what've I told you."

John snarled at his father, the dark shadows under his eyes deepening.

"Ed," soothed Jake, "they were gonna go to a motel. They love each other. Cut em a break, they're just kids."

"They were gonna go to a motel" exploded Ed again, "so you let them use the workshop instead of throwing her off the land and sending him home to his mother and me How fucking dumb are you? You think you get even a tiny say in how I run my son's life?"

"I get more of a say than you think, you bullying prick," said Jake, "when have you ever given a fuck about him, when have you ever taught him stuff?"

"I paid for him for the last sixteen years," laughed Ed, "you think you could've done that on a janitor's salary?"

"Who taught him to drive?" shouted Jake, "who taught him how to wire a plug socket, who taught him the things he's gonna need to know when he gets to be the owner of this place? Not fucking you!"

"No," Ed nodded laughing, "I didn't teach him shit like that. Cos I don't want him to grow up to be a whoring janitor, I want him to be able to afford to pay drunken dicks like you to do the shitty jobs for him."

"Jake," said John watching, "don't let the fat fuck talk to you like that. You taught me plenty of shit. More than that fool ever did."

107

"I thought I told you to take her home," said Jake snapping at the young man, "I'll deal with this."

"Oh will you", said Ed Mason snarling.

Jake turned to John.

"Go," he shouted, "take her home. Be careful."

John reluctantly left the workshop.

The two were silent for a while in the cab of the truck as it drove along Decatur road. That was quite an argument, and they were both a little shocked. Plus, they were concerned as to what would come next.

"Well," he said after a long while quiet, "they took it better than I thought they would."

She tried to stop herself smiling, but couldn't and in a minute they were both laughing hard.

"Yeah," she said with tears of laughter running down her cheeks, "I thought they'd be mad or something."

After a while, the laughing subsided.

"I hope Jake can cool things off," she said, "he cares for you a lot."

"Uh-huh," replied John, finding the turn that led to her street, "he's been like a father to me."

They were quiet for a while longer. Sure the row had taken the wind out of their sails a little, but even that couldn't ruin what had happened before that. The deed was done. She was his now. They both knew it, both knew that they would belong to each other for always after that. They had devoured each other hungrily, he had entered her and made her feel beyond ecstasy. They'd lain there and explored each other's bodies. Of course, they already knew most things. He knew where and when she had gotten that scar on

108

the bottom of her foot. But tonight was the first time he has kissed the scar, and the foot. She knew here the scratches on his chest had come from, but tonight was the first time she had licked them with her tongue as he ran his fingers through her hair. Then her tongue had explored lower.

"Tonight was awesome", he said.

She smiled. It had been awesome. It had been everything she had ever wanted in her life. This was it. This was how her life was going to be, she knew that. With him.

"I hope everything's gonna be ok at home," she said watching the dashboard as she sat there.

"It'll be fine," he reassured her as he drove, "I really don't give a shit what they think any more. I'm with you now."

"John." began Melissa, "about Jake."

"What?" he asked with concern, looking at her, "what is it?"

"I realized something about him," she replied, "something you might not have thought of. Maybe you're too close to see it. About him and you. "

"I'm not too close," he said, "I realized who he was when I was a kid. Just don't go there."

"But if he..." she continued.

"He's never said anything to me," John said, shaking his head, "if that's the way he wants it, then for all intents, I'm still Ed Mason's son. At least until I hear different."

"Maybe someday he'll say something," she suggested.

"I hope so," he admitted, "but I kind of know why he isn't. He wants me to get grandpa's trust fund when I get married. If I'm not Ed Mason's son, then I don't get it."

"But you don't give a shit about that," she said raising her hand, "he should know you better than that."

"I know," John nodded, "but here's the thing. Old Jake has always been a maintenance man, or a ranch hand. Never had roots, or a family, or any money. I guess he wanted his son to be different."

He went quiet for a moment, and they just drove along.

"If I ever do get grandpa's money when I marry you, then I'm giving him half."

She nodded, then was quiet.

"If that's a proposal," she said smiling to herself, "then you're gonna have to do better than that."

"What," he joked, "they whole nine yards? One knee, flowers, everything?"

"The fucking works," she laughed, "If you're dragging me into that family, then I want at least one night of romance before the yelling starts."

He laughed.

"I think you'll be fine," he admitted, "You can probably yell louder than any of them. You sure held your own tonight."

John found her little house, and pulled the ranch truck up outside. It was eleven thirty, and Melissa noticed there was a light on in the main room.

"Figured dad would be in bed?" she said looking at the house with surprise.

"You gonna be ok?" said John, "you want me to come in?"

"No," she said shaking her head, "everything's fine. He's probably just fell asleep in front of the TV again. Besides, you and him don't exactly get on."

It was true. The few times John had met Mellissa's father, they had merely grunted to one another before going their separate ways. Like two big male lions in the jungle, they circled each other warily whenever they met.

"Not tonight," she chided, touching his arm, "we've had enough rows with parents for one night. I'll deal with him some other time."

"If you're sure," he asked, kissing her on the cheek.

She nodded, returning the kiss on his lips.

"You get to kiss me there now," she said smiling.

"And a lot of other places," he grinned.

"Yeah," she remembered, "I don't think I've ever been kissed on the bottom of my foot before."

"I wasn't thinking of there, dummy," he laughed.

"I know," she said slapping his arm playfully, "and don't call me dummy."

"Don't call you dummy?" he said caressing her cheek, "you're the one dating the illegitimate son of a ranch hand."

She kissed him, looking lovingly into his eyes, and got out of the car and ran inside. Christ, how he loved her. For the first time in a long time, he felt happy, despite what had transpired at the house earlier. But he'd been telling the truth, he really didn't give a shit. He cared about Jake. Whatever their history was, the old ranch hand had always been a friend to John, always. He cared about him.

The house was quiet when he pulled up the driveway. The house was in near darkness, and there was no sign of Jake, or his father or mother. He pulled the truck up at the side of the workshop, all locked and in darkness and went inside the house, listening for a sign of life.

"Anybody home," he shouted, not expecting an answer.

"In here," came the quiet voice of his mother. She was in the lounge, sat in the darkness. In the corner he could just make out the figure of his father sat in the armchair.

"Well," John said standing in the doorway.

"We'll talk tomorrow," said mom quietly, "I don't...can't talk at the moment. Just go to bed."

"Where's Jake?" asked John sharply.

Mom sighed loudly, then was silent for a minute.

"He's gone", she said, choosing her words carefully, "he thought it best to leave, what with this being a family matter."

"Gone," said John, "gone where?"

"She doesn't know goddamnit," said his father sharply, "can't you just do what she says and go to bed."

"Ed please," mom pleaded, "There's been enough tonight. I can't take any more. Please, the pair of you, no more tonight."

Something, John noticed, had happened between them after he left for the night. A row most likely. And after his conversation with Melissa about Jake, he kind of suspected what it was about. He wished Jake had stuck around. Sensing there would be no point continuing, he left them alone in the darkness of the lounge and went upstairs to bed. After a few minutes, he undressed and lay on top of the sheets. It didn't take him long for him to put them out of his mind. His thoughts went back to the young woman who he'd made love to earlier tonight, the one who he was in love with, the one who had all but agreed to be his wife, the one who he would live with right here at Belle Starr with and be happy with. The woman would be the true mistress of Belle Starr house. Mrs. Melissa George-Mason. With these happy thoughts, he went to sleep.

1981, July

Morning came, and he awoke in a pleasant, happy frame of mind. At first not realising why, after a minute he remembered her, and what they'd done the night before. Grimacing to himself, this was the day he had to talk to Connie. And talk to Jake. And there was still stuff with mom and dad. Suddenly realising that it would be better to be done with Melissa by his side, he went downstairs to go get the keys to Jake's truck. Technically, he was still too young to drive, but his father had always turned a blind eye. His mom hated driving, and when he was busy in town, in DC with his politician friends, John drove her around. She was already up when John came down to get the truck keys, but his father was nowhere in sight.

"Dad out?" he asked his mom as he went to the kitchen for a quick slice of toast.

Mom nodded, "We all need to talk"

John nodded.

"Sure," he replied, "that's why I'm going taking Jake's truck, to get Melissa. We'll all talk together, like human beings."

Mom sighed.

"Her again." she said closing her eyes. "Can't you do anything without her being involved?"

"Whether you like it or not," he snapped, "she's a part of my life. And she's gonna be a part of this family someday. Any conversation about her, she's being around for."

Mom shrugged.

"I guess you'll have your own way in the end," she said turning her back on him.

"Where's Jake?" he asked. "He come back?"

She turned to face him, and her face had blanched white,

"No," she said. "I don't think he's coming back."

"He must have left a note," continued John.

"I don't know," she said looking down at the floor. "Maybe. He'll perhaps get in touch when he finds a new job. Didn't you say you were going to get Melissa?"

John remembered.

"Yeah," he said. "Yeah sure I did. See ya later."

Mom didn't answer.

As John drove to Melissa's house, he wondered what had gone on with Jake. Probably Dad had fired him and the old ranch hand had gone to a bar or a whore house. He'd press dad about it later. After the Melissa situation was sorted. His parents were gonna accept the situation. There was no other choice for them, and he knew that.

When John knocked on the door, Melissa' father answered. He wasn't properly dressed, just wearing an old vest and a pair of dirty slacks. He looked like he hadn't slept. He seemed startled when he saw John at the door,

"Oh," he said. "It's you."

"She around?" he asked.

"No," her father said, "she's not in."

That was odd. It was still only around ten in the morning,

Her dad sighed.

"She said she was on the way to town," he said, gesturing up the road. She didn't take no money for the bus, so I guess she's walking. You'd probably catch her; she's only been gone about twenty minutes."

John didn't stop to thank him, but got back in the truck and sped off. Something had happened. The guy was pretty much quaking in his pants. Guilty fucking conscience. Something had gone on. He scanned the street for her. Three blocks passed before he caught sight of a figure limping, wearing a grey dirty vest and jeans. The figure was barefoot. He recognised her anywhere, even from the rear. He gunned the truck, and pulled it up on the sidewalk in front of her, jumping out even before the parking brake was properly on.

"Melissa, what..." he began, and then as he saw her, he stopped and stared at her.

Her face was streaked with tears and blood. She had been beaten, and one eye was swollen and shut with a black ring around it. She had several cuts and bruises on her face and body. Her hair was matted with blood, and had been hacked off on top at the front in a crude spiky fashion.

"I'm fine," she said in her husky voice. "I guess they took it better than I thought."

She laughed at her own joke, but her ribs hurt, and she clutched herself in pain. He embraced her, and led her to lean on the truck. He was shaking with fury and yet held it in. He didn't want to show her this, and she didn't need his anger. He held her closely to him, and she gripped him tightly,

"Who the fuck did this?" he said quietly. "I'm not gonna go Charles Bronson on anyone. I just want to know."

She looked at him and nodded.

"It wasn't dad," she muttered. "Least not all of it. Tyler was inside."

"That little fuck did this?" he said, unable to control the anger and the blackness that swirled around his soul,

She nodded. "He was in the house waiting for me. I kinda said I'd meet him, but I guess I got caught up with you and...things, and it went out of my head. Anyway, all hell broke loose. Dad wanted to know what I'd been doing and they both started on me. I kinda blurted it out that I was with you, and we were gonna be together."

"And he beat you?" John whispered, his eyes cast down so she would not see the look of murder in them.

She nodded again.

"Yeah," she said resigned. "I mean, I'm kinda tough, so I fought back. Got a few hits in of my own. But he was too strong."

John nodded.

"Tyler's a big guy for his age," he agreed.

"Tell me about it," Melissa laughed. "He's got a punch like a fucking mule. My face tended to stop most of em though."

He smiled at her irreverence, then stroked her head, running his fingers through the scissored off butchered strands of hair.

"What the fuck happened?" he said.

Melissa closed her eyes.

"I walked through the door," she said remembering, "and there was Dad behind the door, waiting for me, shouting about where the fuck I thought I had been. And there, sat on the sofa was Tyler. I guess if Grandma was still here and not in that home, she'd have kept them calm, but this felt weird, like I was walking into a fucking trap. I made for the door again, to try to wave to back, but he'd stood on the doorway."

"Then what happened?" John said quietly.

Melissa smiled.

"Tyler got up off the sofa and dragged me with my hair into the room. He was mad as hell, the wildcats had lost, they'd both been drinking, and I realised that I better start to duck. He started shouting shit and me, so I just blurted it out that I'd been with you and that I loved you and he could go take a running fucking jump."

"That's how to tell them," he said smiling. "I think you sugar coated it too much though."

She smiled.

"Just rip the band aid off," she remembered. "That's what my mom used to say. I ducked the first punch, but the second caught me in the side of the head. I smacked him back after that one with that wooden thing that we use to keep the living room door closed."

"Ouch," said John.

"Yeah, I know," she admitted. "That one drew blood. So by this time I'm screaming blue murder at him for hitting me, there's blood coming from the side of his head and he goes to hit me again. I go to defend myself and then someone comes up behind me and pins my arms behind me. I thought at first it was the cops."

"But who..." he said shocked, though knowing who it she was going to say.

"Dad," she said quietly, the tears forming in her eyes. "He held my hands so I couldn't move. I saw the punch coming. Couldn't avoid it. Right in the head again. Second one in the gut. I think after that he was holding me up so I could have more. They were calling me names that'd make the fucking devil blush, but that wasn't an end of it."

He stroked her hair, and waited for her to continue. Despite her painful memory, the tears had gone from her eyes as she stood in his arms, and the slight smile had returned to her face.

"They decided I needed a haircut," she said feeling for the short tufts of ruined hair on the top of her head. They'd stopped hitting me by that point, and ordered me to clean up the shit that they'd knocked off the TV table when they were struggling with me. I must have pissed them off, cos the blood was going into my hair as I bent over. I asked him could I go wash it off, and stop it bleeding. Suddenly, he said he would fix it and dragged me to the kitchen. I thought at first he was gonna put something on to stop the bleeding....then....."

She paused and now the tears did come, a flood of them, heavy wracking sobs as she remembered and her body shook at the memory of the night before. He held her hands until the shaking and the sobs subsided,

119

"He went to the drawer," she said, sniffling and wiping her nose on her sleeve. "I thought he was gonna get the meat knife...I thought he was gonna....was gonna...."

She couldn't get the words out.

"You thought he was gonna kill you," he said darkly.

She nodded, sniffling again.

"I know I've fucked his life up, I know that. I've always been a disappointment to him, but I remember screaming at him and pleading with him not to kill me. I think Ty was even scared by that point, cos he ran off up the fucking road."

"Little prick," said John under his breath.

"I know, right?" replied Melissa, the tears drying up. "So he grabs the big kitchen scissors and says something like 'I'll cure those matted bits right up' and chops off a huge lock of my hair, right on top there. He just kept cutting and cutting, right at my scalp. I think he just wanted to fuck me up."

"You're still beautiful," he said kissing her on the lips. She returned the kiss, her eyes smiling,

"There's only you in the whole world would say that this morning," she said. "I look a fucking fright."

"It's not too bad," he said lying, "it's fixable."

"I'm going down to Larry's, get him fix it up for me, good and short. I'll fucking show them. Anybody asks me why a girl with such pretty hair just up and shaved it all off, I'll say my dad and my boyfriend hit me and attacked me with scissors, and this is my punishment."

And he knew she would too. That was why he loved her more than any other person. Her determination, and her sheer force of will. The same force of will that had seen her dip her whole head under the water as a kid just to get an apple out when they had been apple bobbing. Most people, he later came to realise, most people had a point, deep down inside them that was soft and scared, dig down enough and you could make them cry for their momma. Not Melissa. Dig down enough into her character and all you would find was bedrock, strong and tough like solid steel. She would hide nothing of her attack, and wear her wounds and her inevitable haircut like a badge of pride. A kind of 'I've been beaten but still standing' kind of thing. As if reading his mind, she moved away from him and down the street to Larry's muttering airily.

"You think look bad," she shouted back at him, "you should have seen the other guy."

Larry hadn't believed her at first. He chided her, and told her not to tell bad lies. But as she told her story, he knew deep down that Charlie George had temper issues, and, since his wife had died, a drinking problem too. Plus, the kid had always been honest enough. She'd always passed here on her way to school with her momma years ago, and he remembered her looking in. He had always waved back. And so, by the time it came for her turn, he was sympathetic to her, and believed her story. Charlie George had done a job on his daughter, that was for sure. He wasn't sure if her bruises and cuts were his, he was wondering whether or not to call the cops himself or not, but he'd done a job on his daughter's mangy looing blonde hair.

"There not much I can do here, honey," he said. "There's not much left on top here for me to hide the chopped up bits."

"I don't care about it," she said firmly. "Just cut it off."

"I'm gonna have to go pretty short," he replied. "That might not be nice for such a pretty girl."

"I think it'll be cool," she said with a determined look on her face. "Just take it all off. If anybody asks what happened, I'll just tell 'em the truth."

Larry nodded. He knew that look of determination from his own wife. When a woman made her mind up, that was it. No arguing. He picked up his clippers and began to run them across Melissa's scalp carefully, so as not to aggravate her healing scars and cuts. Blonde hair matted with blood and sweat began to rain down on the cape,

"Honey," Larry began as he watched the tall dark haired kid at the side of her holding her hand. "You need to go to the cops with this. Those guys have assaulted you. I know he's your father and all, but you need to think about it."

She gripped John's hand as more hair rained down onto the cape and her scalp emerged.

"It's her word against theirs," John said. "There's no point."

Larry nodded.

"That's true," he said. "I don't know what this country is coming to, when guys can do this to a pretty kid. Her father too."

A dark look from John silenced Larry. As he glanced over, he saw that, as she was being sheared, her eyes were tearing up.

"You look awesome," he said "more beautiful than ever."

Larry finished shearing off the girl's hair.

"I look like a fucking marine," she said ruefully, "but if I had have, maybe I could have smacked them back, huh?"

Larry rubbed her bristled velvety head.

"That's the spirit," he said. "Think about what I said, though."

The kid nodded and she went through the door, thanking him, and rubbing her head as she went. Larry held John back as he followed her.

"They can't be let get away with this," he said quietly. "I know a few guys, who can...you know...quietly. You're her boyfriend; you need to look after her."

John looked at him and the lock in his eyes, the dark blackness that was barely restrained in his very soul chilled Larry.

"It's being handled," he said quietly. "Thanks though. I'll take care of it."

2011

The apartment was quiet. It was Sunday, nearly midday, and John looked idly through the window if the 24th floor view he had over the city. It wasn't a swanky apartment, but as a man with enough money to be comfortable, it had all the things he needed in it. Including, he thought, as he watched the girl pad from the bathroom to the kitchen, a resident female.

He'd been dating Tina for three months. At the age of 46, his friends Errol and Tony from upstairs had been shocked (and a little jealous) when he'd announced he was dating a girl who was 27 years old. Tina was a city cop with jet black hair and nice fat lips, a slim figure with beautiful curves, and a snaking dragon tattoo the whole of her back. They'd met when she'd ticketed him for speeding. Right now she was looking for something in the kitchen, dressed in his red shirt, her pink polka dot panties and knee high white football socks.

"I swear I left it on the side here," she yelled across. "You see it, honey?"

"Huh," he muttered, looking at the paper. The Shuttle discovery had just made its final flight, it was saying. Jesus, he'd just been a kid when the thing was being built. He remembered his father showing him the drawings of it from a magazine or something years ago.

"What's that, baby?" he shouted back.

She stomped over to him, standing in front of him, mock anger on her face.

"I said," she replied, "the apartment is on fire, we need to get out of here in a hurry."

124

"Huh," he answered looking at her and putting down the paper. "You better get your shoes on then and we'll get out of here."

"I'm looking for my diaphragm," she said. "It was on the side there."

"Kitchen drawer," he pointed, "second one down. I moved it. Didn't want the guys to see stuff like that. Neither of those two have dated in a long time. Sex stuff kind of freaks them out."

She laughed, and tuned to go, shrieking as he grabbed her from behind and pulled her to the leather couch he was sitting on. She wiggled in a half-hearted attempt to get away, but laughing, he pulled her across his knee and yanked down her panties. She kicked her socked feet playfully, laughing hard,

"Hey," she yelled, "isn't the game about to start? The guys will be here in a minute."

He laughed back.

"Well," he replied, "I guess I better be quick with your spanking."

Her face made a mock sign of hurt.

"Spanking," she said. "I haven't even been bad? Why'd I deserve a spanking...huh?"

He was silent. For a moment, in another world. As if someone had turned him off.

"Honey," she said, her panties round her knees, "You in, baby?"

"Cradle snatching?" came a voice.

"She's 27," he said to nobody.

Tina looked at him.

"I know I'm 27 honey," she replied. "Are you ok?"

He stared into space, and suddenly remembered his first wife. How long had it been? Nearly fourteen years? He hadn't thought of her in a long while, had closed himself off to thoughts of her, and then bang, there she was in his head, uttering the words "cradle snatching" like she was his conscience or something.

"You ok, baby?" asked Tina again. "Had I better call the doctor?"

John shook himself free from whatever had taken him, and looked at Tina, sitting astride him, concern on her young face.

"I'm fine, sweetheart," he reassured her. "I'm fine. You probably just wore me out. I'm an old man, you know. There's a reason why old men don't go with young girls."

"You're not that old," she said pulling up her panties. "And I'm not that young. You sure you're ok?"

"I'm fine," he answered. "I was just thinking of Melissa."

"Your wife?"

"Yeah."

"Sorry," she said, her young face a mask of concern. "It must have been hard to lose her."

"It was hard for so long," he replied. "I guess I got over it eventually."

She leaned over and kissed him before snatching the paper and stretching herself out on the sofa at the side of him.

"Hey," he said. "I was reading that! What do I do now?"

She flung her white socked feet up from the floor and placed them in his lap playfully,

"You get the feet," she said, turning to the paper.

2012

Glasses clinked and quiet chatter filled the air. The sound of a bar. Somewhere, music came out over a speaker, but nobody was listening to it. Hogan's Bar wasn't in the noisiest part of town; the clientele was slightly more refined: lawyers, judges, business types. Outside, the bar led out directly onto the street, then opposite that was 'wharf walk' where the lovers walked in the moonlight among the boats and the subdued streetlamps to kiss and cuddle their loved ones. John normally had no time for a place like that. A confirmed bachelor of 47, and with one or two business interests, his evenings were either spent alone in his apartment, or with his two male friends who lived in the adjoining apartments.

But not tonight. Tonight was different. Errol, the architect from the room above, had suggested that they all go speed dating. With all three guys either single, or separated, Errol and Tony were desperate to find some female companionship. John wasn't so keen. He never really trusted woman again after Taylor had tried to swindle him, of course there had been Tina, the cop, but that was never gonna last. It was six months before they realised they were worlds apart.

So here he was, in the little meeting room that adjoined Hogan's Bar's dark friendly confines. Speed dating. Each single person spent five minutes at a table, before a buzzer sounded and they all moved round. John felt out of place, like he was on a merry go round. The headaches hadn't stopped, and the doctors hadn't found anything wrong with him. Sometimes he couldn't even remember whether he had actually been to the doctors or not.

"Do you like cats?" a voice said. It was the date sat across from

"Uh, I guess," he replied.

"I have four," she continued. "Their names are…"

What their names were, John never knew. He tuned her out, suddenly jealous of the professional types next door sipping their gins quietly and listening to nondescript jazz music in the background. He found her looking at him, and gave her his attention again.

"Huh," he replied?

"I said," she replied with a look of minor annoyance, "do you have any pets?"

"Oh," he replied nonplussed. They were still talking about pets. John had developed a kind of fearlessness when talking to women these days, either through spending time in the past with Melissa who had always been forthright and direct, or maybe due to advancing years and increasing snarkiness.

"Yeah," he said remembering, "I had a cat once. My girlfriend at the time called him Horace."

"Oh," cooed the woman, "how lovely. Is your friend still around?"

And here was the snarkiness.

"No," he said shaking his head. "The girl swindled me out of millions and got gangsters after me. So I shot her cat in the head. Kind of revenge, I guess. Poor Horace."

She couldn't tell if he was joking or not. The dark look in his eyes told her he wasn't. He was handsome, though his face had a kind of manliness about it, what with the greying hair and all. Thankfully, the buzzer sounded and he moved on. She sighed with relief.

The next girl was no better.

"I just," she said shaking her head, "I just...I'm so fucking sick of men!"

"Should I just go?" he asked. He had meant it to come out as a joke, but kept his face straight, so it looked like an argument was starting.

"No," she said. "Well it's up to you. You all please yourselves, don't you? Away at work all week and then Saturday comes and it's all 'hey, shush down honey, the football is on!"

"What?" he replied, "I work all fucking week, and my one day off, I can't sit and relax and enjoy the game?"

She shook her head.

"It's not going to work for us is it?" she said laughing. "I've known you five minutes and already we're fighting."

"Probably not," he admitted. "But if it's any consolation, this five minutes were the most fun tonight."

She smiled.

"Thanks," she said. "I hope you find someone. That is, if you're looking..."

"I don't know if I am," he replied, "I mean...I should be, I've been single for a while."

"Never found the right woman" she asked?

He shook his head.

"No, it wasn't that," he said pausing, "My...my wife died. Cancer. I guess I got over it, but I always compare them to her. She was..."

"The blueprint," said the woman. "She was the one who they all have to measure up to. Here's a tip. None of them will. Find one who you like for her. Don't stop loving your wife because you never will. But you can love another one in a different way."

She was right. He thanked her, and after four dates, decided to call it a night.

Going out into the cold night air was pleasant after sitting in the darkness. Looking around outside, the night was picking up. Several couples were walking hand in hand along the dockside 'lovers walk' as they called it. John had no times for them, and wished, somewhat bitterly that they could leave their love and romance to behind closed doors. But that wasn't fair. |He'd had his share of happy times, not just with Melissa, but with Taylor when she hadn't been trying to either swindle or kill him, and then later with Tina. She had been a good kid, though too young for him. She needed someone her own age.

Suddenly feeling like he needed a drink, he turned and walked through the dark inviting door of Hogan's bar. The jazz piano music was still playing, but there were only around four booths filled. One person was at the bar, a female in a blue business suit, black nylons and flat patent leather shoes. She sat on a bar stool with her ankles crossed, her hair in a sensible tight chignon at the back of her head. She was sat staring into a glass of bourbon.

He went and stood at the side of her, and the bartender came up to him,

"Bourbon and branch," he said quietly. "Double. No ice."

"Rough night?" asked the woman at the side of him, looking up at him with casual interest. She was late thirties, with a strong jawline and dark features. Her eyes had a look of intelligence, probably a lawyer or a city banker, he thought. She had a nice figure though, good strong hips that the suit tried to disguise but couldn't, and a small chest with a slim waist.

"Speed dating," he said. "What a disaster. You tried it?"

She laughed, shaking her head,

"Oh no," she replied. "I gave up on dating years ago."

The bartender gently interrupted them,

"Your drink sir," he said, "and your change."

He took the change.

"Can I get you a refill?" he asked her.

She nodded.

"Why not," she replied, smiling at him as he sat beside her. He ordered her a drink.

"Hi," he said. "I'm John, the undateable."

She laughed. It was a natural laugh, and one, he imagined that she saved for when she was genuinely amused.

"Maddisen Payne," she returned.

"Pleased to meet you Maddisen," he replied. "If you don't mind me saying so, this isn't normally the sort of place where you meet professional single ladies drinking bourbon at the bar."

She smiled a slight smile again, before turning her body towards him.

"Doctors' orders," she said.

"I like your doctor," he smiled.

"I was having the palpitations," she continued, "and thought I was having a heart attack. Turns out that, what with my job, I was having stress attacks."

He looked concerned.

"I hope you're ok," he said.

She nodded.

"My doctor said it was because I find it difficult to unwind. I'm a defence attorney, and a good one."

"And you'd given up on dating?" he inquired.

She nodded.

"What with taking care of my son, and my job, and a mom who keeps trying to drag me into her women's institute, there isn't much time left for dating."

He nodded.

"I know what you mean," he said.

"How about you?" she replied. "Don't get many men like you speed dating?"

"Like me," he said raising an eyebrow.

"You know," she said gesturing. "Smart, clean, funny, charming. Most of them collect action figures and live with their moms."

He laughed.

"I never thought of it like that," he said taking a drink. "The truth is, my wife died years ago. Knocked me out of things for a while. I'm just getting back into the game, well...trying to."

They chatted for a long while, longer in fact than Maddisen had ever spent in a bar for years. But closing time came, and they both made movements to leave. Seizing the moment, he turned to her as she stood.

"Would you care to take a walk?" he asked.

Fearing she would think herself too old to walk down the 'lovers walk' with him, he watched her for a moment, her dark hair pulled severely back from her face. He could see how people might describe her features as harsh, or angular, but she was beautiful. Her eyes were tender, and filled with intelligence and amusement. The woman in the speed dating had said to find one who he could like in a different way. And he liked Maddisen. She made him smile. Somewhere inside him, he felt a little door close.

"I'd love to take a walk," she said and together they walked the lovers walk arm in arm, quiet in each other's company until at last they returned to their starting point. He held her hand, and she turned into his body. Holding one hand at the back of her neck, he felt her stiff, suited body relax and respond to his touch as he kissed her. It was a hungry kiss, neither of them had felt a kiss for some time and they devoured each other like young lovers half their age, stood there in the moonlight.

1986

The radio blared noisily.

"And in sports, the Boston Celtics again beat the Rockets to win the NBA title…"

Melissa turned off the thing. If it wasn't Reagan, it was fucking sports. She was busy in their apartment pressing clothes, as John brought them up from the laundry in the two baskets. Then he would help fold them. Laundry day, they called it. They had two days off work per week. One day, they would just nap and cuddle and have fun, the other day they crammed in their work in the apartment.

After Melissa's beating, she had never gone home again. Nor had she asked what John had done to Tyler in revenge: although he hadn't touched her father, her dad had never contacted her since. They'd lived at Belle Starr for a while, but his mom and dad were insufferable and clearly hated her for shoving their favourite Connie out of the equation. The trucking company had expanded, and Ed Mason, despite his differences with his son, now employed John to run most of it for him as Ed was busy greasing palms in the capital to try to get himself into politics. Eventually moving out of Belle Starr after yet another argument, the pair had gotten a little apartment on the other side of town, quite modest and run down, but as it was their first home, and they were proud of it.

But this was about to change. Ed Mason had gotten a junior role working for a key figure in local government, and he announced that he and his wife were moving there, at least temporarily. John hadn't cared that much, he rarely spoke to his brother, who was turning into a wiry youth with blonde hair and a mean sadistic streak. Cassie was still a little girl, and still beautiful. Both younger kids would naturally to go with their mother and father,

"I didn't think you'd want to come," said Ed to his son one day at Belle Starr. Besides, you're pretty much CEO of Mason Corp these days. Figured you'd be sticking around."

"You figured right," replied John. "I have people here."

"I don't want to leave the house empty. Not yet. I'm considering selling the place, that is, before it drops around our ears."

"What? To developers?" asked John.

"Why," laughed his dad. "You want to buy it?"

John did. He loved this place. But Melissa and he had nowhere near enough money to buy the old place. They were saving to get married. Not that he'd formally asked her yet, of course.

"Figured you could move back in here," said his dad "and look after the place if you wanted to."

John thought about it. The place was old and needed maintenance, that much was certain. Probably his dad thought he could ask John to move back in and get the work done for free.

"Fine," he said. "I'll tell Melissa to pack our stuff. We'll move in at the weekend. You're gone by then, right?"

"He asked you to move in," his mom said coldly from the doorway, "not her. She's not welcome in my house."

"Are we still on this?" he said, "I'm a grown man, Mom. I make my own decisions. If you don't like her, then that's tough. I love her, and I'm gonna marry her someday."

136

"And that's what she wants," said his mom, "the grubby little gold-digger. Wants you to marry her so she can have half of grandpa's money when you marry. You told the little bitch about grandpa's inheritance when you were a kid, and she'd connived her way in so she can get it."

"You're out of your fucking tree," said John. "This shit has never changed. Either she moves in with me, or pay a fucking house sitter."

"I can't tell you who to see or what to do," she admitted sadly, "but I can still dictate who I want in my house. And she will never cross this threshold."

"Maddy," his father chided, "we need them to look after the house. We have other things to worry about now."

She thought for a moment,

"See," mom said sadly, "she already has him. When he marries her, then she'll have our money. And now you want her to have our house too. She'll have taken it all."

"To be honest," said Ed looking around, "what with the wood rot in this old place, she can have the house. And nobody has grandpa's money yet. Just let the boy look after the house. If he wants to make mistakes, then that's up to him. We won't be around to help him pick up the pieces."

And so one rainy August day, Melissa and John moved back into Belle Starr, unofficially as its Master and Mistress. Ed Junior was upstairs; while Cassie was making sure the movers put the trunks with her toys in the van properly.

"Put them this way up," she said, her voice rising, "so they can breathe."

"They're plastic honey," said dad patting her on the head. "Aren't you too old for dolls anyway?"

"Ed leave her alone," chided mom who suddenly noticed who got out of John's black car.

She met Melissa's eyes,

"You look better," his mom said coldly, looking at the girl up and down. Her wounds had long since healed, and her hair grown back. John's mom had only seen the girl once since her beating. These days she wore it in a slightly longer than chin length bob, and had pale streaks in it. Her clothes were still scruffy though, and she wore an old red and black check shirt, jeans, and brown leather sandals.

"So do you," said Melissa, equally coldly. "You look good for your age. John honey, careful with those bags, those are the plates."

She watched as John wrestled with a huge trunk, blanching slightly at the girl's words.

"You might have his heart," mom said menacingly, "but you don't have his money. And I'd rather this place was demolished than see you as the lady of it."

Melissa laughed.

"I'm no lady, honey", she said, "but tonight when we're tucked up in your bed, he'll be thinking of me and not his momma. You're gone."

They walked inside.

Later, he met his brother on the stairs. Ed Junior was a wiry young man now, also engaged in his father's company, though he and John didn't get on. He was going to study in the capital with his family,

"So," began Ed Junior, "I guess you're pretty pleased with how things worked out."

John looked at him coldly.

"How's that?" he replied.

"House, company," he gestured. "And when you marry her, you'll get grandpa's money."

"I guess," John nodded, "though to be honest, it hadn't occurred to me. The money I mean. Pa pays me well enough for being CEO."

Ed Junior nodded. "You're a pretty lucky guy," he said, looking his brother up and down. "You got it all."

John tapped his brother on the shoulder.

"Your turn will come," he said. "Who's that girl I keep seeing you with?"

"Oh", Ed answered, "Elizabeth? Her dad's a senator. She's pretty cute."

John laughed.

"Who knows," he said. "You guys might even beat Mel and me to the altar."

"Nah," replied Ed Junior hiding a cold look. "That money's yours."

They went their separate ways. John was troubled by his brother. They had never really got along, and had always been jealous of each other. He kept mentioning Grandpa's money. There were millions of dollars, all held in a trust fund. Grandpa had been old fashioned, had wanted his first married grandson to have it, to help him start off in the world. The old fool hadn't seen that it would cause friction between the brothers. Or had he? There were stories of friction between Mason brothers right down through the family line. The truth was, John didn't give it too much thought. He was ok with how his life was working out. He had Melissa, he had a good job, and now he lived back in the home he loved. Melissa had a job too, in a cubicle in an office. It wasn't great, and she still sent her drawings and sketches off to various sources in a hope to break through. But they were doing it together. They were living their lives together the way they wanted to.

It was a Thursday morning when the call came in. John sat behind his desk angry at being disturbed.

"The loads gotta go," the foreman's voice was saying on the other end. "It's a new contract, and if we lose this, there's a lot of work stands to be lost through it. You know how things are?"

John did. The business was successful, but only because their trucks were always on time, and always did what they were supposed to do. This one driver had let him down.

"Go to the damned agency," John replied. "Couldn't Harkness have handled this? I'm due in a meeting with a friend of mine at one. This can't wait. I pay that private dick by the hour."

"Harkness's phone is off," the foreman replied. "I wouldn't have called you, Mr Mason, but I know how important this contract is. There's no available long distance drivers this week."

140

He knew. Previously, the distributor they were working for had used a big logistics chain to transport their products, but John and his father had negotiated a better deal using this company. And in the first week it was going wrong. Damn.

"How far is the run?" John asked.

"Down to Chihuahua, Mexico," the foreman replied. "Local carrier takes it from there."

"Fine," replied John. "I'll take it. Could do with a few days out of here."

The foreman sounded relieved. Melissa hadn't sounded so happy,

"We've not even been at belle Starr a week and you're leaving?" she'd said.

She'd had to refuse going with him. The agency she worked for wouldn't give her vacation time, and so, with instructions as to how to use the boiler at belle Starr, and the water, he kissed her tenderly and left.

"I'll make it up to you when I get back," he said.

"Yeah," she yelled back smiling. "I want diamonds or you ain't getting in!"

He was still smiling as he hit the road in the semi-truck. Leather works, the shipment note said. To be transported over the border to be made into handbags, shoes, and other things before being sent onto Europe for sale in the fashion stores. John's father had insisted his sons learn how to drive big rigs, as that was the business. Always have a skillset, he'd said. Jake had said much the same thing. As he drove for what seemed like forever, he thought of Jake. John nor his family had not seen hide nor hair of the former ranch foreman since the night of the argument. Whenever he'd pressed his father about it, his father just claimed that the foreman had left. Recently, with more resources available to him through the firm, he'd hired a guy to look into things for him, but so far the guy had come up with nothing. Until yesterday, when he'd called the offices. Found something, he'd said.

After days of driving, and feeling dirty, unwashed, and bored, John arrived at the border into Mexico. All hell broke loose as the dogs going over the truck started barking, guns were drawn and the young man was dragged down from his cab, handcuffed, and led to an office.

He sat in the dingy, dusty office for what seemed like hours. The supervisor's desk held a multitude of papers, a typewriter, some photographs of kids and one of those hula-dancing wind-up toys that had faded in the Mexican sunlight. The heat was stifling coming through the closed windows, and John suddenly felt homesick for the damp coldness of Belle Starr. Wrists chafing in his handcuffs, he was glad to see the supervisor return to the office. However, the man made no attempt to remove John's cuffs. Instead, he sat down in the leather chair hard, and the chair made a hiss in protest.

"In a lot of trouble, boy," the man drawled.

"How's that?" John said in his quiet, clipped tone.

"Well," thought the man, lighting a cigarette, "there's all that cocaine hidden in the leather of that truck for one thing. The shipment documentation is wrong for another."

"I know nothing about any of that," John protested. "It's for the Mason Corporation. Call my father, and he'll confirm the job booking."

"We did," said the supervisor, taking a draw in his cigarette. "Nobody at this Mason Corporation knows anything about this load or why the CEO decided to start smuggling hard drugs over the border."

Fuck.

Fuck fuck fuck.

John began to smell a rat. A dirty bit shithouse rat. He'd been set up as a mule? Who by? The foreman? He hadn't seemed the type. Either way, John knew he was in deep shit. A jail sentences for a drug smuggler could be up to forty years? How long had this been going on? And did his father know about this? So many questions. And none of them were going to be answered sat listening to this fool who sat farting in his chair as they waited for the cops to come haul his ass away. He made a decision and stood, as if to stretch his muscles. The supervisor stared at him in alarm, and quickly, John, being an athletic young man, rolled backwards, tucking his hands under him so that they were in front. The supervisor had drawn his weapon, but John, now with his cuffed hands in front of him, knocked the gun away, and barrelled into him, throwing him to the floor. A few seconds later and, hands shaking with fear, John maneuvered the key to the handcuffs, into the lock, and freed his wrists. Taking the man's weapons, he ran from the office. As he got across the courtyard, several other border patrol officers seemed to spot him and they drew their guns. John drew his own stolen gun and fired a couple of warning shots. Heart beating fast, he ran, panicking, to the little delivery van that was just unloading boxes, and jumped in. The keys weren't in, and so he jumped out again, running for the gate. The guards returned fire, and John ducked as he ran to miss the shots. Through the gate he went and onto a dusty side road just beyond the border station, the patrol beginning to start their engines. Along the road from the south was coming an old battered Plymouth. Pointing the gun at the window, he yelled to the man,

"Get out, fucker!" he shouted. "Out of the fucking car. Now!"

The Plymouth slammed on the brakes, and the man muttered something in Spanish and ran from the vehicle. Ducking more gunshots, he got in, spun the car, and gunned the motor. The patrol cars were right on his tail as he sped along the dusty road and into Mexico. The Plymouth was faster that the patrol cars, despite its age, and he began to gain distance from them. The road was free of dwellings, or telephones, only an occasional bush here and there. After a while, with the diminishing presence of the vehicles behind him, he approached a small, dusty town. Flinging the car left with the handbrake, he sped along the main street at seventy, pulling the brake again when he saw some small garages. Hiding the car behind a fence, John held his breath as he watched the patrol cars pause at the entrance to the town, before speeding off down the road.

Stepping carefully out of the car, he looked around. It was a typical south of the border town, with yellow dust everywhere and people who looked like they would kill each other for fresh water and a dust free life. It was like a set from a western, nothing had seemingly touched it since the days of the old west. There was even a bar and saloon. Realising that there would be a telephone inside, he made his way across the dirt street and into the bar. Inside, the tavern was falling to bits, though it still had the air of the

144

old west about it. Everywhere was dirty paint peeled wood, beer bottles, and cigarette ends. A couple of senior citizens sat at one end of the bar,

"You got a phone I could use?" John shouted to the bartender who sat talking to the men.

"Patrons only," he yelled back, not rising.

"Fine," John said throwing down a twenty. "Bourbon and branch. Double."

The man sighed and got off his seat. He served John a Bourbon measure, filling the glass with water from a bottle. It was hardly branch water, but it would serve.

"You got a phone?" he repeated.

"In the corner there," he pointed. "You need change?"

John nodded, and the man took another bill and threw down a selection of coins on the table.

He went to the phone, thinking hard. What the fuck had he done? What was going to happen now? Ran away from the cops, drug charges, a fugitive? Where the fuck was he gonna live, he'd be wanted in the US no doubt. Maybe Melissa could come down here and live with him here. But he discounted that. He wouldn't want her to live in the dirt here. She deserved better. With an increasing grimness, he saw his happy future at Belle Starr disappearing away from him. He couldn't call her. Not just yet. His father then? Suddenly wishing Jake was here, he decided who to call, and dialled the number.

Watching the door for any signs of the police returning from the main road, having realised that their fugitive had gotten away, he put some coins into the payphone. It rung for what seemed like ages, and at first he thought nobody was going to answer. Then the pick-up,

"Yeah," the voice came. "Ed Mason, Junior here."

"Thank fuck," John replied. "It's me, there's been a problem. I need your help."

"What kind of problem?" his brother asked. "Did you get arrested in some whorehouse?"

"No. A big fucking problem. There were bricks of coke hidden in the trailer."

Ed's voice sounded strange, like somehow he wasn't surprised,

"Fuck," he said after a while. "So where are you? In jail?"

"No," he said. "I'm in a town about five miles south of the border. In a bar. Did you know about this shit? You sound less than surprised."

"It's not that," his brother reassured. "It's just....Ron, that foreman that dad uses...he's had money troubles for a while now. Been involved with some nasty guys. This was obviously payment."

"You didn't think to mention it to me before now?" shouted John. "I'm in all kinds of shit here!"

"I'll deal with it," said his brother. "I'll tell dad and he'll check on the situation with the lawyers. Just stay where you are. You set foot in the US, and you'll be in even more trouble."

146

"Fine," John replied. "Tell Melisa what's happened. Take care of her for me."

He gave his brother the address of the town, and the saloon where he would be staying, and went to finish his drink.

The small villa that his family had secured for him was small and modest and, more importantly, discreet, but it was home now. John had gotten used to the Mexican dust, and the heat. He'd started working for one of the local hoods, who trafficked weapons and bootleg booze across the border into the US. But he wasn't working today. On one of his visits, Ed Mason Junior had brought his brother supplies. The legal situation was still not good. John was wanted, both South of the border and in the US. According to his brother, if he returned to US soil, he would face years, maybe decades in jail. The legal team were working on it, and had been for a year now.

That year had been awful. He could only have contact with his brother, nobody else. The police were apparently watching the family and Melissa too. That was the worst thing. He hadn't spoken to her since that day at Belle Starr when she'd requested a diamond ring. His heart ached for her, and he felt the blackness come again for his soul.

"Is she ok?" he asked, as he made his monthly phone call.

"I dunno," the voice of his brother came. "I haven't seen her since she got a job. Company called Telestar I think. She's still in that rattletrap old house. Mom softened a little, but living in the capital with dad, it was hard to offer her much."

"Give me her number," he replied. "I want to talk to her."

"Come on," Ed answered. "You know it's not possible. The news is still talking about you. Dad's trying to get the Governor involved and find out what happened to that foreman, but they're still watching her. I have to be careful where I call from."

"Tell her I love her," said John, feeling the sudden cold bleakness in his heart, "and tell her to write me."

Things were hard below the border. John's brother had contacted his father, who was speaking to friends in DC, try to get the situation dealt with. But it would take time. Money sent by his father got John set up in a small apartment in an area of Mexico city known as Mi-Nezota, a sprawling urban crime- ridden city where a guy could disappear if needs be. And John had need to. The drainage was terrible, the little apartment slum was terrible, the garbage collector that arrived every other Thursday still had a donkey pulling a cart. Gangs roamed the street in broad daylight, though as if they sensed the young American with the dark dangerous eyes was trouble, they gave him a wide berth. John received letters there, and in a local grocery store friendly to him, received phone calls from his family in the back room.

He got the first letter from Melissa a few weeks later.

"My darling John

"I love you. I hope you're ok. I just want to come there and be with you. We could be like Bonnie and Clyde, only without the whole being dead part. But your brother and father say its ok, that you'll be coming home as soon as the heats off. Poohsticks Bridge is weird without you. This isn't how I thought our lives together would start, but I guess things happen in life that challenges couples. I love you, and while you're away, I'll hold onto that. Winter's drawing in and Belle Starr is getting cold and damp. I keep thinking of you all nice and warm in Mexico City. I wish you were here with me to keep me warm. But I have a job now. I'm data entry at Telestar. It's mainly an office with single people, so I have plenty friends. I know you'd love them. I have a little car and a computer and everything. I'm getting used to people there now. I don't think I knew how to interact with people so good, you know? But anyway, we go for drink every weekend and watch the game. Erikkson's head of the Cougars now, I don't know if you're following Washington down there but they're doing pretty good.

Miss you
Love you always
Melissa"

He held the letter, and kept it close to him, in his jacket pocket. In time, and after investigating most of the rabbit warren streets and alleys of the slum, he began to be aware of a protection business going on. Mindful of his brother's warnings to keep a low profile, this nevertheless piqued the young man's curiosity. The gang appeared to pick on the most needy and those without anything. John didn't see the sense in that. The poor folks of Mi-Nezota had nothing to steal anyway, so why take the two pieces of tin that they did have? And so one day, without thinking, he handled it.

There had been a commotion. He had been sat with a small child in the street trying to fix an old pram for her dolly. The kid couldn't get the wheel on. The street was its usual commotion, a riot of color and filth, putrid smells coming from every area, people jostling past kicking through refuse.

"Here honey," he said to her, kneeling. "Let me help with that."

The girl smiled and watched as the young American investigated. The split pin had come loose and now the pram wheel kept coming off, tipping her battered baby doll out into the dirt. He searched around the ground for the split pin, and after a few seconds, found it in the dust and dirt of the street nearby. As he bent it back into shape, he noticed two men go into a nearby slum. By their bulges in their worn jackets, they looked armed.

"Your dolly have a name," he said to the girl tenderly.

She shook her head. The little girl watched as the American pushed the wheel on, and inserted the split pin, bending it so it wouldn't come loose again. All fixed.

John heard a commotion coming from inside. He picked up the little girl's baby doll, smoothed its hair and placed it back in the buggy.

"All fixed, sweetheart," he said rising, "but she needs a name. I'll come by tomorrow and we'll think of one together, ok?"

She laughed and smiled at him, testing the buggy out. But his thoughts had turned to the men and carefully, drawing his own pistol, the one he'd taken from the border guards, slipped quietly inside.

"You can't afford to pay us the money," one of the men was saying, "we break your fucking legs."

"Senor," a woman's voice came, "my husband has no work, we cannot..."

"Then maybe," the man said smiling, "maybe I rape your kid."

She screamed. The scream muffled the sound of John wrapping the barrel of the pistol in a nearby cloth wrap, grabbing the man nearest him in a headlock, put the wrapped gun to his temple and, holding it away from him, pulled the trigger. The spray of blood covered the walls instantly, and John discarded it before it could go over him. The woman cowered, as this new figure extended his gun again to the other man.

"You sign your death warrant, motherfucker." said the remaining gangster, turning his gun on the young American. He was a thick set man with long hair and greasy pick marked skin. Why the hell would these people let a lowlife like this push them around.

John didn't wait around for a war with words. He pointed the gun at the man's knee and fired.

He screamed, falling down instantly, crying like a baby.

"You know who you're fucking with?" he said, screaming. John kicked the gun out of his hands, nodding.

"A piece of Mexican filth," he said with a menacing tone. "I don't give a fuck who you are, I don't rightly give a fuck who your boss is. Go to him and take him a message. Tell him a big tough American fucked you up like a little bitch. Tell him to go work over people who can afford it. These people live in the dirt. All you're gonna steal here is more dirt."

"Why do you care," screamed the man holding his knee.

"I really don't," replied the young man. "But didn't come here to this fleapit to have my peace shattered by trash like you coming in here. I like a little bit of peace, a quiet time for reflection, like a Sunday afternoon listening to the birds in the trees while I read the football scores in the newspaper. You know what I mean? And just as I'm enjoying being here, two pieces of shit come stomping in and try to spoil things. Take a look at yourself? Would your mother be proud? Can you ever go home to a wife who will say she loves you? NO. You gotta go pay for it. How could anybody love that piece of shit? I'd be doing you a favour if I killed you."

"You crazy, man," the man sputtered, struggling to stand, Encilads will kill you!"

John nodded.

"Tell this Encilada you work for that you got fucked up by an American who knows how to handle trash," he said. "If he needs someone reliable, then I'm available for work right now. But not here. There's little kids around here. This isn't a place for business."

March 1988

"My darling John,

I haven't seen your brother for a long time. Well...it's hard with this job. I get to wear a smart suit and have a new haircut (you wouldn't recognise me!!) and I even have a cubicle of my own now. It's like a regular family here.   I'm still sending my artwork off, but I haven't gotten any response, plus...it's hard to get down to it after work. Your dad and brother said last time I saw them that the heat on you was still pretty bad. I wanted to come down and see you but they said I'd be watched. That sucks. I haven't been down to Poohsticks Bridge for a while. It somehow isn't the same without you. But you gotta stay there and keep outta sight. I'm sorry honey, and I miss you, but that's what we gotta do. Can't believe it's been over a year.

Miss you

My Love

Melissa"

He couldn't put his finger on it. Something he was missing, though he didn't know what. Perhaps it was the tone of the letter. Melissa sounded different. Then his mind realised something. They had been apart for nineteen months now. She was moving on, getting on with life without him. What the fuck were his brother and father doing to get him out anyway. He sighed with frustration, and not for the first time wondered whether or not just to go hand himself in, take the jail time and at least get to see Melissa every month through the bars of his cell. That would be marginally better. The work was distracting though. Encilada, the local gangster, had arranged a meeting with the American who had fucked up his hoods, and now John worked for him. Encilada left the folks of the slums alone, and he and John were moving into the narcotics and weapons business. It was exciting, and John found, more importantly, that he could feed the darkness that seemed to descend over his soul nowadays.

October 1988

"My dearest,

I got a promotion at Telestar. I'm a supervisor now. I still draw and stuff, but it's hard to break through. You know, I wonder if that was just a childhood dream? This job pays good and well. I wanted to tell you this next bit in the summer latter, but I didn't know how. Just about August, a sweet guy asked me out on a date. I told him I was with you, but that you were away for a while. Anyway, I said no to him, and we began to be friends. I need someone in my life. It's so lonely here sometimes. But we went together (like we used to do) to a Halloween party...I'm sorry to do this to you. I know what shit you're going through down there, but I kissed him. It seems to have been so long. I feel horrible, but I can't live my life alone! I think that we were doomed anyway, weren't we? So many fucking obstacles in our way...maybe it was just a mistake. And so I'm going to date him. I don't want to lie to you, I'll tell you before 'it' happens, I owe you that. I'm sorry. I'll always be your friend if you still want me to be, always. My best, friend xxxx

All my love,

Melissa"

He dropped the mug he was holding, his hand shaking. Suddenly, despite being alone in a considerably sized villa, he felt like he was trapped in a little box, scrabbling to get out. His brother had told him, barely a week ago, that the family had convinced the Governor to look into John's case, so that, maybe in a year or so he could return. But not until then. He felt so far away. And she had found someone, as he knew she eventually must. He'd found girls, too, that had been interested in him, some local girls and one...one older woman. He'd been tempted especially by her. She was the wife of his gangster boss, Encilada. She was pale, blonde and European with an expensive taste in fashion. At around forty years old, she had attempted to seduce the young man. He remembered the day they had first met.

Mrs Luciana Encilada walked as though she owned all of Mexico City, which pretty much she did, or at least her lover did. Encilada was a dangerous man. She was dressed to kill, in a sharp brown business suit and short skirt, killer heels, and expensively curled blonde hair. She was forty, maybe past forty, but gorgeous. She smiled when she saw the growing bulge in the young man's pants.

"It's hot in here," she said removing her jacket. "Encilada insists on keeping the windows shut: keeps the dust out."

"He nodded, sipping his water. He was waiting for Encilada who was due at any moment.

"I keep telling him that I'll return to New York if he doesn't get this place air conditioned," she said.

He nodded politely, watching her small, but pretty breasts strain against the buttons of the tight blouse.

"That where you're from?" he asked.

Luciana nodded.

"My father is from Marseilles, but we lived in New York and London too."

"I thought there was an accent there," he nodded.

She laughed, slipping her feet out of her heels and rubbing one bare foot.

"I don't exactly fit in with these barefoot in the dirt peasants, do I" she said, "despite his trying to make me into one."

"You're very beautiful," he said quietly.

She ignored his compliment, relishing the cold stone floor beneath her bare feet.

"I ended up with Encilada," she said, "because it got me where I wanted to be."

"In Mexico city?" he said, laughing.

She felt him make fun of her, and she flushed with slight anger. Then, she began to feel the power growing in this young man. Maybe he would be the one. He was going to be somebody; she could feel that.

She went up close to him.

"No," she replied demurely. "It got me close to men like you. Men who know how to treat women."

She moved to kiss him, and for a moment he thought of returning the kiss. At that moment, an image entered his head. The image of a young woman, with blonde rumpled hair and a dirty stained work shirt and baggy jeans. Sat at Poohsticks bridge with him, being all sarcastic and funny. He imagined her lips, the scent of bluebells and aniseed on her breath. He pulled back.

"I can't," he said. "I'm sorry, but I can't."

At that moment, a slim Mexican man entered, wearing a business suit, his hair slicked back.

"Encilada," she said, startled.

He laughed.

"John, my friend," he said smiling. "You're a better man than me if you can say no to Luciana. I couldn't."

"Juan, I…" she said. He waved her off.

"I don't care who you sleep with, slut," he laughed, turning to John and clapping him on the shoulder.

"But I'm glad my favourite guy has better taste than that."

She'd tried again after that. Once only wearing her slim night dress. Encilada had told him that he didn't care. But every time he went close to her, the blonde hair reminded him of the one he loved more than any.

And now she'd sent that letter. She was seeing someone. He couldn't blame her, he didn't want her to live her life alone, he wanted her to be happy and comfortable. He envied her the life she was going to have, and wished beyond hope that it was still somehow going to be with him.

1989, February

"John,

I moved out of Belle Starr after Christmas. Well...before really, I
spent Christmas with Tony, the guy I'm dating. He felt sorry for me
here all alone. I mean...I loved it when you were here, but I need
someone. Belle Starr is shut up right now. I'm sorry. I know I keep
saying that, but I am. And you're so sweet to keep telling me that
you forgive me in your letters to me. I wish I could just hug you like
we used to do when we were small. I really like Tony. I hope that if
you ever get back here, you like him too. I want you guys to get on.
So...Tony and I are looking for a place together. He's left Telestar
now, has a job in the city and stuff. He's commuting, but he wants
us to move there eventually. I don't know...I feel so connected
here. I don't want to be so far away from you and Belle Starr, but in
a way, its time maybe to put our childhoods away."

My love always,

Melissa

1989, October

"Please senor," the man said, kneeling at his feet pleading for his life. "I told Encilada that I lost my job. I can't get the money at the moment."

John watched the man beg for his life, coldly, impassively.

"Ain't my problem," he replied raising the gun. "I'm just here to collect one way or the other."

The man nodded.

"I understand senor," he said. "I feel such a failure. All I've ever tried to do is to protect my family. My wife and I were married way too young. We had nothing else, only love. I thought love would conquer all. How foolish eh?"

John lowered the gun a little.

"I was gonna be married too," he said quietly, fingering the little pack of letters he carried with him.

The Mexican farmer nodded.

"What happened?" he asked. "You don't look like a happy married man."

John smiled, then lowered the gun completely.

"This happened," he said. "I ended up here living in the dirt as a fucking fugitive cos of some fucking foreman who worked for my father got in debt with gangsters. My Melissa got left behind at home. And then..."

The farmer lowered his head and closed his eyes.

"Then she stopped waiting and found someone else," he said quietly.

John nodded.

"She waited longer than most would have," he said.

"Letter?" asked the man.

John nodded, and pulled out the pack of letters. He put the gun in his holster, and sat down in the dirt. Leafing through the letters, he pulled out the last one in the pack and gave it to the man.

"This is the last one she ever sent…"

"John,

This might be my last letter for a good while. The commuting has worn Tony out. We've found a lovely apartment in New York. You'll love it when you see it. I know it's a long way from home, but without you there, I haven't much else to keep me. Sometimes I can't believe it's been three years. I still remember that night, that first night when I thought we were going to be together forever, and live our lives quietly buried out there at Belle Starr. It was a good dream. But it's time to move on from our childhoods. It's never gonna be enough, the words will never cover what I truly feel, but I want to just say thank you. Thank you. All my life I never had anyone else who was prepared to be my friend through anything. My childhood was the best, all because of you. You'll always have a place in my heart. I'll never forget you. Maybe one day we can meet up again at Poohsticks Bridge with our families and our kids. I know you'll find someone one day that will return the love you have, someone who deserves a guy like you. I'm sorry, I guess they were right and it had to end someday. I just wish it could have ended with a hug.

My love always,

Melissa

As the farmer read the letter, he watched the young man's dark shadowed face break, and tears well up in his eyes. Suddenly, their dispute forgotten, the farmer held the young man like he would have his own son until at last his grief subsided.

The farmer read the letter again. "Hmm," he said, "my mother used to say to me... 'Carlos , read the letter. Not the words. That's the way to find out how a person truly thinks'."

John looked up.

"I'd read it a hundred times," he said. "It says the same fucking thing. Somebody else is living my life. Somebody else has her at his side. There's nothing I can do about it. She's happy with him...she..."

"Shhh," replied Carlos. "You're too close to this I think. You're reading the words. Read the letter."

"I don't know what the fuck you mean?" said John exasperated.

The farmer moved to John's side, and put his arm around him. He now understood the boy's darkness, his strange anger. Just like one of his own sons.

"This girl, this Melissa and you...you have such love for each other. She affects you in such a way that I can see the darkness surrounding your soul at the thought of losing her. You cry like a child at the pain of her loss."

"Thanks for pointing that out," John smiled slightly.

The farmer nodded,

"It's nothing to be ashamed of," he said. "Even the brave, strong men cry sometimes. Love is the most powerful emotion of them all. But you're still not reading the letter. Look past the words."

"You mean read between the lines."

Carlos nodded.

"Like I said," he whispered, holding up the letter. "You cried like a baby at the thought of her loss. How do you think she felt when she wrote this to the love she was saying goodbye to?"

John looked at the letter, imagined her bent over to write, as she always did, in her scribbled handwriting. He imagined her wiping her eyes and nose on her sleeve, as her tears plopped down on to the page, along her nose drips. Suddenly he saw the paper, and the neat inked handwriting, the clean crisp sheets of letter writing paper, neatly folded to fit in the envelope. The neat handwriting, without smudges, blotches, tear stains, or scrunches.

And then he saw it. It was a slow realisation, a slow dawning realisation, as a feeling of horror crept over him and enveloped his very soul. He began to smell a rat, as he rifled through the letters. 'Her' letters. He smelled a rat alright. A dirty great big shithouse rat. Carlos looked up at his face.

"You see it," the old man said.

"It's been staring me in the face all along," John whispered. "How could I be so blind?"

"Like I said," said Carlos. "You're too close. You couldn't see the letter for the words."

"I see now," John replied grimly. "She didn't write this. That page is too clean. She never said those things."

Carlos nodded.

"You mentioned being stuck here, that your brother was helping you. Be careful who you trust, amigo. The one you trusted had betrayed you."

And then he saw it. The whole fucking nine yards. Grandpa's money. Keeping him out of the way. His brother splitting him and Melissa up so he would get married first and he would get the inheritance, and as a bonus, the illegitimate son of a ranch hand would end up buried in Mexico forever. His mind saw the plan, saw how he had been played, and suddenly he reread the end of the track with a start. He turned to the farmer.

"So where the fuck is she then?" he said. "Melissa isn't some simpleton. She wouldn't rest if she thought my brother was working something over me."

"I don't know," replied Carlos. "But I think you need to go find her."

"Maybe she really did meet someone else," John thought aloud.

"Did you," the farmer asked?

"I take your point," John answered.

"Look," Carlos replied patting his shoulder. "I have to go through near border in a few days. I'll ask around. My cousin's boy works for border patrol in the US. He's got a good job. We're all proud of him. He owes me a favour. We'll find out, and see if we can get you two reunited."

"I'm sorry," John said, "for all that…that gun stuff. I lost my way. I don't know where I'm going."

Carlos helped him to stand.

"Forget it," he said. "It is done and over. You're going home."

After waiting an agonising three days, Carlos returned with the news from his cousin's son that John wasn't wanted at all. The entire ring of smugglers had been caught two years previously. In fact, there had been an attempt by one or two of them to find the young man. Not without trepidation did he go through the US/South American border. But he was waved through, driving, as he was, In Carlos's pickup truck which he'd bought from him that morning. The drive took another three days, but John didn't sleep, feeling suddenly wired with the anger at what his brother (and possibly others) had done to him, and with concern over Melissa, where she was and what she was doing. He'd released that she could be anywhere. After all, none of the letters had been from her, and most likely none of his had reached her.

As he finally reached his home town, he wondered where to try first. He ignored the changes, the new turnpike, the new football stadium, and what looked to be a huge mall dominating the skyline. Where to try first. The time was just after twelve. He wasn't going to Belle Starr yet. He wondered idly if the place was even still standing, what with his parents apparently living in the capital now. Maybe his brother lived in it. And John couldn't think about him

168

yet. First things first. He had things to deal with first. Deciding to try their old apartment, he turned off at the intersection and through the south part of town. Some of it he just didn't recognise. Buildings had been torn down here and there, and in other places smartened up and painted. There seemed to be more people about, different types of people, different races and cultures. When he'd left. It had been a conservative pacific northwest town, now it was more like a city, more like where he'd just left, a melting pot of cultures. Fast food places had sprung up with strange sounding names that he was eager to try. They would try them together, he thought. The thought of her suddenly made his heart sink, where was she? He ran the pick-up down the street to where their apartment had been and when he got to the entrance, ran up the stairs. Knocking on the door, nobody answered. He hung around outside, looking through the keyhole but could see nothing.

"Can I help you, buddy?" said a thick set man appearing from across the hall.

"Oh," John replied, suddenly aware of how awful he must look, not having slept or shaved for three days, and wearing a dust encrusted suit.

"I used to live here," he began. "I was looking for my …my friend. She lived here too."

The thick set man nodded.

"I dunno, buddy," he replied. "That's been empty for a while. There was a girl used to live here, a long time ago. Heard she got in trouble with the cops. It was empty for a while. Now there's a sweet old lady lives there."

"Huh," answered John. "This girl. What did she look like?"

"I dunno," he said. "Never saw her, really. Heard she got drunk and ran down some kid. Blonde chick I think. Don't hold me to it."

"Nah," John said, turning away. "I won't. Thanks, buddy."

"No problem," the man shouted, going inside. "Hope you find your friend."

It wasn't much to go on. In fact it was less than nothing. He wondered if it had even been her...what was it the guys said? Running down some kid...trouble with the cops? He hoped it wasn't her.

As he drove to his next destination, he turned the phrases over in his head. Running down some kid, trouble with the cops, running down some kid...trouble with the cops.

He hoped beyond hope that she was ok. Suddenly feeling a knot in his stomach, he arrived at the small shop in the seedier side of the commercial district. It was still there, with a peeling sign over the metal shuttered door,

"P.A. Holding. Bail Bonds"

John got out the truck and knocked on the shutters.

"Phil," he yelled. "You home?"

"You got a warrant," a voice said.

"No," he replied. "It's John. John Mason. Do I need one?"

The shutters opened, and a middle-aged man in a vest and sweat pants looked out at him.

"Fuck man," he said. "I thought you were dead!"

John dusted himself down.

"Not bad for a corpse, huh?" he said, smiling a smile that he didn't feel. Holding saw the dark eyes, and beckoned John inside.

"What the fuck happened to you?" Holding asked. "After you put me on that Jake case, the last I hear was that you left town and got busted for drug running. They all said you were dead."

"Dead, huh?" John mused. "Did I have a memorial?"

Holding moved to sit down, looking for his ashtray. He lit a cigarette, and began shuffling papers.

"You want one?" he said, offering a cigarette.

John took it, and for a few moments, they sat smoking.

"Was it a good memorial?" he asked Holding.

"I dunno," Phil replied. "Didn't go."

John was quiet.

"I have the papers somewhere, what I found out about Jake's car. It's been three years and I didn't expect you to come knocking on my fucking door."

"Sorry if I scared you," he said, "what with me being back from beyond the grave and all."

Phil laughed.

"Man," he said. "You look worse than any fucking corpse I ever saw."

John laughed. "Forget Jake for a minute," he said. "I need to know where Melissa is. That's important."

Phil shook his head.

"How would I know?" he replied. "I only know what I read in the papers."

"So what the fuck happened here?" John said riding. "Why the fucks she in the papers?"

Phil sighed, taking a long drag on his cigarette.

"There was an accident," he said. "Sit down, and I'll tell you what I read. I don't know if it's true or what, just what I read, ok?"

John nodded.

"Just after they said you were gone, there was this kid got run down in the road out on the intersection. Bout midnight. Anyway, they found the girl that did it. I recognised her name. Melissa George. They tested her, the cops, and found that she was high."

"She didn't use drugs...well. I mean. We smoked put a little...once, but not..."

"I know, I know," Phil said holding up his hands. "Who didn't, right? I smoked the odd joint myself. But it said in the papers that there was all kinds of shit in her system. Apparently, she'd been to some club. Anyway, she got jailed for five years. Probably got of lightly, Judge Barrow as a good guy."

"I remember Barrow," said john, letting the information sink in.

"Yeah," Phil continued, "a good old guy. You know he killed himself? Wife found him. No, really. Out there in his garage with the engine running. Who would have thought it?"

"So she's in jail?" he said, his voice faltering.

"I doubt it," Phil mused. "A five-year sentence would be over in two and a half, parole probably after two years with good behaviour. She's out there somewhere."

"I need to find her. Quickly."

"Hang on," said Phil, lighting another cigarette. "I need some cigarettes. Damn that bitch, I swear she's smoking me out of house and home."

He found the telephone and called a number.

"Friend of mine on the parole board," he whispered, putting his hand over the mouthpiece. "He owes me a few favours. I found his daughter sucking off some Cholo last year and brought her back for him. Kept it out of the papers. He works for the parole board. If she'd got a job and a place to stay, then he'll know it."

A short phone conversation later and John found out all he needed to know.

"Don't forget," reminded Phil, "I still need to go through this Jake stuff with you."

John turned to his friend as he made to leave.

"There's a more important job," he said, "I'll pay you double when I've handled all this. I swear."

"Go on," said Phil. "I'm always up for double fees."

"Find out about this...this thing with Melissa. This is out of character for her. She wouldn't do this."

"Cops had evidence, man," Phil said. "But I'll take a look. I don't think anyone ever gave enough of a shit before."

"I swear she didn't do this," he repeated, "or if she did, then there's a damn good reason."

As john left, he hoped there was. Either way, he had a name, and for the first time in three years, he was close to her. The name was 'Plukkins.' It was a chicken slaughterhouse that supplied the fast food joints that were springing up all over town. It was a rough job, and only drop outs and ex-cons would ever consider working there. Melissa George had worked there ever since being released on parole from Jail, so Phil had said. She'd served two years in prison.

He was furious, beyond fury, almost. And yet the thoughts of her calmed him. Those who had done this would get theirs, he knew that. Mexico had changed him: he was tough now, street smart, and strong. Nobody would ever fuck with him ever again, or fuck with those he loved dear.

"I'm sorry," said the woman on Plukkins reception as she looked the young man up and down with thinly disguised distaste.

"You hard of hearing?" he snapped. "Melissa George. She works here. Get her."

"I can't really pull people off the floor just because they have visitors," she said emphasising the word visitor. "But I can tell you that her shift finished a good twenty minutes ago. She's probably 'round the corner at the bus stop. The girls wait for the line 11 together."

"Thank you," he said sarcastically. "Have a really good day."

She ignored him, and he jumped back in the truck. He paused for a moment, clutching the wheel. He hadn't seen her or heard from her for three years. What did she look like now? Would she even know him or want him? What had the love of his life been doing? Suddenly his heart ached for her, and he felt the space at the side of him where she'd always belonged. Figuring out which was the main road, he parked opposite a group of woman at a bus stop. There were about ten women there. Some laughing, some joking, a couple quiet with their own thoughts.

He saw her.

His eyes went to her from across the road. Her head was down, as if the world had somehow defeated her. She wore a think pale yellow sun dress and dirty white sneakers, and her blonde hair was cropped short in a severe, but neat style. And suddenly, right there on the street corner all the hatred he had for his family melted away; Carlos, Encilada, and his girlfriend; all the dust in Mexico melted away as he stared at the small figure waiting for the bus, alone in her thoughts. As if sensing that someone from across the street was watching her, she turned and looked into his face. He couldn't hold back the tears of relief that he had found her: whatever she did, whatever happened to them from then on, it didn't matter. He had found her again. He started at her, his whole body shaking and unable to move. She straightened herself, dropped the bag she was holding and walked towards him across the road, her eyes never leaving his. The bus came, and some of the girls called to her, but her eyes remained locked to his. He could see her bottom lip tremble as she met his gaze. Despite the beard, and the dirt, she had known it was him. It couldn't have been a trick; no world would be that cruel to her. And as she got nearer, he still met her gaze, and she knew it was him.

And then she was with him, at the side of the street, and the world stopped its rotation. Time on the little world ceased to exist, every living being held its breath as they embraced. He buried his face in her short hair and kissed her head,

"I...I," he began, unable to speak. "I got letters from you. They said you'd found someone. I couldn't get back to you."

"They said you were dead," she replied, her voice am emotional hoarse whisper. "But I was in jail and couldn't find out."

He held her close, hugging her tightly to him.

"I'm here now," he replied, "and I'm never gonna leave go of your hand again. Not ever. That is...unless you..."

She stroked his hair, and brushed the dirt and tears away from his face.

"I knew you would come back," she said wiping her own face. "I knew inside that we weren't done. I knew it wasn't going to end like that."

He looked into her tearful green, sparkling eyes.

"It's gonna be ok," he said. "Whatever else happens to us, they're never gonna split us apart again."

She smiled. Suddenly the weight that had been on her shoulders for so very long had lifted. They walked along the street for a time hand in hand, feeling so giddy with love and happiness that they

176

didn't know what to do with their excess energy. She felt like running down the street screaming. They were together again.

He fixed himself a drink, necking it hungrily. Since his heart attack, he wasn't supposed to drink. His new wife, Maddisen, kept him on a tight leash in that regard. She cared for him too much to have him die on her. And, he'd decided, life was just getting interesting again. His life finally was picking up, after years of grey and darkness. So much so that he awoke to Maddisen with a smile on his face and in his heart. And his Melissa was now just a memory, a faint echo of an ache deep down in his gut instead of the sharp, stabbing world of hurt that it had always been. And sometimes, nowadays, he never thought of her at all. He loved Maddisen now.

"You want a drink, honey," he shouted. No answer. Perhaps she was on the phone to her office again.

"Maddisen?" he shouted.

No answer.

Cursing to himself, he walked through to the living room. Jacket off, shoes off, there she was, feet up on the sofa watching some TV show,

"I shouted for you," he said, smiling.

She didn't turn her head from the TV show.

"Is that what all that yelling was?" she replied, "I thought it was the TV for a second."

"You want a drink?" he repeated.

"You could have just brought me one instead of coming all the way through here to ask," she said, turning her head.

"Next time get your own," he said with a twinkle in his eye. He reached down to kiss her on the lips.

"Be right back," he said, returning a moment later with her a Bourbon and branch. He sat down beside her.

"My favourite," she said. "A drink and my husband, massaging my feet"

She rested her feet on his lap, and returned to her show,

"Oh," he said disappointed. "I don't mind the feet, but this show is the pits."

She made a face.

"Well just read the magazine at the side of your chair then. Let me watch the show in peace. It's a good episode."

"Why?" he asked, his curios ty peaked. "It's never had a good episode before."

"That's the main character there," she said, pointing to the man in the hospital bed. "He's dying tonight."

"Huh," replied John. "Poor guy."

"I know," she answered, listening to the show. "That's his wife right there. She's going to be heartbroken."

"What's he dying of?" John asked, watching now as intently as Maddisen.

"He was in a car accident," she said. "He rolled his car on the freeway. It was a massive stunt for the show. Rolled the car nine times. He's been in a coma for months. At first, they thought he was gonna come out of it, but recently, he's been getting worse. They're switching his machine off tonight."

John closed his eyes, the sudden glare of the TV making the pain behind his eyes come back.

He didn't remember the rest of the show. Or the rest of the night. He awoke with a start, late, and Maddisen was just stepping out of the shower.

"I have to dash," she shouted from the hall as she pulled on her panties and nylons.

"You in court today?" he yelled, getting out of bed.

"No," she said. "I'm down at county all day. New cases. Getting spat at, called a 'whore bitch' by my client. Fun times all round. Oh, and there's a snarl up on the freeway, so I'm leaving early."

As he made his way around the bed slowly, she was already dressed and ready to dash downstairs to find her shoes. He grabbed her and kissed her hard on the lips.

"I love you too," she laughed. "But seriously, thanks for smudging my lipstick."

He did love her. She was the best thing to happen to him in a long time. His heart attack had left him weak and unable to work. Plus, the doctors hadn't found any explanation for his constant headaches. At least he thought they hadn't. Sometimes he couldn't remember speaking to a doctor. He lit a cigarette and turned on the radio.

"They're backing up all the way to the interchange with I-20 now. Police are saying that that the section of the interstate will be closed for at least two hours."

Jesus, another snarl up. What was with people these days. All those years he spent at Belle Starr and in that little school he never once saw a fender bender on the highway nearby. Fast new world, he thought glumly. His thoughts returned to the little school far away as he dragged on his cigarette, and suddenly, his thoughts turned to the little girl who sat beside him.

And there at the kitchen table, tears welled up in his eyes, for the first time in a long time as he thought of her. He hadn't even been to her grave in what felt like years.

"I wish you'd just get the fuck out of my head," he shouted to nobody. Let me live what's left of my life."

The radio blared again.

"Sources are saying that the car rolled nine times and ended on its roof on the other side of the median where it was hit by a semi-truck. The car driver, a male of around forty years old, was taken to nearby Washington State hospital."

He didn't hear the radio. He was still furious with her, a woman whose image refused to leave his head. He needed Maddisen, and thought for a moment of calling her, but seeing as she was probably in traffic, he decided against it. He lit another cigarette, and massaged the pain in his head.

1989

He had made love to her for a long time. Firstly, she had let him sleep, for he was exhausted. Then, she had shaved his face and trimmed his hair. And then they had made love hungrily together. And then they had simply lain together. She had lain on the bed with him naked, her head on his chest, as he caressed her softly with his fingers.

"I need to tell you some stuff," she said after a long while.

"If it's about the jail," he said looking at her, "then I already know. Phil told me."

"Who?" she replied, looking up. "Oh its ok, it doesn't matter. I couldn't understand it. I don't do drugs, except for that time when we..."

"I remember," he nodded, caressing the short hairs on the back of her head.

"How come you got a haircut?" he asked absent-mindedly.

"I dunno," she said, rolling over onto her tummy on top of him. "Just seemed easier, that's all."

"I got Phil looking into the jail thing," he said, playing with her hair.

"Who is this Phil guy anyway?" she said, closing her eyes.

"I don't mind it," he said. "The hair I mean. It's a little short for my tastes. But you do look cute. And neat. You never looked neat as a kid."

"I don't do neat," she answered. "Not really. But its only five bucks every month and five minutes in the morning. You were telling me who Phil was."

"Oh," he said, suddenly distracted by her naked body. "He's a private detective that used to work for my father. When I took the company, I kept him on."

"I still can't understand what happened. I remember not being able to see, and the whole thing being hazy and hitting that kid. And then jail."

Melissa fell quiet.

"Did my family help?" he asked quietly. This was the first time he'd thought of them.

"Never seen 'em," she said, distracted from her sudden quiet. "I was arrested and held, and when I got out...well, the house was boarded last time I saw it. Ed Junior is still around. Think he runs things for his father since you...you know."

"Since I died," he said grimly. "I'm guessing he married that girl, who was the daughter of that politician."

"Just this last year," she said. "That's what it was all for, isn't it? That money of your grandpa's?"

He nodded playing with her hair.

"You're seriously going to have to grow this out," he said laughing, "I used to love playing with your long hair."

She rolled over again, and sat up, lying down the opposite way so that her head was at the bottom of the bed. She placed her feet on his chest.

"Play with these for a change," she said laughing.

"So Junior and my dad split us up, sent me to Mexico, and you to prison," he said thinking. "Faked some letters to end the relationship. Then he cleans me up, and cleans me out. Illegitimate son of a ranch hand gets nothing, not even the girl."

"I wonder what ever happened to Jake," she mused, falling quiet again.

"I'll find out soon enough," he replied. "Phil has some stuff he wants to talk to me about. First things first. You keep going far away on me. Something's eating you. I wanna know what."

She smiled to herself. Even though he was staring at the bottoms of her feet, he knew her too well. The smile faded as she remembered.

"It was while I was in jail," she said quietly, her voice barely a whisper. "By the way, you don't need to stop."

"Huh?" he replied. "What...oh, sorry."

He'd taken his hand off her foot as she spoke, but now picked it up again and gently massaged her toes as he knew she enjoyed.

"Huh," she replied. "That's better. I've missed that. Weird huh, the things you miss."

He continued to play with the foot.

"You were saying," he prompted.

"Oh yeah," she continued, sighing, "I was. So there I was, in the bathroom, in the showers. I'd been inside about four months. I wasn't a bully or a hard nut, but you know...I can look after myself."

184

"Yeah," he said, running his fingers between her toes and making her smile again. "I got the bruises to prove it."

"So anyway," she said, going serious again. "I dunno what I'd done, or said, or whose territory I'd walked across, or whose toes I'd stomped on, but there they were, one sitting on me, the other stomping the living bejesus out of me."

"You got beat?" he said, suddenly gripping her foot.

"Ow," she said. "Not so hard."

"Oh," he realised, letting go and going back to massaging the foot more gently. "Sorry. So what happened?"

"I got the shit kicked out of me, that's what happened. You know it isn't my first beating, and in jail, they have to be careful. Nothing on the face or the wardens know. Tell the wardens and you're dead. I didn't know why they were doing it. They stood me up and started kicking me in the stomach."

Her voice faltered, and he sat up in bed. She sat also, and he held her hand as she spoke,

"I felt it go," she said. "I felt something break inside me."

She held her naked belly with her hands.

"Right here," she said pointing, her eyes sad. "They broke something, something's broken in the little oven. I felt it go."

"Jesus," he said softly, holding her to him. "You're safe now. We're together now. Nobody's gonna hurt you again."

"I'm really ok," she said. "It was a while ago. I had grief counselling for it. I'm...I...I can't bear children any more. At least they don't think so. But I'm ok now. I kind of got over it. I got over it a lot today."

She looked him in the eyes.

"Something happened today," she said smiling. "I got something back today, something that I thought I'd lost."

He held her close.

"I'm not letting go of your hand again," he said.

He stared at the house sadly, and he gripped her hand a little tighter. The red and white sign plastered over the iron gates, keeping them out, sounded the death knell for Belle Starr.

"Demolition Order," it read. "Keep Out."

She gripped his hand. The house looked in a terrible state. All the windows were boarded, and as they peered around the side, it looked as if part of it around the back had fallen in.

"I guess Dad sold it," he said sadly.

She nodded.

"I didn't come here," she said. "It hurt too hard."

"Can't even get to the bridge," he said, turning to her.

"You know what," she said. "It doesn't matter. None of it does. The house being gone, your grandpa's money being gone, the house being demolished, none of it matters. I found you when I was a little kid, and we kept hold of each other. That's what matters."

He smiled, and kissed her on the lips.

"You're right again," he said smiling. "You're making a habit of that."

"Well I am female," she said returning a smile. "Come on. I gotta go start work. I still have a job, at least until we can persuade those chickens to commit suicide."

He laughed at her as they walked back to the pick-up truck.

"You're not working there for long," he said. "I'm back now. We'll find something better. I just have some stuff to do."
187

"With this Phil you spoke about?" she asked

He nodded.

"He's a good guy," John replied. "I can't pay him yet, but I have a good idea how I'm gonna get the money. He was my dad's private eye for years."

He dropped her off at work at Plukkins, and then, after refuelling the beat up old pick up, returned to Phil's place. This time, the shutters were up and Phil was dressed in a suit.

"Ah," Phil said. "by the look on your face, you found your lady love."

"Yeah I did," he replied. "That's another one I owe ya."

"All being tallied up, my friend," he laughed. "All been tallied up."

"About what I owe you," John began, but Phil held up his hand.

"Hey," he started. "I know you're good for it. You never saw me wrong when you worked for your dad."

"I appreciate it," John said quietly.

Phil nodded.

"That's the secret to life," Phil laughed. "Store up favours with folks, then when you end up tied to a chair in a warehouse, you've always somebody to call."

"That's good advice," John mused.

They went inside. Phil lit a cigarette and offered John one, but the young man shook his head.

"Nah," he replied. "I don't think Melissa likes it. She never said; she just pulled her face when she caught a smell of me."

"Wow," laughed Phil. "Two days back with her and under the thumb already. This girl's good."

John laughed back.

"She's the best thing that's ever happened to me," John said seriously.

"So I take it you want to know what I found out about her first then?"

John nodded, with some impatience.

"OK", began Phil. "First of all, security tapes. Lots of em. Took me twelve hours watching footage of that seedy backstreet club she came out of. Never saw so many drunk people in my life. Finally, about 2:30 there she is, she appears. Here, I'll show you."

He inserted the tape into the VCR and wound it to the correct spot. It took a while.

"You think she did this," he asked while they were waiting.

"She ran that kid over," Phil returned. "That's a certainty. "But the rest of it...just watch."

He watched a grainy black and white screen. A girl, that was Melissa came in and after looking around near the bar, began to speak to a man to her right. She appeared to argue with him then watched as he ordered her a drink. They chatted for a while."

"Here," Phil said. "Watch really close."

He stared at the screen. The man she was arguing with dropped something in what she was drinking. Unaware, she finished the drink quickly, and she and the man left the view of the camera.

"That guy spiked her drink," said John, his face angry. "Find him. No matter how long it takes."

"You know what," Phil replied. "I'm that good. Three years ago, some grainy footage of a random guy in a bar, and guess what? I have his address right here. I'm better than fucking Magnum, dude."

"Who is he?" John asked. "What'd you get?"

Phil rifled through the files on the table.

"I left it right here," he said. "Oh hang on - here it is."

He pulled out a file.

"Well alrighty. Here's what I did. I wound back the tape about forty minutes. Nothing. Then, I watched the entrance foyer tape around the same time. Our guy here, the guy that's talking to Melissa later, left the bar area forty minutes before to make a telephone call. Then he returned to the bar, and forty minutes later, Melissa appeared. I was curious, so I drove it. Allowing for the goddamned traffic these days, it's around forty minutes to get from Belle Starr to here."

"He called her," John realised, a sudden chill going through him. "Who the fuck is he and why hasn't she said anything?"

"You know...I wanted to know that too. Of course, this kind of exonerates her as it is, but I needed to know myself. I got sucked into this. Guess what? Turns out that the phone calls from those machines were all recorded, at the time. Cops were having problems with gangsters making meets for drugs using those exact phones. Anyway, one of Mom's friends has a kid who works down the PD, and he got me the tapes. You won't believe the shit people talk about to their boyfriends."

"Who's the guy?" said John firmly.

"Find out for yourself," Phil said, pressing play on a machine.

He listened.

"I need you to come pick me up," came the voice of his brother through the machine, slurring his words. I'm..."

"Why the hell have you taped my brother?" said John, still not getting it.

The tape continued.

".. stood up, and what with John being missing and mom and dad and.....I just...I need a ride. Can't find my wallet...didn't know who else to call. I just need a ride."

The voice sounded very drunk. Then another voice. Phil stopped the tape.

"I pulled the phone records. He called Belle Starr."

John listened some more, this time to Melissa's voice

"It's late," came her husky voice. "Get a cab. I'm not coming over there. I'm going to bed."

"Come on," slurred the voice again. "It'll take you a half hour. Have a drink, you need to loosen up."

"I don't wanna loosen up," said Melissa exasperated. "I want...well...you know what I want. I want him back so we can start our lives."

She sounded close to tears. Suddenly John wanted to be with her.

"I just need a ride," came the voice of Ed Mason junior again. "Please. He'd want you to help his brother."

Apparently, that did the trick. She curtly agreed to come pick him up, and the receiver went down.

Phil stopped the tape, and sat back. Both men were silent for a while.

"My brother," John said, exhaling deeply. "He set me up to get trapped in Mexico, and he sent my girlfriend to prison."

"There's no evidence that he had anything to do with the drugs in that truck," said Phil sadly. "But there's no doubt about Melissa. He lured her to the club, and spiked her drink. Poor girl wouldn't have known what day it was."

"She didn't tell me," he said.

"Of course not," Phil replied. "I guess she figured it best if you found out what an evil bastard your little brother is on your own."

John nodded.

"She went through all that, just because of me. This is all my fault."

Phil shook his head.

"How is it your fault?" replied Phil looking at the young man. "How are you to blame for your family being a set of douchebags?"

"And where's my dad in all of this?" he asked. "And my mom?"

"Who knows," replied Phil. "My guess is that they found out about it after the event, but when it meant that their blood soon could get his hands on Grandpa's money, they let it ride. Especially knowing how pissed you'd be."

They have a day of reckoning coming," John replied grimly.

"Not yet kid," replied Phil. "There's the other matter. Jake."

"You found him?" asked John.

"No," said Phil, shaking his head. "And I don't think we're going to."

"How's that?" asked John, puzzled and hurt from all the revelations

"It took a while," said Phil. "In fact, I called you on the day you'd left. Been sitting on this information since then. It took about six months in fact. I traced Jake's car to a lady in Fayetteville."

"Yeah," John nodded. "Dad sold it when Jake didn't come home."

"Hmm," replied Phil. "Well first of all, your father sold the car two days after the day you said that Jake left."

"He said it was in the garage at Mason Corp for storage," said John.

"I checked," said Phil. "More than once. The foreman has no knowledge of it. Course at first he said yeah yeah, it was there, but...I lied and said it was a felony to lie to a detective, and he bought the lie. Car was never there."

"So dad lied?" asked John.

"Ed Mason lied to you," nodded Phil. "Mrs Bracewell bought the car two days after Jake left your ranch. Her husband had recently died.

and she couldn't handle the Buick, so the little Datsun seemed perfect. But there was a problem with it."

John watched his friend, intently,

"It was all shiny and clean, been cleaned inside and out. Vacuumed and everything. But she had to take it to the shop. Brakes were corroded, exhaust hanging off, the works."

"Dad swindled her?" he asked. "Jake's car was always a wreck. He probably cleaned it to trick her."

Phil shook his head.

"No, that's not it. You just failed your detective test, son. When the garage guy went under it, he found it covered in a black, grey sludge, like a kind of dark gravelly mud. Car was covered in it. Garage guy reckoned the car had been driven through the stuff and got stuck. Mrs Bracewell had to have the whole thing cleaned out."

John waited for the next bit.

"You said that you left to take Melissa home. That takes about an hour on the Interstate, round trip. Now, for your detective test pass, what's twenty minutes southbound from Belle Starr where the trucks on the Interstate are coming from?"

"Milner's quarry," replied John.

"Now...why the hell would Jake go there?" asked Phil.

"He used to know a guy there," John admitted. "Years ago. But it was closed. I remember that night. It had been raining for weeks. Melisa and I had gotten soaked in the woods that night. The black silt flows down out of the rocks and makes the quarry too hazardous to work in."

194

Phil sat back.

"I have nothing more," he said. "There's no more trail, nobody's seem him or heard from him. This is all I have. I think it's pretty clear. Sadly, it's not even close to being enough evidence."

"It's enough for me!" John said standing. He left.

His head swam with the torrent of new information. His brother, his father...his entire family. The fury and the blackness threatened to engulf him, but the thought of his Tweedle-dee, off to work at Plukkins, calmed him and made him think. And, sitting in the pick-up truck for a moment, he formed a plan.

It had been easy to get through the chain link fencing that surrounded Belle Starr with its "Danger Demolition" notices everywhere. The house's condition was worse than he thought. As he made his way round the back of the derelict house, he could see the windows were smashed and, around the back, the kitchen roof over the single storey kitchen addition had caved in completely. The garden looked overgrown, as if the house had been empty for some time. He thought back to his childhood and remembered how he and Melissa, as young children, had walked hand in hand down the garden to Poohsticks bridge.

And...

If his plan went the way he wanted it to, this place would be theirs again.

The inside of the house, stripped of furniture, was beginning to look its age. Empty, cavernous, and unloved, it stood as a silent tomb for its many memories, which it would carry with it until the wrecking ball would sound the gong of its destruction. He made his way upstairs, to what, several years before had been his bedroom. The battered wardrobe was still in place, and he knelt. Moving aside the broken door, his hands felt for the crack in the floorboard. There. Lifting the floorboard, he pulled out a package wrapped in a white cloth. His father's gun. The gun that had been used in the slaying of the two gangsters years eight years earlier. Carefully he stowed it in his coat pocket.

The Mason Corp offices were grander these days. Grandpa's money had obviously bought Ed Mason Junior a swanky new base from which to run his father's company. All smoked glass and brushed steel. The girl on the desk had been checking her hair, which was slicked back, and her crisp suit when he'd walked in. His clothes were old, and looked like they belonged on a ranch hand, but this guy wasn't a ranch hand. Noting the vague resemblance to her boss, Ed Junior, she watched the darkness swirl around in the man's deep brown eyes as he walked straight towards her.

"Can I help you, Mr …errr…." She began, as he came to the desk.

"No," he said ignoring her veiled question regards his name. "No you can't. Direct me to Mr Mason's office please, if you will."

She shook her head politely.

"I'm so sorry," she said sympathetically. "Mr Mason isn't taking calls without an appointment this afternoon."

"Please call him," the man said quietly. "And tell him that a man from Mexico is here to see him. It's most urgent."

The girl nodded, and John listened as she made the call.

"He's standing right here," she whispered into the handset. "I can't, he's right here."

"Edward," John shouted. "Your brother is here. Time for a family reunion. Should I just come up?"

The girl put the receiver down.

"He says to go on up," she said nervously. "20th floor."

He bowed his head in her direction.

"Thank you, Olivia," he said noting her name tag.

She sighed with relief as he left the entrance foyer. Olivia had heard there'd been a feud between the two brothers, and that the

197

elder brother was a drug dealer and a fugitive or something. She wondered whether she should call the police. Better not get involved, she thought.

For Ed Mason Junior, the day had started so damn well. He'd taken over another trucking company, and taken on the staff (at a much-reduced wage of course) and over the course of the morning, had made more money for himself and his father. Things were going great. He and Lizzy were enjoying their marriage, and their life of opulence, and dad had even said that he might be able to get him a job in the capital. Maybe even President someday, he'd joked. Ed Junior hadn't thought of his half-brother in a long time. Buried him in Mexico somewhere. Wasn't so fucking superior now, was he. Now the rightful son had the inheritance. It had been a shame that dirty conniving bitch of a girlfriend hadn't gotten longer in jail, but that couldn't be helped. And then THAT call. He'd hoped that the bastard would get killed in South America, but he hadn't. Ed Junior steeled himself as his brother came up the stairs suddenly feeling trapped up here on the 20th floor penthouse office.

The door opened, and he walked in. He looked dirty and dangerous. More dangerous than he'd looked when he had suits and nice clothes. He looked like a gangster now.

"Brother," John said holding his arms open. "It's wonderful to see you."

"It is," said Ed nervously, remaining seated.

"After all you did for me?" John said, still holding open his arms. "I owe you my life."

Ed thought fast, and nervously. Could the guy be so dumb he didn't know he'd been set up. He stood and went to return his brother's embrace.

They held each other for a second, then he looked directly and deeply into his brother's dark angry eyes.

No. he wasn't so dumb.

"Now," John said releasing his brother. "Here's what's gonna happen. You're gonna get my wonderful father on the phone. He's going to sign the house and the company over to me. Right now."

"What?" said Ed Junior, smiling somewhat. "Mexico has done something with your brain, brother?"

John held up his hand.

"We haven't much time. Its 1:30 now, and I arranged for the police to come down here at 1:45, so we have to be fast."

"Cops?" said Ed nervously. "What are we doing with cops? You know they're still after you."

John shook his head.

"No," he said decisively. "No they're not. I checked. Or at least a Mexican acquaintance of mine checked for me. No brother, the police are here to talk to you. But that's later. First, get my dad on the phone. Tell him to sign the old belle Starr over to me, and the CEO job that I had before."

"But that's my job now," replied Ed.

"Not for long," said John. "Please call dad. You haven't much time."

"Fine," sighed Ed, speed-dialing the number. His father's gruff voice came over the speaker.

"Dad...," ED Junior began. He was cut off.

"Hi, daddy", said John, sounding like a cat that about to kill a canary, "guess who's home"

"Son", the voice came curtly, "I didn't know you were home. I...that is...we..."

"Save it, daddy dearest," replied John. "Here's what's gonna happen. First, you're gonna sign the house over to me: land, deeds, everything."

"Impossible," his father's voice came. "We've sold it for demolition. You couldn't afford to match their price, and I can't just give it away."

John sighed.

"The second thing," he continued. "After you've given me the house, is the CEO job here. You're gonna give me that back."

Ed Junior laughed.

"Just one problem," he laughed slightly. "I'm still here."

John looked at his watch.

"1:30," he mused. "Yeah, for about fifteen minutes. So, dad, in about a quarter of an hour, there's gonna be a vacancy in the boss's seat right here. I figured I did pretty good before, so..."

"John," came the gruff voice. "The house is out of the question. But now you're home, why don't I fly over, and we'll talk. We'll talk and find you something."

"Here's the thing, daddy dearest," answered John. "Point one. The detective I hired to find Jake located his car. Turns out it was covered in shit from that quarry. Now, he tells me that you sold the car two days after Jake took off, while we still thought he might come back."

John's dad sighed loudly into the phone.

"It's not what you think," he said angrily. "And if this is blackmail, then you know you haven't enough to prove anything."

"I know," countered John. "I know that. It's just...you know, what with you being involved in politics and all, mud has a nasty habit of sticking. Plus, there's the second thing..."

"Go on," said the voice, quieter now.

"It's a colt pistol," came back John. "Silver, nice piece. Registered to you, I believe."

"You little bastard," the voice said. "I lost that eight years ago."

"As I remember," laughed John. "You didn't report it missing. Turns out that two days before it went missing, two drug dealers were shot to death behind your eldest son's school with a weapon matching the description of yours. Be a shame of that weapon turns up in the hand of the cops, wouldn't it. Like I said before, there's hardly enough to send you to jail, but...there's that mud again, sticking to that nice shiny grey suit and ruining a political career."

"John, listen," came the voice.

"Time for talking is over," John said harshly. "I've had three years sitting in the dirt in Mexico to think this through. I'm cross with you, Ed. And I'm through with both you and mom. Give me the house and make me CEO again. I'll make you money like a good dutiful son and, as a bonus, I'll keep fucking quiet about all your backroom underhand shit."

"You know nothing, you ungrateful little ..."

"I know enough," laughed John looking at his watch. 1:34. "Now let's wrap this. You send me a signed document to the effect...fax a copy over right now. Then put the original in the post and I'll learn to keep my mouth shut. Maybe I'll send you a nice silver Colt pistol for Christmas."

"John, don't hurt him...," came the voice of his father.

"Relax," laughed John. "Your golden son is safe. He's gonna be real safe. Just relax."

John cut the connection and the line went dead.

"You're crazy," said Ed Junior, shaking his head in fear. "You can't blackmail dad."

"Brother," said John, picking up a fresh fax off the machine. "Turns out I can. You know what though...three years sitting in the dirt in a piece of shit farmhouse tends to make a guy sort out his priorities. You know what? I missed rain? Can you believe that? Fucking rain? I never had a dry day all my childhood life at Belle Starr, and there I am sitting in the dirt crying because I forget what it feels like to have rain on my tongue? Can you figure it?"

Ed Junior shook his head and watched his brother move around the side of him.

He read the fax copy.

"I guess dad think more of his political career than he does you," he said showing him the fax. "You're in my seat."

"You won't get..."

"We have about seven minutes left," he said looking at his watch. 1:37. "Maybe eight, depends."

"What the fuck are you gonna do?" Ed Junior said nervously. "Come on, we can work together. You screwed the old man, he deserved it for the shit he put you through. You and me, brothers. Together, back to back."

"We're gonna sit down," said john, sitting in the visitor's seat. "It's ok, stay right there in my seat, I don't mind. I'm gonna tell you a story."

"John I..." broke in Ed Junior

His brother held up his hand.

"We have six minutes for me to tell this story," John said. "Now...if you keep interrupting me, then it's gonna take longer, I'm gonna have to keep stopping and starting, and it's gonna get all disjointed and ruin things, ya know? So do me a favour...keep your pecker closed. Let me tell the story. If there's time, we'll have a question and answer later."

"John, please," pleaded his brother. "I don't wanna die."

John shook his head.

"Me neither," he laughed. "I think we're both too young. Anyway, |I promised Dad. Like I said, I'm telling a story."

Ed Junior was quiet, and his mind raced as he wondered how to get away from his obviously lunatic brother. He had the money, sure, lots and lots of it. But it wasn't worth this. His elder brother had a murderous look in his eyes. And he'd taken Dad down without even thinking about it. This guy wasn't the guy they'd sent to Mexico to be rid of him for a while, this guy was someone who'd learned how to handle the world, someone dangerous.

"We begin years ago. A nice young man – let's call him John - and a girl: every story needs a girl. Let's call her...oh I don't know...let's call her Melissa."

"Please," Ed Junior broke in. "What happened was...unfortunate... but..."

John held up his hand.

"What did I just say?" he said looking annoyed. "Let me tell the story, for fucks sake. Anyway, John and Melissa were friends. Good friends. Best friends. Later on, they fell in love, but not before they learned one thing. They were stronger together. There's a proverb 'no man is an island,' and you know fucking what? It's true. John and Melisa figured out that, if they stuck together, nobody could hurt them. The knights in medieval times figured this out first. If they fought back to back, they were safe: if they split up, they were dead. So, back to our heroes. People tried to split them up. John's father tried to split them up and...you know what?"

John paused for effect.

"You know what?" he continued. "It cost him. Cost him his son, and his son's respect. And the father knew, deep down, that by treating his son badly, and forcing his son to fight for himself, that he'd taken away a part of his son's humanity, part of his gentleness, for in the future, the son…John…would be hard against the world. But the worst sin was committed against our hero and heroine by John's brother."

John looked at his watch. 1:43.

"John," began Ed Junior. "I…"

His elder brother ignored him and continued.

"Not only did the brother try to take Melissa away and put her somewhere that she could never be found, when she was away, she got hurt. Hurt badly. Now…the hero of our story knew that he could find her wherever she was, but to hurt her…to cause her pain and suffering. That was inexcusable."

"I had nothing to do with her being in jail," he began. "There's nothing you can prove…"

"Be quiet," ordered his brother standing up, "You had her put in prison. You set her up. For money that I was due and that you wanted. Truth be known, all I ever wanted was her. If you wanted Grandpa's money so bad, you could have had it if you'd have asked. We could have run dad's firm together. Done up the house like brothers. I'm ashamed of you."

Ed Junior was silent, and he watched for John's hand going for the gun in his coat, but there was no movement, except from the elevator outside.

"Anyway," John continued, hearing the noise, "the story concludes. The hero's brother, having chosen illicit wealth over love, realises too late that love is the most powerful emotion of them all, stronger than either money, power of any amount of wealth. I need you to realise what's important in life, Ed. I really do. That's why I called the police, and gave them the tape yesterday."

John opened the door and several police officers walked in, straight to Ed Mason Junior.

"Mr Mason," the sergeant began. "I have a warrant here for your arrest. You have the right to remain silent..."

Downstairs, Olivia waited a long time. What a day. What a job. Did she even still have a job? Her CEO and boss dragged off in handcuffs by police, and his elder brother, who looked like a cross between a gangster and a hobo had been upstairs alone for a half hour. Then the buzzer rang. It was the CEO's office.

"Olivia," the sharp voice came. "Come up here, please."

This was it then. The end of a good job. Fired. She wondered what Ed Mason Junior had been doing to get hauled off by the police. She'd always thought the young man was a little smarmy and creepy, but this new guy was just plain scary. She went upstairs and knocked on the walnut door.

"Come in."

She peeped around the door.

"Mr, err...Mr Mason, sir."

"Come in, come in," he replied.

He was sitting in her boss's seat, looking through files on the desk.

"Olivia, right?" he said, pointing at her with a smile on his face.

She nodded.

"OK," he replied. "here's the thing. My brother has stepped down from his…err…post. I'm in charge now. I need a PA that I can trust. I don't need a stupid girl that's gonna run her mouth to her boyfriend, or sell me down the river, I don't need some bimbo who's gonna flash her tits at me, I need professionalism, respect, and integrity. Can you give me that, Olivia?"

"Of course, sir," she said, nodding. A promotion!!

"One more thing," he said. "There's probably a lot of guys like me gonna come knocking on my door, trying to get to me. I don't have time to throw them all out of the window. I'm gonna need you to toughen up a little. If you tell them they aren't comin up here to see me, I want you to mean it. You got me?"

Ye sir," she said. "I got you. You won't regret it."

He nodded.

1991

She hugged him close, staring at the water.

"You think this really is the end of the soviets?" she asked, staring down into the water.

"I dunno," he replied. "It's weird though, isn't it?"

"Mmm," she murmured. "It's like when we were kids, the Russians were always the bad guys, our opponents in everything. Did we win something?"

He shook his head.

"I dunno," he answered, resting his head on hers. "It's a changing world, I guess."

She nodded, and kissed him softly. It was autumn, and for once the rain was holding off. They sat with their backs to the deck rails on their favourite bridge, their feet overhanging the edge listening to the sound of the birds in the autumn air.

He turned to her suddenly.

"I love you Mrs Mason," he said, looking deep into her green eyes.

"Mrs George-Mason," she corrected. "And I know. You tell me every day."

"I said I would," he reminded her.

She laughed.

"Yeah," she replied. "You did tell me that."

She kissed him softly.

"I love you too," she said.

"I'm sorry the wedding wasn't grander," he said stroking her blonde hair, grown out now long and down past her shoulders.

"I don't care about a fancy wedding," she said laughing. "I care about having a marriage. A marriage to the one person who's a part of my soul. A house that doesn't leak would be good too, though."

He laughed and kissed her again. It had been a busy year, since he had won back the house and gotten control of his father's business. The first order of the day was to make the house habitable. It had been a slow process: the boiler and heating had cost thousands, the floors had to be replaced, and several of the windows and roof tiles too. The money had run out to fix the caved in roof and side wall of the kitchen extension, and so, in true pioneering spirit, they had rebuilt the wall themselves using rescued timbers, and slung a truck tarp over the whole lot to keep the room dry. It was a little jury-rigged but it worked, and kept the electrics dry enough to operate. According to Melissa, it was romantic. They were fixing it up bit by bit. She'd left her job at Plukkins, and had a nice little office job in a cubicle, what with her prison record being overturned. Plus, she was back doing art again, with John's encouragement. And sending art off everywhere to be considered for publication. And then there had been the wedding. It was a small affair, in the local council offices. She would remember it forever.

They had been painting the living room when he'd done it. He was doing the lower half of the walls, and she was up the ladder doing the high half.

"Are you busy after this?" he asked absent-mindedly.

"Hmm," she replied. "I was just gonna take a bath for a while," she said, painting a high section. "You wanna join me?"

"I thought we could go into town," he said. "Maybe get a bite to eat?"

"Nah," she said. "I'm covered in paint."

It was true. They both wore identical work shirts, old jeans, and sneakers. She came down the ladder suddenly, stretching. He stood and massaged her shoulders.

She laughed.

"We're not doing that," she chided.

He made a face, but she stuck out her tongue.

"If we keep breaking off to go have sex, the room will never get painted. We gotta be strong."

"I don't want to be strong," he said. "I want to…"

"I know what you want to do," she laughed. "But you're gonna paint."

He made another face.

"But we have to go out later. Don't need to get changed. It's just a little surprise."

She looked at him.

"What kind of surprise?" she said going back up the ladder.

"Wouldn't be a surprise if I told ya, would it?"

"Can't be so good if I can go in my painting duds," she remarked laughing.

"Hey," he said. "What the hell? Paint footprints on the floor where you just stood."

She came down the ladder and looked around. On the wood floor that they'd spent weeks sanding there were now little sneaker prints.

"It's you," he said. "They're Converse."

"Fuck," she cursed, kicking off her sneakers and padding through to the kitchen for a cloth. They both fell to their knees and began scrubbing. He looked at her and kissed her on the nose.

"This is how I love to spend my weekends," he said. "Scrubbing floors with my best friend."

She was silent, but her green sparkling eyes said what she wanted as she returned to the scrubbing.

"Come on," she chided. "We gotta focus. We're never gonna get this done."

"I nearly had you then," he said smiling. "You're gonna give in."

"I'm not," she laughed, climbing up the ladder in her white socks. "We've been decorating this room for weeks, and just end up having sex all the time."

"You make it sound like a chore," he said.

"This is the chore," she said coming back down the ladder having forgotten the paint pot. "When we get the chore done, then we can have fun."

"You're mean," he said, sticking out his tongue.

She ignored him, trying not to smile. She loved him so much. It would be so easy just to fling herself down the ladder and go have fun, but this was important. At least have one room nice and finished.

"You're still doing it?" he laughed at her. "Look on the floor: little socky footprints now."

She looked. Damn. More paint footprints. It was all over her socks now. She looked down, a little sheepish.

"Guess the paint's on the ladder rungs huh?" she said coming down the ladder and taking the socks off.

"I'm gonna have you stripped in a minute," he laughed, kissing her again.

They scrubbed the footprints off a second time, and she was returning up the ladder once more when he got down on one knee.

"I miss a bit?" she said, scrubbing the ladder rungs.

"No, idiot" he said. "Come down here."

"Oh," she replied, realising what he was doing. She came over to him. He had a box in his hand.

"Is that..." she began, but he ignored her.

"Melissa," he said. "Since I was a little kid, and you gave me that biscuit, I knew that I wanted to spend my whole life with you, by your side. Will you marry me, will you be my wife? Will you laugh and cry with me? We've grown up together, you and I. Will you spend the rest of your life with me, until we're so old that we sit on the porch swing outside and reminisce about when we were kids? Will you make a lifetime's worth of memories with me?"

She was in tears, and didn't answer, so he opened the box and put it in her paint covered hands. Shaking she looked at it. It had cost him plenty, but it was the biggest diamond rock she had ever seen.

She sniffled, wiping her nose on her sleeve.

"That's a hell of a rock," she said, laughing.

"So," he replied. "You gonna leave me on my knees forever?"

She knelt with him, holding his hands.

"I love you," she said. "I wanted to be with you. You made me...I dunno, it was like I knew I had to be by your side. That's why I gave you the biscuit. I'll love you forever, I'll never be anywhere else, only by your side. Yes. Your answer's yes!"

She wiped her nose again, and put on the ring. It fitted her perfectly. Of course, he'd known her finger size for years. He knew every inch of her.

"Guess we better get married then?" he said looking around at the paint and decorating hell that was their living room.

"What, now?" she laughed. "You'll do anything to get out of this decorating."

"Just so happens," he said, smiling. "I booked a place in town, a little council place. We can do it in an hour. If you want to."

He looked in her eyes, and saw the sparkle.

"If you want to wait," he said, "and plan things, do it right, then that's ok too. Well do that."

"You mean," she said smiling again. "I can go out this afternoon and come home in an hour as Mrs Mason?"

He nodded and she rose. Following her, she turned.

"Get the car keys, buddy. We've got a wedding to get to."

He followed her out the door.

"Shit," she replied realising as soon as she got outside. "I need shoes. I have no shoes on."

"You're beautiful as you are," he said laughing and bundling her into the car. "Besides they have paint all over them."

"Hmm," she laughed. "Barefoot and covered in paint. That's not how I imagined it, but I wouldn't want it any other way."

And that was how they'd done it. To them, it was the most romantic thing they'd ever done.

2014

He stared at the little blue piece of plastic and wondered what it meant, what it was. He was upstairs packing for a vacation with Maddisen, and had been distracted tidying up and tossing some stuff out. He turned the blue piece of plastic over in his hands and

214

suddenly a vague memory came to him. A vague memory of a little girl.

"They're subway trains," she'd said in her earnest little voice.

Where had she said it had been going? For the life of him, he couldn't remember what she'd said now. That's what this tiny blue piece of plastic had been. A section of an abacus he'd bought her as a joke gift once. They hadn't had any money back in the first few years they spent married. Not that they needed any, or expensive gifts for that matter. They just bought each other gifts that mattered, a gift that meant something. He'd always loved trains, always stopped at the toy store, even as an adult when they'd walked around town hand in hand at Christmas time. He'd stopped and looked in the window at the train display. That year he knew what to get her straight away. He turned the piece of blue plastic over in his hands. He remembered the day he'd smashed it against the wall, the day his grief overcame him, and he took the pistol from the drawer and put it into his mouth. So long ago, it seemed. The blue piece of plastic made him remember...

1993

"I can't believe you found one," she said excitedly, sitting cross legged on the floor. He watched her face as she unpacked the abacus from its cardboard packaging. She looked adorable, dressed in her red Christmas sweater, cosy fleecy pants, and white socks with red pom-poms on the toes. They sat together, alone at belle Starr, opening their Christmas gifts to each other.

"I can't believe you're so excited," he said, gazing at her.

She laughed, shifting position and resting on her belly.

"Are you kidding?" she squeaked. "I've remembered this damned abacus since I was a kid. This is just the same."

"They still make em like that," he said, lying down on his side next to her. "What were the colors?"

"Who knows?" she said, removing the last of the packaging. "We can make some new ones."

She clicked the little coloured pieces from one side to the other.

"The red one," she said, her husky voice full of merriment, "is going to Yonkers."

He turned to her and kissed her on the lips, watching her green eyes sparkle.

"The yellow one," he said with happiness, is going to Harlem."

"Yeah," she said. "I remember now, the red one had to wait for its connection."

He laughed as she clicked the little plastic counters back along the rail.

216

"Ha-ha," she laughed. "They missed their train."

"We are such kids," he said, stroking her hair.

She smiled at him some more, then reached her hands in his pants, stroking his manhood gently.

"We didn't do this when we were kids," she smiled.

He kissed her again, then he watched as a thought occurred to her as she rolled nearer.

"Where's the blue one going?" she asked with happiness as she kissed him under the Christmas tree.

2014

"Blue one goes to the airport," he said, still fingering the piece of plastic in his hands.

He tossed it in the trash, then went back to sorting stuff out. That part of his life was done now, over. Time to throw out the old. Maddisen was his wife now, and he loved her. Of course it was love in a different way, but he loved her just the same. Rummaging through the box, he found a picture, in a frame. They'd bought this together at a charity jumble sale that year. It was a picture of two little fat cartoon characters, hand drawn. Underneath it was labelled in gold lettering.

"Tweedle-dum and Tweedle-dee."

"That's us," Melissa said.

"What?" he laughed. "Two old fat guys?"

"No, idiot," she said, poking him in the ribs playfully. "Tweedle-dum and Tweedle-dee. Always together."

"I get it," he said stroking her hair. "Our gift to each other."

She nodded. "We'll look at this when we're old and all wrinkly and remember where we got it."

Together forever. The words suddenly sounded hollow. He tossed the picture into the same trash bag, aware suddenly of how his head hurt again. He seemed so damn tired lately. Dog tired, all the time. Maybe it was his heart. He took a pill for it every so often now. Or at least when he remembered. His memory wasn't what it used to be. Rummaging once more, he pulled out a small ticket stub, and his hands began to shake. He dropped the ticket stub back into the drawer. Not that. Never that. He would never part with that. That was the one thing. The last thing. After that little ticket stub, their lives had never been the same again.

1995, March

It had been a cold winter, but now the tendrils of spring were beginning to stretch from the frozen earth and light the dead ground with life. The forest next to the house was beginning to come to life again, and the birds return.

"It's magical here," she said one spring afternoon as they sat lazily together on the bridge deck.

As usual, Melissa had packed snacks for them to eat and peck at while they sat and dreamed out here and spent their days together. Biscuits, fruit, cans of soda and tissues for a cold that Melissa hadn't been able to shake since winter.

"You need to see the doctor," he said. "You've been sneezing for over a month with that cold."

"I'm fine," she said, rubbing her nose that was red raw with constant blowing and tissues. "Quit being an old fuss britches."

"Fuss britches?" he laughed. "Where'd you hear that?"

"Fuck knows?" she replied. "Heard it on the TV I think. I like the word though. Kind of describes you to a tee, don't ya think?"

"Hey cheeky," he said poking her in the ribs. "You wanna find out just how cold that water really is?"

"Try me, big man," she laughed. "You want to start a poke war with me, then go right ahead."

She sat up and crossed her legs ready, but instead, he hugged her with amusement.

"God help any guy who attacks you in the street," he laughed.

"Yeah," she said, lying back down. "I'll poke em to death."

"Or talk em to death," he muttered, just loudly enough for her to hear. He smiled to himself as she kicked him hard. Grabbing her sneaker, he pulled it off her foot playfully.

"Hey," she began, folding her other foot under her protectively as he pulled off her sock. "That's mean."

"What happens to girls that kick?" he said, his eyes sparkling.

"I dunno," she said reaching for her sneaker unsuccessfully. "Their husband takes them out for yummy burgers for dinner?"

"That's not the right answer, sweetie," he said, keeping her sneaker and sock out of her reach.

"Girls that kick have their shoes and socks confiscated," she said with her head down in mock apology. "I'm sorry sweetie, but lefty is real cold. He needs his sock and shoe back on. Its only March."

"I love that," he said laughing as he tossed her the footwear. "You called him lefty."

"Yeah," she said, pulling on her sock. "Guess what I called the other one?"

"I'm guessing 'righty'" he said.

"Ha," she laughed, pulling on her sneaker. "Wrong, Mr Clever Clogs. I called *her* Natalie."

He collapsed into laughter as she stuck out her tongue, before she leaned over and rested on top of him. This was how their lives were, how they both wanted their lives to be. They were largely alone out here, and happy to be left alone in each other company.

John worked his father's company, and was largely successful and making a growing concern. Melissa had been successful in her art, and was now working with a writer, illustrating a series of children's books. The first book had been a best seller and, though work wasn't flooding in yet, her publisher told her that it soon would be. And so Melissa quit her soul destroying job in the office cubicle to concentrate on her art. The beauty of this was that, during the day, she could take a break from her illustrating to call him, or text him on her cell phone. Their lives were pretty blissful. Of course, she still couldn't have children, but ...neither of them felt they were ready for that commitment yet anyway. He didn't want to share her with anyone, and she only had time for him and nobody else. The time would come, they realised, when they would want to share their lives with someone else, but that day wasn't today. Winter had worried him though. She 'd had a bad dose of the flu, and, to him anyway, it wouldn't shift. She had seemed to grow less rosy-cheeked and healthy than usual, and he felt determined to take her to the doctor.

It was hard to persuade her. Never one to cause a fuss, he'd only managed to convince her to go by telling her they'd make a day of it. Go on the bus. And pretend they were silly kids again. Call at the ice cream bar outside the high school on the way back. The doctor had seemed as concerned as John himself had been. He'd done tests, listened to her chest as she held his hand, chided the pair as they began a poking war as soon as her top was off, and then, the thing that had scared him, an appointment at the hospital for tests. The doctor wouldn't commit himself and say what the hell the tests were for, but the look of concern seemed to show on his face, despite the assurance that it had just been a precaution.

The tests went without a hitch. They were on the other side of the city, in a sombre medical center. They'd spent the last week or so re-walling the downstairs of the house, so they were both filthy and covered in paint and dust. She could see he was worried sick as she sneezed and coughed her way through the tests. To lighten the mood, she'd worn her Christmas pom-pom socks, but she could see he was worried sick about her. Melissa didn't let things worry her any more. She had everything she wanted, and she was happy. Nothing would spoil that, nothing. After all, she mused, some people never ever find any happiness, whereas she had been happy in her idyllic life for nearly thirty years.

And so when the results came of the tests, she was happy. Not because it would give her the all-clear from whatever horrible unpronounceable disease the doctor thought she had, but because it would make him smile again. Her Tweedle-Dum had been way over-protective, and she could see his mind was working on all sorts of horror scenarios. She cuddled him, and they laughed and joked at the bridge all summer long, but it was no good. But finally, this letter from the medical center would do the trick. She opened it.

2015

"Are you ready, sweetie?" he yelled. "Maddisen?"

No answer. The headaches had finally subsided, although they had been replaced by a kind of listlessness and lack of energy.

"Maddisen," he yelled again.

"Quit yelling," she said appearing at the door holding a luggage bag. "I'm here. Jesus."

He smiled.

"Sorry sweetie," he said. "I just want to get going. It's our first real vacation together."

She smiled.

"I can't wait," she replied.

He looked at her with pleasure. Maddisen was a traditional dresser, and he had been surprised to note that she didn't own a pair of pants.

"I'm a girl," she had said defiantly. "I wear skirts. Why should I have to dress like a man just to be successful?"

He loved the way she looked. Quirky, he called her privately. Always wearing her hair in that harsh pulled-back chignon she liked so much, teamed with either a suit and blouse, or a smart skirt. Never had he seen her in trousers. Or high heels for that matter. Maddisen had expensive tastes in nylons and shoes, but there were all flat heeled and, like her, quirky. He decided that he loved her. The rest of him was nearly shut away now; finally the hurt seemed to have gone.

"Better avoid the Interstate," she said, getting into the passenger seat. "I heard there's a big snarl up on the 49 again."

"What?" he said, getting into the driver's seat. "Again?"

"Yeah," she replied, shaking her head. "Some guy rolled his car nine times, so it says on the news. Guy was airlifted to the hospital, but he's in a coma."

"Poor guy," John muttered. "You never know when your life is over, do ya?"

"No," Maddisen sighed. "They said he's probably going to die."

John was quiet for a while. Despite his listlessness, he was looking forward to this vacation. He couldn't remember the last time he'd had a vacation. Even though his mind tended to play tricks on him these days, he felt sure that he and Maddisen had never had a vacation together. They were going to Maddisen's mom's cabin, by the lake. Maddisen's mom, widowed two years previously when Maddisen's father had died, had invited them, along with her eldest son, Maddisen's brother Jake, whom John only knew in passing. It sounded to be a nice relaxing weekend. They both needed it. John hoped that, now he'd finally put his first wife to rest, this listlessness and his memory issues would clear up. He hoped they would. Certain things still flashed in his memory though. Like now. Avoiding the I-49 had turned them down past Greenacres and the Woodhouse Medical Center. Normally, his stomach would have turned as he thought of seeing this place again, but now...now it didn't have the same effect. He was finally getting over what had happened here.

1995, December

They were making the best of it. She'd shouted at him when she'd found him crying to himself locked in the bathroom, shaking with fear. They tried really hard to make it a good Christmas, just the two of them. But he could barely remember any of it. He remembered going into the bathroom with her four days before Christmas and helping her to shave her head as her hair began to fallout in clumps.

"Guess what I got for Christmas?" she said in her laughing way. "I got a mean new haircut."

"Yeah," he said hugging her. "You got a Kojak."

1996, August

He was looking through some papers: doctor's appointments, medication. Their lives had been full of it for the past year. All of it for nothing. None of it had worked. Every week he listened and watched and prayed to whatever gods would listen for a bit of good news, for a slight glint of hope, something to cling to. But nothing. Every time it got worse: it had spread, and slowly her body began to lose its fight. Melissa grew thin and weak. She grew so weak that she could no longer leave the house, and padded about the bedroom and along the landing. He simply stopped going into work one day, and stayed with her. They were together twenty- four hours a day now. Eventually, he had oxygen installed in the bedroom for when she felt short of breath.

Brushing aside a sudden stabbing headache which he put down to stress, he placed the papers back in their wallet, jumping as he suddenly sensed her behind him. She was like a living skeleton, pale and bald, her skin as delicate now as tissue paper. It had become an effort to walk around upstairs now.

"Hey," he said tenderly. "What are you doing up?"

"I heard you rattling around," she said, her voice bright despite her sick appearance. "You find anything good?"

"No," he replied shaking his head. "Just medical stuff."

"Phooey to that," she laughed.

It had been two weeks before, that the specialist had said the words he had dreaded. The words that he had buried deep down in the pit of his gut, words that he dared not even think about. But the specialist had said them.

"There's not much more we can do."

He had known it was coming. They had both sensed it was going to end this way. The treatments hadn't worked, and her cancer had spread to several of her organs. At the time, they'd gone home hand-in-hand, gone straight to bed in the middle of the afternoon, and cried themselves to fitful sleep.

In the end, that wasn't going to do any good, and so they both tried to be positive. The doctors estimated that she would live, without treatment until September at the latest.

"I want to see the fall," she had said. "It's my favourite month. I want to sit at Poohsticks Bridge in the fall. That was always my favourite time."

He watched her as she peeped into the box, then finding nothing to hold her attention, she began to shuffle back to their room.

"You need the toilet?" he said following her,

"No," she said. "Not right now. I need to go lie down though."

Her voice was almost a whisper. The little walk through to the other room had exhausted her frail and dying body.

"I'll come with you" he said, holding her and steadying her until she got into bed.

"Man that's better," she laughed weakly. "Feels good to be in bed."

"You always were lazy," he joked.

She smiled, looking out of the window.

"Leaves are starting to turn," she remarked, watching the trees from their bedroom window.

"fall's coming," he said quietly.

"Good," she whispered. "I like fall. How is Poohsticks? Still beautiful. Seems so long since I was able to get there."

"Its fine," he nodded. "A little overgrown maybe, without our heavy feet treading stuff down."

"We'll have to cut things back…I mean…you'll have to…"

Her voice tailed off, and he looked at her as he lay beside her on the bed.

"I will," he nodded, his eyes suddenly filling with unshed tears. "I'll keep it beautiful."

"Yeah," she nodded, gripping his arm weakly to comfort him. "Cos it's still our special place. It can still be your special place."

"It will be," he said, feeling his lips tremble with the effort of keeping his face straight. "I'll still go there, I promise."

"You should," she nodded, looking directly at him with those deep green eyes. "You should be happy again. Meet someone else, take her there someday."

Tears trickled down his cheek and he trembled.

"I will," he said. "We'll go there."

She looked at him with sad eyes, her thin hand gripping his.

She nodded.

"Good," she whispered. "It should always be a happy place. You'll be happy again. I know it."

He suddenly shook his head.

"I'm not taking anyone else there," he said turning his head away from hers. "I'm not going to meet someone else, I don't want anyone else."

"I know," she replied sadly. "And I know it sounds selfish, but I don't want you to meet anyone else. I know it's the wrong thing to say, but I don't. I don't want my last memory to be the thought of you going down to our place with someone else."

He looked at her again, square in the eyes.

"There'll never be anyone else," he said, choking on his words. "I don't want anyone else, I never did and I never will."

She closed her eyes.

"I don't mean that," she said. "What I just said. Of course you need to go have a life, meet someone else. Have a happy life. You deserve it. I know you. You'll let this hurt eat you up and it'll destroy you."

He didn't answer, but hugged her close.

"What if there was a way," he whispered, still choking on his words.

"A way for what," she answered, pulling away and looking up at him.

"For us to be together," he said, sitting up straight, his face firmer now. "When...you know?"

"Oh Jesus, no!" she said closing her eyes and placing her head on his chest. "Just...no. Never. I'm never gonna agree to you doing that. Not ever."

"There's no other way," he said, shaking. "What the hell will I live for, what will I do here without you? We'll do it down at the bridge. Together."

She shook her head.

"Promise me you won't," she said sadly. "You need to seriously promise me that you won't put a gun to your head when I ...when it's time. I need to know that. You can never do that!"

"I need to...be with you..." he said quietly.

"If you're not here," she said. "Who'll remember? Who'll ever know about Poohsticks bridge, how we made tents there and slept there, how I gave you my biscuits, how the abacus subway trains went to Yonkers and Harlem? Who will ever know? You have to live your life. Maybe you can tell your kids about the abacus subway, and it'll make them laugh. You gotta promise me this. That you'll live your life, and not do something stupid like put a gun in your mouth. Promise me!"

She looked at him with sad earnest eyes, straight into his soul in that way she had, and he nodded.

"I promise," he said softly.

1996, September

She sat by his side in a folding chair. The day had started in a happy way. She had seemed somehow brighter, and at first he had thought it was the miracle cure that he had prayed for. She had suggested a trip to Poohsticks Bridge. It had been a struggle. She was too weak to walk far now, and he had to carry her, after making a prior trip with blankets and folding chairs for them to use. And so he had helped her dress, and carried her in his arms to her favourite place, her frail body bundled up against the cold. She was quiet now. Speaking took so much energy, energy that she no longer had. They sat in their little chairs, and watched mid-morning turn to lunch time (though neither of them ate), and lunch time turned to afternoon. Melissa shivered, and he realised that soon it would be time to take her inside.

"Fall is so pretty," she whispered. "I wanted to see fall."

"It's beautiful, isn't it?" he said to her. "The thrushes are collecting sticks. I think they're building."

"Make sure to come down here with some food this winter," she replied. "They'll be hungry."

He touched her hand. And there it was, the reminder. The reminder that their days together were limited. The doctors said that, if she was lucky, she'd get to see the fall. And it was here, the long and painful summer had begun its decay and was turning into Autumn cold. The forest around them was dying, and even the forest creatures were beginning their migration or hibernation. She was so quiet, sitting beside him, motionless. For the first time, his heart turned to a chill and he looked to see if she had died, but she had not. Suddenly feeling his lip beginning to tremble, he reached out for her hand suddenly and gripped it. She feebly returned his

232

grip. She was weaker now, he could see that. Her eyes closed with the exhaustion of simply being here.

"I think it's time to go," he said, his voice husky and cracked.

"No," she began a protest. "Another minute."

"He could see her lip tremble too, and he knew why. This was her happy place: she and he had grown up here and lived here, laughed here and cried here. She knew this was the last time she would see this place, the last time she would be here with him. Neither of them wanted it to end, though he knew it must. It would weaken her so much to leave her in the cold afternoon air. And yet his courage failed him time and again.

He never saw her look so beautiful as she did now. They both knew that fate had finally defeated them, no matter how they tried to stay together, to huddle close against the gentle tendrils of life and death, it would be no use. Life is finite, it can end in the blink of an eye. He could barely take his eyes from her, in an attempt to etch onto his brain the very image of her, here in her happy place, in their happy place, so that in years later, when her memories would fade, this moment would remain stamped forever onto his brain and still bring the stabbing pain of loss that he felt now. No matter how much time would pass, in years to come he knew he would still smell the sweet scent of the trees as they sat there in silence waiting for those final moments, the quiet hush of the birds as they watched in revered peace as the pair waited to be separated forever. Not just yet, he pleaded silently, as his courage once again failed him, let there be a few minutes more. He studied her face again. How beautiful she was.

The time came to take her into the house, and, leaving their things, he carried her frail body inside the house, as quiet as a pallbearer.

233

He was dimly aware of people in the house, his sister was there, and friends, it seemed. To help him with her. He imagined they'd been here for a while, but he barely noticed them. He carried her upstairs and slipped her into bed, climbing in silently beside her and holding her tightly. She was quiet now, and he held her for a long time. He watched through the window as the afternoon began to turn into early evening, and the sun began to enter its death throes. The tendrils of night began to cast shadows of evening across the window and into the room, and after a while, the room grew dark. All was silent in the house. The friends and family downstairs were occupied with their own thoughts, their own sadness and left Tweedle-dum and Tweedle-dee to their final moments together. As he lay holding her, now the final afternoon was drawing into evening, and the long shadows of the fading autumn sun had darkened the bedroom, he knew that the way they protected themselves, to hug each other till the bad things left, would not work today. He held her tighter as the room grew darker, and closed the covers over them both as her body grew cold in the autumn evening. He wondered for an idle minute what Tweedle-Dum would do when Tweedle-Dee was gone, as she surely would be today. He felt it was ending here, he knew in his heart that the embers of her life were slowly going out and the fire of her existence was fading to ashes. She had felt it too. That was why she had insisted he carry her to Poohsticks bridge that very morning, not because she felt better, but because she was saying goodbye. His Tweedle-Dee had known she was at the end of her path. He hugged her tighter still, and closed his eyes against the blackness that threatened to envelop his very soul.

The day had seemingly started so well, he thought, only to end in what would forever be the blackest day he would encounter in his life. The stabbing pain of this day would be etched into his heart forever, he knew that. As he held her, he knew it wouldn't be long. The spark of life which ignited her soul grew dimmer with each passing second. He held her close, and often heard her murmur, though she was barely conscious. She no longer had the strength to fight for life. She suddenly stirred.

"Be happy again," she whispered. "You promised me."

He couldn't speak, but kissed her softly on the cheek as way of an answer.

"It was a good day," she whispered. "The happy place."

"Our first place," he said gulping for air. "I first loved you there."

"I love you," she replied softly.

He could no longer speak, and so held her again, close, and kissed her cheek. She was quiet now, and her breathing softer. The evening had turned to night, and still he held her. Her body grew cold, and still he held her close, Tweedle-dum holding his Tweedle-dee possessively. She had been his. She had always been his. She had never belonged to anyone else, only him. And they had been happy. Since they had been five, they had been together, every day, everything alike. They had shared everything, from fun, laughter, games and toys to later on love, passion and togetherness. He had known her like he would know no other. And nobody else would know her. She had been his, and his alone. And now, she always would be only his. He hugged her as tightly as he could, for he knew this would be the last time he would ever hold her, there would be no other times, no more memories to make. This was the final one. The flame of life inside her had flickered out now, he knew that. She was gone, he could feel it. And yet, while he still held her, it didn't happen. Just another minute, he pleaded, one final minute with her. Just another minute. And while he held on, she couldn't be gone. One last minute of holding her, the last time he would ever hold her. He didn't want to let go, and not for the first time did his thoughts go to the revolver in the desk drawer. To put the gun in his mouth and join her in whatever afterlife there was. Together again in death as they had been in life. His hand reaching for hers once again, hand in hand as they always had been. But he didn't, couldn't. She'd made him promise not to. And, though it was the hardest thing he would ever do in his life, he put the thoughts of the gun aside, and released her cold body from his grip, and rose from the bed. He felt blackness wash over him, and as he looked at her body, he suddenly grew more angry than any man, he let the darkness wash over him, a monolith of hate and anger against a world that had cruelly snatched away the only thing he had ever cared for. He became faintly aware of the stabbing pain in his head returning as he made his way downstairs.

A voice, who was it? Who the fuck knew? Who cared? He heard his own voice in his head as he sat down in the living room chair. His father's chair. Tears filled his eyes and he could neither see nor speak. Hands touched him, a female body held him, but he remained a silent monolith. He cast his head down to earth as they spoke to him, their voices a mass of sympathy. He felt his breathing grow laboured as he sat in the chair. He couldn't bear to utter the words to them, the conformation of her death, he couldn't say it. Wishing he was back in bed at the side of her holding her, he cast his head down and felt the blackness come.

2015

John and Maddisen arrived at the cabin. Part of a huge national park that was littered with cabins, those of the rich and wealthy were multi story affairs with balconies, garages, and solid construction, whereas those of the less well-off were single story, and resembled the trailer parks that dotted the landscape in poorer parts of the country. Maddisen's parents' cabin was certainly one of the former, it was a two-story affair, and, to John's eyes, kind of resembled Belle Starr ranch house, only with a rich dark brown wood finish. It was surrounded by conifers and other large trees, and one side, a large balcony and veranda overlooked an expanse of water, Boavista Lake. It certainly looked tranquil: the only road was a cinder path affair with a low speed limit.

John pulled their car into the driveway. Maddisen's mother was certainly well off. Margaret Payne had been the wife of Bruce Payne, a wealthy self-made man. Far from being a lawyer born into riches and Harvard educations, Bruce Payne was barely literate, a ditch digger with an idea and a lot of ambition. An industrial accident left him with a large settlement and an inability to work. So he put the money to good use and set himself up in business. Twenty years later, he had a wife who was welcomed into all the lady's circles in town, and three children with Harvard law degrees Jake, the eldest, was in the middle of a nervous breakdown after his wife had left and had quit his job as a successful commercial lawyer to write poetry. Middle child Marilyn had also quit law to raise her family with her banker husband after she grew pregnant. And then there was youngest daughter Maddisen. A brilliant defence attorney, Maddisen had fallen pregnant at seventeen whilst studying. Her son Leo, now in college himself, had caused a rift between mother and daughter. Maddisen, since her son had been born, had eschewed men and relationships and thrown herself into

237

her career and the care of her son. Thus, it came as a surprise when, at the grand age of 38, Maddisen had announced she was getting married to a former nightclub owner.

Feeling out of place amongst the lawyers and bankers, they got out of the car,

"I'm not sure I feel at home with such intellect and riches," he admitted to his wife.

She nodded.

"Me neither," she said laughing. "I've always felt out of place in this family. Least now I have an ally."

He laughed with her, and together, they walked inside. Three cars were already in the driveway, he assumed Jake and Marilyn were already here. Maddisen walked along the hall. He watched her sway appreciatively. Maddisen had lovely hips. She was dressed in her blue two-piece business suit, the hemline of the skirt just above her knees, expensive black hose and her funky maroon leather flat T-bar shoes. Her hair, as usual, was pulled back into a tight chignon. He watched her walk away, then heard a voice, a disagreeable voice coming from inside.

"Maddisen," it said in an annoyed tone. "Shoes! How many times do have to go through this. All you do is trample the red clay in."

"Hi, Mom," she said, retreating back to the door. She looked at her husband with a look of exasperation on her face.

"The red clay tramples in," she hissed. "I'd like to trample the red clay into her face sometimes."

He watched her slip out of her shoes.

238

"Oh," he said. "I'd have brought my slippers if I'd have known."

She touched his arm.

"You're funny," she said, touching his arm. "You're fine. It's me she bullies, not you."

"Are you gonna be out there all day," mom shouted from inside.

"Coming, Mom," replied Maddisen, allowing her husband to follow her inside the main room of the cabin.

"I was just explaining to John," continued Maddisen. "That he's fine with his boots on inside; it's me that you like to bully."

Margaret sighed.

"Sometimes, Maddisen," chided her mom. "Your sense of humor seems to escape me. But yes, he's fine. You're the heavy footed one around here. Even as a child, you were such a big clumsy girl."

John blanched at the insult Maddisen's mom had given her. Maddisen was slim and fit, and anything but clumsy. Apparently, his wife was used to this kind of carrying on.

"Good to see you, Mom," said Maddisen, kissing her mother gently on the cheek. "You look older. Did your regular hairdresser die, or something?"

Margaret ignored her, and turned to John.

"It's good to see you," she said warmly. "It's nice to finally meet the man who would take on Maddisen. I feared she would get left on the shelf."

"I'll take good care of her," he assured her.

"Not that good a care of her I hope," came an abrasive voice from the kitchen. A man emerged, with wiry red hair, a tall athletic man. He held out his hand.

"Jake Payne," he said. "At your service. Or at least I'm at your service if you need a poet. Did they tell you I had a breakdown and I'm poet now?"

John shook the hand.

"No," he said. "They didn't. Congratulations on all the...umm...poetry, guess."

"Where's Marilyn?" Mom asked looking at Maddisen.

"What a shame," she continued, looking Maddisen up and down. "Still putting weight on? Look at those hips."

She turned to John.

"She was such a fat little girl," her mom said. "We thought she would be the size of a house by the time she was eighteen. But then she lost it all and went really slim. Now each time I see her, it's creeping back on. I guess you might end up the size of a house after all, huh?"

Maddisen threw her a look.

"Look on the bright side," she said with her lawyers acid tone. "I'm thirty and you're past sixty. You'll be long dead by the time I am."

Jake grabbed John's arm.

"Come on, guy," he said. "That's our cue to leave. They'll be arguing full tilt in a minute."

John let himself be taken from the room. The room they had been in was a large living room, with a teak wood floor and walls, and rugs hanging. One side there was a set of patio doors that opened onto a balcony, and it was these doors that John and Jake went through. Outside was a woman, sitting on the recliner. She was similar in features to Maddisen, with a strong jaw, dark brown eyes and long dark hair. But somehow her features weren't quite as harsh and masculine as his wife's. her hair was long and loose, though some of it was concealed beneath a grey knitted hat. She had on a brown cardigan, buttoned up, and a dark brown skirt and matching thick tights. Like her sister, she was shoeless.

"Ha," said Jake, motioning John to sit down. "The shoe Nazi got you too."

"I swear to god," the woman replied. "One day that woman will go into the lake head first."

"See," laughed Jake. "We're all big fans of Mom down here."

"Hi," said the woman holding out her hand to John. "I'm Marilyn. Marilyn Payne-Osarc."

"John Mason," he replied. "Pleased to meet you."

She nodded, then turned to Jake.

"She gave Tony a blast down the phone this morning,", she said. "Blamed him and what she called 'his kind' for Obama. Said it was his fault we were addled with what she calls a 'joke president'. He came in the bedroom and had a go at me for it."

"His kind?" asked Jake. "Bankers? Jews? What's the old battle axe on about?"

"Who knows?" Marilyn replied. "Besides I kind of like Obama. What do you think, John?"

"Barrel would probably be better," he suggested.

"Better than Obama?" asked Jake. "A barrel would be a better president? Are you a Republican, John? Maz, John and Tony will get on real well."

"No," John corrected. "For your mother. You said you were gonna throw her in the lake. Put her in a barrel first, add some rocks, and it'll sink right to the bottom."

Jake and Marilyn were quiet after that. If he were joking, then they hadn't got the joke. The place sure was peaceful.

It was later, though he didn't know how much later. It was well after dinner, he knew that and the sun was lowly going down. He was sat alone on the balcony, alone with his thoughts. After what seemed like a long while, Margaret came out with two candles and a lighter.

"You guys called a truce?" he asked.

"Don't take us the wrong way," Margaret said smiling. "I love my children. Maddisen especially. This is just the way we've always been. It sounds malicious, but I promise you, it isn't."

He smiled.

"Fair enough," he said.

"What ya got there?" he asked, motioning to the two candles.

"Oh these," she replied, placing them on the deck rail. "I always ask my kids up here this time of year. Their dad loved it. His hard work built this place. I always light a candle on the anniversary of his death. If he's watching me from wherever he is, then he'll see the light. I just sit here while it burns, and watch the sun go down. I feel closer to him."

"I'm sorry," he said genuinely. "How long has it been."

"He's been gone two years," she replied sadly. "Lung cancer."

He was silent for a while. She turned to him, holding out an orange candle to him.

"We'll light one for your wife too," she said quietly. "Then she'll see it and know you're thinking of her."

He fell silent. Suddenly it was last week that he had said goodbye to her and held her for the last time, and not so many years ago that he'd begun to forget what her voice sounded like. He closed his eyes.

"I'm sorry," said Margaret. "I asked Maddisen. She said it sounded like a good idea. I'm sorry if it hurt you."

He opened his eyes and stood, taking the little candles from her.

"No," he assured her. "No, Maddy was right. It a lovely idea. Maybe they're standing together, watching us?"

Margaret nodded, lighting the two candles that he had set down on the railing.

"How long has it been," she asked him, placing a hand on his arm.

"Feels like two days," he muttered. "But no. Nineteen years. 4th of September 1996, just before seven in the evening."

She was silent, and they sat together and watched the candles burn. He wondered if they were watching them, the loved ones that they'd had to part from. John had been kidding himself. He realized that now. Forgotten her, he'd thought. Over her at last. Ha. What a joke. The pain was as fresh and as raw as it had been nineteen years ago. It was so painful that even now he couldn't remember her funeral. Blocked it out, along with so many other things. Life was such a blur. He sat there for a long time until Margaret whispered to him that she was going in.

He nodded and was alone. The little orange candle that he'd lit for Melissa had just about burned out. He watched it flicker and fade in the dying light of the afternoon.

Just another minute. Another minute won't hurt. Let him hug her for one more minute. And let the minute last for all eternity. Let them bury me living at the side of her, let me hold her lifeless body for the rest of my days. The pain in his head had returned now, worse than ever, and he stood and went to the balcony, where the little orange candle was going out.

"I'm sorry," he said, gasping for air. "I couldn't do it. I broke my promise."

He paused, as if waiting for an answer, but of course none came.

"I know," he continued. "I know you said to be happy again, that someday I could find someone. And I did. It's not the same, but I did. I found someone. I know you'd like her, that you'd approve of her. I didn't take her to Poohsticks. I just can't be there anymore. I didn't go back again. That was our place."

He sank onto his haunches, and gripped the railings, and gripped them. the pain in his head was worse than ever.

"I tried to be happy," he said aloud. "I tried. I just couldn't do it."

"You're not kidding," she replied. "Your face'll frighten the milk sour."

He laughed a sarcastic laugh. "Great," he said to nobody. "Now I'm hearing you in my head. You know what, I'm nuts."

"Well," she said smiling. "I'm not arguing with ya. Miserable, and crazy. It's a good job we're together. We'd ruin two normal people's lives, wouldn't we? Bet they leave us alone."

"But that's it," he said gesturing to her. "We're not together, are we? You had to go and die. The one thing I ever loved in the world, the one thing I wanted, the one person I needed to spend my life with and guess what, you went and fucking died. Now I'm here alone and scared, and I don't know where you are. I just want you."

"Well then," she said, touching his arm. "It's time to come back to me."

He gripped the railings, the pain in his head rising like a crescendo until his brain threatened to smash his skull to pieces. The blackness came and threatened to take him.

"Come back to me," she said again. He could feel her hand reaching for his.

Hand in hand. They always held hands. He would hold her hand till he died. Which might just be now. The pain in his head exploded. The figure gripping the railings in the little cabin collapsed to the floor, and was motionless.

PART 2

Undated

He awoke to a blinding light.

Am I dead?

He remembered collapsing in the cabin. Kind of half remembered it. It seemed so unreal somehow. His vision was blurred, and the light blinding. Angels walked around beside him.

I'm not dead, he thought. I'd know if I was dead.

Damn.

As he came to, he closed his eyes against the blinding light. He realised that he'd either had a heart attack, a stroke, or a brain haemorrhage. Probably the latter. Might be the blinding headaches he'd suffered for what seemed like years. Something in his brain was foggy, something he couldn't put his finger on. Then sounds. Noises from the angels. Only they weren't angels. They were people, fussing over him.

"Doctor," came the voice. "He's awake."

Then more voices. John attempted to speak, but found he couldn't. Tubes, breathing apparatus, all kinds of things stopped his speech, and it came as more of a gargle. More voices, and the doctors and nurses began to fuss over him some more. He could barely move, and felt foggy and strange.

"Call his wife," a voice came. "She's outside I think."

"She's sleeping in the corridor," came another voice, "I'll go fetch her."

Maddisen. The thought of Maddisen sleeping in a corridor amused him a little, and some more of his brain began to turn back on. Maddisen. The whole thing seemed strange to him, a fogginess that wouldn't lift.

"Your husband's awake, Mrs Mason," came a voice.

Then a flurry of movement, footsteps, and he felt a body near him. Maddisen, he thought? He fought to open his eyes, but the light was still blinding. Then a hand reached out to touch him. A soft hand. He shivered at its touch, for he knew the hand instantly. Knew its touch. He'd never thought to touch it again, remembered the last time he'd touched it as she had lain in death. He reached for the short, neatly manicured nails and knew who they belonged to. He felt the hand grip onto his, and he attempted to grip back, but his grip was weak.

"He gripped my hand," came a voice. That voice. His heart almost stopped as he heard it. Husky and low toned, it had sounded concerned and full of anguished love. So familiar. It was a beacon of crystal clarity instead of the murkiness and uncertainty of his life since he had lost her. But there was her voice again.

It didn't belong to someone called Maddisen. The whole painful foggy soup of that life was fading and fraying around the edges at the sound of that voice. Despite the blinding light he opened his eyes and forced them to focus.

Melissa looked back at him, her face a mask of concern and worry, dark shadows under her sparkling green eyes. He wanted to laugh, he wanted to cry, he wanted to shout to her, to cry that he had watched her die. Everything was such a fog. At last his vision began to clear and he looked at her. Somehow she looked older, about late thirties, he estimated. Melissa. His Tweedle-dee, the love that had never faded, the pain of her loss that had burned in his soul. He looked into her eyes. What was happening to him? This was real, he knew that. His Tweedle-Dee was sitting by him, his Tweedle-dee. His beloved. They were somehow reunited.

He thought for a moment of the other one, what was her name, Maddisen? He couldn't even remember what she looked like now. None of that even felt real any more. He had so many questions. There was so much he didn't seem to know. But that would have to wait. He still couldn't speak, and was barely conscious. So he gripped Melissa's hand as hard as he could, and let his fingers interlock with hers. Their eyes met, and the concern in those eyes left her face as she saw him recognise her. She smiled.

"He knows me," she said to the Doctor.

He nodded.

"It's gonna be a long job, Melissa," he said, consulting some kind of chart on the wall, "He's been in a coma for eight months. His brain's been active, so there's no telling what he's been going through. We've been seeing spikes of activity within the brain. He'll be disoriented, and probably remember things in the wrong order, or maybe remember things that haven't happened. It's hard to tell. There may be memory loss."

John tried to remember something, but the foggy memory was falling apart as he gazed at his Melissa. He remembered a sense of horrific loss that he couldn't put his finger on. Had he watched her die? It had felt so real, the pain of being at Poohsticks Bridge without her. And yet it was fading into the murky soup that was his memory as he looked into the eyes of his beloved.

How long had they been apart? He didn't know. Right now, it didn't matter. Nothing did. It had felt so real, and yet…how could he have forgotten what reality felt like?

"Never letting go of your hand," he managed to gurgle out, despite the tubes down his throat. She gripped his hand, and kissed him softly on the cheek. She looked tired, with dark rings under her eyes. She looked as if she hadn't slept for months. She pulled her hand away from his, and he tried to grip it, but was too weak.

"It's ok baby," she said. "I have to go pick Lola up. I'll be back"

Damn her. She smiled that green-eyed smile she had. He screamed to her not to go, that the moment he shut his eyes she would be gone again, and he would be back in that dark world of pain and loss, a world that he didn't seem to know anything about. Not that he knew anything about this one much yet. The focal point was her, she was the anchor. He focussed on her, and watched as she kissed him, and left. Begging that the darkness wouldn't take him again, he felt himself fall into deep sleep.

Voices again.

"There was brain activity, so it's doubtful that he'll be brain damaged," said a voice.

"No more than normal," returned a female voice, laughing. It was her! His heart sang. She was still here. This place he was in was real. What was the other ones name? Maddisen? What did Maddisen even look like? He couldn't remember. She seemed so unreal now, like a blurry ghost made from smoke and imagination.

His eyes opened, and there, smiling at him, was his Melissa. He found the tubes had gone from his throat. He tried speaking.

"Melissa," he said softly.

She smiled.

"You remember me," she said, her eyes watering.

"You were...I dunno," he thought. "I was lost. Did you die? Did you get cancer? Or did I die?"

She looked at the doctor with alarm.

"It's not unknown." the doctor assured her. "Your husband is disoriented. "His mind fixed on something important and traumatic in his life. Did you ever have a cancer scare?"

She nodded.

"They thought I had leukaemia," she said, stroking John's head. "It was years ago. Turned out I didn't. It was just the effects of painting and doing dry wall in a damp house kept my colds coming on."

"His mind's fixed onto that," the doctor said. "A fear of losing you. It's likely replayed in his head while he's been in a coma, his mind working out the outcomes. It's difficult to tell. A dream for six months can feel like a lifetime. It's likely that the memory of you is what's kept him alive, along with your voice telling him to come back. There'll definitely be memory issues. I'll have to keep an eye on him for a while."

"Can I take him home?" she asked, "I can get him well again at Belle Starr?"

"Soon," the doctor said. "Soon. I'll go check on some readings for you right now."

"Home," he said. "Home with you? I want to go home with you. I want to live my life with you. They said I couldn't, and you went away, but I still loved you. I knew that you couldn't be gone from me; I knew the world wouldn't be that cruel to take you from me. I couldn't find you. I'm never letting go of your hand again."

She stroked his hand, her eyes filling up.

"I'm sorry," she choked. "It's too much for me. I swear to god …I thought you were gone. I thought I'd lost you, I was walking in here to say goodbye to you…I could never do that, but I was planning how to as I walked through the door."

He stroked her face, with his feeble movement.

"It's ok," he said softly. "We're holding hands forever now, like we did when we were kids. Never et go."

She nodded, tearfully.

"We're never letting go again," she smiled.

He blinked away the tears and looked into her face. Relief washed over him as they gazed at each other, reunited.

"Do you remember someone else," she said suddenly in that husky voice that he seemed to have forgotten. "A small person?"

He thought hard. It was so foggy and distant. His life at Belle Starr had seemed so long ago. But there was a person in his mind. A child. A little blonde gir .

"We turn right at the intersection," he remembered. "You hate her riding the school bus. Leave the house at three, get to school for half past, ice cream on Fridays."

"You remember," she said looking at him with love.

He was surprised at where the memory had come from.

"You'll start remembering things when you least expect it," she said. "At least that's what the doctors said. Who do we pick up at the school?"

Then he remembered her. The little one.

"We had so much love in our lives," he said quickly as if he were desperate to get it out of his head before he forgot it again. "We wanted to share it with someone else, teach them how to play with Lego and abacuses and Poohsticks. We adopted her. The little quiet one at the back who thought she was sullen and silent and ugly. You thought she had a beautiful name. I thought she had the most beautiful, sour, mean looking face I ever saw. We loved her instantly. It's always our joke the first time we said it."

Melissa nodded, holding his hand again.

"'I love Lola,'" he murmured, remembering. "It reminded me of that show my dad used to watch with Lucille Ball. Someday we were going to open a café or a bar or something called I love Lola. Is she...is she here?"

Melissa shook her head.

"She was scared to come. Too scared. They said you were getting weaker. I sent her to Nancy's. Sometimes she goes to school with

Josh, sometimes she goes back to Nancy's and helps around the house."

"I have no idea who Nancy or Josh are," he said racking his brains. "But I know Lola. I know it took a long time to get her to call me daddy. It was a rainy day, and she was crying for no reason, right there on the bridge. She thought I was gonna scold her for being miserable when she had a house full of toys and nothing sad in her life. And I didn't. I knelt in front of her, and hugged her, and held her hands. And I said that's its ok to be sad. And when you're sad, I'll be right here being sad with you, until you're happy again."

Melissa nodded, remembering the memory.

"And then she looked at me," John continued. "And she said 'I don't want you to be sad, Daddy. So I guess I can smile for both of us.'"

"She didn't even know she'd said it," answered Melissa. "It just came out all natural."

"I want to go home," he asked her. "I don't remember much. In fact, hardly anything. Part of me is still afraid to go to sleep, in case I wake up again and you're gone again. But the other part of me wants to go home, to you, and to Belle Starr, and to Poohsticks Bridge. The few things I do remember."

"I promise you," she said bringing her face close to his. "I'm real. I didn't die, ok? Take more than Leukaemia to get rid of me from your life. You dreamed it. I've never left you. When you go to sleep, I'm gonna be right there beside you till you wake up again. I swear."

He smiled, and kissed her on the lips.

"Speaking of sleeping," he said to her. "You don't look like you've been doing much of that."

He brushed his fingers over her soft skin, noting the dark circles under her eyes.

"Yeah," she smiled weakly. "My husband's been in a coma for eight months. Nearly died. They said he might be brain damaged or even brain dead. Makes ya not want to sleep, ya know?"

"I'm coming home," he said firmly. "I don't give a shit if I to walk out of here in this nightdress thing, with these tubes attacked, but I'm going home. And I'm going home today. You need to rest."

She laughed.

"You're volunteering to look after me?" she said. "You've been awake two days. Can you even remember where we keep the coffee in the kitchen?"

"I don't give a shit," he said, still firm. "I'm taking you home, putting you to bed, and you're gonna sleep."

She closed her eyes, and stroked his face.

"That's sounds so good," she laughed. "But I'd better ask the doctor."

"Tell the doctor," he insisted. "I'm going home to take care of my family. I've lain here dreaming all sorts of crap for too long."

He paused, something suddenly worrying him. He looked at her.

"Can I just ask you," he said. "Something suddenly occurred to me."

"What?" she replied, gripping his hand again.

"Do I..." he began. "I mean... are we...are we solid. I mean, you and me. I remember that I love you more than anything, my heart aches for you. But I don't remember anything for a long time, not since the cancer thing. Are we good, you and me?"

She felt a tear fall down her cheek, and she closed her eyes.

"I don't know how I've carried on," she said sadly. "How do you do something like that, when they said that I had to think about maybe you weren't coming out of it, and that you might .,...you know..."

"I'm sorry," he said. "I shouldn't have asked. It's just...if there's something that I did, that I can't remember, then I..."

"What you can't remember is that we finish each other's sentences. They call us Tweedle-dum and Tweedle-dee. We call each other's cell phones thirty times a day. We go to the bathroom together. Some people talk to their shadows."

"We talk to each other," he finished, remembering.

"We never hurt each other," she said smiling into his eyes. "Not ever. In mean...It's not perfect all the time, we have arguments and shit, everybody does. Its fine, we worked it out."

"Arguments about what?" he asked, curious.

"I dunno," she said, regretting mentioning it. "Just stuff."

"What stuff," he persisted.

"Just work," she continued. "You know, like... I dunno. Sometimes I wouldn't see you till nine o clock, then you'd come home all excited cos you'd closed some deal for your company, and it'd be all 'yay you', but I'd been at home all day drawing stupid pictures for the publisher and hadn't seen you. So we'd fight about you not coming

255

home for dinner sometimes, and cos we weren't listening to each other. But we worked it out and it's good."

He kissed her.

"I have no idea," he continued. "What publishers are for, or books, or ever what the hell I do. Am I still working for my dad's company?"

She nodded.

"Still CEO," she confirmed. "But you bought your dad's stock out a couple years ago. It's your company now. You've built it up. It's something to be proud of."

He nodded, but his face was sad.

"I'm sorry," he said. "I don't know what kind of asshole I've been, that I put a company and business in front of you, but it's not a mistake I'll ever make again. Besides, I have no idea what I did there, I just can't remember being a CEO, or what that does."

She was silent, but gripped his hand.

"Go see the doctor," he said. "I'll be disentangling myself from this goddamned mess. And I had better find some pants. Can't really go wandering the streets in a nightgown."

She laughed. Through the tears of relief, and love, she laughed loud, long, and hard. Then he laughed too. And as he sat up in bed, and began removing tubes from himself, they embraced. He was never going to let go of her again.

November 2003

"Not as easy as I thought," he laughed, trying to get out of the car and manoeuvre the walking frame.

"Let me help, idiot," she replied, running round the other side of her battered Toyota.

"I'm fine," he laughed again. "And don't call me idiot, or I'll hit you with my walker."

She leaned on the trunk and laughed.

"You sound like a senior citizen," she said, choking through sudden laughter.

He watched her laugh, seeing the pressure she had been under for months suddenly release.

"Well," he countered. "I don't see how you can call me a senior citizen; I'm not the one driving a Toyota."

She looked at him with sparkling eyes.

"It's not me that totalled the classic car," she shot back.

That was a comment too far, and she regretted it the instant the words came out. The black 1950 Chevrolet Coupe had been in his possession since he had been fifteen. He'd built it up from a wreck. And now it was a wreck again...worse than a wreck now. She saw the look in his eyes.

"I don't remember," he said. "The Chevy...is it...?"

"It's dead, honey," she said, going to his side of the car and putting her arms around him. "But it died saving your life."

"It's just a car," he said, rising onto his walker and looking around. "I have you back. That's more important."

It was the most important thing. Everything else would wait. He watched her unlock the door, and run back to help him inside.

"Daddy's home," he muttered to himself.

"I'll just get you settled," she said locking the car. "Then I'll call…"

"Shhh," he motioned to his lips with his finger.

She placed her hands on her hips, smiling.

"Did you just … just shush me?" she said with amusement.

He hobbled over to her.

"Damn this walker," he said. "The sooner I get rid of this fucker, the better. But yeah, I shushed you. Cos you ain't doing anything except going upstairs, getting into bed and sleeping."

He put a hand on her waist.

"You haven't slept for months," he said. "Have you?"

She shook her head and felt the tears well up in her eyes.

"It's just been so damned hard," she said looking down at her feet. "There's bills beyond bills, your brother's replaced you as CEO, the insurance has covered your medical bills just about, but my artwork barely covers the heating bills. I got a part time job in a cubicle at Testors in town, but with Lola, I can only work part time. The Toyota's running on fumes as it is…I just…it was coming to a time when I was thinking I'd have to sell this place…"

She buried her face in his shoulder, shaking with sobs, and he held her till she was quiet.

"There's a realtor person coming around," she said, "Tuesday next week."

"Hmm," he replied, stroking her hair. "Looks like I woke up just in the nick of time. Look, everything's gonna be fine, I promise. I don't know how it's gonna be fine, it just is. Didn't we always say we were stronger together and when we're apart it all comes unstuck?"

She nodded, wiping her nose on her sleeve. They helped each other inside.

"Someday," he said. "I'll buy you a box of tissues. Save those sleeves."

"You sound like my grandma," she shot back.

He didn't recognise the house. It wasn't the house he remembered. Things were different. The walls and décor were finished in some parts of it, the floor was shiny polished wood, but the walls in the hallway were still cement. Light fittings were missing in places.

"I haven't been able to do much," she said sitting down on a chair in the hall. "Lola and me decorated some walls upstairs, and finished the flooring in our bedroom."

"I can't wait to see," he said, noting a chair opposite the one she was sat on. He shrugged aside the walker and sat in it. She looked across at him and smiled.

"You don't remember what these chairs are for," she laughed. "Do ya?"

He shook his head.

"I don't remember any of this," he replied. "Last thing I remember, the house was ...different. My sister lived here I think?"

Melissa shook her head.

"Cassie lives in LA with her girlfriend," she replied, bending down to yank off her cowboy boots.

"Girlfriend" John asked, "I don't remember that, either. Here, let me help with that."

She put her booted feet in his lap, and he easily pulled the boots off in a practiced motion that he seemed to remember doing before. On instinct, and though he struggled with the movement, he placed his own feet in her lap.

"That's what these chairs are for," he said decisively, pulling off her socks.

She smiled.

"We spent so much time last year waxing that floor, we decided to have a space to take our shoes off. Instead of bending down and doing shit the hard way, we...ya know?"

"Do it together," he said watching as she unlaced his sneakers. She grabbed their discarded footwear and padded to a cupboard at the side of a coat rack, stashing their coats and footwear in there.

"We've done this before," he said smiling. "I can feel it." He stood, a little unsteady without the walker.

She put her arms around his waist again, and hugged him tight.

"Hmm," she said, her eyes twinkling.

He looked at the floor in the hall. She released herself from his grip and did a graceful pirouette on the floorboards, her bare feet leaving sweat marks on the wood.

"I've made love to you here," he said laughing. "Right here. Were we playing with Lego or something?"

She laughed,

"I knew you would remember that," she said laughing, hugging him again. "Lego sex. Who could forget that?"

"I don't know the details," he replied. "You're gonna have to show me that."

She nodded.

"Oh yeah," she replied laughing. "There's a lot of things I'm gonna be showing you."

"First things first," he said, noting the tiredness creeping into her face. "Bed, Mrs Mason."

"You can be so masterful sometimes, Mr Mason," she giggled. "What time is it?"

"Just after eleven," he replied looking at his watch. "We did promise the doctors that I'd get plenty of rest. And you need some rest too. Bus drops Lola off at three, so you can sleep till four, and I'll get dinner."

She held him tight, and helped him upstairs.

"First," she said. "You just remembered something else. About Lola, I mean, that she finishes at three. Second, you can't make dinner. You probably don't remember where anything is."

"And third," he broke in grinning. "In my house, my word is the law. So go to bed. Now."

"You're word is law," she giggled again as she supported him into the rear bedroom. "Your memory is definitely screwy if you think that's gonna happen."

He grabbed her around the waist, and kissed her softly on the lips.

"I'll be fine, cooking dinner," he said. "My little girl hasn't seen me for eight months. Won't that be fun when she comes in and sees me cooking..."

"Or alternatively running for her life as the house burns down around her ears...," broke in Melissa.

He laughed, and she kissed him back. Then she collapsed down onto the bed, and waited for him to join her. He closed the curtains and lay on the bed, holding her in an embrace that they'd held for many years. He saw her eyes close in grateful slumber, the exhaustion and stress of the last few months had truly worn her out. She snored a little as she lay in his arms. He was tired too, and certainly not well enough yet to be one hundred per cent. And yet he forced himself awake.

He watched her in slumber, his precious love. He remembered bits of the coma, the dizzying pain, the sense of loss the death. Her loss he remembered that. The feeling of being trapped. He remembered a vague hint of a memory that he had held her in death, the late afternoon autumn taking her life. He held her tight as he watched her breathe. It had seemed so real in parts, and yet in other ways it had not. The sense of loss had seemed real, and at the thought of it, he held her even tighter, and kissed her sleeping form softly. She opened her eyes to find him hugging her tightly, tears in his eyes.

"Are you…," she began sleepily.

"I'm fine," he nodded. "I'm fine. It's just…some of that …where I've been…seemed so damn real. I remember being without you, I don't know how I could bear to lose you."

"I'm not letting you off that easy," she said. "You still owe me for pushing me in the dirt that time."

He smiled at the memory, hugging her closely to him, their faces a mere inch apart.

"Don't worry about it," she said. "The doctor said your false memories will fade as your real memories return. Come on, let's get to sleep."

"I promise," he said cuddling down with her. "I'm never letting go your hand again. No matter what."

"Even to go to the toilet," she said half asleep. "Cos we tried that, and it didn't really work, except to wash our hands and clean our teeth and stuff."

He kissed her, and together they fell asleep.

November 2003. Later.

He lay dozing in the bedroom. At first, John wondered where he was. Then he awoke, and found he was still holding her. As he breathed in her scent, he suddenly remembered the pain of loss. He seemed to have lain in a different bed then. One at the front of the house. He hugged her closer. She was here, real. The pain of loss felt real, too. Yet it was not. And as he gazed at her, deep in slumber, he realised the pain and loss was being replaced by a sense of relief, almost euphoria, like waking from a nightmare only to find that the monsters that were chasing you weren't real after all. As quietly as possible, he rose from the bed, leaving her to sleep. The magazine on the side table said "October issue 2003." The years had seemed to blur into one before, as though he was on a dizzying merry go round. He started at the date. 2003. He stopped trying to remember, remembering the doctor's words to let it come on its own.

Melissa had looked so exhausted. He crept out of the bedroom and stood a while on the landing. He didn't recognise the house at all; somehow it all seemed different. He walked around the landing to the front of the house. There was a door to a child's bedroom with a sign "keep out adults" written in crayon. John obeyed. Lola. He remembered a little pale faced blonde girl in tattered clothes, and something in his heart smiled involuntarily. He remembered her, or the love he had for her. He moved along the hall, and it took a sharp right turn towards the bathroom and the back of the house. He paused at the point where the hall turned. Here was where he'd imagined his and Melissa's bedroom had been. Right here on the corner of the house. And yet...it was outside wall. There had never been a bedroom here. He remembered the idea of loss here, the idea that he had lain beside her and felt great grief here. He touched the wall. It was real. He remembered the little girl again suddenly,

"What have I told you, Lola," he said frowning.

She planted her feet wide and placed her hands on her hips.

"Not to run in the hallway else I'll trip."

He nodded, smiling.

"If you're gonna run in the hallways, then either tie your laces or take your sneakers off, honey," he said bending down. "I don't want you to squish your pretty face in."

"I'm not pretty, John," the little girl said. "All the other kids said I was pale and plain. Not pretty."

"Hey," he said touching her nose. "Mommie Melissa's pretty, right?"

The girl nodded.

"So," John reasoned. "I know a pretty girl when I see one. So when I say you're the most beautiful little girl I know, then you know I'm right?"

The little girl screwed her face up as she thought about it. The logic of his words puzzled her little brain, and he took that moment to depart and leave her to play.

"Don't run in the hallway, Lola," he shouted back as he heard the thudding footsteps of the girl...

Lola

He watched the empty hallway as he remembered a snipped of a memory of his life. The doctor had been right. The coma-induced memories would fade, as his memory returned. That was a memory. Suddenly aching to meet Lola, he glanced at his watch. Three fifteen.

"Bus gets here three thirty-five," he remembered, murmuring alone to himself. Just a phrase in his head, but it came again. He remembered.

"Crumpets with Jam, Daddy John."

That was what she liked to come home to, a little snack before they called for a take-out dinner or found something to cook. Reaching for his walker, he inched his way quietly downstairs, so as not to wake the sleeping Melissa.

It took him a while to find the kitchen. It wasn't where he remembered it being. It took him so long that Melissa had awoken and appeared behind him. He was still surprised at the sight of her.

"Should've drawn you a map," she said laughing and poking him.

"Oh," he said feigning annoyance. "Are we poking again?"

She nodded.

"Yeah," she said defiantly. "I'm poking ya. See."

She poked him again, harder.

"That a fact," he retorted. "You starting a poke war, huh?"

She nodded again.

"Guess I am, big man," she laughed. "What ya gonna do about it?"

"Maybe I'll poke ya back," he said reaching his finger out towards her breast. He was too slow, and she grabbed his finger and playfully twisted it a little.

"Hey you little bitch," he laughed. "Quit that."

She didn't let go the finger, but she used it to pull him towards her. He entered her arms and kissed her hungrily on the lips. Their tongues met, God how much he had dreamed of doing that. He felt the scent of her threaten to overpower him as they devoured each other stood there in the kitchen. They closed their eyes, and for a moment, there was nothing. No country, no world, no universe, nothing, only the two of them being as one. Finally, the moment ended and for a long time they simply embraced, gazing into each other's eyes. He still seemed a little woolly, and his eyes seemed to glaze over and tear up slightly as he looked at her.

"Penny for em?" she said.

"I love you," he said. "That's the strongest thought in my brain. I can't remember so much, a lot of it is still confused, but I Love you. As long as I keep hold of your hand, we'll be fine."

She kissed him softly, looking into his eyes.

"And this kitchen is a fucking mess," he laughed.

She snorted into laughter too, and together they looked around the Belle Starr Kitchen. Originally, the kitchen had been in the middle of the house, but John's father had turned that room into a den, and had a single story extension fitted on the back, a large affair, with sliding patio doors that led out to a large garden and terrace. Right now, the place looked worse than a ruin. The single storey roof was either gone, or collapsed, and a truck tarpaulin was fixed in its place where the roof had been. Exposed timbers were in varying states of repair, and cardboard packing cases littered the worktops. A camping gas stove sat in a corner where the electric oven had been. The plaster and dry-wall on the left side wall of the kitchen extension was all cracked and the outside timbers of the house were exposed.

"What he fuck happened?" he said. "I can kinda remember vaguely a storm? Christmas time?"

Melissa nodded.

"The roof fell in during the rain storms last Christmas," she replied. "And the side wall too. We fixed it together. The three of us. I hope it will come back to you. It was fun."

John looked around sceptically.

"Yeah," he nodded. "It looks like it was a whole lot of fun."

She hugged him.

"It was the best time ever. The three of us in a big adventure at Poohsticks Bridge on Christmas eve."

His eyes lit up as he remembered his happy place. Their happy place.

"Let's go there," he said. "It seems like it was so long since I've been there."

Melissa looked at the clock.

"Lola's due," she said.

"We'll surprise her," he said eagerly. "We'll leave her a note...say Mommie Melissa wants her down at Poohsticks Bridge. And when she gets there..."

268

Melissa beamed, her green eyes sparkling.

"Daddy John will be there waiting for her!" she said.

He nodded. And so they wrote the little girl a note, pinned it to the door and set off to the bridge. To him it had seemed to have been years since he had been there, but in reality it was barely ten months. Suddenly he remembered the early summer, the young birds, not knowing the ways of humans as they had sat on the ground looking at the pair of humans walking down the path. Now it was October, he had missed the summer, and the younglings were more wary, but still down here in the little wood they were unused to humans and sat on the near branches and watched as the man made his way down the forest path with the walker, holding onto the girl as he went.

"I remember...do I remember stables in the garden?" he said. "There was a gate here? Or am I remembering it wrong?"

She kicked away the loose fence panel that was so familiar in the bottom of Belle Starr's garden, and crawled through. Walking was difficult for him yet, and it took him a while.

"Curse this thing," he said kicking at the walker.

"Hey," she shouted, doctor said it would take a while. "It's only been a day."

He nodded.

"I feel like an old man," he muttered.

"You're still late thirties," she replied. "I'm not far off that myself."

He smiled.

"Still beautiful," he said looking at her.

"Knock it off," she laughed. "I'm well into the mom zone."

"The mom zone?" he asked as they walked the oh-so-familiar path.

"Yeah," she nodded. "We talked about it. Guess you forgot. The time of life when young guys just see girls as 'a mom' instead of a sexy girl they can fuck. When a guy comes up to you when you're in the mom zone, he's probably asking for directions, rather than for your number."

"Never thought about it," he said, using her shoulder to steady himself.

"Me neither really," she admitted. "The truth is, I never really cared. About being sexy and wearing tight clothes and attracting guys. Guess it was cos I always had you. I got to just be me. Still busy being me."

He laughed, as they came closer to their bridge.

"Yeah," he answered. "That was why I first wanted to be more than just your best friend. You're so beautiful. You were always the most beautiful girl around. Still are. The best thing is that you knew how to be you, you never had to act like 'I'm so gorgeous.' You were just so natural and scruffy and you have such a cute smile and those eyes."

"And I'm a mom," she said, turning to him. "In the mom zone."

He hugged her.

"I always loved that," he said kissing her. "It was the same when you need a haircut. Other girls would spend hours getting some fancy shit done and be all 'don't touch it don't touch it.' You were

270

gone an hour, had some cut off and came back and we went out for a walk."

She shrugged.

"When I was a kid," she said quietly. "My mom died. I realised then that I gotta concentrate on the important shit in my life. Not the bullshit. It doesn't matter. All I had after mom died was a new best friend, who looked after me and made me chuckle."

"The red one goes to Harlem," he said quietly, remembering the abacus trains.

"ha ha," she laughed. "You remember that?"

He nodded, thinking of the broken plastic part from his fractured memories.

"Does the...does the abacus...do we still have it?" he asked.

She giggled.

"It's in Lola's room," she smiled. "We gave it her. I mean, she's eight. She doesn't need it, and always looked at us as though we were stupid when we said it was hours of fun playing with it."

"Then it isn't smashed?" he said smiling.

"No honey," she answered. "We'll steal it from our daughter later. Maybe after we go to bed."

He hugged her again.

"Hmm," he mused. "Sex on the Harlem subway?"

"Hey," she laughed. "We never played that game when we were kids."

"This is the adult version," he shot back amusedly.

"I'm not complaining," she replied holding him steady. "It's been eight months. Momma's getting some tonight."

He kissed her as they arrived at their clearing.

"Yeah she is," he said. "Momma's getting a lot tonight."

Then they were there. The trees parted and revealed the little wooden bridge that had been the focal point of their lives. Whatever else his mind had lost, he knew this. He walked out onto the deck and touched the aged wood with his hands. How many years had he spent there with her. He looked across at her, still standing on the mud bank and saw her face change, her eyes suddenly filling with water. She ran over to him.

"I'm sorry," she said sobbing. "I know I'm such a wimp. But it's just...I came here with Lola and we just sat here. And when they said you weren't gonna come out of it, I had visions of..."

He kissed her.

"Visions of what?" he asked.

She blinked, gulping down her sobs.

"Scattering your fucking ashes here," she replied angrily. "God I'm such a wimp."

"I love you," he said. "See? It's like we always said. Separated, you and me are nothing. We're less than nothing. We can't survive. But I'm here now. A little forgetful and a little wobbly, but I'm back, and I'm here. In the flesh. Nobody's gonna be scattering any ashes, nobody's gonna have to sell Belle Starr, everything's gonna be fine. We seem to have always been holding each other in tears here at this place. Well here what's gonna happen. I'm never letting go of your hand again. I mean it. You need to go the bathroom, I go right with you. You go to the kitchen...we go together."

She nodded.

"When we were little kids," she said nodding. "We always held hands. You remember that? Then we let go for a bit. And then, a bit later we held hands again...when we first....you know?"

He nodded.

"I'm never letting go again," he said. "Someday we'll be coming down here when we're eighty years old."

"We're gonna spend our lives here."

"Yeah we are," she said leaning her head on his shoulder.

She kissed him long and hard on the lips, suddenly directing his attention to a little bench on the mud banking.

"You like it?" she asked.

"I do," he answered. "That's new. It is new, isn't it?"

She nodded.

"Lola and I built it this summer. It saves us sitting down on the deck of the bridge. A nice bench overlooking the bridge, the water, and the berry bushes. We even put a plaque on it."

"Really?" he replied.

She nodded.

"Come see," she said.

It was a little bench, with wooden slats and wrought iron metal end pieces that were painted bright red. The little plaque read:

"John and Melissa's bench."

"Lola decided the name," she said, sitting down on one side. "Come sit. It's quite safe, even though it was built by an eight-year-old."

He laughed, sitting down beside her. It was only a small bench, but there was room enough for the two of them on it, plus two others besides.

"I love it," he said quietly.

"Yeah we are," she said leaning her head on his shoulder. "Lola wanted a bench big enough so she could sit here too. Right in the middle."

He smiled to himself. Three thirty pm. Lola would have seen the note by now and would be trotting down here.

And then he remembered, and it all came back like a lightning bolt.

2000, February

They were nervous during the car journey. Both John and Melissa had been quiet the whole way, wondering what they would say when they finally got to meet her. They'd got to a stage in their relationship and their marriage when they both realised they had enough love to share with someone else, and with Melissa unable to bear children, they'd looked into the possibility of fostering children, maybe leading to adoption if everything went well. They lady that dealt with them was really nice, and interviewed them several times. Privately, though she realised that they had a good stable home and a loving environment for a child, she thought the pair of them very quirky indeed. They would dress alike sometimes, and had a habit of finishing each other's sentences. And so, when it came to her choice of a child to foster, she thought immediately of Lola.

Lola had been abandoned at birth and spent time in several foster homes and different children's centres. As she grew from a baby into a little girl, it became harder for prospective parents to deal with her. She has quiet, moody, and sullen. And quirky. Very quirky. Lola would sit quietly for hours coloring a picture in a book if the mood took her, but if it did not, the mere suggestion of coloring would lead her to scream and cry and threaten to kill herself. She needed a loving home, but her quirks of character usually proved too much. But this time, with these two...Tweedle-dee and Tweedle-dum the city worker called them, the little girl might stand a chance.

"You're quiet," Melissa said as he hunted around for the street. "What?" he returned. "No. No, I'm fine. I'm just...thinking about stuff. What I'm gonna say. I don't have much experience with little kids."

"Me neither," Melissa nodded. "I just know that we should have one. And we both were kids, so it shouldn't be too hard."

He held her hand as he found the street, turning the black car into the driveway.

"Me too," he replied. "It's time for us to share our lives with someone."

"I thought it would be strange," she said looking at him. "You know? Having a child that's not our own. But it doesn't matter, does it? What matters is that we make her our own and love and care for her"

"Yeah," he nodded. "And hey. I thought I was the heir to the Mason fortune. Turns out I was only the illegitimate son of a ranch hand."

She touched his arm as the care worker met them.

"You turned out pretty good," she said.

Nervously, they went inside. Lola was up in the play room. Denise, the care worker, suggested that John and Melissa see her on her own territory.

"I'm sorry," she said shaking her head. "Lola's been in a tantrum all morning. Today isn't a good day. She wanted to be really good, was all excited about you both coming. And then she knocked off the toothbrush glass, got all upset and angry, then she ripped the page by accident when she tried to color a picture for you both. She's sitting with the dolls now. Just don't expect too much."

They nodded and crept upstairs, barely daring to breathe.

"I'm really scared," laughed Melissa nervously.

"Yeah," John laughed. "You think she's gonna attack us with scissors or something?"

That made Melissa laugh as they reached the landing.

"I didn't mean scared like that, idiot," she smiled.

And so, when they put their faces around the door, they were still laughing. Lola had heard voices coming upstairs. She figured it was them. The ones who Denise was trying to persuade to take her. They wouldn't. Not for long, at least. They never did. Lola had tried really hard, but things were always set against her. Like this morning, the stupid glass, and the stupid picture got all ripped. But that was strange just now. Laughter. Despite her misery, and her intent on not looking up and being sullen, when a blonde lady with sparking merry green eyes poked a head round the door, she looked up.

"Get inside, idiot," came a male voice, and Lola watched as the blonde woman, being pushed by the man, stumbled inside the room. Lola laughed.

"I swear," said the woman, laughing to the man who had also come onto the room. "You call me idiot one more time..."

Lola watched as the woman saw her, and, coming over, knelt to her level.

"Hi honey," she said. "That's a beautiful laugh. I'm Melissa. And this idiot behind me is my husband John."

"Hey, Lola," he said coming over to her. He sat on the floor, legs crossed.

"What ya got here?" he asked. "What ya playing with?"

"Barbies," said Lola, her face still laughing at the way the two grown-ups had come in.

"They're a little worn out," the girl continued. "Their hair is all ruined and I think the dog ate the face of one of em. But they're ok. I can't wreck them."

"Don't give em to him," said Melissa, taking one of the Barbies and stroking its hair. "It's head'll probably fall off."

"Hey," he laughed. "I'm good with toys. I like Lego. Do ya like Lego, Lola?"

The little girl sat in between the two of them. She didn't know what to make of them. They both smiled and laughed, and sat with her.

"I never played with Lego," she said quietly.

Melissa looked at John, and Lola watched as the two of them shared a look. Lola cast down her head. She'd done it. Said something wrong already and that was the end. She thought of the drawing that she'd screwed up in the dustbin.

"She's never played with Lego," echoed John.

"A Lego virgin," whispered Melissa, suddenly noting the girls downcast and suddenly teary face.

"Yeah," John agreed in a conspiratorial voice. "That means we have to train her ourselves. Buy her tons and tons of them to play with.

"Maybe make her bed out of it?" suggested Melissa. But the girls face was still downcast.

"Nah, stupid. She has to have a proper bed. Maybe a four poster one, like a princess one? You like princesses, Lola?"

No," said the girl suddenly. "I'm not one. I'm not pretty enough, and I'm not nice."

Melissa took hold of the little girl's hand, and squeezed it. John took hold of the other one.

"Honey," she said. "I think you're beautiful. When you laughed when we came in, you were the prettiest girl in the world.   And we were only kidding about the Lego."

"Yeah," John continued. "When we were both your age, we'd sit in my room for hours playing with the stuff. Making houses and campers, and space stations and stuff."

Her eyes widened a little.

"Yeah," said Melisa. "There ya go. There's that Lola smile."

Melissa tickled her under the chin and the girl chuckled a little. Then she was sad again. She looked to the dustbin, and began to cry a little.

"Aw hell," said John, sitting closer to her. He put the little girl on his knee. Melissa came next to him, and they held her.

"What's the matter, baby?" she asked the crying girl.

"I did a picture. They asked me to. Cos families like me at first, then don't like me and bring me back. So I did a picture so you'd like me for longer. And I ripped it by accident. Then I ripped it some more on purpose and thought bad things."

Melissa kissed her on the forehead, moving over to the bin and fishing out a crumpled [piece of paper. She brought it back, and unfolded it.

"See," said the little girl crying. "I ruined it. And now everything's miserable and ruined."

John laughed, cuddling the girl, and in puzzlement, she stopped crying,

"You're a regular little ray of sunshine, aren't ya," he said, his face full of mirth. She studied him intently.

"I love her," said Melissa, her own eyes growing teary. "I just love her so much."

"She's ours," he replied looking at the tear stained face of the child. "She's perfect for us."

Melissa looked into the girl's eyes.

"Will you have us, honey? Will you put up with us and come live with us?"

"They always send me back," said the girl, fingering the drawing.

Melissa shook her head.

"No baby," she said. "If you come with us, then if you want to, if you like us enough, then you can stay. You can be our little girl."

"It's not the most modern house in the world," John continued. "It's a big old wooden ranch house. With a big garden and a bridge..."

"Poohsticks Bridge," broke in Melissa.

The little girl forgot her tears as she watched the two adults finish each other's sentences.

"Poohsticks," repeated the girl. "Denise read that to me in a book."

"We have the book," said Melissa. "We named our bridge when we were your age. We had adventures there and…"

"…camping out, and barbeques, and stuff," continued John. "Would you like that. Come try it out. See if you like us enough."

Lola looked from one to the other.

"Can I stay if I like it," the little girl asked John. He nodded.

"If you like it," he replied. "You can be our little girl for always."

2003, November.

"For always."

Lola had liked it, and it hadn't been long before things had been finalised, and Melissa and John adopted Lola as their own little girl. It had all suddenly come back.

Lola had gotten off the bus as normal, at the bottom of the driveway on Decatur road. It was cold, and although Momma Melissa had made Lola promise to wear her mittens and scarf, they were stuffed in her bag. Odd though that Momma Melissa hadn't met her on the drive like she normally did. The car was there. As she got near the house, there was a note pinned to the door.

"Lola," it read. "Come to Poohsticks. Surprise. Momma."

Lola dropped her little schoolbag and trotted off to the bottom of the garden. She hoped Momma was ok. The two of them had been ok without John, but it had been weird. She knew Momma Melissa had been upset sometimes. Lola could always tell. Momma Melissa usually gave her extra cuddles when she felt sad, or arranged lots of activities for them. Lola didn't mind. She was sad that daddy John was going to die. He was nice, but it was typical of her luck. She'd finally found people who liked her, and one of them died pretty much straight away. Lola kicked through the leaves as she made her way to Poohsticks. At first, she'd been closer to Mommie Melissa. She smiled a beautiful smile, and hugged her tight. Daddy John hugged her too, and smiled. But at first Lola had been a bit scared of him. Like he was fierce of something. Which he wasn't. And just as she got not scared of him, he did something to the car and didn't come home again. What was Mommie Melissa doing down here.? She only came here with Daddy John, and they hadn't been here in a few months. But Lola knew the way, and pretty soon she neared the clearing. She rounded the corner, and saw Mommie Melissa sitting in one corner...

And saw something.

Saw someone.

Someone else sat beside her.

A man.

At first, she thought it was a new boyfriend. Daddy John had died. But then she saw the black hair, and that sideways smile, and the look in his eyes as he saw the little girl. He stood shakily.

She didn't hear his words.

282

"Hey Lola," he said softly. "Haven't you got a kiss for your daddy?"

She flung herself across the path and into his arms. He sank to his knees and embraced the girl, tears streaming down his face.

"I remembered you," he said, studying her face after, at long last, their embrace had ended. "Your little face. You kept appearing to me. My little Lola. I love you so much, my little Lola."

Then Lola was sat between them, and they both embraced her. She was crying now, but they were tears of happiness.

The day after, they kept Lola away from school, and played with her all day. The happy day began at seven thirty, when, deep in contented slumber, John and Melissa were awakened by a happy little girl begging to be allowed into their bed. They relented, and she nestled down between her adopted mummy and daddy happily. But she was too excited to sleep.

"Sing me the song, Daddy," she said looking into John's face.

John's mind was a blank, and he thought hard to try to remember it.

"Lola honey," began Melissa. "He doesn't..."

"It's ok," said John touching his wife's arm gently, "I'll figure it out. There's something there in the back of my head. Let's just see if it's the right one."

Lola propped herself up John's chest and watched anxiously as John thought. There was only one song in his head, right there at the back of his mind. He watched his daughter and began to sing.

"Oh give me a home..." he began.

Lola closed her eyes with pleasure. He'd remembered.

"Where the buffalo roams," he continued softly. "And the deer and the antelope play."

"You remembered," said Melissa, squeezing his arm.

"Can I continue the song?" he asked, a gentle smile playing across his face. They nodded.

"Where seldom is heard," he sang watching the little girl's eyes as they studied him. "A discouraging word. Come on honey, join in"

"And the skies are not cloudy all day," they all sang together.

They lay there singing *Home on the Range* till gone nine. At just after ten, sitting in the leaky kitchen with the collapsed roof eating breakfast, a knock came on the door. Lola jumped down from her stool at the breakfast bar, but John held her arm.

"No honey," he said. "Finish up your breakfast. The man of the house is home now. Let me answer my own front door. It's been a while."

Melissa watched him as he grabbed his walker and edged his way to the door. The knock came again. Bell must be burnt out again, she thought. She added it to her mental list of jobs to do.

In the hall, her husband had reached the door, and opened it. There was a woman standing there, slight of frame, with pulled back dark hair. She was wearing a uniform, all black with a logo on it that John didn't recognise.

"Oh my god," said the woman, slightly faint. "I...you're....oh thank god!"

She hugged him suddenly.

"When Melissa didn't call," she continued. "I assumed the worst, that you'd...you know? I had to come around just see to see if Melissa was..."

"Hey," said Melissa from behind John. "Guess who's home?"

The woman came inside, and embraced Melissa.

"I'm so happy for you," she said. "When did this...Is he...?"

"Yesterday," said Melissa rubbing Johns arm. John felt vaguely bewildered. Who was this woman? Did he know her?

"He's fine," said his wife. "It's gonna take a little time. There've been some memory issues with him, and having spent eight months laying in a coma, he has to learn to walk again. But we're getting there. I have him home."

"Tweedle-dum and Tweedle-dee," said the woman. "God help us all. Have you started going to the bathroom together again yet?"

Melissa giggled.

"Sure," she said. "Why wouldn't we?"

The woman shook her head.

"You're still weird," she laughed. "And you still creep me out."

"Are you coming in for coffee," Melissa asked.

The woman shook her head.

"No," she replied. "I gotta get to work. Besides, your no shoes rule pisses me right off."

"Can I just ask," interjected John still feeling bewildered. "Who are you? Sorry - I don't know much. I mean…I'm remembering shit, but not that much."

The woman looked him up and down, smiling,

"You remembered enough to wear the same clothes as your dipsy little wife," she said sarcastically.

John looked at him and Melissa. The woman was right, Melissa and john looked identical in red and white check plaid work shirts and jeans. The only difference was that he wore socks, and Melissa did not. It had seemed natural to be the same as her, something in him told him that this was what they did. When they had a chance they wore the same clothes. It had made them both laugh during breakfast.

"You're both very strange," laughed the woman. My name's Nancy. Despite your horrible weirdness, I'm friends with you both."

"Huh," said John. "That's nice. How'd we meet?"

"Hmm," said the woman, retreating to the doorway and winking. "You and I had an affair, then we all agree to be friends. Threesomes…"

"We had an…" he started, but Melissa broke in.

"Hey," she said. "Don't mess with his mind any more. I tried it this morning over breakfast. That's my thing."

"You messed with my…" he started.

"You made him do chores," laughed Nancy.

"He made the breakfast," laughed Melissa.

"You said that I always liked to make the breakfast," said John feigning sternness. "You lied to me? You fiddled around in my head?"

"Hmm," said Melissa shrugging. "Just a little. It was fun. I wouldn't do it with anything serious. Just chores."

"Yeah, well," he said with a twinkle. "You've got a spanking coming."

"Good lord," said Nancy rolling her eyes. "And that's my cue to exit."

"No," said Melissa grabbing Nancy's sleeve and dragging her back inside. "Come in, have coffee and be weird with us."

Nancy was serious.

"I have to go to work, honey," she said holding Melissa's hands. "But I'm so overjoyed for you both. I mean that. Seeing you both together here again...despite your icky weirdness. It's good."

She touched John's arm.

"I'm glad you're home, big guy," she said. "I hope you know how many tears she's shed for you."

He nodded,

"I shed a few for her too," he said.

"I gotta go," she said trying to get her sleeve free from Melissa's grip. "I swear to god your grip is worse than a ...some gripping animal...I don't know."

"Have coffee with us," said John.

"We have Lego" said Melissa, losing her grip on the sleeve, "and shiny floors. Come slide with us."

"Yeah," replied John. "Let's have a sliding contest. Lola's home."

"Listen, you two," said Nancy sternly. "You stay home all day and have sock sliding contests. I gotta go to work. Do adult things. Lola has to go to school tomorrow. I'll see you guys soon, ok?"

She left.

"She seems like a nice person," said John watching the car fly down the driveway.

Melissa nodded.

"She's lovely," she replied. "We met cos she's Josh's mom."

"Oh," nodded John. "That explains it."

"You have no idea who Josh is, have you?" giggled Melissa as they went back inside.

"Not a clue," answered John, picking up his coffee.

Melissa laughed, and hugged him.

"Lola's best friend," she said.

"That explains it," he answered. "She thinks we're weird?"

Melissa nodded.

"We finish each other's sentences, and go to the bathroom together, and..."

"Dress alike," John finished.

288

"Yeah," continued Melissa. "I guess we are kinda weird."

"You know what else?" he added. "We have a little girl home from school all day."

"Yeah we do," considered his wife. "Home all day."

"And we have some really shiny floors," he continued.

"Real shiny," she nodded looking down. "I bet a person could slide a long way, if she tried hard enough."

"I guess he could," he nodded.

"Well Nancy told us we could," she countered. "If we wanted to."

He turned to her.

"So, we play today," he said. "And be responsible adults tomorrow?"

She nodded.

"There was just one thing," she added. "In case you forgot. I was bad before...you said..."

"I haven't forgotten," he continued, swatting her on the rump as she fiddled with the laundry to find a pair of clean socks. "You have a spanking coming."

Just then Lola entered.

"Who's being spanked?" she asked. "Have you been bad, Mommy?"

Melissa and John both blushed.

"Rule of parenting number forty-nine," he whispered.

"Don't talk about spanking your wife's butt in front of your kid," she finished.

"Who's being spanked, Mommy," Lola persisted.

"Nobody honey," replied Melissa. "Nobody. Just some bad kid down the street."

Friends. He suddenly remembered. Friends. They had some. What were their names? He knew about Nancy now...but there were more of them...he closed his eyes and thought.

2000, May

Dee managed to avoid most of the potholes, swerving the car along Decatur road carefully.

"Damn girl," said her husband Errol. "You nearly took off the tailpipe!"

"Sorry baby," she replied. "Always miss that one. I remember the first time I came up here."

"Me too," he said remembering. "I hadn't seen the guy since high school. We were on the baseball team. I swear when I knocked on the door, he was terrified, some big black dude knocking on his door."

Dee laughed.

"He didn't recognise you."

Errol laughed.

"I put on a few pounds since then," he said patting his huge chest. "John's a good guy, though. A few minutes later we were like old buddies. Even tried out a few balls out the front."

Dee shook her head.

"What is it with you guys and sports, anyway?" she laughed. "Truth is, Mel and I never really spoke much in school. Who would have imagined her and me could become best friends?"

He shook his head.

"Nobody," he replied. "Guess we turned into adults."

They reached the main door of Belle Starr, but it was locked and closed.

"Hey you guys," shouted Errol. "You home?"

No answer.

"Where the hell they at?" puzzled Dee. Then a voice.

"Up here, doofus," screamed Melissa.

"Oh Jesus Christ," shrieked Dee. There was Melissa, high up beyond the second floor windows, sitting suspended on a small swing high above the ground. The swing was a short thick plank, to which was attached a rope. The rope ran around the chimney to fix it in place. Melissa, at the moment, was busy reattaching the wooden shingles to the side of the house, about forty feet off the ground. As Dee looked up, John was walking about precariously on the spine of the roof itself, handing her down the tiles as she reached up for them.

"You guys," screamed Dee. "You're gonna kill yourselves. Have you never heard of tradesmen."

Melissa looked down, and Dee gulped as she took her hands from the ropes that held the swing in place.

"These tiles," Melissa shouted down. "Cost fifty bucks a hundred. The guy to come fix em cost five hundred an hour, plus the fifty. We figured that we'd take turns on the swing, do it ourselves, and spend the money we save on other stuff."

"Come on up," John shouted. "The ladder to the attic is open. It's perfectly safe. Bring the beer?"

"They got beer?" asked Melissa. "Hell yeah. Come on up. I'll get off this swing and we'll have a beer on the roof."

Errol and Dee went into the house through the unlocked back door and up the stairs. At the top of the central stairway and landing where a small trapdoor was open in the ceiling, and a metal runged ladder was propped up.

"I'm not going on the goddamned roof with those two," said Dee. "I'm no good with heights."

"Come on, Baby," Errol cajoled. "I'll get a crick in my neck. Besides, we help em get finished, then we can get down and sit on the porch."

Errol climbed the ladder and disappeared into the attic.

"Come on up, Baby," he shouted to Dee.

The attic was full of stuff, boxes, old toys, clothes, and photographs. The pair of them had boarded it, so it could be walked on. Plus, they'd fastened insulation to the inside of the roof to keep in the warmth. It was fascinating for Errol to see the interior framework of the belle Starr house. Over in the corner beyond the boxes and the stored memories he could see new wooden supports that replaced the old.

"Did you replace these beams, buddy?" he shouted through the open skylight.

"What?" John's voice came. "Yeah sure. We did that last year. Come on up."

Errol, making sure Dee was safely in the attic, climbed the little stepladder and popped his head out onto the roof.

Jesus it was high. But the view from the roof of Belle Starr was amazing. You could see the intersection, and the truck yard, the

293

quarry, and as Errol turned his head, you could see the forest, and beyond that, you could follow the property line and see where all the other big ranch houses had once stood.

"Man, the view up here," said Errol, climbing out on the roof. Belle Starr's roof was a traditional A-frame roof, but had an added walkway on its crest, about two feet wide to walk on when performing maintenance. The walkway ran from chimney to chimney. John was leaning on the eastern Chimney leaning over the side to Melissa, who was dangling on the swing.

"Jesus," Errol said, getting his balance. "I wish you guys wouldn't do this."

John laughed.

"Where's your pioneering spirit, buddy," his friend laughed. "It's ok after a minute when you get your balance. Could you hand me that stack there? She's almost done."

Gingerly, Errol bent, putting down the six pack of beer he'd brought, and picked up a case of wall tiles, handing them to him."

"You replaced that beam, Jay?" asked Errol.

John nodded, taking the tiles from his friend,

"The house was sagging down at one end," he said handing down a tile to Melissa. "You're welcome, honey. Anyway, the foundations in that corner needing shoring up as well."

"That why your toilet didn't flush?" asked Errol.

John nodded.

"Anyway," he continued. "They quoted us twenty five thousand for the work. I mean, we had it, just. But then I found out that if I hired a crane for a week to support the house, plus materials, we could strip the side, shore up the foundations and the drains ourselves, and replace the load bearing strut for less than half that."

He handed her another tile.

"You guys are crazy," said Errol shaking his head, and turning to the open skylight.

"Are you staying down there in the attic?" he shouted down.

"I don't do rooftops," shouted up Dee. "I'm not a monkey, and I ain't no bird either, sitting on a roof."

"We got beer up here," said John laughing.

"I'm in heels," the voice shouted. "Can't you guys take a break?"

"Come see the view, Baby," Errol called. "You can see the truck yard."

"Well whoop de doo," called up Dee. "I can see the goddamned truck yard, all the time without risking my life on the roof wearing heels."

"Hey," shouted Melissa, using the swing to move from one side of the house to the other, high off the ground. "Why is she in my house wearing heels? Dee, you're re-waxing that floor, honey."

"Oh hell," shouted Dee. "Who rattled her cage? OK, I'm coming up. Without the heels."

She slipped off the heels reluctantly, and ascended the ladder. After about ten minutes of heart pounding terror, she popped her head out. Seeing how high it seemed out there on the rooftop at Belle Starr, she felt her stomach do a backflip. Then she saw them, sitting there. Melissa had climbed back onto the roof off the swing, and was leaning against the chimney with John next to her and her feet resting on his lap.

"Hey," shouted Errol from beside the skylight. "Look who joined the fun."

Dee shakily climbed out onto the roof, and gingerly sat down beside Errol.

"It's all right," he reassured her. "You get used to it after a few minutes."

Together, they sat on the roof and drank their beer.

2003, December

"Errol," he said to nobody in particular. "We sat on the roof."

"Beer and heights," laughed Melissa. "You remembered?"

He nodded.

"Is Errol still…" he asked.

"Sure," she reassured him. "Came to visit you in the hospital. I'll tell them you asked about them. They wanted to come see us, but figured to give us some time first. See…things are coming back now."

The first few weeks were slow going. Gradually, John learned to walk without the walker again, but his memory remained hazy. Not that any of them really cared. They were together again. But a couple of things bothered him. First, the finances. They were coming close to being forced to sell Belle Starr, despite Melissa's efforts to work twenty-eight out of every twenty-four hours in a day. He remembered being in an office, but barely enough to be able to answer a telephone.

"What the hell does the CEO of Mason Corproration do anyway?" he'd asked.

And that wasn't his only concern. Melissa, he remembered, had been an artist, he knew that much. Since he'd returned from hospital, she'd reminded him about the children's books she'd illustrated. The money wasn't enough to take it up full time, but the books had sold well. And yet… with her job in this anonymous office cubicle and repairing this old house, there wasn't much time for it.

One morning, he wandered into Melissa's art room. Her secret place. Her special place. Where she indulged her very soul. Sometimes, he would come in here to get closer to her, if that were possible. To find out the inside of her soul.

It had once been the children's den. But now the walls were whitewashed, and there was just a huge table, some cupboards and art materials everywhere. A stack of books lay on the desk. Not remembering, he turned one over. It was a new book, made to look old by its embossed cover. The title read "The Adventures of Mouse," in gold letters across the top. The cover was patterned, and he felt it beneath his fingers. The sketch on the front was simple, but beautiful, and was of a red mouse. Initially looking simple, the attention to detail, color, and shade was spectacular. He started at the cover for a long time. It was his wife's hand, he knew that. He turned the first page. Even the paper felt quality, like an old manuscript. 'Written by Maggie Brown," it said. "With illustrations by Melissa George-Mason."

He smiled inside, and he felt a warm beam of light radiate from within his soul. 'She' had done this. This was her thing, the one thing she had always wanted to do. He couldn't remember her doing it – that memory had, for the moment, been lost – but as he leafed through the book, he remembered every one of the beautiful colored sketches. Including the one with the cow. That one reminded him of a coloring exercise at school years before. What a pity she had seemed to step away from her art, having this stupid office job she had.

He explored some more. Stacked at the side were paintings, oils, and each one looked, to his eyes, amazing. Lifting one, he stared at it. It was the two of them, locked into an embrace. Her head was down as though she were desperately sad, and his eyes were closed. He thought it breath-taking, and marked it in his mind to ask her whether it could be hung in the house. And then he saw the little clay creatures. The red mouse he recognised. The robots, the goldfish with legs he didn't. Wonderfully detailed, exquisite in paint and texture. She had been busy. Everything just looked to be laying around, forgotten about. He saw some plates stacked neatly, a design on each. They were painted with scenes from the books, painted to look like they'd been sketched. Each one different.

As he looked around at this stuff, it gave him an idea. Not just an idea, a feeling. If, he reasoned, If I'm this CEO person doing all this office shit, and leaving her at home to do all this, then why doesn't she do something with it? And then the idea came fully fledged into his mind. This was something they could do together…an art shop maybe? Perhaps a bar. He knew nothing of this corporation that he was supposed to run. Presumably, his shares, or stock would be worth something, that might be enough to get them started. But why had he not thought of this before. Maybe he had, and the accident made him forget about it. Maybe, just maybe, he reasoned, I was too blind to see it before, too caught up in this CEO business, to notice what she was doing here. Too busy with my passion to give a thought for hers.

"Am I that much of a douchebag?" he said aloud. He really couldn't remember, and made his mind up to ask her about it.

A few days later, she decided it was time that he was re-introduced to his office and the company that he'd been CEO for a long time. John had agreed to this, though he still could remember nothing of the business, or what he was supposed to do. And, he added a proviso that they went downtown, as he had some business there, though, to Melissa's annoyance, he wouldn't say what. For once, and largely for old times' sake, they took the bus that's stopped on

299

the corner of Decatur Road into the business district. Sitting together on the front seat of the bus, the town still looked so strange and different to him.

"Ice cream store," he suddenly shouted as they passed their old high school haunt. Every passenger looked around at him, thinking him a little bit simple. Melissa nodded.

"We took Lola there to celebrate the adoption being finalised," he added, suddenly remembering. "She had strawberry sprinkles. Good god, the tiny bits of bullshit that I can remember, but other stuff...I just haven't got a clue."

"Patience, Baby," reassured Melissa, as the bus turned towards the business district. After a while, Melissa reached over and rang the bell to signal the bus to stop.

"Is this it?" he asked. "Are we nearby?"

Melissa grimaced inwardly. He must have walked the length and breadth of the business district main street a hundred times or more, but there was no recollection. This was a problem. His brother Ed Junior had been granted control in John's absence. And he wouldn't be keen to give it back. Meanwhile bills were piling up, and Belle Starr was threatened with having its water and gas cut off. John's brother had hated him ever since he'd been to prison years before. She held her husband's hand. Now, he had no recollection of his brother being released from jail, or the subsequent burying of the hatchet between the two. Another problem.

"Here we go," said John, bounding up the steps to a tall building.

"You remembered it?" asked Melissa hopefully.

"Nah," he replied. "I read the nameplate on the door. Mason Corp. Let's get this over with."

They were met in the foyer of the building with many people glad to see their former CEO up and seemingly well again. But she could tell he was bewildered and knew nothing of the place. She took him up to what had been his office on the 24th floor, where they were met by Olivia, his long term PA. Olivia hugged him, weeping a little.

"We thought we'd lost him," she admitted to Melissa. "You must be so relieved."

Melissa was, though when she looked around, he had wandered off.

"I like the view," he said, having disappeared around a corner to look out of a side window. "A little bit impersonal though. I'd have thought management would rather be closer to the shop floor, you know? Keep contact with the line staff."

"This is your office, honey," she said, going over to him and pointing towards the open door of a huge, seemingly empty office suite.

"Was his office," came a nasal voice from behind them, coming out of a room. "With you doing your whole Rip Van Winkle bit, It's been left to me to run things."

John studied the bald-headed, bearded man intently. He looked slightly older than John, wiry and thin. Too thin in fact. He saw a flicker of something across Melissa's face...was it anger, distrust?

"So you're running things for me, John asked, studying the man's face and nodding. "Thanks for doing that. From the looks of things, we seem to be doing pretty well."

The man nodded, offering out his hand.

"I'm sorry," said John refusing the hand momentarily, before turning to Melissa. "Who is this guy again, honey? I seem to know him."

"Brother," said the man, feigning hurt. "I'm heartbroken you don't recognise your own brother."

John shook his head.

"First, you lost your hair," he said. "Second, you're supposed to be in jail."

Ed Junior shrugged.

"What can I say?" he laughed. "I have Dad's genes, not the field hand's like you. And really? Did you forget about me coming out, the whole forgiveness speech, and the embrace?"

John shook his head.

"I don't know any of that," he said.

Ed Junior smiled sardonically.

"Well," he replied. "That's annoying I guess. My apology speech was so damn good. A couple of jokes, a bit of pathos, some tear-jerking apologies. Am I really gonna have to do all that again?"

"No," said John distracted. "I'm not sure I'd want to hear it. Things have changed, for me anyway. I do have a couple things I need to be straightened out though."

"Oh?" asked his brother.

"Yeah," continued John. "First thing. You running my company, which I guess is ok if I've forgiven you. What I don't understand is how come my fucking house is falling to pieces with bills dropping through the letterbox every damned day."

"Well," shrugged his brother. "I don't pay your bills, seeing as I don't have ownership of that pile of junk you guys lovingly call Belle Starr, or Poohsticks, or whatever childhood memory you guys have going on. So while you've been having sleepy time, I guess there's nobody to pay them."

"Couldn't you have helped?" john asked.

"Hmm," replied Ed Junior, "I believe I did. I made a sensible offer to Melissa for your remaining stock in the company, to buy you out, so to speak."

"And take control of my company?" John snapped back.

Ed Junior nodded, then looked around as another man came bursting in, pushing past Melissa and Olivia in the doorway,

"You lousy set of bastards," he shouted. "Going back on you fucking word to my men! It's all about the dollar with you, isn't it?"

"Look," said Ed Junior, holding up his hands to the man. "It's all business, Doug. The guys have to accept changes, be flexible."

"Flexible!" snorted the man. "After what you two sharks have done to them! When you offered to buy my company, and keep the guys on, you said there'd be no changes!!!"

Ed Junior shrugged.

"Market forces," he said. "It's an employer's market."

"Can I just…" broke in John.

"Honey," replied Melissa going to his side. "Maybe we'd better leave this to…"

He silenced her.

"No," he said. "No. I need to know what's going on here."

He turned to the angry man.

"Who are you, first of all?"

"Forgot me already, Mason?" said the man rounding on John. "You piece of shit."

"Hey," shouted Melissa. "He just got out the hospital."

"Yeah, well," said the man balling up his fists. "A return visit can be arranged."

"Look," interjected John. "Whoever you are. I rolled my car on the Interstate nine times. What memory I have has more holes than a TV soap opera plot. Please fill me in."

The angry man looked into John's earnest face.

"Okay," he said. "I'm Doug Atchison. Owner of Atchison Transportation. Took over from my father Brian Atchison. Most of the guys who work for me worked for my dad. You two guys made me an offer. I'm getting close to retirement so I took it, on one proviso. You guys promised, and now you've broken that promise."

"Like I said," broke in Ed Junior. "Market forces."

"Look," appeased John. "Tell me what I did. Please. Like I said, I have memory issues."

"My guys all have paid lunch breaks. Full sick pay, plus benefits. Keeps the loyal long term guys on the payroll, and rewards hard work. That's the way I like it. I don't want to have to keep training young new guys, I want old, dependable guys. So my benefits package is fair, and keeps 'em working for me."

"Sounds good," agreed John. "I don't see your problem."

"My problem," said Doug Atchison. "Is you two guys. You've threatened to take all that away from them, given them a token cash settlement, and the shaft. And you've made me out to be a liar."

"Is that true?" said John sternly turning to Ed Junior. "Is that what we do here? Take money from good hard working folks?"

"John," appeased his brother. "Don't make me out to be the bad guy here. You constructed the deal, you worked on the terms."

"Well then," agreed John turning to Melissa. "I guess I did learn something today. I was a bigger douchebag than I thought."

"The profit made it seem worth it," muttered Ed Junior.

John shook his head, before turning to Doug Atchison.

"Here's what I propose," he said. "A two-year takeover package. Your name stays on the trucks for that whole time. We install a manager to run things so you can go off on your cruise. And your guys keep their benefits package for a further two years. At the end of that, we'll talk again. If we make enough money, then they can keep their benefits packages, plus a little wage increase."

"John what the hell are you…" began his brother, but he was hushed.

"Are you happy with that?" John asked Atchison. The man nodded.

"I'd have to see something on paper," he admitted. "But it's better than I'd hoped for."

John shook his head.

"I'm sorry I put you through this," he replied. "An accident like the one I had puts your priorities into perspective. I'll get the paperwork locked in before I depart as CEO."

"What," said Melissa and Ed Junior together.

John nodded.

"I don't like this place," he said to her. "It makes me think I spent more time here than I did with you."

Her face suddenly had a flicker of sadness upon it.

"What?" he asked her. "What's wrong?"

She put her head down.

"That's why you had the wreck on the Interstate. I'd called, for what had been the ninth time, to ask when you were coming for dinner. And then..."

"I crashed the car when I was answering the cell?" asked John. She nodded.

"It's all my fault," she said quietly, going ashen white.

He embraced her, and the others watched them.

"No," he shook his head. "I'm guessing I could be a little preoccupied with this place when I wanted to be. Otherwise, how

306

would I not have noticed that it's you that has the real talent around here? Yeah, I went into the art room and saw all that stuff"

"You've seen it before," she said looking up at him.

"Yeah," he replied. "I guess. But I never noticed it before. Like I said, too preoccupied. In that coma, I lost you. I know that, I felt it. There was so much more I wanted to say to you, so much more I wanted to do with you, to be with you."

"This is all very touching," broken in Ed Junior. "But…"

John ignored him.

"I'm not doing this anymore," he said, shaking his head. "This bullshit is meaningless. I'm spending my time with you. He can have the stock. I don't really give a royal shit. That's what our second appointment downtown was. I had an idea."

She held his hands and looked into his eyes.

"Idea?" she said laughing. "You can't remember shit and you're having ideas?"

"Yeah," he nodded. The whole room had faded away for the two of them. Now, as always, there had only ever been the two of them. The others in the room were, and always had been, incidental.

"An idea," he repeated. "An art shop, to sell your stuff. A studio upstairs, and we sell the stuff downstairs. I can work in the shop."

"Together," she said quietly, looking into his eyes.

"Together," he confirmed. "And … we can sell coffee, and cakes and stuff, turn it into a bar at night. And have all your artwork on the walls and sell it. No more working in that fucking cubicle."

Her eyes shone as she began to work on his idea.

"You see," he said. "I realized that you were the one. Not my family or this meaningless bullshit. You. You and your little talent. This is something we can do together. I said I was never gonna be separated from you again, and I meant it. We'll buy a little shop with the money we get from the sale of this stock, pay the bills on Belle Starr, and…"

"…and have our own little shop together," she finished.

They looked at each other for a long time, saying nothing but realising the pleasure they both felt at each other's side.

Later, Melissa had been trying to trigger memories.

"You remember any of these," she asked as they walked past the paintings that hung in the main hall, "When I first came here as a child, you told me who they all were."

He looked at the oil paintings of the people that hung there. He shook his head.

"I...they look familiar," he replied, his hand seeking hers, "but I dunno. Just faces."

"This one," she said pointing, "Great Uncle Feargal."

He looked up at the painting. It showed a youngish man with a shock of red hair and a vista of land behind him.

"He won the Belle Starr land in a poker game," she said, "Came from Ireland for the gold rush in the Yukon."

He shook his head.

"Vague recollections," he said, "I dunno. Maybe I didn't pay much heed to these things before. I just had eyes for you."

"This one," she said leading him to an old framed photograph, "This is Sam Mason, and his wife Nan. Sam and Nan built the house here, and our bridge. Nan Mason and her sister Jeanie were chorus girls in some gold rush town. She ran off with Feargal to find the land that he'd won here, but after a short while, he left her high and dry."

"Nice guy,"

"Yeah, right? Sam Mason was Feargal's brother, he built the ranch here, and Nan married him."

"You know more about this family than me," he remarked, pulling her close to him, "I'm sorry, I don't much remember. Not yet. Where's our picture?"

"We never got round to it," she said kissing him on the nose, "We were always too busy."

"Well let's do it," he said, for once let's dress up in our best goddamned clothes and get a picture taken of us. Me and you. The lady of Belle Starr house and her decrepit husband."

He smiled that sideways smile that always seemed to find that place inside her, and she kissed him again, this time on the lips.

"Thank you," he said looking into her eyes, "Thank you for remembering this stuff. Nobody else would have ever cared enough to do that. I love you so much."

She smiled at him, and they hugged.

"You're not so decrepit," she said laughing, "But it would be nice to have us up there too. The next custodians of this place."

They stayed in their embrace for a moment, neither wanting to let go. He stared at her, scrutinised her face, the face that he'd known since he was five. Melissa had owned this place since she first walked in here as a little girl. He suspected she cherished it even more than he.

"We have to stop just standing here hugging," she said, laughing.

"Time to be adults, huh?"

"We got stuff to do. If we be all grown up now, we can dick around later."

"I don't want to dick around later. I want to dick around with you now. At least until Lola gets back from school."

"That's about…"

"Four hours twenty five minutes."

"You worked this right out."

"I always did have smarts."

"Couldn't drive for shit though. You couldn't just hit the barrier and leave it at that. Had to go roll the damn car nine times."

"What can I say," he laughed, "I was auditioning for an action movie."

"So…" she said looking at the floor, "how we gonna spend those four hours twenty whatever minutes?"

"We could go into the attic and you could show me some more of those old dusty paintings?"

She made a face.

"Or we could just…you know…go upstairs and do stuff. Fun stuff."

His eyes met hers and they shared a look.

"Well that's what I meant. I mean…start off with the paintings and…"

"In the goddamned attic? Fucking in the attic?"

"It's one room of the house we haven't done it in."

"Really? We've lived here so long and never….huh. Let's go remedy that."

311

They grinned at each other and scampered off to the attic, laughing.

"Be quiet, Doofus," she hissed as they crept into Lola's room.

"Quit calling me Doofus," he said trying not to laugh and wake the little girl in the middle of her night's sleep, "This is your idea to come and steal our kid's toys at midnight."

"We're just borrowing them," she whispered, poking him in the ribs as they tiptoed across Lola's room, "it isn't fair. Just because we're adults we don't get to have Legos anymore."

"So all we need to do is come steal our kid's."

"She'll never know. We'll just borrow the box, build some shit and put it back before morning."

"She'll know it was us crept in here at midnight. I think sometimes she's the adult."

Suddenly Melissa yelped.

"Geez Louise," she shouted as her bare foot stood on a Lego piece, "this fucking stuff is just…"

"Be quiet Doofus" he said, gulping to stop himself laughing, I have the Legos crate."

Lola stirred a little in her little bed.

"Shhh,"Melissa hissed, "Let's just drag it into our bedroom. We'll put it back before breakfast and she'll never know we played with it."

"The perfect crime. Who'd have thought stealing from your own children was so easy?"

312

The crate was almost to the door when Melissa's other foot found the Lego piece on the floor and she yelped again.

"Holy mother of fuck…"

He couldn't hold it in any more, and he sat down on the crate laughing. When the pain in her foot wore off, his infectious laughter spread to her and she sat down on the floor in the doorway laughing with him.

They hadn't noticed a little person sat bolt upright in bed watching her parents with inquisitiveness.

"Mommy," said Lola?

"Cheese it," said John, "It's the feds, we're rumbled."

Melissa's laughter started again, her wet eyes glistening.

"Lola, it's all a dream, honey. Go back to sleep."

"Are you throwing my Legos in the garbage, Mommy? My other folks did that when I was bad."

John and Melissa's laughter suddenly stopped. She came to sit on her daughter's bed, and her husband sat on the other side.

"Honey, no," said Melissa, "We would never do that."

"Then why were you taking it?"

The little girls face looked straight at her mommy, with puzzlement.

"Cos we're grownups," said Melissa, "And sometimes daddy and me don't want to be grownups, we want to play with kid stuff like we used to do."

"Being grownup sucks ass and balls," said Lola suddenly.

They both laughed at her with surprise.

"Where the hell did you hear that?"

"From you, Daddy. I can usually hear stuff through the wall. I know when Mommy sees a spider in bed cos she yelps and shrieks late at night."

Melissa's face blushed deep red and they looked at one another.

"We're sorry to wake you, honey. You go back to sleep. We can play tomorrow after school if you like?"

Lola nodded, and after a kiss from her Mom and Dad, and a careful look that her Lego crate was returned to its position, they put out the light and left her.

"I told you that your shrieking would wake the dead," he whispered, grinning. "You scream like a goddamned banshee."

"Well if you hadn't have woke her in the first place," said Melissa as they went into their own room, "We could've been playing with her Legos by now."

"You were the one who shouted when you stood on the Lego piece."

"You woke her in the first place, Doofus."

"You know what, Mrs. Mason; I never did give you that spanking for fiddling around in my head the other week."

"Have to catch me first, Doofus," she said scampering around the bedroom.

2004, January

He sat in the chair in the den trying to make sense of things. The family attorney had put the wheels in motion for the sale of John's stock in Mason Corp. That at least had kept the wolves from the door of Belle Starr and enabled Melissa to pay some bills. But things were still foggy. He still looked at her sometimes as though she were a phantom. And at night, in bed, he hugged her tight as though she were going to be, at any moment, snatched away. But now he sat in the den. It was mid-morning, and he'd been looking through the commercial property section of the local newspaper to try to find a shop for them to run. He wasn't promised a heap of money from the sale of the stock, but it would be enough to pay off the debts on Belle Starr and get a deposit on a small shop. The rest of it was up to them. If it didn't work out, they were both getting regular jobs. It had to work. They were a team, the pair of them. It would work.

Later

"Huh," he said to himself, wandering around the house on his crutches. Nothing was where he remembered it to be. The house and the contests of every cupboard and drawer seemed moved around somehow. Of course, some of what he remembered wasn't real. One or two things had come back. He remembered the old leather couch that had a green and grey throw covering it, he remembered an image of cuddling her on it, an image of rubbing her cold feet one night as they sat watching the TV when the heating had been out of action. The house in general seemed dilapidated, like it needed money to fix it that they just didn't have. He guessed that this CEO job of his didn't pay that well.

He eventually made the coffee and stumbled along the hallway to the den. He missed her presence in the house, but she insisted that the job was important. To pay the bills, Melissa had taken a job in a cubicle in the city, answering calls on the telephone. It was a soul-destroying job. Of course, she said outwardly that she enjoyed it, but he could see her soul being slowly crushed by it. It wasn't something that he was going to allow to happen. If he could only remember more. The bills for the house were mounting up, she was right about that. Everything was in the red, the little car was on the verge of being taken away, there were bank loans on top of bank loans just to keep this damned old place upright. The sale of his Mason stock would help, if it ever came through. He idly wondered why his mom and dad hadn't helped. He remembered some of it, some of the arguments and unpleasantness, but it was more of a feeling of distaste than anything else: no real memories came. Not yet.

John sat with his struggle, felling about a hundred years old, when there suddenly came a knock on the front door. Odd. Who the fuck was this? He wondered if there was a maid or someone, but remembering the pile of bills, suddenly felt it unlikely that his wife had hired help, and he struggled to his feet.

"Just a goddamned minute," he muttered grumbled as the knock came again.

"Melissa?" came a male voice. "You home?"

Who the fuck was this? He wondered why a guy would be visiting Melissa. Not that he was worried about her fidelity. If nothing else, he remembered the faith he'd always had in her. She would never do that, inside both their hearts, they knew the other would never cheat. He was curious though. The Melissa he remembered had, apart from allowing him into her life, had always been something of a loner. Came with the territory of being an only child, he reflected. He reached the door with a struggle, and remembered thankfully that he left it on the latch. He opened it to find a smart looking well-groomed young man at the door. Wearing a bright colored purple suit and matching tie, he had product on his hair. Too much product. John reflected on his own somewhat dishevelled and grizzled appearance; after all he'd only just gotten out of hospital. I used to look like that, he thought. At least I think I did. He rubbed the two days of stubble on his chin and watched the man.

"Yeah?" he asked curtly. "Whadda ya want?"

"Uh...I...that is," stammered the man. "I was...Is Melissa home?"

Curious. Who was this ratty little fuck?

"No," replied John curtly. "She ain't home. Who the fuck are you?"

The man found his confidence, and held out his hand, which John ignored.

"My name's Russ," he said with a smile/ "Pleased to meet you."

"What the fuck do you want with my wife?" said John, irritated by Russ. Mainly because he remembered looking like that himself, and not this crippled, grizzled wreck he now was.

"Are you..." began Russ. "Are you John?"

"No," said John sarcastically. "I'm the fucking tooth fairy. Are you gonna stand there asking questions or are you gonna stand still while I shoot you for trespassing?"

Russ laughed. It was a genuine laugh.

"Man," he said, "Melissa didn't tell me you were up and about! Man, that's fantastic!! We've all been hoping and praying that you would, and you know...she's been pretty much a wreck. I dreaded to think what would happen if you'd...well...hey...here you are!"

John, taken aback by this guy and his niceness, resisted the urge to be even snarkier.

He nodded.

"How do you know my wife?" he said quietly.

"Oh...yeah, I better explain. I'm from Purple Realty. Melissa and I have been discussing the possible sale of Belle Starr."

The bottom dropped through John's world at the mention of the phrase "sale of Belle Starr"...Melissa was selling it? How could she? He felt suddenly woozy again, like his body wasn't strong enough to support his head. He swooned a little.

"Hey fella, you ok?" asked Russ with concern. "Come on, let's get you inside. Here, take my arm."

Somehow they got inside and Russ sat John down.

"I know where the kitchen is", said Russ. "Let me get you some water."

John waited until Russ came back with the water. He took a sip, and as the shock of the man's words faded from him, he spoke.

"Belle Starr isn't for sale," he said, his voice almost a whisper. "No matter what Melissa has said."

Russ nodded.

"I know," he replied. "She's told me that a hundred times. She'd let this place crumble down around her ears before selling it. I know cos I've asked her to let me sell it a hundred times."

He suddenly felt relief. She hadn't let him down. She had clung to Belle Starr like he had done. It was hers as much as his. Then he felt guilt at suspecting that she might have sold it. How could he have suspected her of such a thing? This place ran in her blood. And, looking around and the ramshackle old ranch house, he couldn't have blamed her if she had been tempted. Place should have been demolished years ago, like most of the other ranch houses on Decatur Road had been. So what was this weasley fuck pestering her for then?

"The thing is," began Russ. "Melissa's main objection was the potential value of the land as opposed to the house. Her words were that seeing the house pulled down would have broken her."

His heart skipped as he heard that, and more than ever, he wanted her at his side, so he could squeeze her and feel her comforting presence.

"Anyway," Russ continued, "I had to come down and see her again. I've had a couple of people come looking around for real estate, and they expressed a strong interest in this place."

"The house isn't for sale," John snarled. "Nobody's demolishing my house."

"That's the point," Russ continued. "Nobody will. The people that are interested are representatives of a children's charity. Disabled kids. Some rodeo star set it up years ago. Says riding horses is good therapy for kids with disabilities. They live at this retreat for a couple of months and the staff and nurses teach them, and there's riding and activities and stuff. See,. Here's a prospectus."

Russ placed a glossy pamphlet down on the coffee table.

"They need something here up north," continued Russ. "This is one of only two or three big old ranch houses that are suitable. The plan would be to keep and renovate the house, turn it into a school with dormitories and classrooms, and rebuild the stables, so there'd be horses and riding. The woods at the side can be tidied up and used for nature walks, and stuff like that. At least that's what they said when they saw it from the road."

Later

The house was quiet now Russ had left. John had sat and watched the morning turn into noon and read the prospectus. Children. Laughing children. Teachers everywhere, parents, and cowpokes. For some reason he remembered Jake suddenly. He was surprised at himself. For an hour, he'd been sat there considering the potential offer. No, not considering it. Trying to think of a reason to refuse it. And he could think of none. The money would help with the shop thing, they could even afford a nice little house in town, just the three of them, a cosy little family home where the heating worked everything was nice. They could even afford the trendy part of town, and go out and have a social life with their friends. With difficulty, he stood, replacing the prospectus on the coffee table. Taking a pen, he wrote on it.

"Gone to Poohsticks"

It was so peaceful here. Somehow now, it was associated with bad memories. He saw the place he had knelt down and cried at the thought of the little hand of his Tweedle-Dee slipping away from his. This place had become a sad, lonely place for him, and sitting here alone, he just wanted to sit and cry again. But as he sat there on the little bench and watched the water rushing by, he felt an excited feeling come over him. The sadness wasn't' real. She wasn't dead. He gripped his hands together. Tweedle-Dee still ran at his side, as she had during the long months that he'd been in a coma.

Could he leave this place? Sell it? The place where everything had happened in his life?

He'd spent his life by her side, her breathing was the soundtrack to his world, her voice was the one sound that he can imagine even when he was far from her. Which was not often.

He spent his childhood days foraging in the woods with her, the scruffy little kids with their woollen mittens and fluffy hats.

He spent his teenage years learning about how to love her, and learning how to tell her that he loved her. And he learned how to touch her.

He spent his adulthood building a life with her, he would watch as she changed from being an excited newlywed to being the family matriarch that everyone respected, and someone that people would always turn to when they needed advice.

He would spend his golden years relaxing and snoozing by her side, laughing in the sun as their dogs frolicked with their grandchildren, loving every laughter line on her face, laughing with each other as they would become eccentric in their old age.

Neither of them knew how they would spend the afterlife. But they both knew we would spend it together

And it had been here. Always here. Poohsticks had seen the very best of them, and it had seen the very worst of them. They had laughed here, they had cried here, they had fought here, and they had been intimate beyond ecstasy here. Here was where she had such pleasure as he entered her that she knew she would never in her life want the touch of another man upon her. Here was where Lola had called him daddy. He had this vision of the three of them, years from now: Lola as a grown woman and her aging parents, still hand in hand, sitting here on the deck, united in their love for each other. Suddenly he wanted her. Suddenly he cursed the realities of the practical world which meant he lost her for eight hours at a time for work. The sooner this shop and house thing was done the better. Which brought him back to the realities. Could he face never sitting here again with her? Could he do it? Could they do it?

As if to answer his pleas for her to come to him, he heard footsteps down the path. He turned.

"I brought a sweater," the husky voice said as it approached. His heart lifted. It was her.

"Yeah cos I forgot," he replied ruefully as she approached. "My memory's been a little screwy."

"I'd never have guessed," she laughed, sitting down at the side of him on the bench.

He laughed, partly at the relief of her appearance, and partly at her dress. She was smart. Office smart in a black skirt and top, black hose, and practical flat shoes.

"Whatcha lookin at," she said cocking one eyebrow as he regarded her.

"Nothing," he said, smiling at her.

"Huh," she replied wiping her face. "Have I got snot on my face. I just sneezed after sniffing at the paper in that prospectus thing."

"No," he laughed, reassuring her. "It's just…I dunno. I don't see you smart so very often. You went to our wedding in dirty jeans and bare feet."

"Yeah," she said, putting an arm around him. "Always rocking the hobo look huh?"

He kissed her on the nose.

"That's how I love you" he said, "I hate you having to do this damned job. Things are gonna change soon, I promise."

"Yeah," she said. "I know. We go to look at those shops on the weekend, don't we?"

He nodded.

"About that prospectus," he said. "What d'ya think?"

"I think that Russ is very persistent," she replied.

John nodded, taking her hand.

"It seems a nice organisation," he continued.

She looked at him, her eyes widening.

"Are you seriously considering this?" she said, slightly shocked.

He nodded again.

"I dunno," he replied. "It'd have to be a decision we made together. Wouldn't hurt to consider it. On the one hand, Belle Starr is pretty run down, it's way out of the cool part of town where we want our little coffee and art shop to be, it's a long way from our friends, and its cold, draughty, and damp."

"Yeah," she said reluctantly. "You got a point. But we've got all this."

She pointed to the bridge.

"Could we really not come here anymore?" she said softly.

"I dunno," he said looking in her green eyes. "I once would have said no. But now I dunno. In a way, I think I'd like to live in a little house with you, a little comfortable warm house, with our little girl, and within walking distance of our shop. Maybe a little garden where we can plant vegetables and have roses growing and stuff."

"You're planting vegetables and getting roses?" she said, raising an eyebrow, "you're quite the little gardener aren't you?"

He laughed.

"You know what I mean, idiot," he said smirking. "A nice little comfortable well-built place that isn't gonna cave in around us. Plus, it would solve all our problems. We could buy the shop outright instead of having to rent. Plus we'd have some to put away."

"Sounds like you've already made the decision," she said sadly.

He shook his head.

"No," he confirmed. "No. Definitely not. This is something we need to talk about. When I married you, this place became yours as

324

much as mine. This is our decision, not just mine. It's just…that Russ guy went out of his way to find people who would not only keep the house, they'd look after it."

"And," continued Melissa reluctantly. "They'd give it a purpose. A good purpose."

He nodded.

"We gotta think about it, weigh it all up."

She nodded.

"Remember when we first sat here," she said pointing to the bridge.

He nodded.

"I kicked off my sandals and dangled my legs over the edge. You were obsessed with staring at my feet."

He nodded, laughing.

"It was like…" he said. "That cemented our friendship. Like, I thought, its fine, she knows me well enough to take her sandals off at my bridge. There's a girl barefoot on my bridge."

She laughed, hugging him tight.

"You were a weird kid, you know," she laughed.

"I remember lots of times here," he said kissing her softly on the lips. "It's always just been us. Us saying that it's our last time here together, and then we get all sad and I always realised how I felt and it welled up inside me and I knew, only ever here, I knew how much I loved you, I loved you every single time we came her, more than I loved anything in the whole world. I just wanted you, nothing else, never anything else. The whole world could go to hell

325

in a wicker basket for all I cared, as long as I had you to hold me and laugh and me and tell me that it was ok."

She hugged him.

"There was never anyone else," she said pressing her face to his sweater. "As soon as I came her with you, it was like...I was right here. I never considered anyone else in my life, or even knew anyone existed. I'd felt from being a small kid that there was something missing inside of me, a part of me missing. When I came here for the first time, hell even before that, when you sat down beside me on the school bus that time..."

"Green sandals, white socks," he remembered.

"Always with the feet," she laughed. "And yeah, call the fashion police. I know. But yeah, even back then when you sat your bony ass down beside me, I knew that was right, that the piece I'd been missing was sat right there."

He kissed her.

"It's gonna be hard to sell this place, isn't it?" he asked.

She nodded.

"It's practical," she said. "And who knows, perhaps we're just scared of change. But we're together so its ok. Things only start going shit shaped when we're apart."

"So we'll think about it?" he asked.

She nodded.

"I like that," he added, smiling. "Shit shaped."

"Yeah well," she replied rising. "I've said it a million times. If you weren't so dumb as to wreck your car on the freeway, you might remember. Come on, my ass is going numb sitting on this hard bench."

"Yeah well," he shot back sticking out his tongue. "It'll squash your brains."

She kicked him playfully.

"I'm starving," she said hungrily, then adding as an afterthought. "what we need is a picnic table!"

"What?" he replied in a mocking tone. "To eat? I'm not a fucking beaver."

They laughed hard, their hands gripped together as they walked back to the house.

During the week that followed, the two of them spent a great deal of time noticing things about the house that they hadn't before, almost like they were paying more attention to it somehow. Deep down, though they had not spoken of Russ and the offer, both of them knew what the outcome was going to be. The money from John's sale of stock in Mason Corporation had filtered through, and they'd used this to settle the worst of the bills. The rest of the money would pay the rest of the bills, and no doubt pay a good chunk towards a shop somewhere, and finances to fund Melissa's art business. That would leave a little to help with the house repairs, though John was beginning to notice things. Things like, not only the canvas-covered kitchen roof, but a nasty hairline crack at the top of the wall in the den, which could only be caused by the failure of one of the main supporting timbers. As he sat alone in

327

the house, attempting to recuperate from the accident, he began to mentally tote up the bill for the repair work to the house. The kitchen roof, the main beam repairs, the garden, the boiler and heating systems, rotten and leaky windows in the back upstairs...it all added up to more than they had. He knew it and, he suddenly realised, she knew it too. She'd worked it out while she'd spent so many weeks sat home alone while he was in a coma. Even with the sale of his stock, there wasn't nearly enough. For a moment, he regretted closing the door in Mason Corporation. He'd certainly miss the money. The sale of the stock would help, but in a way, it had been a strange moment, the last of his connections to his family, his business, his father's business. He was finished with it forever. But on the other hand, it was exciting. His wife had a talent, he knew that to watch her. And for years, she'd supported him and gone about it quietly.

It reminded him of a conversation he'd had with Jake all those years ago, working on the car. Jake had spent a huge chunk of money on a large boring chunk of metal. Young John had wanted to spend the money that week on an exciting set of mag wheels he's seen in a catalogue, not a boring bit of steel. Jake had put him right,

"That bit of steel," he'd said in a conspiratorial tone. "Will make the difference over a quarter mile with that car. Without it, you'll look like an old man going to draw his pension...with it, you'll be the hero of the street."

And he had been. The performance clutch had performed beyond John's expectations. It reminded him of Melissa and her art. For so many years, she'd just sat there quietly, supporting him, painting and sculpting a little, but mainly playing the good wife, and being there for him and his business. Doing her job, but never being noticed.

Fuck that.

That wasn't happening any more. She was centre stage now. They both were.

It all seemed so strange to him. So many things he couldn't remember yet, things that he didn't know were real, or false. Then he remembered Christmas.

December 2001

"A little higher," Melissa said, stretching almost onto her toes to pin the gold decoration on to the wall.

"Careful," he said, holding her legs. "I don't want you to fall from the stool."

"I'm fine, idiot!" she laughed. "I'm ticklish. You grip- me like that again, and we're gonna end up in a heap! Is it straight?"

"It's good and straight," he said smiling. "At least...it's as straight as the house is."

"Straighter than the house," Melissa muttered, stepping down off the stool and looking for Lola. "Lola, did you turn the stove down, sweetie?"

Their daughter was silent. At least they assumed so. It was Christmas eve, about eight pm and the weather was wild. It was the worst storm to hit their town in a decade, wind, rain, and sleet battered the ranch house. They'd decided to wait till Christmas Eve to hang the decorations, to surprise Lola. The little girl had loved it, and for the past two hours, the three had been busy transforming the house into a Santa's grotto.

"Lola," said John, "You with us, sweetie?"

The little girl came bursting through the door, a worried look on her face.

"Daddy John," she said, "I turned down the stove, but the kitchen is making weird noises."

The kitchen was a single storey wooden extension on the house, added after John had been born. The old kitchen had been turned

330

into a rumpus room for the boys and their little sister, and John's parents built a big kitchen on the back of the property.

"Its fine honey," John reassured the worried girl. "It's an old house, it makes noises."

"The roof joists need their anchors redoing," said Melissa tying up some tinsel. "We need to get those metal brackets made."

"I can probably have it done in one of the truck workshops," he replied, nodding. "I'll do it after Christmas."

She handed him a bauble for the tree.

"Yeah," she replied. "Do it before the freeze sets in. Otherwise were gonna be having snowmen on the inside."

"It might not be that bad," he laughed. "You know what that local weather station is like. They were predicting monsoons this summer, and there we were waiting for Poohsticks river to burst its banks sitting there in our oilskins and everyone else is at the beach in shorts and thongs."

Melissa laughed.

"All the same," he continued. "I think we better get it done. I'll phone Phil on the 27th."

"He working so soon?" she asked.

"Yeah," John nodded accepting another bauble. "Says he needs the overtime. And god knows, I need the staff."

John stopped what he was doing at that moment and scrutinised his adopted daughter. She was sat on the floor, having abandoned her post of sorting out and untangling the baubles.

"Honey," John said beckoning Melissa to look. "What ya doing?"

His little girl ignored him. She was peering into a shiny blue bauble and studying the reflection.

John sat cross legged on the floor next to her, and Melissa sat on the other side of her. Ignoring the howling of the wind and the alarming creaking coming from the roof of the house, they watched the little girl.

"You ok, Honey?" Melissa asked.

The girl nodded.

"I'm looking at Christmas," she said. "When you look into a bauble at a Christmas house like this one, you see it shinier and brighter when you look through a bauble. It's more colourful and bright that it is normally."

"You know," said Melissa, picking up a bauble. "They say that if you're real good, you can close your eyes and go inside the reflection, and go into the magical Christmas world in there."

Lola looked at her adoptive mother.

"Yeah," John added pointing his reflection. "We can go inside. There we are, look."

"There we are," said the girl laughing. "You see us, Momma?"

Melisa nodded, suddenly looking round the room.

"It's Christmas," she said. "It's looking good in here again. And we have people here."

"Yeah," he nodded, hugging his wife and daughter, "It's good to have the family growing again. I mean, I'd have been happy here
332

alone with you as long as I lived, it's where I was meant to be, but...I dunno...it's good to have Lola here. We're a family now."

"Our own little family," added Melissa.

Suddenly, the lights went out, and there came a loud electrical hiss and pop.

"Damn fuses," said John standing. "I'll just go check the..."

But whatever he was going to check, he was stopped in his tracks as there came the most horrific splintering crashing sound from behind the closed kitchen door. The vibration from the sound of broken splintering wood made him look up, as it sounded like the whole house had come crashing in on them. Melissa stood, alarmed, and Lola screamed, hiding behind her dad's legs. Another crashing sound, louder this time, followed by the sound of shattered glass and falling masonry and the entire house shook.

"Kitchen," he said, going for the door. "We better take a look."

"Daddy! No, I want to hide," screamed Lola. "The house is falling down."

"Well then," said Melissa taking her little girl's hand as the crashing sounds continued. "We'll just have to rebuild it. Come on honey, you're safe with us. We won't let anything happen to you."

And it was true. No matter how old Lola grew, this was the most important lesson she was ever to learn. Face your fears head on. Open the door, take a look. The reality is much less fearful that the imagined terror. Lola always remembered this, and her parents' fearlessness when all she had wanted to do was to run from the devastated house screaming.

The main house, and the den in particular, had seemed fine. But when they stepped through into the kitchen they found only devastation. The entire single story roof had been torn off completely, the wind and rain howled around the exposed room. Where the roof joist had been secured to the side wall, it had torn away a section of wall. The crashing splintering noises had been the kitchen being nearly destroyed. John clambered through the wreckage towards the ruined side wall, where the side joist of the roof was still attached to the main house proper with a bent and buckled metal bracket. The wind and storm buffeted the ruined room.

"Stay here honey," instructed Melisa to her daughter, planting the child in the den doorway. She clambered over the ruins of her kitchen in the howling rain to her husband.

"That side bracket's gonna bring the whole house down if the wind catches the roof," she shouted, being soaked by the rain.

"Yeah," said John climbing higher on the ruined timbers, to get a foothold, and at the same time avoiding being crushed by splintering masonry. He ducked back as a gust of wind caught the remnants of the busted roof and lifted it. The bracket connecting it to the house groaned, but held firm. The joist that his father had connected it to was a supporting beam for the house. Melisa was right, if a gust of wind caught the roof section, it would pull the joist out and simply tear down the house.

"Lola," he shouted to his daughter. "Run to the front shed, honey. The door should be open. Go get the small saw off the bench, and the big tire lever on the floor there."

"Daddy, I'm scared," Lola shrieked.

In the midst of the maelstrom, John noticed that she'd called him "Daddy" and not "Daddy John." He smiled for a moment. But another creak from the main beam of the house spurred him into action.

"Honey," he shouted. "You can do this. Go get the things, sweetie. You'll be ok. Daddy's relying on you."

Reluctantly, and after considering for a moment, Lola fled through the house towards the shed.

"I'll go check the roof upstairs," Melissa said. "See how the beams are in the attic."

"There's the big flashlight under the sink there," he shouted over the wind. "Should have taken it back to the garage yesterday."

"I'm glad you didn't," she laughed. "I kind of regret giving you shit about it now."

"Be careful up there," he shouted to her.

Then she was gone.

The storm howled, and the timbers of the house creaked and groaned alarmingly. John, now bereft of his family, held onto the roof section with all his might, as if he alone could hold up the entire house, his house, his home. His family's home. What would he do if it were torn to flinders tonight. What if Lola and Melissa....no. Not that thought. Never that. The metal bracket was bent and twisted, and yet held firm, as it had held for thirty years. For thirty long years, it had sat squarely and held the kitchen extension firmly onto the side of other house. Now that firmness threatened to destroy the very thing it had protected.

"Daddy," came a small voice. "The tools."

As he came down from his position halfway up the wall, the little girl dropped the selection of tools as his feet.

"Good girl," he said. "I'm proud of you."

She was soaked through, as was he. He watched as she reached into her pockets and fished out some fluff covered sweets.

"You want a jelly?" she said.

He nodded, hugging her to him.

"Yeah," he said. "Yeah I do. I'd love a jelly."

"Ooh," came a laughing voice behind him. "We got candy? I love candy!"

He turned around and Melissa beside him. Lola gave her a jelly from her pocket, equally covered in fluff and together they stood for a moment, surveying the wreckage and eating their candy. Whatever else happened, John reflected, nothing else mattered. They were together.

"How's the roof?" he asked.

"Fine," she said, looking up at the ruined kitchen wall. "The main house seems ok. It's goddamned noisy up there, but it's only leaking in the places that it leaked before. I've put those pans down that we have behind the dresser."

He nodded, staring at the ruined kitchen.

"I have to cut this free in about four places," he said. "Else it'll tear that supporting beam out."

She nodded.

"I'll climb up and do the top two," she said, clambering up the ruined and battered shingles.

He took hold of a big steel saw, and waited while she climbed up the nearby drainpipe and anchored herself against the wall. Taking the saw, Melissa began to cut the first anchor hinge.

"Ugh," she groaned. "It's a metal hinge. Why'd I volunteer for the hard job?"

He laughed, taking the larger chainsaw and finding his footing on the ruined kitchen floor.

"I dunno," he said. "Though I was kind of pleased when you did."

"I don't suppose," she added. "That you want to change saws, and give me the gas-driven beauty?"

"Hmmm," he said considering. "Let's see: you wedged halfway up the side of the house in the rain, upside down, with a chainsaw. What could possibly go wrong?"

She laughed, the rain streaming off her face.

"I dunno," she shouted, the storm suddenly gaining in intensity again. "It'd almost be worth losing a limb or two to make this job easier."

He laughed back, turning to Lola.

"Go into the den honey," he ordered. "This could be dangerous."

Lola set her little chin, and simply stood there.

"I want to help," she said slightly sulkily.

337

"It's dangerous, baby," he said. "Be a good girl now."

"I want to stay with my Mom and Dad," she said, tears coming to her little face.

He turned to Melissa. Sawing the metal brackets was hard going, and several times, she nearly slipped down the wall. He turned back to Lola.

"OK honey," he said. "Mom's busy up high. We're gonna cut the joists out where they attach to the anchors. I want to hold up the beam as I cut it. Stand well back though, ok?"

Lola nodded, and John fired up the chainsaw.

It took a long while, and the thunder and rain thrashed them repeatedly. They were soaked to the skin, Melissa had slipped several times and had wood splinters in her fingers, and John and Lola were covered in sawdust from where he cut the beams off. But finally, they were done, the ruined section of kitchen was cut away from the main anchoring beam of the house, and the roof section where it had come away had been cut into harmless smaller pieces.

They were at the front door, with their coats and hats on. They had both agreed that they couldn't stay here tonight. No electric, no heat, the house would need serious repairs. Lola was quiet as Melissa locked the door and the three of them dejected, dirty and tired, and made their way to the car. Suddenly Melissa heard a sniffle come from Lola, and the little girl's parents got down on their knees to speak with her.

"It's ok," said Melissa. "It's all over. We're going somewhere warm and safe."

338

Lola, tears flowing freely now, looked at the face of her mom.

"I don't want to," she cried. "Santa is coming here. He doesn't know we're gone."

"Honey," replied Melissa. "Santa is magic. He'll know where you are."

"Besides," John added. "I left him a note in the den with directions to the motel."

Lola nodded sadly, and they walked away from the dark, empty house. As they got to the car, Melissa shuddered.

"She's right," she said.

"What," replied John quietly. "About Santa? Aren't we technically the grown-ups here?"

Melissa nodded. "I guess we have to be, though Lord knows I wish I didn't have to be sometimes. But that's not what I meant. Look at it."

"What?" he replied.

"Belle Starr," she continued. "Look at it. It's always shielded us, or tried to. It was this house that we began in, you and me. Right here. It's given everything to us, and we just lock it up on Christmas eve and walk the hell away. I'm probably too tired to think straight and sentimental, but ...John...I just can't. I feel like I'm locking it up for the last time, like when you were in Mexico that time."

He hugged her close.

"I know what you mean. I've always loved you for that. The way you love my family home just as much as I do. You're right. We can't leave. Not now."

"We'll have Christmas in the den," she said. "I'll get us some woollies. We can keep warm and dry."

They walked back into the house. John looked around, staring at the den wall.

"We don't need to," he said thinking. He handed Lola his keys.

"Honey," he said, go back to the big shed, and where you found the tools, go get daddy's big mallet."

Lola ran off.

"Are we knocking more walls down?" said Melissa laughing.

John felt the wall with his palm.

"Upstairs there's a chimney. So there's obviously a fireplace behind here. Dad walled it up before my time, I guess, but it's here. The chimney goes right down."

An hour and a half later, the little family sat in the big tent Melissa had pitched in the den just next to the Christmas tree. The room was lit with an old oil light, and the newly found fireplace was lit with a roaring fire. All three were in the special Christmas pajamas Melissa had bought weeks before.

"Here honey," said Melissa turning to Lola. "Have another baked potato."

Lola took the food from the offered fork, and ate hungrily.

"It's good," she said scoffing noisily.

340

John smiled, stroking the face of his wife.

"I love you," he said.

"I love you too," she said. "Good thing I'm not materialistic and want a nice house, isn't it?"

"I'll get you a nice house," he said earnestly. "I swear we'll fix up this piece of shit!"

Melissa shook her head as Lola watched the fire.

"No," his wife replied, cuddling up to him. "I don't want it. I want this. I feel more comfort in this little tent next to you than I would in any fucking mansion."

Lola turned.

"Mom said a swear," she said giggling.

"Dollar in the swear jar, Mom," said John poking Melissa.

"Ah to hell with you all," she said laughing. "Most of the dollars in that jar are mine anyway."

He hugged her tighter.

"That fancy life shit doesn't mean anything to me," she said. "As long as I have you and Lola, I'd rather have ruins and rags."

He looked around, before kissing her on the nose.

"Well," he laughed. "You certainly have ruins and rags."

2004, January

He looked at the room. Where had that memory come from? Bang, there it was. Probably while he'd been sat here thinking of selling the house. And the memory of the most recent Christmas was still in his head, with Lola and Nancy and Josh and Errol. All the well-wishers who had come to celebrate with Melissa and John.

Sunday came, and, still not talking about Belle Starr, they dropped Lola off at Josh's house and went into town in the Toyota. John was still prohibited from driving following the accident. The DMV wanted to interview him or something, to make sure he was fit. Privately, he was putting it off. The thought of sitting where Melissa was sat now behind the wheel terrified him.

"You got the address?" she asked, taking a turn at the intersection before honking at a truck.

"Yeah, right here," he said. "That truck drivers gonna get out in a minute."

"Fuck him," she replied. "Should learn to drive. Third road off main street, right?"

"He's probably sore about working Sunday," John answered. "Must've left his wife all tucked up in bed."

"That's where we should be," Melissa agreed. "Where am I going here?"

"Sorry, Denver street, yeah. Straight to the bottom and turn right, along there till the schoolhouse and turn left again. The "village" as they call it is right there."

"I've been once or twice," she remarked. "All full of cool type people. Students and old folks. I went to see what it was all about. Needed some art supplies. Everyone thinks they're really hip."

"I remember when we were hip," he said. "Did you get the art supplies."

She shook her head.

"It was all way expensive," she acknowledged. "Kind of like it was just on sale for posers. No way impoverished artists could afford to shop there."

He nodded.

"I know the type," he said, "The types that think they're good at shit they don't understand cos they haven't lived long enough."

"And we were never hip," she continued laughing. "I think the word was 'cool' though. We weren't that either. I think we were bordering on cornball."

"Yeah well you were the arty type," he shot back smiling. "You were the nerd. I was a football player. We would've been cool if it were up to me."

"We were never gonna be cool," she laughed out loud. "We were the fucking Adams family. Two

freaks who finished each other's sentences and slept in a big old house."

He smiled at the memory.

"Yeah well," he said. "Cool or not, we got to have sex before anybody else."

She smiled softly at the private memory that they so rarely spoke about. They didn't need to speak about it. It was one of many moments in their past that they cherished.

She came to the schoolhouse, and turned left. There was "The Village." It was a street, a long street, with big storefronts both sides, and brick-built individual shops. Trees lined the sidewalk that had posters and placards hanging from them, and colored lights were strewn across the street, which would light up the [pavement cafes and bars after the sun had gone down and nightlife in "The Village" began. The shops were eclectic and individual. Predictably, there were a couple of big chain coffee shops, and one or two bars. There were numerous art shops, retro and designer clothing stores, numerous attractive looking goodwill stores, a bicycle shop, and a tattooists/barbers. Some of the shops and stores were traditional brick-fronted old-fashioned looking things, and others seemed so full of things that you lost the image of the shop front at all. Several were former warehouses converted into small shop units. The main street on one side backed onto the river, once used for extensive trade where it met the railroad yard further down into the main part of the town. But now the industry had gone away, and the brick warehouse buildings had been converted into small shop units.

They parked the Toyota and walked down the street, resisting the urge to peer in through the windows. It was Sunday, and early still, but the streets were already full of life, students on their way home from Saturday nights festivities, and early morning coffee addicts. They came to a two-story block made of brick. A former warehouse, it had been converted into four shop units. The end one sold guitars and musical instruments, the next one was a bakery, selling beautiful looking pastries, then there was a door seemingly leading to nowhere, then an empty unit, and their final shop on the end was a sort of craft shop, selling hand-made artsy-crafty things. Miniature witches hung in the window on springs, doll houses, sign boards. Melissa was fascinated and peered through into the Aladdin's cave.

"Look at this," she said pointing, "it's a fish, holding a fishing rod. How cool."

"Hmm, yeah honey, whatever amuses you," laughed John, "This is the empty unit."

"A fishing fish", she said again, "How cool is that. It's like a fucking cannibal fish? Wouldn't you have thought that fish should just stick together? How does the rod ever work underwater anyway?"

He smiled at her. She belonged here, he knew that right away. Her artistic nature would thrive here.

"I'll get you the fish in a minute," he laughed. "Let's take a look at this place. The agent's inside by the look of things."

"Ooh," said Melissa, excited. "I didn't know she was here. Let's take a look inside then, at our new empire."

"ha ha ha," laughed John. "Easy, tiger."

They entered the door, jokingly pushing and shoving each other out of the way to get in first. It was an empty unit. Apparently, it had been a book store. Now it was just a massive empty shop, with a small kitchen and bathroom at one side.

"I'm so glad you could make it," gushed Melinda the realtor. "Are you guys ready?"

They nodded.

"OK so here it is," she said standing back. "A large floor space, plus a small kitchen and personal bathroom. The kitchen door opens up onto the lake in back, so I guess when it's quiet you can sit outside."

John looked around. Somehow he couldn't see this place as their art shop/coffee place. Melissa spoke up suddenly.

"Can we knock the back wall out?" she said.

Melinda looked surprised, but she checked her notes.

"The shop at the end has already done that," she replied. "A large open area. I think they were going to have impromptu music concerts there, but the bookstore complained about the noise."

"So we could open it up?" she asked.

Melinda nodded.

"What are you thinking," asked John, noticing the sudden gleam in Melissa's eyes. He knew she'd seen it, he knew she had an idea. This was her type of area, her artistic temperament had kicked in.

"I'm thinking coffee shop out front, kitchen to serve, bathroom for the customers, and knock through
the back wall and build a patio. After hours, we turn it into a bar. The guy at the end has his impromptu concerts, we sell next door's cakes and pastries and..."

"And make a whole heap of money," John replied, "but what about upstairs. We need to get you that studio so you can work, and sell your stuff."

Melinda nodded,

"I think you'll like the upstairs. If you'd care to follow me?"

They followed her, surprisingly, outside, and watched as she opened the secret door. Inside the door was a wooden passageway about ten feet long leading to a set of stairs. Dark wood panelling was on the walls, and Chinese lanterns hung on hooks. They continued up the small wooden staircase, which twisted around upon itself twice until they ended up on a landing. The passage continued to a small door which overlooked the lake and the rear. Melissa peered through the tiny window.

"Hey there's an upstairs balcony out there."

Melinda nodded.

"Sure is. This used to be the upstairs of the warehouse. The door there leads into the upstairs of the shop, your studio. The construction of the building, and the fact that its historic, means that this unit is unique. They owners weren't allowed to move the staircase into the shop itself. The staircase is the original Electric company warehouse staircase and landing."

"This place is wide enough for a couple of tables," murmured John. "Prop that back door open and people can get access to the upstairs balcony. Have their coffee and beer out there."

"Can we have a staircase in the store too," she asked. "I like this one. It's kind of like a whole separate magical place, but …just to be convenient."

"I don't see why not," the realtor admitted. "The bookstore never saw the need for it. But if you need access quickly, and as long as you don't disturb the fabric of the building."

John nodded, turning to his wife.

"This little staircase and landing is like a bonus area," he said. "We can fill this with people. It's individual, unique, and it'll sell. And you have the entire upstairs as your art studio."

Melinda looked at Melissa.

"Oh, you're an artist," she said nodding. "Then I guess you'll fit right in here. The guy next door does sculptures and stuff like that. The lady next door makes her own cakes."

I like it," Melissa nodded. He could see that she more than liked it. He saw in her eyes that she loved it.

They knew it was futile to view the other properties in their list. She had built their little shop in her head, with its two balconies, and its lanterns. As he watched her driving the car, she was building it in her head.

"With a staircase in the shop," she said out of nowhere. "I can shout down to you."

He nodded.

"If you're just gonna shout, he laughed. "I'll just tear a hole in the upstairs floor."

She snickered.

"You know what I mean, idiot," she said. "I'll come to the top step and shout."

"Then I can come up," he finished.

They were quiet. Imagining. This was happening. Something good coming out of his accident. He reflected as they drove to their next appointment. Before he had been in the crash and the coma, from what he could gather, he and Melissa had been having problems. Not insurmountable ones, but he'd been at work all day, and she was frustrated getting nowhere with her art. Though he still had little recollection of most of it, she'd hinted that they'd fought a little. He'd never take her for granted again, if indeed that was what he had done. Much of what had happened in his coma was just hazy memory, but that particular memory wasn't. The aching pain of loss was still fresh in his mind. In fact, the pain of his loss, for he had nearly died, was still in her mind also, and since, they had had clung even more tightly to one another.

They arrived at the next appointment. Honolulu lane. A pleasant suburban street, there were trees on the sidewalks, and pleasant little detached bungalows with side garages in a neat row down both sides.

"Which one is Errol and Dee's?" he asked.

Melissa frowned at his memory loss.

"Forty-eight," she said looking at him. "You've been in there a hundred times."

"I know," he nodded. "Some stuff comes back right away. I guess it's the important stuff."

She nodded.

"Yeah," she replied. "I was glad you remembered the bathroom thing. That's kind of...the thing we've always done. I would have hated to lose it."

He touched her arm.

"That's one of my favourite things," he said, smiling. "Even though other people think we're weird."

They did. Their friends often referred to them as Gomez and Morticia. They went to the bathroom together. Really. If one of them got up to go to the bathroom, the other would get up and be right alongside. At first, she imagined that post-coma, he would have forgotten this. But the first time, she got up to go to the little girl's room, instinctively he had gotten up and followed her.

"Here it is," she shouted, drawing the car to halt. "Number 89 Honolulu lane."

"Is it our new house?" he asked.

Melissa thought for a moment, and started through the car window, the rain battering on the glass. The brown bungalow looked nice and friendly, small but cosy. A grown up sensible house, a family home. Unlike the ramshackle Belle Starr house, this was sturdy, smart, and strong. Sure, it didn't have Poohsticks Bridge, and it didn't have their memories in it, but they had each other. The memories came from within them.

"Maybe," she said with a faraway look. "Let's go take a look."

The little house was nothing like Belle Starr. It was a bungalow with a small add on room upstairs that overlooked the little garden. The garden was closed in on all sides: on one side was the garage and on the other side a fence and some conifer trees. Various bedding plants were laid out in a pleasing pattern, some low bushes, a patio with a bench and a small pond.

"It's kinda nice," Melissa nodded. "Can we afford this?"

"Yeah," he confirmed. "If we get the deal on Belle Starr. We can pretty much pay cash."

"I dunno," she said. "It's the nicest house I can think of seeing, and it's the first. I like it. It's not that I don't, it just…"

"…just that we've spent our whole lives living up at Belle Starr," he finished. "You grew up there pretty much, like I did."

She nodded.

"I can't imagine coming down the highway from town and getting off this exit instead of the turnpike for forty-one," she said, her head down.

He went over to her as they looked at the small pond, put his arm around her and kissed her.

"How many times is it gonna happen?" he chuckled. "I'm waiting here with dinner on the stove and you're all the way out at 41 going to Belle Starr."

She looked at him, cocking an eyebrow.

"You're cooking dinner?" she said with a hint of incredulity in her voice. "So we're burning the house down already?"

He laughed,

"It's gonna be weird," he admitted. "Everything happened in that house. You and me, dad and mom. Hell, I remember which room I was in when Reagan got shot."

"I guess you were playing with Lego in your room?" she murmured.

"I was in the kitchen porch, mirror writing on the frosted glass. Mom was cooking a roast. You were on the other side of the glass trying to figure out what I was writing."

She laughed.

"I got confused and kept running outside," she began. "I forgot to put my shoes on..."

"And stood in a puddle and came back in with your socks all wet and filthy," he finished.

"Your mom asked what we'd been doing," she laughed. "She scolded us."

He hugged her tight.

"We have so many memories in that house," she said quietly. "But you know...it doesn't matter where it is, I don't think..."

"As long as we make them together," he finished.

"Course, we have a few properties to see yet," he added.

"Yeah," she replied. "I like this one though. I know Lola will like it too."

They stepped outside and there on the corner, hand in hand, were Errol and Dee.

"Hey guys," they said together, seeing their friends.

"Are you visiting us?" asked Dee. "What you park way down here for?"

"No," began John. "We're here to..."

But Errol had put it together.

"You guys are looking at houses," he said. "Don't tell me you finally threw in the towel on that falling-down old rattletrap of a house?"

John looked sad for a moment, and Dee, seeing his face, nudged Errol in the ribs.

Oh," he said. "Sorry I...are you guys really selling the ranch?"

Melissa nodded.

"I think so," she said softly. "We weren't sure, were we?"

She turned to him and they hugged,

She continued.

"But this place is nice. Close to our new project in The Village, and it's nice. I think it's time."

John nodded.

"Yeah," he said, his voice a little quiet too. "Belle Starr is falling down around us. It's no place to bring up a child. And the money will come in handy starting off a business."

"Whoa," replied Errol. "A business? What business?"

John told their friends about their idea, and they walked back to Dee and Errol's for coffee and some advice. Strangely enough, their friends were against them selling Belle Starr. John thought that strange as they'd always thought it was a falling-down old dump.

"I guess I'll get used to the idea," admitted Errol. "It's just...I can't think of you guys anywhere else. Sitting out there at that little bridge every weekend when we were kids instead of being around town. You guys belong there."

 John nodded.

"We can still walk to Poohsticks," he said. "It's gonna be open as a pathway for people to walk down, like a nature trail. Mainly for the kids that'll live in the house I guess, but for ramblers and wildlife guys too. Besides, Belle Starr is no place for a kid as it is. It needs too much doing to it."

Errol nodded sadly.

"I guess," he said. "I just thought of you two always living out there, all alone, cuddled up together."

Melissa smiled a faint smile.

"We'll always have our memories," she said sadly. "But now we'll be closer to the town, and to our friends around here."

Dee nodded.

"Yeah," she said. "At least now you can come join in some of the get-togethers."

That was true. Their circle of friends often had parties, and meet-ups in town that were just too damn inconvenient for John and Melissa to be able to get to, stuck out at Belle Starr. This would be better. So many things were being added to the plus column. And yet….and yet, as they sat in Dee and Errol's front room, John went quieter and more taciturn than usual, and was glad when they got home.

2004, February

The phone was ringing in the house, and when Melissa went to answer it, he opened the side door and stared out over the fields to the woods beyond. How many years had he had this view? All his life. And yet it meant little to him without her. He could barely remember a time when the place hadn't been filled with her, her sound, her scent, her very presence. As a very young child, he'd hung around with Jake, or one of the other hands, bored out of his tree, until she came along and he began to see the world through his own eyes at last. Through her eyes. He sensed her approach behind him.

"You ok?" she asked. "Standing here brooding again?"

He laughed, shaking his head.

"It's not that," he said. "I'm just thinking. About this house. About you and me."

She nodded.

"Maybe you were right," she said. "At one time we lived in that little apartment on the other side of town."

He laughed,

"I remember that," he said. "We had to hang the washing on that pulley thing. And those old folks upstairs..."

"With that television that was always tuned to ABC, and turned up real loud. We endured The Cosby Show whether we wanted it or not."

"We were just kids," he said. "It didn't matter, did it?"

She laughed.

"NO," she said. "It didn't. Cos half the time we could pay em back when we fucked."

"Yeah," he remembered. "You used to shriek like a fucking banshee."

"Why did you shriek, Momma," said a little voice, as Lola's earnest face appeared.

"Oh," said Melissa, embarrassed. "I didn't hear you come in, honey. You walk so quietly."

The little girl hugged her mom.

"So why where you shrieking?" she persisted.

"Ummm," she said thinking hard. "Daddy was cuddling me real hard and he squeezed a little too tight."

"Oh," said Lola, thinking. "Like he does at night sometimes when you shout out? I hear you shrieking then."

Now John joined Melissa in glowing bright red. If Lola noticed, she didn't say. She started to set the table for dinner, noticing that her mom had a bag full of take-out food ready.

"Anyway," Melissa said, changing the subject. That was the realtor. Those people who want to buy the house and land want to come see it. Meet us. Kind of like to reassure us that they're not just gonna tear it down and build an apartment block."

Oh," said John. "I guess that's fine. "I don't know when that'll be though, cos we want to make a move on that shop, don't we?"

Melissa nodded.

"Sure," she said. "Like we agreed. If you're sure."

He nodded, hugging her.

"It's our little dream," he said.

"They said they're coming in two Sunday's time," Melissa continued.

"I guess that gives us time to see the store again next week. And perhaps see the house too."

He turned to Lola.

"With Lola this time," he said grinning at the little girl who was carrying a stack of huge dinner plates.

2004, March

They were all smiles as they walked around the house. The house that was to become THEIR house. The woman, in her mid-fifties, had her gray hair in a tight bun and was wearing a pant suit, held a clip board, and occasionally wrote upon it, while the man, in a light beige suit, had receding hair and an amiable smile, had no clipboard, and spoke in a lively manner to John and Melissa as they walked around the house.

They had explained that the main skin of the house would be entirely removed, and, after shoring up the foundations, the wood skin would be replaced by cinder block before replacing the wood on the outside to retain the wooden ranch house feel of the place. Round the back, where the single-story extension was, there would be a huge double story extension, as well as stables taking most of the back garden.

"We're going to move the garden round to the side," he explained. "We'll fence it in nicely, so there's a place to go for prospective parents. Take a few trees out of the wood, so that the garden leads directly to the forest path and to that dear little bridge."

"Poohsticks Bridge," Melissa corrected.

The man nodded continuing. "We're going to make a feature of that area, lanterns, new plants, that sort of thing. Make it more magical."

"It's magical already," Melissa muttered under her breath.

The woman turned to them.

"It's a beautiful house," she said. "You both obviously love it very much. Nobody is trying to force you out here. This is …perfect for us. Truly perfect for our business, but it has to be right for both of you too."

Melissa shrugged.

"It's right for us, too," she said slipping her hand into John's. "It's nice to see that the old place is gonna be cherished."

"Poohsticks Bridge is a magical place," the man continued. "It's obviously a very personal place for the both of you. I can promise that the kids are gonna love it there. Any changes we make will be sympathetic to the area, I promise."

John nodded, squeezing Melissa's hand.

"We know," he said.

Sundays had always been so quiet. Today was no exception, and the pair sat on the bench seat in the kitchen together. The door was open so they could see Lola playing with Josh in the garden, and there was a nip in the cold air. They were quiet. On the little low table in the den was a whole mess of paperwork. Two contracts were for the little shop, already signed and sealed by the pair. They had agreed to take the shop on, the shop with the stairwell. They still hadn't decided on a house, but were looking at a few more yet. Tina and Errol had agreed to house the pair after the sale of Belle Starr. And as for that…the last contract on the table, the one as yet unsigned. The contract for the sale of Belle Starr. It had to be signed by Monday at the latest, and for the last two weeks since the visit of the company that were buying it, the contract had lain on the low table while the pair had talked about everything else under the sun and avoided the subject almost entirely.

It had to be signed, they knew that, to guarantee a secure future for their business. The Belle Starr house was dilapidated and needed too many repairs. But they clung on for the final remaining days before knowing what it was they had to do. Suddenly Melissa stood, and began to pull on a pair of old boots that were just inside the doorway.

"Mom and Dad will be at Poohsticks, honey," she shouted. The little girl nodded, deep in her own conversation with her friend Josh.

"Come on," said Melissa holding out her hand. "You coming?"

He nodded.

"I guess I know what it is we're gonna talk about," he said, pulling on his own boots, plus a thick plaid shirt that hung behind the door. "You got a sweater?"

She shook her head. He handed her an identical plaid shirt from the same hook, and they began their walk down the path to the fence.

The wood was alive with birds, scurrying insects, and small animals, suddenly afraid of the human feet in their world. The pair were quiet, and gripped hands as though they would lose each other if they let go. After a few minutes on the path, Melissa stopped.

"You remember stuff now?" she asked.

He hugged her to him.

"Some things," he said. "Some things not so much."

"You remember this place?"

He nodded.

"This is where we started," he said, his eyes glazing over slightly as he looked at her. "This is where I saw you, defeated, the weight of the world on your back, soaked through. You were gonna walk home in the rain, our friendship was done and we were nearly over."

She nodded, almost burying her head in his shirt.

"I thought my world ended," she said. "You know, like when you suddenly become an adult and things aren't gonna be how you imagined they would be when you were a kid. I suddenly saw my life with you and here, and us being here forever all gone in a heartbeat. You were gonna be here with that...what the hell was she called?"

John didn't remember, and shook his head with a laugh.

"I don't know," he said, "When you turned and walked away down that path, I realised that, no matter where I was in the world, unless you were there at my side, I was never gonna have any kind of life."

"Old friends that said hi in the street," Melissa muttered, remembering.

"That was never gonna happen," he said holding her closer. Rain started to drop on their heads as the sky clouded over.

"It nearly did," she replied. "I could feel our strands coming undone that night when I wanted to walk away home. I couldn't do it any more, watching you going off with another girl and playing the friend who has to step back."

He kissed her forehead.

"You were never gonna be that," he said. "I was never gonna let you go like that."

She smiled, as she remembered the rest of the memory.

"That was our first time together, that night in Jake's shed."

"Well," he replied. "Our first time when we knew what we were doing."

She laughed.

"Yeah, that's true. But it was our first proper time."

"I don't think he expected us to be so long."

"Well, we did fall asleep on that sofa bed."

"You looked so cute, all happy and sleeping."

"I was a little sticky," she laughed.

"It turned out ok, didn't it?" he said. "In the end. Here we are. Whatever the fuck we've been through, we made it together."

She nodded.

"Come on," she said, and the pair continued down the path to the bridge. The rain came on heavy now, and the plaid shirts were of little use.

"Why is it always raining?" he said laughing, soaked through.

"I guess if we lived in Malibu," she began. "We'd have some dry days too."

"It doesn't matter," he replied. "I've kinda gotten used to sitting here in the rain with you."

They sat down on the bridge deck, as they had for so many times before, and watched the water flowing under the bridge. The rain made the water flow faster, and made the surface of the water look as though it bubbled.

They sat cross legged on the deck, and she reached out and they held hands. He studied her, soaked through as she was, with rain streaked strands of hair whipping her face. The lock of hair at the front always fell first when it rained, and he held up his hand and ran his fingers through her hair to stop it.

She smiled.

He held his hand in her hair for a long time. She was as much a part of this place as the water that flowed, she belonged here as much as the very foundations of the house belonged here, indeed, if a person were to look up the deeds and ownership of "Belle-Starr Ranch, Decatur Road, Shoreline WA, they would see her name ahead of his on the ownership deed. As he watched the rain-soaked face looking back at him, Melissa George-Mason had owned this place since she had first set foot on it as a small child. It had belonged to her then, and she had belonged to it.

Were they doing the right thing in selling? In some ways, it felt the practical thing to do, the right thing for their family, and their new business. Pointless to stay wedded to the past, to hang onto something because of old memories. He didn't need the old memories. He noticed the hair in his fingers, he didn't need the memories while he had the real thing sat right there in front of him…

And yet…he hesitated. She was practical, and sarcastic, and, the older she got, her head ruled her heart. To a point. The time would always come when Melissa's practical side could no longer hold her

363

emotions inside, and she would explode in a torrent of emotional outburst. She was quiet now, shivering as the rain soaked through her shirt and through to her underwear, and he felt she was close now.

"Do you want to do this," he said simply.

She was silent.

"I mean, I did, until a minute ago," he said. "But I dunno. I just keep thinking back, and remembering stuff from our past. For some reason, I can remember Ronald Reagan being on the radio."

"Your folks always had the radio on," she said quietly.

"I remember the driveway, walking down it that day and seeing the little friend for the first time since her mom had died, I remember…"

"Don't," she said softly, holding her head against his. "It's not worth torturing ourselves over."

They were quiet for a long time.

"It…it's not that I'm afraid to leave," she began. "It's not that my time with you is somehow linked to here. It's not that. It's something else. I didn't want a house and a husband and a baby and a town job and all those things that you're supposed to want as a kid. I wanted someone who would understand me. Someone who would love me for me, flaws and all. And I'm pretty fucking flawed."

"I think you're just perfect," he said softly.

"That's what I wanted. I wanted to be scruffy, and spend my time laughing and happy in an old house in the dirt with that one person

364

who understood me in the whole world. With the one person who thought things were strange and scary when I wasn't around him. That's a pretty fucked up dream for a young girl to have. I guess it was cos my mom was a hippy."

"You got your dream," he said kissing her on the forehead.

She nodded.

"It's like...suddenly becoming grown up and you realise that your dreams are just that: just castles built out of mist and air. The romance of living in a broke-down house with the love of my life forever is beautiful, really fun, but practically..."

"It's hard," he said quietly. "I know. And cold. And then there's Lola. I know she loved it here, having a giant house to run around in, but it's cold and damp."

"The dream is just a dream," she said, her voice quiet. "We have to be sensible. Think of money, and practical stuff."

"So you're decided?" he asked. "You're ok with saying goodbye to all this."

They were silent again, and she remembered.

It had been a hot day. Real hot. One of the first days of summer. They both had seven weeks away from school. Seven weeks to spend playing. They were both nine years old. He was in his usual plaid shirt and jeans, and, feeling girly for once, she had worn the sundress grandma had bought her, along with some new sneakers, which at that moment were kicked off at the side of the bridge deck. Nine-year-old Melissa had smiled as he had complimented her, proud of his friend and how smart and cool she looked. His own mom had helped the girl out a little, buying her one or two new sets of clothes, and taking her off to get the long lank mop of blonde hair cut into a nice short summer haircut.

They sat cross legged watching a beetle scurrying about through the cracks, going about its business and predicting where it would go next. At first, they had been concerned there was a spider hiding at the bottom of one of the bridge spars, but it appeared to be either dead or asleep.

"I wonder where it goes at night," mused John as the pair studied it.

"I guess it goes to sleep," she replied. "I dunno. Maybe it has a little house."

"With a momma beetle?" asked John.

"Definitely," she replied. "Probably a whole bunch of kid beetles too."

"I can think of worse things."

"What, than being a beetle?"

"Yeah."

"What about spiders though? They're pretty scary if you're a beetle."

"That's why I'm gonna be nice to them," he said. "So if I ever come back as one..."

"Then," she finished. "A human will be nice back."

"Exactly," he said proudly.

"Wonder if they can swim?" she said.

He shrugged.

"Cos if they could, we could have them as little pilots."

"For our Poohsticks?"

"Yeah, and build them little cockpits to sit in."

"They'd just run off."

"Just put some sugar there, and they'll stay."

"Yeah sure," he laughed. "They'll sit right there just as the river rapids are going all around them."

"Yummm," she said making an eating noise with her mouth. "Who cares about this HIUGE river? This sugar is YUMMY!"

They both laughed.

The rain had soaked them through, as they watched the soaked wet deck of the bridge. So many memories. There had always seemed so much time. Now there was no more time. The contracts were due to be signed today, they would be gone within a week. No more time.

"Come on," she said. "Let's go."

She stood looking at the bridge, and the little place where they had lived, and for a long moment was silent. Her body shook slightly as she stood in the rain. Then she turned and walked off down the path away from Poohsticks Bridge. Her shoulders were hunched. At first, he thought it was the rain, and the wet, but it wasn't. It was defeat. He watched her, as he had watched when she had been sixteen and their friendship had almost become too hard, and they had nearly ended it on this very path. They walked up the path in silence and back to the house. A quick call to Lola from mum to confirm the girl was upstairs with her friend, and she went, still with her soaked boots on, into the den.

"Let's get this done," she said without emotion.

She picked up the pen from the bureau and opened the document to the last page where the signatures should be. Her hand shook so much she dropped the pen twice. Rain streaked her face, and made her eyes water. She blinked, and screwed her face up tightly as she finally got the pen to work and signed her name in the box. Melissa George-Mason. It was done. She banged down the pen and turned away from him.

"Get it over with," she said, her voice hoarse.

He stared at the document, the paper that signified the end of his life here, that signified the end of the eternal childhood they had both enjoyed. She had her back turned away, and was breathing heavily. He knew she could not bear much more.

After a moment or two, he put the pen down, and hugged her from the back.

"That's it," he said.

He felt a sigh come from her, a deep sigh, and, her legs giving way, she sank to the floor on her knees. Facing her front, he sat on the floor and hugged her close.

"I didn't sign it," he said, his eyes filling up. "I can't. I can't do it. I can't do it to you. To us. We belong here in the dirt and the damp. What the hell is our life if it isn't living out the dreams we had when we were little kids? What the hell lesson is that for Lola? What the fuck? I'm teaching the kid to give up on what she believes in and what she wants just for greenbacks? Who the fuck is going to look after those berry bushes on the banks of the little river if we're not around?"

She closed her eyes.

"Is it even possible?" she said. "The money...there isn't enough."

"We can still have the store. I think. It won't be as elaborate at first, and we can't do squat to this place. I think we can get materials in time to do t ourselves, like we always did."

She smiled, but was quiet.

"I always thought I had such a long time here, back when I played here as a kid. I imagined that one day, I'd still be here as a real old lady, you know? My kid's mind could hardly understand how long that would be. I guess I was too young to comprehend it."

She smiled again and kissed him on the lips.

"We can grow old here," he said. "We're gonna spend our whole lives here, and have it to give to Lola when she's grown."

Melissa nodded.

"I knew," she said. "Deep down inside me that I had years and years to spend here. We have so much time. So much wonderful time to live our lives here."

He kissed her again, and they stood.

"Our house," he said taking the contacts in one hand. "Our home together."

He tore the contract in two.

2006, April

"Its fine," he said into the cell phone. "Have it there Thursday. No, it's ok, I'm taking a day off. Ralph's running the store. I have a personal thing to do that day. Yeah, he knows what to do. It's doing good, it's doing good. It's only been a couple of years, but we're doing ok. Even had some of the house fixed up. Just send the bill to the store whenever, is that good? Fine. I'll speak to you soon."

He pressed a button on the cell and put the phone in his pocket. The call had been one of their suppliers. Things had been going great, good profits, good customer base, it had all worked right. The coffee bar was full, Melissa's art was selling, and she'd had a ton of commissions. They'd even had some spare money to fix the house up a little. Things worked better, they realised, when they were both in the shop themselves. Ralph worked Tuesdays and Thursdays daytime and evenings in the bar, but the takings were up when John and Melissa were in there together, though neither of them could imagine why. So things had been going great.

Had been going great.

Then a moment that John, at the back of his mind, deep in the locked away shadows at the back of his head, had dreaded. He remembered it from the long nightmare coma dream from a couple of years ago. Of course, he was pretty much recovered from that now, but still, he remembered it. He remembered it started with a cold. She'd had a cold for weeks, and he molly-coddled her to such a degree that she got frustrated with him. But then it got worse. She'd haemorrhaged blood a couple of times, and started being violently sick just after waking. Naturally, what with her medical history, she could rule out pregnancy, she'd always known it was impossible for her, ever since the prison incident.

This was worse. They both knew it and both felt it.

She had an appointment at the specialist in town at four. After taking Lola to school, they decided to distract themselves with a walk to the Bridge. In the end, it had rained torrents, so they contented themselves with a walk halfway, to where they'd rigged up a small shelter last summer. Made from half an upturned rowing boat fastened to a tree with a bench seat across, this kept the rain off when they wanted to be out of the house.

She pressed closer to him, huddled inside her warm black overcoat.

"Sometimes," she said watching the rain falling through the trees in torrents. "I think we should move to California. I don't think it does this there."

He watched her.

"I like the rain," he said. "It matches my mood right now."

She touched his arm.

371

"Don't," she replied. "Don't go there. Not yet. It might be nothing. Let's not worry."

She was quiet, and gripped his hand.

"Yeah," he said softly. "Let's not worry."

They sat and watched the rain falling through the tree canopy. He moved a hand to her head, and brushed away the stray lock of hair that fell in her eyes whenever it was wet. He stroked her face.

"It's not gonna happen," he said. "Whatever I'm thinking, it's not real. It isn't gonna happen."

She squeezed his hand.

"Things like that happen in life," she said watching the puddles. "When you had that accident, we were alone. You and I. You're not alone now: you have Lola. If I were to – "

"Don't," he begged, kissing her hand to stop her. "Just don't."

"You have Lola," Melissa said, insistent. "The two of you need to love each other, and look after each other, in case it's bad news this afternoon."

"Do you think it is?" he asked.

She watched his face, the dark soulful eyes and black hair that hung messily and wet now over his forehead. They all saw only a man, a strong man, clever, wise, a businessman with a hint of danger about him. She saw that too, but under that, she saw the boy, the little boy that had pushed his friend in the dirt and been so close to crying. She saw the sudden pain behind his eyes, the emotions that boiled so fiercely just beneath the surface of calm.

"I love you," she said simply, and kissed him on the forehead.

And that was enough. Her touch, her words of comfort were enough. That would always be enough. This afternoon was an unknown, danger, blackness, despair. But for now, he had her close to him. He had his home, and he had her at his side.

2006, April 3:08pm

This is KBBL radio. It's just after three, you're listening to Mike Sorento in the after – "

He turned the radio off. Damn this clinic. Who the fuck decided to build the motherfucking place here, next to a school, and a small row of shops. Their own business wasn't too far away at the bottom of nearby 3rd street. He couldn't park anywhere near the clinic, and so, risking the ire of other traffic, had dropped her off on a crossing and gone to find somewhere to park the car. Driving was still weird for him. even now nearly two years since the accident. But today was terrible. There was a bus broken down across the intersection, and so the entrance to the Lionel Avenue carpark was blocked. After about twenty minutes, he managed to squeeze the Toyota into a place at the side of the road, despite cutting across another driver who had been aiming for the space.

The car's driver had honked the horn noisily as John got out the car.

"What the fuck," shouted John shrugging his shoulders. The guy got out of the car,

"That was my space, buddy, I outta come over there and – "

"Yeah," nodded John, suddenly feeling the rage and blackness come over him. "Yeah, you should. Then your kids can go to their momma tonight and say 'Mom? Why is daddy not coming home tonight? Why did that man smash his head against the curb until his face was pulp? Why did daddy have to say something to that man on THAT day? Why couldn't Daddy leave him the fuck alone so the man wouldn't have had to kill him right there at the motherfucking curb side?'"

"Hey man," said the guy backing away. "I don't want any trouble, man."

He got back in his car and drove away quickly. John stood there for a moment, lost without her by his side. He walked along, to the clinic. Is this what his life was going to be like. Was it reality catching up with his horrible fantasy. Was the blackness coming to engulf his in real life? He suddenly felt an empty space by his side, as he walked along the street. The empty space. Tweedle-dum left alone. It was happening, just like he dreamed it would. He watched his feet on the sidewalk as he walked up the path to the clinic, barely able to see beyond the black of his boots. This was it. She'd never be by his side again, not without the death sentence that he knew was coming. In a trance, he met her worried face in the waiting room, and they walked into Dr Solzac's office together.

The doctor talked for a while in an amiable voice, about random nothings. Forgoing the screen at Melissa's behest, he had her strip to her socks and underwear and, giving her a blue robe to put on, he examined her. At one point Dr Solzac had to forcibly remove

374

their clasped hands from one another so that he could examine her properly. He held his hand there, open now, staring at the place where her hand had been only a moment before.

"That's it," he murmured. "Is she slipping away from me again?"

"Huh?" asked the Doctor.

"Does she have cancer, doctor?" he asked. "We thought it was. Had to be."

Dr Solzac stared at them both and their worried, almost childlike faces. He thought hard for a moment at what John had said. Watching their hands gripped together. He laughed slightly.

"No," he said reassuringly. "No, of course not."

"Then what has she got?"

"Your wife has gotten pregnant, Mr Mason," he said with a smile. "She does have a bad cold, probably from getting wet in all this rain."

"I can't be pregnant," she said. "My history …"

"I can read, Melissa," he said chidingly. "The truth is, those jail doctors aren't normally the best. And in some cases, where the woman is healthy and relatively young, your insides can repair themselves enough to be able to bear children."

"So I'm actually pregnant?" she asked, suddenly beaming.

"Yes you are," he said nodding. "Now you can both breathe again. You haemorrhaged a little, but that's fine. That's natural in your case. Your baby is fine and healthy. I'll need to keep an eye on you both, especially since she had her incident those years ago, but I see no complications."

John looked at her.

"We're pregnant," he said.

She laughed suddenly, a laugh of love and relief.

"I'm gonna be getting fat," she said smiling.

They didn't feel like driving home so soon. So instead, and almost skipping along, they went hand in hand part way down 3rd street, to where their old high school was. There on the corner was the Ice Cream shop where they'd sat so many times.

"I can't believe it's still here," she said.

He shook his head.

"Better placed business than ours," he said jokingly. "All these kids."

"Yeah, well its after four - they should have gone home now."

"Lola should be at Nancy's. We wouldn't be too long."

"Time for an Ice-cream?"

He nodded.

"Why the hell not?"

So they sat there, eating their Ice Cream like they had done when they had been children.

"I hope you like fat women," she said, almost under her breath, a big grin on her face.

"Always said that you had child bearing hips," he said laughing.

"You better watch out or you won't live to see your kid born."

They were silent after that. He looked into her eyes and she looked into his. They already had Lola, and now they would have another child of their own. He started at her happy, ice-cream smeared face. He knew that he could stare into that face forever.

2041, December

It was getting cold. Winter was drawing in, he realised. The elderly man drew his scarf up around him with frail hands, and huddled into the warm coat his daughter had bullied him into wearing. He'd had the impression she hadn't liked him shuffling off down here every day, not at his age, but he always won the argument in the end. He was 75, not 5, and made his own decisions. And so every day here he came, down to the little bench.

"So many happy times," he said to himself, remembering.

Though these days he tended to forget details, he never forgot the happy times. The old man smiled at the thought of them, it had seemed to him that they would last forever. And in his mind, they had lasted an eternity. He knew it was at an end, he could feel it in the air, could feel the chill like never before. Every morning a sense of increasing uselessness in the world, and every day an increasing struggle to fight the advances of old age.

He looked at the empty spot on the bench beside him and remembered, smiling.

2016, July

A knock came at the door of the beautiful Belle Starr house. It'd taken them years, but the house was now fully rebuilt and restored. Looking around, with all the noise and celebration in the living room, nobody had heard the door. Sighing to himself, John went to the door, opening it. It was three of Lola's friends. But not the right one. Not the one she wanted. Today, his adopted daughter was twenty-one. That sure as hell made him feel old, seeing all these damn kids. Not that they were kids, by their ages. He and Melissa had already been through a lifetimes worth of emotions. He greeted Lola's friends, and watched as they made their way through into the main room. There was laughter, and cheers as the birthday girl greeted her friends. But he only had eyes for one. Not the twenty something kids who shrieked and giggled, but the elegant blonde woman in the centre of the room, presiding over everyone: Mrs Melissa George-Mason. The lady of the house. Her hair was shorter these days, and tinged with gray. But that just made him love her more. The laughter lines around her sparkling green eyes reminded him that they were not just growing older, but growing older together. He watched as she presided over her daughter's party majestically, the absolute matriarch of the house. He felt so proud of her, and what they had achieved together. He looked around for the twins, and as he peered into the room further from the doorway to find his two sons, now twelve years old, his wife caught sight of him,

"You do have an invite to come in, you know," she laughed beckoning him in.

He smiled and joined the fun, noticing that every set of eyes were on him, Mr Mason, the family patriarch, his elegant wife at his shoulder and his two young sons at his other. He smiled a slight smile as he saw his beautiful daughter, resplendent in her silver dress, her long blonde hair cascading down about her like an angel's. She would be the lady of this house one day, he thought as she came over to him to kiss him.

"Are you ok, sweetie?" he asked.

She nodded, but hid her eyes from him. Not that she needed to. Something had happened between her and her old friend Josh from childhood. His mother Nancy, her own hair streaked with gray, had tried to persuade him to come, but he had refused.

"She's putting on a brave face," whispered John to Melissa after taking his wife to one side.

She nodded.

"I wish it hadn't have been today," admitted his wife. "I wanted everything perfect for her."

He hugged her, feeling her familiar form close to his side.

"It is perfect," he said. "It is. I love you."

"I love you too," she said, kissing him on the cheek.

Sometime later, just as the buzz from one too many measures of bourbon with Errol and the guys in the study was beginning to make his head buzz, he heard the door again. Someone answered it apparently, and he tried to drown Errol out as he listened to the voices. One belonged to his daughter.

"I'm sorry I said anything. I fucked everything up, I know that. I guess...I guess I just wanted to see. If I hadn't have asked..."

The other voice shushed her. It was Josh.

"Shhh," he whispered, "I'm sorry I ran out. You just…it was kind of a bolt from the blue, you know? I know you were being weird, but I didn't know why? I never would have imagined…"

"That your best friend from school has a major crush on you?" came Lola's voice again.

John silenced the guys, and crept to the door. Peeping through the crack, he saw the lounge door slightly ajar too, and though he couldn't see her, he knew Melissa was watching from inside the lounge in a similar manner.

"Is that what it was?" said Josh. "A crush? I thought you said you loved me?"

"I dunno," Lola admitted. "Growing up here, with the parents I had. I mean…they have more love for each other than the whole fucking world, you know? I just thought that if I loved you I could automatically have you. I never thought you wouldn't feel the same way. I just figured it'd work out for me like it did for them."

"I never said I didn't feel the same way," replied Josh, reaching out for Lola's hand. "You just surprised me. It isn't every day that a beautiful woman tells me she loves me."

He kissed her, and John watched as the living room door closed with a click. Things were going to work out just fine, just as his wise wife had said they would.

2041, October

The old man smiled at the memory. That had been Lola's first kiss with Josh.   He'd been a good husband to her, and the two of them had been very happy together. He smiled again at the thought of his grandson.

The water flowed down the creek as the old man turned to his young man.

"Don't be sad," he said patting the young man on the head. "And don't be afraid."

"I miss her, Grandpa," the young man replied sadly.

 The old man nodded.

"Me too," he nodded. "Me too. But I spent more than fifty years by her side. I can't be sad. I've had more than half a century of her company. Not many people can say that. And...I know she isn't around anymore, but you know what?"

He looked at his grandson.

"No Grandpa," the boy replied. "What?"

 "I'll see her again someday. You see, we made a deal, your Grandma and me. Whoever died first would wait, right there at the gates. She'll wait till I get there, then we'll go in together, holding hands, just like we did when we were little kids."

The boy cast his head down.

"You shouldn't talk like that, Grandpa," he said sadly.

"Ah, don't be so sad," Grandpa chided. "It's not gonna be for a while yet. And when I do go, you know I'll be with your Grandma again. And you know I'll have a smile on my face."

"Yeah," sniffed his grandson. "Unless she's tearing a strip off you for being late."

The old man laughed, nodding.

"That's true enough," he said smiling. "Besides, if you need to come talk to either of us, after were gone, then just come down here, anc sit on the bridge. We'll always be close by. This place was always in our blood. Yours too."

The old man put his arm round his grandson and they watched the water as it flowed down the creek.

Thinking of his grandson made him think of her. In the end, there was only her.

How long had they sat here, on the small bench near the bridge? The years had seemed to melt away, children, grandchildren, the house, the Belle Starr ranch, none of it mattered as much as she, the one who lay snoozing in the sun's rays while she leaned upon his shoulder. Though folks might have considered them old, past it, and put out to grass, he could have told them that they both knew more about passion and love than anyone would ever know. For he had been by her side now for seventy years. It was the place he was born to be, and it was by her side that he would die.

They only saw 'Grandma' or 'Mom' or 'Be careful with that hip.' He saw his beloved. He saw the other half of his soul, he saw the smile and the eyes of the little girl he had first met when he was barely six years old, and who had shared a biscuit with him in a playground. He saw the one who had helped him to fix the collapsed roof in the rain one Christmas eve decades ago when Lola had been small, he saw the one with whom he had relaxed on the porch seat when their children had gone off to begin their own lives and left the big house quiet, he saw the one with whom he had been intimate a million times and yet each time was as wonderful as the first day he had touched her. John stroked the side of her face as they dozed in the sun sat by the side of their bridge.

The day was drawing to a close. He pulled up his muffler and thought about heading home. It took longer now that it had when he was young. The walk was quiet now without her shuffling along at his side. He chided himself as a moment of sadness crept into his heart, as he remembered their final day together on earth. It had been a Thursday. She had just recovered from a nasty illness, the diabetes that had found her later in life meant that a slight illness became a major one. That plus her age had meant a summer recuperating from poor health. The illness had left her thin and pale. Lola and her husband had expressed concern as they saw her mom beginning to get her coat and woolly boots on.

"Where d'you think you're going?" Lola asked, her hands on her hips, and in the next breath, shouting "Jordan, the school bus is here!"

"We're going out," said her Mom firmly, struggling to lace the boots.

Her dad appeared, pills in hand.

"Here," he said to Melissa. "You forgot your pills. Let me tie that for you."

He wheezed as he struggled down onto his knees, to tie her boot. She took the pills from him.

"There's so many of these I swear I'll be rattling," she grumbled, downing them without a glass of water. "Damned diabetes."

Her husband tied the boot, and tried to stand up. He struggled and Lola went to help him.

"Thank you, honey," he said. "Like she said, we're going out. Taking a walk to the bridge."

Lola's brow furrowed. "It's cold, you guys," she said. "It's almost winter. Just stay in here. The snooker is on TV. I thought you liked snooker?"

"Hmm," answered Melissa. "I did like snooker, but then that nice blonde man got knocked out. I don't like the Chinese guy. He takes too damned long."

She wrapped her muffler around her throat, then struggled on with her coat. Her husband helped her with it.

"Just don't be there all day and get cold," Lola chided. Her father turned.

"Don't treat us like babies," he said softly. "We need to be on our own. Just for today. I'll take care of her today, I promise."

Lola was quiet, watching her dad's eyes. She was silent after that, as if she saw something in her father's face. Suddenly she hugged him tightly, and watched as her mother fastened the coat.

"Be careful," said Lola quietly, "I only nag because I love you."

Melissa nodded a pale-eyed smile. She was still weak, and now way too thin. Her appetite was small these days, and she ate little. She hadn't even packed them a picnic. But evidently Lola had.

"I found this," she said, her voice strangely light. "Remember this?"

It was the hare bear bunch lunch box, battered now after its years in the Belle Starr attic, its paint nearly all faded away and crumbled.

"I'll pack it with things for you to take," she said to her mom. "Biscuits and stuff."

Her mother smiled another pale smile as she held onto her husband.

"I can't believe you found that old thing," she said. "My mother bought me that on my fourth birthday."

"How old is it…about seventy years old?" he laughed, holding her hand while he waited for their daughter to pack the box.

Jordan ran past, a boy of around eleven, Lola's eldest. He bade his grandparents goodbye, glad that his grandma was up and seemingly looking better after her long weeks being bedridden, and flew outside to catch his bus. The little hare bear bunch lunch box packed, they set off. John walked with a stick now, and though Melissa didn't, she was still weak, and Lola worried as she saw her aged parents set off shuffling to the forest

"Seventy-five years," Melissa said softly as they made their way through the forest.

"I know," replied John wheezing a little, "They barely manage five these days. I don't know what the hell these kids are thinking. They give up on their relationships far too easily these days."

"They don't know how to do it," she replied. "I think we learned a lesson the day you pushed me down in the dirt."

He looked at her.

"I'm sorry I did that," he said.

"I forgave you decades ago," she smiled, and they continued their walk. "But that was it, wasn't it? We learned that it was awful when we upset one another…"

"And so we didn't do it again," he finished.

"They all said," considered Melissa. "When you're grown up, your life seems to go so fast, that time flies. I don't think it seemed to do for us, did it?"

"No," he shook his head. "It's strange, isn't it? I seem to have been walking down this path with you for an eternity. It hasn't gone fast at all."

"Some folks hate getting old," she said as they reached their special place. "I dunno. I kind of enjoyed it."

"I've enjoyed every part of it," he said nodding, helping her to sit. "Being a kid, growing up, being an adult, getting over the accident, and spending time with you remembering stuff...."

"...watching our kids grow," she continued. "And then enjoying the peace when they'd all left..."

"Then enjoying the grandchildren when they returned...," he followed. "And here we are."

"Here we are," she agreed.

They were quiet for a while, contented just to be in each other's company. Her breathing seemed heavy these days, and he knew she was still sick. Matter of fact they both were. It came with getting old. He wasn't sad though. What other guys get to spend more than seventy years with their best friend? He'd been retired over fifteen years now when they finally sold their little café, and since then he's spent every waking minute by her side.

The old man stirred. He looked around at the empty spot beside him and despite himself, he was sad. He remembered that final day he'd spent with her as though it were yesterday, and though he was pragmatic about it, had accepted that it would happen, and got on with what remained of his life. When he sneaked off alone here, they knew it was because he wanted to be near her still. He knew Lola and Josh came here, as did Jordan and that girl he was seeing...what was her name? He couldn't remember, but she was a pretty black girl. He'd brought her down here more than once. The place was in good hands. It wasn't 'their' place any more.

He remembered their last day together clearly, the Thursday. 24th June, 2039. They'd already discussed what would happen when one of them died. If there was an afterlife, then the one who went exploring first would wait for the other one before going in. And so he wasn't sad. As Melissa had pointed out, they'd once been separated for over three years.

"You'd better not live for more than three years after I go,' he'd said gruffly.

"What makes you think you're going first?" she had replied, laughing,

In the end, as they had both known deep down inside them, it was happening that day. He could tell that morning, with her pale face and the way the sparkle had faded from her eyes a little. They'd stayed at Poohsticks for a long time, taking it all in, sitting quietly and contently by each other's side. At last it had all been said. There was nothing more left to say, no more observations about the world, no more jokes, nothing. They knew it was done, and all either of them wanted was to feel the presence and the warmth of the other one at their side. At tea time, they had both shuffled home, Melissa announcing she needed a lie down.

Lola had looked concerned as her parents made their way upstairs, undressed and climbed into bed. Still quiet, and like she had done every single day of their marriage, she turned and kissed him, said she loved him, and closed her eyes. Snuggling up to her, he closed his eyes.

She had died that night in her sleep, quite peacefully. He sat on the bench, cold now, reflecting on his life. He closed his eyes and remembered her, etched as she had been, on his memory.

"Those bushes are dying back," she said, her blonde hair catching the last rays of the fading sun. Her voice. Its sounded real again.

He nodded.

"Birds'll all be hibernating," he replied. "Or going south. I never did figure out which."

She was quiet for a moment.

"I've enjoyed it here," she said. "This has been good."

"Is it time?" he asked looking at her face.

She looked so young, like he remembered her when he looked at old photographs of them together. Waited for him. Come back for him.

She nodded.

"Thank the lord for that," he said, his voice sounding younger in his head now, younger than his seventy- five years.

She held out her hand, and he took it, and their fingers interlaced as they held hands. They stood together. Looking back to their bench, he saw the figure of an old man that had been sitting there, his muffler wrapped tightly around him. As he watched, the old man's head bent forward, and he slumped slightly, and was still. He was dead. John grasped Melissa's hand tighter.

"Together forever," she said, her green eyes sparkling as she smiled.

"You and me," he said, kissing her on the lips.

May 2042. **And so to the Breeze**

Lola sighed. The house was quiet. She hadn't gotten used to the quiet. Back when she'd first come here as an orphan, the house had always been noisy. Truth was, it still usually was, but today they were all out. She went into the lounge where the two urns stood on the mantle, along with photos of her parents, and looked at them. It had been six months since her father had died, sitting on his bench. She removed the lid from the urn that held her mother's ashes, and picked up the other urn, the one with her father inside. Carefully, she emptied her father's ashes into her mother's urn, replacing the lid. She picked up the full urn and looked at it.

"Together again," she said softly.

At that moment, her husband Josh appeared, stroking his beard.

"Hey," he said. "Are you ok? I thought we were doing this together."

She nodded.

"It's time," she replied. "It feels like the right time. Let's do this. Zach and Tom wanted me to do it. They're coming over at the weekend. Zach wants to say something for his mom and dad."

"Are you sure about this," he asked, embracing her. "Keep them in the house if you'd rather. Be close to them."

Lola shook her head.

"No," she answered. "It's not what they would want. They spent their lives down at that bridge. They'd want to be down there. And if I need to be with them, I can go down there, too."

"I'll always be with you, you know," he said, rubbing her shoulder.

Sometime later, Lola stood on the bridge. Josh was stood a bit further back. Lola had wanted to do this alone. She stood on the deck looking down at the water as it flowed between the rocks. It had been her mother's little painted sticks that had given the bridge its name. Poohsticks Bridge, her mother and father had called it, when they had been children.

She gripped their urn in both her hands. They would have wanted this. Now, whenever she missed them, whenever she needed her mother's guidance or her father's wisdom, she could come down here, sit on the bench and think of them and all they had taught her. She opened the urn, and slowly, reverentially, scattered the ashes down into the flowing water. Lola closed her eyes and listened to the creaking of the wood in the trees as the breeze blew. She almost imagined she could still hear them.

"Spring is coming," Melissa said, digging him in the ribs.

"Hey," he laughed. "Quit poking. Water's flowing fast today."

"There's wind in the air," she replied. "Change on the wind."

"Change," he repeated, looking at Lola standing on the bridge. Josh had approached her, and was embracing Lola as she thought of her parents, and finished scattering their ashes.

"It's going to be okay," Melissa said putting her arm around her husband.

"I love you."

"I love you too."

Josh kissed his wife as she stood there with her eyes closed.

"C'mon honey," he said, kissing her softly on the top of her head. "Let's go home."

Lola listened, as the voices she had heard turned into a birdsong on the breeze. As she turned to her husband to leave, the leaves whistled in the trees as they always had. All was quiet.

Poohsticks Bridge.

For Helen.